BARBARA BRETTON

Shore Lights

BERKLEY

$6.99 U.S.
$9.99 CAN

ISBN 0-425-18987-2

T

"AN AUTHOR OF IMMENSE TALENT"*

Acclaim for the novels of Barbara Bretton . . .

"Bretton's characters are always real and their conflicts believable." —*Chicago Sun-Times*

"Soul warming . . . A powerful relationship drama [for] anyone who enjoys a passionate look inside the hearts and souls of the prime players." —*Midwest Book Review*

"[Bretton] excels in her portrayal of the sometimes sweet, sometimes stifling ties of a small community. The town's tight network of loving, eccentric friends and family infuses the tale with a gently comic note that perfectly balances the darker dramas of the romance." —*Publishers Weekly*

"A tender love story about two people who, when they find something special, will go to any length to keep it."
—*Booklist*

"Honest, witty . . . absolutely unforgettable." —*Rendezvous*

"A classic adult fairy tale." —*Affaire de Coeur*

"Delightful characters . . . thoroughly enjoyable."
—*Heartland Critiques*

"Dialogue flows easily and characters spring quickly to life."
—*Rocky Mountain News*

"No one tells a story like Barbara Bretton."
—Meryl Sawyer, author of *Unforgettable*

"Highly entertaining . . . sparks with rapid-fire repartee . . . unforgettable." —*Romantic Times*

Please turn to the back of this book
for a special preview of Barbara Bretton's

GIRLS OF SUMMER

Available from Berkley Books in November 2003!

Shore Lights

BARBARA BRETTON

BERKLEY BOOKS, NEW YORK

This is a work of fiction. Names, characters, places, and incidents either are the product of the author's imagination or are used fictitiously, and any resemblance to actual persons, living or dead, business establishments, events, or locales is entirely coincidental.

SHORE LIGHTS

A Berkley Book / published by arrangement with the author

PRINTING HISTORY
Berkley mass-market edition / May 2003

Copyright © 2003 by Barbara Bretton.
Excerpt from *Girls of Summer* by Barbara Bretton copyright © 2003 by Barbara Bretton.
Cover illustration by Wendy Popp.
Cover design by George Long.
Interior text design by Julie Rogers.

All rights reserved.
This book, or parts thereof, may not be reproduced in any form without permission. The scanning, uploading, and distribution of this book via the Internet or via any other means without the permission of the publisher is illegal and punishable by law. Please purchase only authorized electronic editions, and do not participate in or encourage electronic piracy of copyrighted materials. Your support of the author's rights is appreciated.
For information address: The Berkley Publishing Group, a division of Penguin Group (USA) Inc., 375 Hudson Street, New York, New York 10014.

ISBN: 0-425-18987-2

BERKLEY®
Berkley Books are published by The Berkley Publishing Group, a division of Penguin Group (USA) Inc., 375 Hudson Street, New York, New York 10014.
BERKLEY and the "B" design are trademarks belonging to Penguin Group (USA) Inc.

PRINTED IN THE UNITED STATES OF AMERICA

10 9 8 7 6 5 4 3 2 1

Acknowledgments

Many thanks and much love to James Selkirk; Kay Butler; Jeannie Perrin; Robin Kaigh; Cathy Thacker; Dottie Martin; Mary Preisinger; Shelley Wester and everyone from Open Your Heart; the Hurts; Rabbi Sheri; Fredericka; Doreen Babott, M.D., and Carole; Inez and Beth; and, as always, my husband for just about everything.

And, last but not least, thanks to Squirt for keeping me company during the run for the finish line.

Chapter One

ONCE UPON A time in the Emerald City there lived a woman named Maddy Bainbridge who believed she could move back home with her mother and not lose her mind.

Now, Maddy was old enough to know that the things that drove you crazy when you were seventeen would probably drive you even crazier when you reached thirty-two, but her mother's offer came at a moment when her defenses were down and her options extremely limited.

"I need help and God knows you need a job," Rose said during the fateful phone call that changed their lives. "The Inn is doing turn-away business, and I'd rather share the profits with my daughter than a perfect stranger."

"I appreciate the thought, Mother, but I'm just going through a dry spell here." An eight-month dry spell, but Maddy wasn't about to put too fine a point to it. "I'm sure the voice-over work will pick up any day now."

"You're an accountant, Madelyn. You have a degree. You can do much better than voice-over work for a used-car dealership."

"I *was* an accountant," she reminded her mother. "Not much call for bean counters when there aren't any beans left to count." The great dot-com collapse of a few years ago had littered the landscape with the fallen careers of fellow accountants from Washington down to Baja.

"Be that as it may, you have a child to take care of and no husband to help you out. You need a chance to get back on your feet, and I need someone I can trust to help me with the business. Give me one good reason why this isn't the perfect solution for both of us, and I'll never broach the topic again."

Are you listening, God? Just one good reason . . .

On any other day Maddy could've given her twenty, but that evening she couldn't come up with a single one.

"Hannah has a brand-new dog," she said finally, knowing her mother's negative stance on anything furry or four-legged. She had spent part of her childhood wishing she could turn Rose into an Irish setter. "Her name is Priscilla and she has a few issues."

"What kind of dog?"

Oh, how she longed for something large and prone to drooling. Bulldog! Saint Bernard! Irish wolfhound with an overbite!

"A poodle," she mumbled, praying it sounded like bull-mastiff on Rose's end of the line.

"Did you say poodle?"

"Yes," said Maddy. "A poodle."

"How big a poodle?" Rose sounded amused.

Maddy glanced down at the tiny bundle of curly fur asleep in her lap. Sometimes the truth was a royal pain. "Too soon to tell," she said, "but her paws are gigantic." For a stuffed toy. There was always the chance Priscilla might make it to a whopping five pounds if she pigged out on Purina.

"No problem," Rose said calmly. "Just so long as she doesn't piddle in the common areas."

Was this her my-way-or-the-highway mother talking, the woman revered in three counties as the undisputed Queen of Clean? Rose had been known to change her

sheets after a fifteen-minute nap. "Okay," Maddy said,
"now I get it. My real mother is trapped in a pod in the
basement behind the washer and dryer."

Rose's answer was a surprisingly long span of silence.
No snappy comeback. No withering maternal observation.
Just enough silence to unnerve her only child.

Maddy would have liked to match her mother silence
for silence, but Rose had thirty years on her and she had
no doubt her mother could stretch that silence until Christmas if she felt like it. "I was making a joke, Mother. You
were supposed to laugh, not take me seriously."

Rose cleared her throat. "Quite frankly, I don't see
what's holding you there in Seattle now that Tom has . . .
moved away."

"He didn't just move away. You can say it. I promise
I won't fall apart. Tom married somebody else. I've made
my peace with it." Which, of course, was a big enough
lie to grow her nose to a size worthy of the men of Mount
Rushmore.

"Maybe you have," Rose said, "but Hannah certainly
hasn't. She's the one you should be thinking about."

Instant guilt, supersized with fries. This was no pod
person; this was her mother.

"Hannah is the main reason I'm staying in Seattle. This
is the only home she knows." She paused, waiting for a
response from her mother. Rose, however, remained silent. Rose had never been one to play silence to such
advantage. "Besides, Hannah will be starting preschool in
a few weeks."

"We have schools here in New Jersey."

"All of her friends are here."

"She's four years old, Madelyn. She'll make new
ones."

"Seattle's our home."

"Home is where your family is. What Hannah needs
right now is to be surrounded by people who love her."
People who won't leave her. Oh, Rose didn't say those
words, but then, she didn't have to. She had already

wheeled out the heavy artillery and aimed it straight at Maddy's heart.

Oh, God, Mother, you're right ... of course you're right.... I can't argue the point with you.... Was this how you felt when Daddy went back to Oregon ... ? Did you lie awake every night and stare up at the ceiling and worry about me the way I worry about Hannah ... ? It's been so long since I heard her laugh ... I can't even remember how long it's been.... I don't go to church anymore, but maybe I should because I'm beginning to think it will take a miracle to make Hannah happy again.

But she didn't say any of it. The words were trapped behind all the years they'd spent away from each other, all of their differences both large and small. The ghost of the lonely little girl she once was rose up between them and she wouldn't go away. Only this time the little girl looked like Hannah.

How Hannah adored her father! Her world had revolved around their Sunday brunches, their excursions to the Space Needle and Mariners games, strolls along the waterfront where he taught her how to eat crab. The loss of those weekly visits had turned her happy child into a sad-eyed little girl Maddy barely recognized. How did you tell the child you loved more than life that not every man was cut out to be a 24/7 father?

"This wasn't part of the plan," Tom Lawlor had said the day Maddy told him she was pregnant. It hadn't been part of her plan, either, but sometimes life handed a woman a miracle and trusted her to do the rest. Tom's children had children of their own, and he had been eagerly anticipating retirement from the company he owned and a life that didn't include potty training and the Tooth Fairy.

Not that Maddy had been ready to punch her ticket on the Baby Express herself. Children had been out there somewhere in the shadowy future, a concept to be dealt with at a later date. She had never doubted that somehow, some day, Tom would warm to the idea of another child, but until then she was quite content with the life they shared. She took her birth control pills religiously, popping one each morning with her orange juice, trusting her future to God and country and modern pharmaceuticals.

A fierce bout with the flu—and one tossed pill—had shown her the folly of her ways.

The easy carefree relationship she and Tom had enjoyed before her pregnancy was soon nothing more than a memory. He still cared for her and she knew he loved Hannah, but sometimes it seemed to Maddy that he loved their daughter the way you would love a golden retriever you had to send to college. A part of his heart remained distant and not even the sheer wonder of their little girl had been able to change that fact.

Why didn't they tell you the truth when they handed you that squalling, slippery, precious newborn? They congratulated you and wished you well. They gave you coupons for disposable diapers and baby wipes, but they didn't so much as whisper about the things that really mattered. Why didn't they tell you that the feeding and diapering were the easy part; a baby cried when she was hungry and she fussed when she was wet. Even the newest of new mothers could figure that out without too much trouble. If only someone, somewhere, could tell you what to do for a little girl with a broken heart.

"Promise me you'll think about the idea," Rose urged as they said goodbye.

"I'll think about it," Maddy told her mother, and then she did her level best to put the entire idea from her mind.

But a strange thing happened. The more Maddy tried not to think about Rose, the more often her thoughts turned to her mother. Twice in the next few days she found herself reaching for the phone, only to catch herself mid-dial. What on earth would she say? It wasn't like she and Rose were friends. They didn't share the same tastes in books or movies. Their child-rearing methods were poles apart. Rose was a realist who believed only in what she could see and hear and touch. Maddy believed in those things, too, but she knew there was more to this world than met the eye.

The first time Maddy brought home an invisible friend, Rose put the entire family into group therapy so she could figure out where they had gone wrong.

When Hannah showed up with her first invisible friend, Maddy set an extra place for supper.

Still this odd yearning for her mother lingered. Rose was the last thing she thought about at night and her first thought in the morning. So much time had passed since they had last lived together under the same roof. So many things had changed. Maybe the idea of moving back home again wasn't quite as crazy as it sounded.

"Leave Seattle for Jersey?" her cousin Denise e-mailed her when she first got wind of Rose's offer. "Are you nuts?" What woman in her right mind would trade life in the Emerald City for a one-way ticket back to the Garden State. *Crazy* didn't begin to cover it.

"DON'T DO IT!" Her cousin Gina's warning practically leaped off the computer screen. "You're the only one of us to make it west of the Delaware River. Don't blow it now!"

The senior members of the clan also weighed in with their opinions.

"You'll make your mother so happy," Aunt Lucy IM'd her, then surrendered the keyboard to Aunt Connie, who added, "I don't know why you moved out there in the first place. We have coffee in New Jersey, too, Madelyn."

Every morning Maddy woke up to an in box stuffed with e-mails with subject headers like "Come Home Maddy" and "Don't Do It!!!" until she began to feel like she was being spammed by her own family.

The weeks passed and she was still no closer to making a decision than she had been the day Rose made the offer.

The day before Hannah started preschool, Maddy was rummaging through a huge trunk of old clothes that she'd stashed in the condo's storage area when she came across the beautiful fisherman's sweater Rose had knitted for her when she started grade school. The thick cream-colored wool was still supple and lustrous and smelled only faintly from Woolite and mothballs. Large bone buttons marched smartly down the front, fitting neatly into the beautifully finished buttonholes. Rose was a perfectionist and her needlework showed it. Every stitch, every seam was meticulously crafted and designed to last. Only the pockets showed serious signs of wear, faint ghostly outlines of small fists jammed deep inside, of crayons and candy bars and half-eaten PBJs.

That sweater was probably the last gift Rose ever gave Maddy that didn't come with strings attached. Even the presents for the baby had come with warnings about the perfidy of men, about the impermanence of love, about how if Maddy had half a brain she would stop wishing on lucky stars and start pumping up her 401(k). All the things her nine-months-pregnant daughter hadn't wanted to hear.

All the things that had turned out to be painfully true.

September waned and she continued to duck Rose's demand for an answer, but the yearning for something more than they had shared before lingered and grew stronger. In early October she packed Hannah and Priscilla into the Mustang and drove down to Oregon for her father's seventieth birthday party. He knew all about Rose's offer and Maddy's reluctance, and his take on things surprised her.

"It's time you went home," Bill Bainbridge said as they watched Hannah pretend to have fun with his neighbor's children. "You need your mother. You both do."

Maddy pondered his statement. Was that possible? She was a grown woman, the single mother of a small child. She was long past needing anyone. She was the one who wiped away Hannah's tears, the one who lingered at the bedroom door, listening to the holy sound of a sleeping child. Rose hadn't done any of those things for Maddy when she was growing up. At least, not that Maddy could remember. Rose had been too busy selling pricey real estate to people with more money than brains, sure that the example she was setting for her daughter would put Maddy on course for success.

Nothing had prepared Rose for the rebellious underachiever who sprang from her womb with a mind of her own.

"It's not that I don't love Rose," she told her father as they wiped away the remnants of cake and ice cream from every surface in his kitchen. "I just think we do much better with a continent between us."

"She's reaching out to you," Bill said as he tossed a used paper towel into the trash.

"The way I reached out to her when I was pregnant with Hannah? She didn't even show up for the birth." Nothing Rose had ever done hurt Maddy more than that.

"Did you ever ask her why?"

"I don't care why. There's nothing she could say that could explain not being here."

"People act in strange ways sometimes, Maddy. Sometimes they're just not thinking clearly."

"How come you always take her side?"

"I'm not taking sides. I'm just saying maybe it's time you gave her another chance."

"Easy for you to say," Maddy grumbled as her father pulled her into a clumsy hug. She was desperate to change the subject. "You were only married to her. I'm her daughter: I'm doing life."

They both laughed, but Maddy sensed Bill's heart wasn't in it. She wanted to kick herself for making such a thoughtless remark. It was no secret that her father had never quite managed to get over his first wife. He had gone on to make a successful second marriage that had ended with the death of his beloved Irma, but there was little doubt that the love of his life was the fiercely independent redhead from New Jersey who didn't believe happily ever after existed anywhere but in the movies.

"We don't get a lot of second chances in this life," Tom said when he kissed her goodbye. "Go home, Maddy. Give it a try for Hannah's sake if not your own. You won't regret it."

"Hannah and I could move in with you," she said, only half kidding. "I'm a pretty good cook and Hannah's great company."

He smiled and shook his head. "You know your old man's hitting the road next week. I promised Irma I'd make that trip we'd been planning, and it's a promise I intend to keep." Oregon to Florida and back again, with scores of stops along the way. Irma had been working on the last of the itinerary when she lost her long battle with breast cancer.

Maddy's eyes filled with tears at the memory of her stepmother. "Has it gotten any easier?"

"Nope." He glanced away toward the curb where her Mustang idled loudly. "Didn't expect it to."

"You'll stop by and see us in Seattle during your travels, won't you?"

He grinned and tugged on a lock of her hair. "Not if you're in New Jersey."

"Fat chance."

"Six months," he said as she hugged him goodbye. "Give your mother six months. What can you lose?"

"My sanity," Maddy said and they laughed, but the truth was out there and she couldn't take it back. She wanted one more chance to get things right because sometimes even the most independent woman was only a daughter at heart.

Chapter Two

ROSEMARY DIFALCO SWORE off men in August of 1992, and as far as she could tell, that was when Lady Luck finally sat up and took notice. All her life Rose had been waiting for her ship to come in, and when it finally sailed into view she swam right out to meet it.

You didn't get anything in this world by being shy, and you sure as hell didn't get anything by waiting for some man to hand it to you on a silver platter.

For longer than she could remember her mother, Fay, had rented out rooms in her ramshackle old Victorian house, sharing their living space with retired schoolteachers, penniless artists, and an assortment of hard-luck cases whose only common ground was the bathroom on the second floor. When Fay died almost five years ago, she left the house to her four daughters, three of whom wanted absolutely nothing to do with it. Rose, however, saw possibilities lurking behind the cracked plaster and faded carpets, and she bought out her sisters' shares and settled

down to the hard work of building a new life for herself
at a time when she needed it most.

She took early retirement, then traded in her fancy
condo on Eden Lake. She cashed in her 401(k), then
plowed the proceeds into the house where she had grown
up, a wreck of a Victorian that just happened to boast
ocean views from almost every bedroom.

The Candlelight Inn was born and Rose never looked
back. To her delight, she found that she enjoyed the constant parade of guests. She loved the challenge of staying
one step ahead of the needs of a nineteenth-century house
with a mind of its own. Most of all, she loved the fact
that the Candlelight's success had made it possible for her
to offer her daughter a way out of the mess her life was
in.

Anyway you looked at it, this should have been a slam
dunk. Rose needed help running the place; Maddy needed
a job. The perfect example of need meeting opportunity.

So why did Rose wake up every morning with the sense
that she was preparing for war? She had created an oasis
of peace and tranquillity for her paying guests, a place
people came to when they wanted to leave the stresses of
the real world behind. You would think at least a tiny bit
of that tranquillity might spill over onto the innkeeper's
family. Take this morning, for instance. Maddy had been
holed up in the office working on the Inn's Web site for
hours now. Rose hadn't seen hide nor hair of her since
they'd laid out the breakfast buffet in silence. They had
exchanged words late last night over something so trivial
that Rose couldn't even remember what it was, yet the
aftermath had left her wondering for the first time if she
had made a terrible mistake inviting Maddy and Hannah
to come back home.

It was painfully clear they weren't happy. Her daughter
was prickly and argumentative, more reminiscent of the
seventeen-year-old girl she had once been than the grown
woman pictured on her driver's license. And Hannah—
oh, Hannah was enough to break your heart. The delightful little girl who had entertained Rose with her songs and

stories last Christmas in Seattle was now a withdrawn and painfully sad child whose smiles never quite reached her stormy blue eyes.

Rose knew that Tom and Maddy's breakup had nothing to do with her, but decades of guilt were hard to ignore. She hadn't prepared Maddy for the real world of men and women. She had taught her how to balance a checkbook, shop for the best auto loan, and make minor plumbing repairs, but she hadn't taught her the fine art of living with a man.

The truth was, she hadn't a clue herself. Rose had grown up in a world of women, with an absentee father, three sisters, and more aunts and nieces than you could shake a bra strap at, and between them all they had about as much luck at keeping a man as they had at the slot machines in Atlantic City.

Some women were lucky in love. Some were lucky in business. One look at the bare ring fingers and flourishing IRAs of the four DiFalco sisters, and you knew which way the wind blew. Lucy, the eldest, said a DiFalco woman couldn't hold on to a man if she had him Krazy Glued to her side. Over the years Rose had come to realize the truth of that statement.

In the best of times love was a puzzle Rose had never been able to unravel. She had married a wonderful man, the salt of the earth, and still hadn't been able to find a way to hold on to love for the long haul. He offered her the world, and she had found herself longing for the stars. She had a beautiful daughter who was bright and talented and loving, yet somehow that wasn't quite enough for Rose, either. She wanted Maddy to have everything she never had, to be everything she could never be, and when Maddy had turned out to be lacking the ambition gene, Rose's disappointment knew no bounds.

Maddy was a dreamer, same as her father. She followed her heart wherever it led, and she never thought to leave a trail of breadcrumbs so she could find her way safely home. Maddy's unplanned pregnancy had filled Rose with a combination of elation and dread. She hadn't known

Tom Lawlor well, but she did know that he had already earned his parenting stripes and wasn't in the market to add a few more to his sleeve. He was her age, after all, and she understood him even if she didn't approve.

But not Maddy. Not her daydreaming, foolish optimist of a daughter. She hadn't seen it coming, not even when he spelled it out for her in neon letters a foot high. She had still believed they would find a happy ending, believed it right up until the moment Tom and Lisa flew off to Vegas for one of those quickie weddings in a chapel on the Strip.

She longed to gather Maddy and Hannah up in her arms and kiss away their tears, mend their broken hearts until they were better than new.

All of the things she didn't have time to do when Maddy was a little girl.

Instead there she was, a successful sixty-two-year-old businesswoman with the hottest B&B between Rehoboth Beach and Martha's Vineyard, trying to summon up the guts to knock on the door to her own office and see how her daughter was getting on with the Web site. Rose had bearded wild bankers in their lairs, charmed free advertising out of jaded local radio stations, spun pure gold from straw. Spending five stress-free minutes with her only child should be a piece of cake.

So what if she and Maddy had exchanged words last night. It wasn't the first time and God knew it wouldn't be the last. They were mother and daughter, hardwired to get on each other's nerves. Nothing was going to change that fact, but she could make it better. She knew she could.

If she could just bring herself to knock on that door.

"OH, NO!" MADDY hit the backspace key three times, then retyped the number. This was no time to screw up, not when the auction was sliding into its final minutes and she was struggling to maintain high bidder status over some surprisingly stiff competition from someone named FireGuy. You wouldn't think there would be so much action over a dented teapot, but she'd had to raise her maximum bid twice in the last hour just to stay in the game.

The computer screen went blank. The hard drive grumbled, then groaned. She held her breath until the screen refreshed itself and her new bid appeared.

"Okay," she said, grinning at her reflection. "That's more like it." Now all she had to do was ignore the fact that her mother was lurking in the hallway like your average peeping Tom and keep her mind on making sure that old samovar was waiting for Hannah under the tree on Christmas morning.

Priscilla pawed at the door. She looked up at Maddy with limpid brown eyes, then yipped one of those high-pitched poodle yips capable of breaking juice glasses two towns over.

"Yes, I know she's been standing out there for the last ten minutes, Priscilla, and no, I don't know why."

The door swung open on cue.

"Very funny," Rose said, her cheeks stained bright red. "I was polishing the hall table, for your information."

"I polished it yesterday," Maddy said, one eye locked onto her computer screen.

"We polish daily around here these days," her mother said. The usual edge to her words was absent. "The paying customers expect it."

Maddy forced herself to relax. "I have a lot to learn about being an innkeeper. I bumped into the Loewensteins in the upper hallway last night and almost lost five years of my life."

"You'll get used to it." Rose hesitated, then stepped into the room. She smelled like Pledge and Chanel No. 5, a combination that suited her mother down to the ground. "I don't want to interrupt you if you're working on the Web site."

Maddy reached for the mouse to click over to a different, safer screen, but she wasn't quick enough. Her mother leaned over her shoulder and peered at the image and the accompanying information.

"For Hannah?" Rose asked.

Maddy nodded, wishing she had faster fingers or a less curious mother. Asking for both might have been tempting the gods. "You know how she is about Aladdin. The second I saw this, I thought it would make a perfect magic lamp."

"I thought you'd finished Christmas shopping for Hannah."

"I thought so, too, but she came home bubbling about a magic lamp she saw in a coloring book at school and—well, it's Christmas and she's my only child." She looked up at her mother. "You know how it is." *Didn't you feel that way when I was little? Didn't you want to gather up the stars and pour them into my Christmas stocking?*

"You spoil that child."

"She deserves a little spoiling. She's had a tough year."

"That teapot won't change anything."

Maddy had the mouse in such a death grip that she was surprised it didn't squeak in surrender. "I think I know what's best for my child." How could one five-foot-tall woman reduce her adult daughter to the emotional level of a sulky teenager just by breathing?

"I thought she had forgotten all about Aladdin."

"I don't know what gave you that idea."

"She's too old for this kind of make-believe."

"I suppose you would have advised Stephen King to get his head out of the clouds, too."

"What's that supposed to mean?"

Keep your mouth closed, Maddy. For once in your life, just shut up.

She peered more closely at the computer screen in front of her and prayed Rose would take the hint. You spend three hours wrestling with cascading style sheets for the Inn's new Web site and there was no sign of the boss lady, but the second you flip to Shoreline Auctions, she appeared like magic right over your shoulder.

Well, there was no hope for it. Hannah, a devoted fan of all things Aladdin, needed a touch of magic, and Maddy was determined to make at least one of her wishes come true. This samovar had seen better days, but, polished and repaired, it would delight her little girl and that was the most important thing. With only five minutes to go until the auction closed, she wasn't about to lose high-bidder status now.

"You're going to give her unreal expectations, Maddy. The sooner Hannah learns she can't have everything she wants, the better off she'll be."

Ignoring Rose was like ignoring a tsunami when you were trapped one hundred yards from shore in a rowboat.

"It's only a teapot, Ma, not the keys to a Porsche."

Rose made a sound that fell somewhere between a snort and a sigh. "That child needs a teapot like I need more rooms to clean."

Rolling her eyes in dismay over her mother's pronouncements had become a reflex action. The figures on the screen changed. Maddy groaned and quickly typed in a new high bid of her own. "That'll teach you to mess with JerseyGirl."

Rose whipped out her eyeglasses from the pocket of her pale blue sweater, then slipped them on. "Tell me that's not the price."

"That's not the price." Unfortunately she wasn't lying. The final price was bound to be higher. She refreshed the screen and watched as the numbers changed one more time. "You're a tough one, FireGuy, but you're not going to win." She typed in yet another bid and pressed Enter.

"FireGuy?"

"That's his screen name."

"What's wrong with his real name? Does he have something to hide?"

"I'm sure his entire life's an open book, Mother, but everyone on-line has a screen name. That's how it's done."

Rose peered at her over the tops of her glasses. "Do you have one?"

"Of course I have one."

"I hope it's nothing embarrassing."

When Rose was in one of these moods, the name Betsy Ross would be embarrassing.

"I don't understand this obsession with on-line auctions," her mother went on. "You could drive over to Toys "R" Us and buy one of those sweet Barbie teapots for half the price."

"You're welcome to drive over to Toys "R" Us anytime you feel like it, Mother. I'm perfectly happy with Shoreline Auctions."

"Nobody should pay that much for a battered teakettle." Rose's sigh sent middle-aged daughters across the Garden State ducking for cover. "Sometimes I worry about that child."

"Because she has an imagination?"

"You've filled her head with fairy tales. Where is that going to get her in life? She should be making play dates with her school friends, not dreaming over magic teapots and flying carpets."

And people wondered why she had left home at seventeen. Maddy bit her tongue so hard she almost drew blood.

"Have you heard a single word I've said?"

"Every last syllable." Maddy turned from the screen. "Mother, if you make me lose this teakettle to some bozo who'll use it to store fishing lures, I'll be forced to tell everyone in Paradise Point that your naturally red hair quit being natural around 1981." Rose opened her mouth to protest, but Maddy raised her hand. "I have less than four minutes left in this auction. You can finish the lecture after I nail down the kettle."

It was the wrong thing to say. Maddy knew it immediately. If she was looking for the pathway toward peaceful coexistence, maybe it was time to stop and ask for directions.

"Mom, I'm sorry. If you'll just—"

But it was too late. Rose wheeled and stalked from the room, and Maddy had no doubt the rest of the clan would know about her latest transgression before it was time to rinse the radicchio for the dinner salads.

She knew she should run after Rose and apologize. Give her a hug and crack some clumsy joke to try and break the tension that had been building between them, but the clock was ticking on the auction, and if she left her desk for even a second, she would lose the kettle, and her only chance to make Hannah smile again would be lost with it.

She had waited fifteen years to mend fences with her mother. Another fifteen minutes wouldn't hurt.

Chapter Three

O'Malley's Bar & Grill—the other side of town

YOU HAVE BEEN OUTBID BY JERSEYGIRL.
TO PLACE A NEW BID, CLICK HERE.

Aidan Michael O'Malley slammed his fist down on the shiny surface of the bar and sent the mouse skittering over the edge. He grabbed the gizmo just before it hit the floor and quickly repositioned it on the stack of cocktail napkins that served as a mouse pad. Ninety more seconds until the auction closed. If he didn't type in a new dollar figure right now, as in this second, he'd lose the auction and face the wrath of his daughter.

"You have to win," Kelly had instructed him that morning as she shrugged her narrow shoulders into her bright red down vest. "This is just like the one in the picture of her and Great-grandpa Michael at the old restaurant."

He knew the photograph well. It was the last one taken of Irene and Michael O'Malley before the Easter Sunday hurricane of 1952 roared across the inlet, taking everything in its path. The dock. The boats bobbing next to it.

The restaurant they had built up from nothing.

And Michael O'Malley himself.

"What do you think?" Kelly asked. "Maybe it'll bring back some happy memories for her on Christmas morning."

He hadn't the heart to remind her that it had been a long time since Grandma Irene had cared much about dented teapots. Or her family, for that matter. Holidays had become nothing but another way of counting down the years.

It was a feeling he understood too damn well.

"You sure she'd want something like this? Looks like a piece of rust to me."

Kelly sighed loudly. "Oh, Dad, really. It's perfect. You'll see. All you have to do is log on to the auction site and make sure nobody outbids you."

"Whoa," he said. "Let's establish a few limits here."

Kelly gave him the I-can't-believe-you're-really-my-father look she had perfected over the last seventeen years. "It shouldn't be more than seventy-five dollars," she said casually. "But you can go up as high as one hundred."

He widened his eyes. "You have a hundred dollars to spend?"

"I have a lot more than a hundred dollars," she said, grabbing her books from the kitchen counter. "It's from the money I've been saving for college expenses."

Other kids begged, borrowed, and stole money from their parents. His kid could open a savings and loan with what she'd put away baby-sitting, waiting tables at the clam bar during the summer, and tutoring. Sometimes he wondered why, in a life that had featured more than its share of shit, he'd been given this gift of pure gold.

Other times he just thanked God.

"Be careful," he said as she plucked her car keys from the pegboard near the door. "It's icy outside. Maybe I should drive you to school."

The look on her face was one of complete horror.

"Okay," he said, laughing. "I rescind the offer. Just take

it slow and remember those are all-wheel brakes."

"You worry too much." She rose up on tiptoe to kiss him on the cheek. A second later she was gone, leaving behind the faint scent of maple syrup and herbal shampoo in her wake.

You'd be proud of her, Sandy. She's everything you were at that age . . . everything we prayed she would be.

He had pretty much gotten over the habit of talking to his dead wife years ago, but lately he'd found himself wishing Sandy could come back for an hour—even fifteen minutes—just long enough for her to see the wonder their baby girl had turned out to be. Kelly was bright and pretty and kind-hearted. She was popular at school; the other students as well as the teachers loved her. It hadn't been easy for her growing up without a mother, but you'd never know it by the way she sailed through life with a smile for everyone.

"You've done a great job with her," his sister-in-law, Claire, said the other day when he told her about the full scholarship. He would have liked to take credit for it, but he knew he had about as much to do with his daughter's success as he had to do with the last presidential election. Kelly was a force unto herself. All he ever had to do was point her in the right direction and trust her to do the rest.

Lately he'd had the feeling that he had been doing too much of that over the last few years. Since the accident, the focus had been so clearly on Billy's death and his own recovery, that Kelly's needs had been put on the back burner. *Don't worry about Kelly,* they all said. *That girl was born knowing the right thing to do.*

He should be proud of that fact, but there were times when what he actually felt was guilt. She was such a good kid, so dependable, that sometimes he thought he hadn't paid as much attention to her as she deserved. She seemed to float above the fray, always making the right decisions, always exceeding expectations while her old man fought the world on a daily basis and more times than not came up the loser. What the hell could he tell her that she hadn't been born knowing?

He tapped in a new bid, wincing as he saw the numbers creeping uncomfortably close to triple digits. What did Kelly want with this piece of junk anyway? His grandmother would take one weary look at it, muster up a criticism, then drift back into her memories of a world long past. Kelly's excitement would swiftly turn to disappointment, and he would be left trying to explain to her that it was nothing personal.

The irony would be lost on a bubbly seventeen-year-old girl with a heart of gold and enough enthusiasm to light the world. She believed she could make a difference, his little girl did. She believed that good people could do great things, and when he looked into her eyes (eyes so much like her mother's) he could almost believe it, too.

What difference did another twenty bucks make? If she wanted that teakettle for Irene, he'd make damn sure she got it.

He tapped in the number, pressed Enter, then sat back to see what JerseyGirl had to say about it.

MADDY COULDN'T BELIEVE her eyes. One minute to go and FireGuy topped her bid by twenty bucks. There were names for that kind of bidder. What kind of louse would lurk in the shadows until the very last second, then leap into the fray with an over-the-top bid designed to snatch that treasure out of your hands before you could type in one last set of numbers.

She quickly scrolled down, tapped in a totally ridiculous figure, one that would have sent Rose flying to the phone to dial 911, then hit Enter.

"Take that!" she hurled at the screen. A number big enough to give even the most rabid bidder pause. She leaned back in her chair and glowered at the monitor, almost daring FireGuy to up the ante one last time. She'd show him how it was done. Nobody got the better of JerseyGirl, not while there was still breath in her typing fingers. FireGuy hadn't a clue what he was up against.

Eighteen seconds. Seventeen. Sixteen . . .

*   *   *

CLAIRE MEEHAN O'MALLEY, Aidan's sister-in-law and business partner, leaned over his shoulder and surveyed the scene.

"FireGuy!" she said with a bark of laughter. "Don't tell me you're prowling the chatrooms, Aidan!"

"Can it," he said, furiously tapping away at the keyboard.

Fifteen seconds . . . fourteen . . .

"Shoreline Singles, right?" Claire could barely speak for laughing. " 'Where the Elite Go to Meet . . . true love is just a click away.' "

He shot her a look. "Sounds like you've been there yourself."

"My lips are sealed," Claire said. "Come on. 'Fess up. Loneliness isn't a crime, brother-in-law. I don't blame you if you're chatting up somebody on-line. About time you got back in circulation after—" She stopped. There was no need to finish the sentence.

"I'm not in a chatroom."

"Fine, fine." She backed away, hands up in surrender. "Don't tell me. You know I'll find out sooner or later. We O'Malley women are relentless."

"Stow it, will you?"

"If it isn't a chatroom, then it must be an auction." She laughed again, louder this time. "An auction! The guy who thinks shopping is cruel and unusual punishment. I can't believe it!"

Ten seconds . . . nine . . .

What the hell was wrong with the computer? He pressed Enter once, then twice, and nothing. He reentered the figures and hit Enter again.

"Not now," he muttered to the screen. "Come on . . . come on . . . gimme one more second . . . yeah!" The screen flickered and he held his breath while it refreshed itself.

THIS AUCTION HAS ENDED
WINNING BIDDER: JERSEYGIRL (53)

He groaned, then fixed Claire with a baleful look. "I lost."

"You look like it's the end of the world," Claire remarked as she began pouring salted peanuts into a dozen red plastic bowls. "What were you bidding on: *The Secret History of Captain Kirk*?"

"Not funny." He clicked over to check the tides on his favorite South Jersey site. His fondness for all things *Star Trek* was the basis for much of what passed for humor at the O'Malley. "It was for Kelly."

"Oh, honey, I'm sorry." She snagged a peanut from one of the bowls and popped it in her mouth. "Shopping for a teenager is hell. You'd be better off giving her a gift certificate."

"Not this time. She asked me to bid on a teakettle she wanted for Grandma Irene."

Claire's normally cheerful features contracted into a scowl. "I don't know why you two bother. It's not like that old lady ever did anything for anyone in this family but herself."

It was an old argument. "She's my grandmother. She took Billy and me in after our parents died. She's Kelly's only link with—"

"What a load of crap. That bitch doesn't have a sentimental bone in her body."

"You don't know that."

"The hell I don't. The old bat didn't so much as send a mass card when Billy died. Her own grandson—" Her voice broke and she took a moment to regroup. "You don't forget things like that, Aidan."

He could have reminded Claire of the incident at Billy's funeral when she turned Irene away, but what was the point. There was enough guilt and blame and pain for all of them.

"She's an old woman. She's been through a lot."

"And we haven't? She's all for herself. Always has been, always will be. Kelly's been trying since the day she was born to make that cow love her—what makes you think it's going to work now?"

He pushed back from the counter and stood up. "I don't think it's going to work now, okay? I don't think there's a chance in hell Irene's going to change. Not for your kids and not for mine."

"Listen, I—"

"I'm not going to fight old battles with you, Red." He reached out and ruffled her mop of silver-dusted auburn curls, but she pulled away.

"I'm serious, Aidan. Don't waste your time on that old battle-ax. You don't owe her anything. None of us does."

Her pain and anger filled the room, edging out everything else. Claire had grown up in a large and happy family who had never known an emotion they didn't express. Even during the worst of times (and there had been plenty), she took love as a given, the one constant upon which everything else depended. Irene's indifference to her grandchildren and great-grandchildren was beyond Claire's comprehension.

Aidan had long since abandoned dreams of some great familial epiphany that ended with a group hug and a chorus of "Home Sweet Home." Irene had opened her house to Aidan and Billy after their parents died, but she had never quite managed to open her heart. He had spent a great part of his life wondering why his own grandmother didn't love him, but he had come to realize the answer would remain hidden away with the rest of Irene's secrets.

"Kelly has to figure it all out on her own," he said finally. "If she wants to give Irene a teakettle for Christmas, I'm not going to stand in the way."

"And Kel thinks a teakettle will bring about this miracle?"

"She hopes it'll bring back some happy memories of when Irene and Mike owned the restaurant."

Claire sighed loudly. "I didn't think O'Malleys bred optimists."

"Me neither," he said as he reached for a bar towel. If it wasn't for bad luck, the O'Malleys would have no luck at all.

Chapter Four

"YES!" MADDY LEANED back in her chair and admired the notice on the computer screen. "Oh, Hannah, wait until you see this!"

CONGRATULATIONS, JERSEYGIRL! YOU WON ITEM
#5815796
GENUINE ANTIQUE RUSSIAN SAMOVAR
CLICK HERE TO USE SPEEDPAY

She hit Enter, typed in her password, clicked YES YES and YES, then waited while the screen dissolved, then reassembled itself. The seller promised to ship within forty-eight hours, and with a little bit of luck, Hannah's magic lamp would be wrapped and tucked away in the closet by this time next week.

She exited the program, pushed back her chair, then dashed down the back hallway into the kitchen, where her mother and her aunt Lucy were slicing orange segments for the guests' salads.

"Congratulations are in order, ladies!" she announced as she reached for a slice of orange. "I'm a winner!"

"You won the Lotto?" Lucy asked, deftly slipping her paring knife between the membranes. "Which one: the Pick Three or Pick Four? Pick Six I would've seen in the paper."

"Not the Lotto," Maddy said, kissing her aunt's Estée Lauder'd cheek. "I won a samovar."

Lucy turned a puzzled face to her sister. "A what?"

"A rusty teapot," Rose said, shaking her head. "Can you believe it?"

She kissed Rose's cheek for good measure. *I'm trying, Mother, but you don't make it easy.* "It's almost an antique."

"It's a piece of junk."

She ignored her mother's jibe. "FireGuy gave it his best shot, but I was a woman on a mission and I wouldn't be denied."

Rose looked over at her sister. "You wouldn't believe what they get for junk on those auction sites."

"It's for Hannah," Maddy said, wishing she didn't sound quite so apologetic. She was a grown woman, too, and a mother. She didn't have to apologize to anyone for the choices she made for her daughter, no matter how ridiculous they might sound to the rest of her literal, practical, no-nonsense family. "She's always wanted a magic lamp, and this is the next best thing."

Aunt Lucy frowned. "I thought you said it was a teapot."

"It is a teapot," Rose said. "A plain, ordinary, rusty, overpriced teapot."

"Yes, but it's a rusty teapot with magical powers." Hey, why not? They already thought she was out of her mind. She might as well add a little more fuel to the fire.

"Magical powers?" Aunt Lucy crossed herself. "I don't like the sound of this."

"Oh, don't be an idiot," Rose said, swatting her big sister with the wet end of a dishtowel. "The only magic thing about that pot is the way it made Maddy's money disappear."

Lucy burst into laughter while Rose looked like a one-hundred-pound cat who'd caught a particularly tasty canary.

"I'm glad the two of you find this so amusing." Maddy glared at her mother across the bounty of food strewn across the worktable. "Nothing you DiFalco girls like more than stomping on someone's imagination." She almost said "dream," but she was afraid they'd launch into a medley of Frank Sinatra songs.

"Maddy, really! Why do you always take things so seriously. I was only—"

Who said time travel was impossible? Thirteen words uttered by a woman with dyed red hair, and Maddy was catapulted back to the glory days of her adolescence when the mere sound of Rose's voice was enough to send her running headlong into the night. Racing down the back hallway to the office didn't have quite the same impact, not when you were thirty-two and a mother yourself, but a slammed door still made a statement that even the most stubborn woman on earth couldn't ignore. Her heart was beating so fast she sat down on the edge of the desk and wondered if the Paradise Point rescue squad had a defibrillator.

"Hello?" A soft voice sounded at the door she had just about knocked off its hinges.

Oh, God. Not Mrs. Loewenstein again. Didn't the woman know she was supposed to be off somewhere with Mr. Loewenstein, reveling in the romantic wonders of the Garden State.

"Is everything all right in there?"

Maddy swallowed a string of words not usually heard at the Candlelight. When was she going to remember this was no longer Grandma Fay's house but Rose's tribute to the romance of capitalism?

"Everything's fine, Mrs. Loewenstein." She opened the office door a crack and smiled up at the elderly woman. "Sorry if the noise startled you. A gust of wind slammed the door shut."

"Wind?" Mrs. Loewenstein peered over Maddy's head into the room. "Your windows are shut tight."

She inched her smile up another notch. "Oh, you know how drafty these old houses can be."

"You need more insulation," Mrs. Loewenstein said with a sage nod of her head. "I'll give you my son Buddy's card. He'll take good care of you."

Maddy thanked her, then closed the door. She considered locking it, but that was probably against the innkeeper's code of ethics.

"This isn't going to work," she said out loud. "Not in a million years."

ROSE SIGHED AT the sound of the office door slamming shut a second time. "She used to do that when she was a teenager. I was hoping she'd grow out of it by the time she turned thirty."

Lucy turned to face her sister. "Did I say something wrong? I probably shouldn't have said that about the Pick Six."

"No," said Rose. "I said something wrong." She attacked one of the oranges with a cleaver. "Everything I say is wrong these days."

"Maddy always did have a flair for the dramatic." Lucy finished sectioning the last orange in her bowl, then rinsed her hands at the double sink. "I'm surprised she didn't end up in the theater."

"Ma always said Maddy was one tantrum away from winning an Oscar." Not at all like the relentlessly practical, fiercely earthbound DiFalco sisters. If Rose hadn't endured twenty-three hours of labor to deliver the child, she wouldn't have believed Maddy was her own flesh and blood. Maddy was mercurial, emotional, impulsive. All the things her mother wasn't and never would be.

All the things Rose didn't understand.

"Maybe it's a good thing I never had children," Lucy mused as she dried her hands on a snowy-white kitchen towel. "I don't know what I would have done with a daughter like Maddy."

"You couldn't have done any worse than I did." The sharp edge of the counter dug into her hipbone as she attacked an orange with wild swipes of the knife. "I feel like I'm walking on eggshells."

"In other words, nothing has changed."

She considered bashing one of the oranges with the meat mallet, but thought better of it. Orange bits in the hollandaise would be unacceptable at the four-star Candlelight. "It's worse than ever, Lucia. We're at each other's throats every second. It's like the last fifteen years never happened and we're right back where we were."

Lucy busied herself with an invisible snippet of pith. "Nice atmosphere for Hannah."

"Tell me about it. I wanted this to work. I wanted her to love what I've done with the old house and throw herself into growing the business with me."

"She seems enthusiastic enough."

Rose jabbed the orange with the tip of her knife and said nothing.

"You want her to be you," Lucy observed quietly, "and that's just not going to happen, Rosie."

"Is that so terrible?" Rose swung around, knife slicing into the air between them. "I'm a successful businesswoman. I'm well liked in the community. I meet interesting people every day of the week without leaving home, and I have enough money in the bank so that I could say to hell with everything tomorrow and never have to worry." She paused for effect. "Is that such a terrible fate to wish on my only child?"

"Maybe it's not what Maddy wants."

"She doesn't know what she wants. If she knew what she wanted, she wouldn't have——" She stopped, ashamed of what she had been about to say. Ashamed that she could have thought such a terrible thing.

Lucy took the cleaver from her and placed it safely on the counter. "This is Maddy's life, Rosie, not yours. She'll find her way sooner or later. We all did."

"She had it all right there for the taking," Rose said, her frustration boiling over like an unwatched pot of soup. "She was climbing the ladder at her job. She and Tom had a solid long-term relationship with a real future and then . . ."

Lucy sighed. "Hannah."

Rose felt her expression soften. "The little girl who turned my little girl's life inside out." She thanked God for her granddaughter every day of her life. Hannah was a bit of heaven on earth, proof that angels sometimes deigned to mingle with mortals. She couldn't imagine a world without Hannah in it, but how she wished Hannah's arrival hadn't exacted such a high price from Maddy.

"Maddy's doing a great job with her," Lucy said, pouring them each a cup of coffee from the decaf pot. "She's a good mother."

"Of course she is. That's never been an issue."

"You've told her that?"

Rose hesitated. "Not recently."

"Ever?"

"I'm sure I—" She deflated like a failed soufflé. "I don't know."

"I know you mean well, Rosie. I know you love that girl more than life itself, but you'd better take a step back before you lose her all over again."

"She doesn't like me." It hurt to say the words. Much more than Rose had imagined it would. "She never has." Even when Maddy was a little girl, Rose had sensed the distance between them, a barrier she couldn't break through no matter what she said or did. "You would think after thirty-two years I'd learn to accept that but"—she dragged the back of her hand across her eyes and winced at the sting of citrus—"I thought it would be different this time. I thought if we approached this as partners, we'd strike a balance."

"You hurt her badly," Lucy said. "When you didn't fly to Seattle to be with her when Hannah was born, you almost broke her heart."

Rose's temper flared. "You of all people know why I couldn't."

"Yes," Lucy said calmly, "and it was a valid reason.

But the one person on earth who deserves to know the truth is still in the dark."

"I know," Rose said, her voice breaking. "I know."

"So do it."

"I've tried. I can't seem to find the words."

"Then write her a letter."

Rose laughed despite herself. "Oh, Lucy, how did it all end up such a mess?"

"Blame it on the five-hundred-pound gorilla in the room."

Rose couldn't help but laugh.

"You owe her the truth, Rosie. She's been carrying that burden around with her since Hannah was born. Help her out. Tell her why you weren't there for her."

"I wish I could, but it would only make things worse."

"You don't know that."

"That's the one thing I'm sure of."

Lucy draped an arm around her little sister's shoulders. "It's only been three weeks, honey. Things will get better before you know it. I promise you."

"I hope so," Rose said. If they didn't, she would be the first winner of the New Jersey Innkeeper of the Year award to run away from home.

"ENOUGH ALREADY," CLAIRE said as she finished slicing hamburger rolls for the lunch crowd. "You're staring at the screen like you lost your best friend. So you didn't win the auction. So what. Kelly's a smart kid. She knows you can't win them all."

"I've forgotten all about the auction," he lied. "I'm checking tomorrow's tide. Amos might come out to repair the dock and I want to—"

"I wasn't born yesterday, brother-in-law. You're still ticked you didn't nail the teapot."

"The hell I am."

"Fine," she said, brushing the crumbs into the palm of her hand, then tossing them into the sink. "Whatever." She piled the rolls high on a platter. "I'll bring these out

for Tommy to toss on the grill before the natives start
eating the bar rags."

He mumbled something but didn't take his eyes off the
screen.

"I have a dentist appointment in fifteen minutes and
then I go to pick up Billy at school. I'll be back around
three-thirty, four o'clock."

The second she left he flipped the screen back to the
auction site, and the big, full color picture of Kelly's teapot appeared. He felt a tug of emotion as he looked at it,
and he wondered if Kelly had experienced the same thing
when she first saw it. The original O'Malley's had been
a neighborhood restaurant with a regional reputation for
good food and great atmosphere. There was a box of
memories up in the attic, filled with newspaper clippings
from the hundreds of articles that had been written about
O'Malley's in its heyday, before the Hurricane of '52
swept it all away.

Kelly said the teapot she was bidding on reminded her
of one of the many teapots Grandma Irene had had on
display at the restaurant years ago, but that was like saying you liked one grain of sand over another grain of sand.
Who could tell the difference? Still, he couldn't deny the
way the thing pulled at him.

"Hey, boss," Tommy greeted him as he pushed through
the swinging door that separated the kitchen from the bar
itself. "I thought you were back there getting the books
ready for Bernie."

"He's coming tonight," Aidan said, moving swiftly to
the framed photos nailed to the wall above the cash register.

Tommy glanced up at the television screen. "How
many times are you gonna marry the wrong guy, Erica?"
He sounded more like a lovestruck teenager than a sixty-
year-old retired cop.

"You talking to Susan Lucci again?"

"Damn straight and one day she's going to answer
and"—Tommy made a *va-room* noise like a fast-moving

car—*"hasta la vista*, baby. Send my last paycheck to Pine Valley."

"You're a sick man, Kennedy." His own glance bounced quickly over photos of his late parents on their wedding day and his brother, Billy, the first day he reported for duty at the firehouse. Where was the one of Mike and Irene and the old restaurant? "Good thing Jean's an understanding woman."

"Works two ways, pal o'mine." Tommy's eyes were glued to the screen. "She'd leave me in a New York minute for Harrison Ford."

It was bar room bullshit and they both knew it. Tommy and Jean Kennedy were one of those till-death-do-us-part couples who were happy to be in it for the long haul. During forty years of marriage the Kennedys had been hit by just about everything life could possibly throw at them, but somehow the good times always managed to outnumber the bad in their eyes. They were lucky and they knew it, which made them luckier still.

Sometimes Aidan wondered what he and Sandy would have been like ten or fifteen years down the road. Would they have grown together like the Kennedys or lived parallel lives in the same house like so many of his old friends? He liked to think that what they had shared would only have grown deeper and richer with the years, but the truth was he would never know. Intimacy required an openness of spirit, a willingness to risk heartbreak. O'Malleys seemed to have the ability to bypass intimacy and go straight to heartbreak without passing GO.

"You need anything?" Tommy asked. "I already made the drop-off to the bank."

"Didn't we have a picture of Irene and Mike's old restaurant hanging up here?"

"The one taken the summer before the Easter Sunday hurricane?"

Aidan nodded.

"The nail gave a couple weeks ago. I stashed the picture in the drawer under the register."

Aidan slid open the drawer. Rubber bands. A crumpled

Canadian dollar. Two Frank Sinatra CDs, one Pink Floyd, a well-thumbed copy of last year's *Sports Illustrated* swimsuit edition. He slid his hand under the magazine and poked around.

"It's not here."

Tommy tore his attention away from *All My Children* for a minute. "I think that's where I stowed it."

Aidan checked the drawers, the cabinet adjacent to the dartboard, even unlocked the utility closet hidden behind the rack of pool cues and looked behind mega-sized bottles of Clorox and Mr. Clean.

"I know it's somewhere," Tommy said.

"You didn't throw it out, did you?"

"What the hell kind of question is that? Why would I throw it out?"

"Beats me," said Aidan, "but it's not hanging on the wall, and so far it doesn't seem to be anywhere else."

"It'll turn up," Tommy said as he upped the volume on *All My Children*. "Wait and see."

Not much else he could do. He went back into the kitchen, poured himself his sixth cup of coffee, then stared at the open laptop on the table. No matter what Kelly hoped, that dented teapot wasn't going to change anything. It wasn't about to undo years of neglect and turn Grandma Irene into the kind of cozy, nurturing figure both he and his kid secretly longed for. It wouldn't bring Sandy back or save Billy. It wouldn't make him whole again.

But his kid had seen something in it, the possibility of something wonderful, and that was reason enough to give it one more try.

Chapter Five

THERE WAS NOTHING like a guilty conscience to keep a woman from settling down to work. Maddy missed the old days when these fierce skirmishes with her mother had left her feeling exhilarated and morally victorious instead of ashamed of herself. It wasn't like she had really expected Rose to cheer her auction win. A mild display of excitement would have been nice, but this was her mother she was talking about. A woman who saved her displays of excitement for the really important things like a reduction in the prime interest rate.

All Maddy had been looking for was a simple "nice going." Or, if that was too much, she would have settled for a look of benign maternal amusement. Unfortunately, neither was in Rose's limited repertoire of responses. Maddy knew she wasn't being fair, but she couldn't help herself. The truth was Rose had been genuinely baffled by Maddy's determination to win the teapot. She could've talked herself blue in the face down there in the kitchen, laid her heart on the table with the arugula, and Rose still wouldn't understand. You either believed in magic or you didn't, and everyone knew on which side Rose cast her vote.

But Hannah still believed and the thought of her little girl's excitement when she first saw the teapot, all polished and gleaming like new, filled Maddy's heart with delight. Even Rose would have to admit she'd been right to pursue it when she saw how happy the ersatz magic lamp made her granddaughter.

First, though, there was some work to get done. It felt good to have a purpose again even if it wasn't quite her heart's desire. She settled back down at the computer and tried to wrap her brain around the ongoing task of updating the Inn's Web site. Her plan to add voice-overs to the site was still in the early stages, but she'd been tinkering with the idea of designing a Flash page that featured flickering candles that would lead you to the area you wanted to explore. Unfortunately her experience with Flash was limited and she needed to contact one of her geek friends in Seattle for direction.

So much for working on the Web site. She could always check the upstairs bathrooms and see if they needed some spot cleaning. Rose's standards were higher than the ones imposed by the Board of Health, and it took a lot of hard work to maintain the place to her satisfaction. The rewards, however, were undeniable, and Rose deserved all of the credit for the Inn's overwhelming success.

She clicked on her e-mail program and was instantly rewarded with six invitations to repair her credit history; three reminders that it really was time to lose that excess weight; and one promise that she could (pick one) enlarge either her breasts or her penis in forty-eight hours simply by popping a magical herbal preparation made from powdered Siberian goat tails.

And there was a note from FireGuy.

TO: JerseyGirl@njshore.net
FROM: FireGuy@njshore.net
DATE: 4 December
SUBJECT: Samovar—Item #5815796

I know this is a long shot, but would you consider selling the teapot for a $25 profit? I was bidding on it for
my kid and she'll be real disappointed when I tell her I
lost out. Let me know.

She read the note twice, then started to laugh. The guy
had a lot of nerve, but she couldn't help admiring his
style. Any man who wanted to make his daughter happy
was a winner in her book. Her fingers flew across the
keyboard. The spellcheck hiccupped on "fuhgedaboudit,"
but that was only because it wasn't programmed to speak
Jersey. She bypassed the error message, pressed Send,
then waved goodbye to FireGuy.

AIDAN WAS IN the bar kitchen adding more of his special spice mix to the huge vat of chili bubbling away on
the stove when he heard the bell that signaled new mail.
Wiping his hands on the dishtowel looped into the waist-
band of his jeans, he made for the laptop on the table.
   Point. Click. Damn, he was getting good at this. Next
thing you knew he'd be asking Santa for a pocket protector and a laser pointer.
   JerseyGirl hadn't wasted any time answering him. She
must have some kind of office job where she could play
around on the Internet and still look like she was working.

TO: FireGuy@njshore.net
FROM: JerseyGirl@njshore.net
DATE: 4 December
SUBJECT: Re: Samovar—Item #5815796

Nice try but fuhgedaboudit. I bought the teapot for MY
kid and believe me, she's going to be very happy
Christmas morning. Better luck next time.

The *fuhgedaboudit* was a nice local touch. He limbered
up his index fingers and started pressing keys.

TO: JerseyGirl@njshore.net
FROM: FireGuy@njshore.net

DATE: 4 December
SUBJECT: Re: Re: Samovar—Item #5815796

Sorry. Wrong answer. What does YOUR kid want with
that dented piece of junk anyway? (How does an extra
$35 sound?)

"Poor FireGuy," she said to the screen. "You're spending way too much time at the keyboard." *Unemployed*,
she thought as she started typing. Who else would have
so much free time? Probably an ex-dot-comer like herself
who suddenly found himself on the outside looking in. If
she didn't want the teapot for Hannah, she'd almost be
tempted to sell it to him.

For a small profit, of course. She was, after all, her
mother's daughter.

HE DIDN'T BOTHER getting up to check on the chili or
mix a batch of blue cheese dressing for the Buffalo wings.
JerseyGirl would be sitting in his in box before he reached
the stove.

He grinned at the sound of the new mail chime. He
grinned even wider when he read her response.

TO: FireGuy@njshore.net
FROM: JerseyGirl@njshore.net
DATE: 4 December
SUBJECT: Re: Re: Re: Samovar—Item #5815796

An extra $35 sounds great, but you're not getting the
teapot. (And, since you brought it up, what does YOUR
kid want with MY dented, rusty teapot anyway????)

He clicked on Reply and started typing. Who knew you
could type so fast with just two fingers? (Who knew he
had so much to say to a stranger?)

FIREGUY DIDN'T DISAPPOINT her. She fiddled with
the screen brightness, deleted a half-dozen spams, then

started grinning like a fool when the new mail icon started
flashing.

TO: JerseyGirl@njshore.net
FROM: FireGuy@njshore.net
DATE: 4 December
SUBJECT: Re: Re: Re: Re: Samovar—Item #5815796

My kid wants to give it to her one-hundred-year-old
great-grandmother for Christmas.
Top that, JerseyGirl!

Her reply seemed to appear on her screen by magic.
She hadn't had this much fun since her senior prom. She
hit Send, then leaned back to wait for his answer.

TO: FireGuy@njshore.net
FROM: JerseyGirl@njshore.net
DATE: 4 December
SUBJECT: Re: Re: Re: Re: Re: Samovar—Item
#5815796

Oh, please. I can do better than that with my typing
fingers tied behind my back. Maybe you were bidding
on a teapot, but I was bidding on Aladdin's magic
lamp. Would YOU take a magic lamp away from a four-
year-old child? I think not. . . .

She had a four-year-old child.
He stared at the screen as the fizz went out of the enterprise. If she had a four-year-old child, she probably had
a thirty-four-year-old husband.
He caught himself and laughed out loud. What difference did it make? All they were doing was exchanging
some e-mail banter about an old samovar. They weren't
flirting. They weren't baring their souls. It didn't matter
if she was twenty-five or seventy-five, married or single,
mother of eight or not mother material at all. The only

thing that mattered was the fact that she had won the auction and he hadn't.

He glanced up at the clock. He'd wasted enough time already. Slayney would be there any minute with a delivery, and once that was squared away, he needed to get the wings started and the ribs ready. The late lunch crew wandered in around two o'clock, followed by the happy-hour gang from the docks around five, who paved the way for the serious benchwarmers who began streaming in around eight and stayed until closing.

Still, he couldn't leave her hanging like that. He wasn't sure what exactly e-mail etiquette entailed, but it seemed to him that dropping the ball now was a lot like not returning a phone call. Besides, there was nothing wrong with keeping the lines of communication open. There was always the possibility that her kid might turn up her nose at the bucket of rust, and JerseyGirl would turn to him to bail her out.

He clicked on Reply and was about to start typing when Slayney's voice rattled the rafters.

"O'Malley! Get your ass out here! I got six other stops and there's snow coming."

Walt Slayney was standing in the doorway, looking pissed as hell.

"Hey, Slayney," he said with forced geniality. "Gimme a second. I need to send something out."

"Quit screwing around on the goddamn computer. If you want your Guinness, you'll get your ass out here now."

He muttered something Slayney could probably sue him for, then got up to join the man out back.

Sorry, JerseyGirl. It was fun while it lasted.

WHERE WAS HE?

Six minutes had passed since she had hit the Send key and still no reply from FireGuy. Was it something she'd said? She had been enjoying their rapid-fire exchanges and wouldn't have minded volleying a few more notes with him. FireGuy, however, had apparently exhausted the limits of e-mail chat and vanished into the ether whence he came. *Easy come, easy go.* When it came to men, she could give Houdini a run for his money. She was great at making them disappear, and she didn't need a magic wand and a Vegas stage to do it. She had inherited her mother's chin and her bad luck with men. Traits shared by all four DiFalco sisters and most of their descendants.

She fussed around with the Web site, but her heart wasn't in her coding and she screwed up twice and had to start over from scratch. Thank God it was nearly two o'clock. Hannah's preschool let out at two-thirty. At least when her daughter was around, she and Rose had a common interest beyond business.

At her feet Priscilla let out a whimper, followed by a frantic scratching motion that Maddy instantly recognized as trouble.

"Oh, no, Pris, no mistakes today!" She swooped the puppy into her arms and dashed for the back door, pausing only long enough to grab her jacket and shoulder bag from the brass coat stand in the corner.

Priscilla hated being leashed, but the days of neighborhood dogs running wild on Main Street were a thing of the past. "Good thing you're a pedigree," she said as she snapped the lead on the poodle's tiny collar. "Before long they'll be passing a law against mutts." She slipped into her jacket, then grabbed the pooper-scooper and bag she kept stashed behind the trash bin near the garage.

Priscilla made straight for her favorite spot by the stand of dogwoods. A sharp wind whistled between the house and the garage, nearly lifting the puppy off her paws. She looked up at Maddy with an expression that managed to be simultaneously forlorn and indignant. Who could blame her? Maddy was a fan of indoor plumbing, too.

"There you are!" a male voice boomed behind her.

She turned to see a short, round man in a Philadelphia Eagles windbreaker bearing down on her. He seemed familiar. Where had she seen him before?

"I've been looking all over for you." He completely

ignored the fact that she was standing there with a loaded pooper-scooper in one hand and two pounds of growling poodle in the other. "The wife needs more towels tonight. She's planning to wash her hair after dinner."

It took her a few seconds, but she finally realized where she had seen him before: coming out of the second-floor bathroom. "Mr. Armagh," she said, jiggling Priscilla to stem the growling. "You and Mrs. Armagh are in the Ocean Room, right. I'll make sure she has plenty."

"Make sure you knock twice," Mr. Armagh said with an exaggerated waggle of his thick gray eyebrows. "We're on our second honeymoon."

Which definitely fell under the heading of Too Much Information.

Maddy disposed of the pooper-scooper and its accessories, then checked her watch. Hannah's bus would be at the corner in fifteen minutes. She considered popping into the kitchen for a quick glass of milk and a chocolate chip cookie, but the thought of another round with the DiFalco girls was a strong deterrent. She'd do without the cookies; her thighs would thank her for it.

She bent down and deposited a reluctant Priscilla on the sidewalk in front of the Candlelight. Priscilla sniffed the concrete delicately, took two hesitant steps forward, then slammed on the brakes.

"Sooner or later, you're going to walk," Maddy said as she once again scooped up the puppy. "We all do."

The dog looked appropriately smug as she cuddled against Maddy's chest and closed her eyes.

Paradise Point's Main Street ran parallel to the shoreline. Five blocks of wide sidewalks, tall trees, and a score of quaint gift shops, boutiques, and craft stores redesigned with the tourist trade in mind. A glittering crown of B&Bs reigned supreme over the south end of the street, benevolent despots that set the tone for the entire town. With the expansive porches and gingerbread trim, the beautifully restored Victorian ladies served as time machines that invited visitors to step back into a more gracious era.

Gone were the days when you could park on the street

and race up the lawn to the front door. Now you had to drive around back to a tiny eight-car lot near the garage and pray the paying customers hadn't taken all the best spots. It was like living in an upscale Motel 6, except if she were really living at Motel 6 she would be able to park at her door and somebody else would be worrying about clean sheets and fresh bath towels.

The B&Bs soon gave way to a block of charming single-family dwellings that whispered old money. No taking in boarders for those houses, thank you very much. They were holding the line between the raffish charm of the north end of Main Street and the upscale trendiness of the south end and doing it quite well. She crossed the street in front of Upsweep, her cousin Gina's hair salon, and joined the knot of women at the corner of Main Street and Paradise Point Lane. She was related to almost every single one of them by either blood or marriage, and the ones she wasn't related to she had gone to school with.

"Hey, cuz!" Gina greeted her. "Were your ears burning? We were just talking about you."

"Nothing awful," her cousin Denise quickly added as she rocked the stroller back and forth while her son slept. "You look like we jumped you in an alley somewhere."

"Bad day," Maddy said, placing an unwilling Priscilla on the sidewalk by her feet. "A really bad day."

"Uh-oh," said Gina. "This might change the odds."

She didn't like the sound of that. "What odds?"

"They were taking bets," Joann Colarusso said with a laugh as she patted Priscilla's furry head. "How long until you buy a one-way ticket back to Seattle."

"So far it's split evenly between Christmas Day and New Year's Eve," her second cousin Delia Sweeney offered. "Personally I think you'll be gone a week from tomorrow."

Maddy opened her mouth to say something she probably shouldn't, but was saved by Claire's arrival.

"Advil," Claire said with a loud groan. "My kingdom for an Advil." She placed a hand against her cheek and rolled her eyes.

"Cramps?" Gina asked, digging through the pockets of her down jacket.

"Root canal." She groaned again. "I'm telling you, childbirth was easier."

The knot of mothers burst into laughter, and Maddy felt some of her tension ease. It felt good to stand there on the corner in the brisk winter wind with a group of women she'd known and loved forever. The only one she hadn't grown up with was Claire, but they had already formed an easy waiting-for-the-school-bus relationship that she enjoyed.

"I have Tylenol," she said to Claire, "if you don't mind reaching around Priscilla and digging through my shoulder bag."

"Bless you," Claire said with a grateful smile. "Bless you and all of your descendants!"

Fran and Gina were engaged in a lively debate on the relative horrors of dental surgery versus hard labor that had the other women cheering them on. Claire pulled a sports bottle of water from her tote bag and washed down a pair of Tylenols with a healthy gulp.

"Thanks," she said to Maddy. "I owe you."

Claire launched into a very funny story about her first experience with nitrous oxide that had the other women literally holding their sides with laughter. Beneath her own laughter, Maddy found herself inexplicably close to tears.

This was the life she would have lived if she had stayed in Paradise Point, the same world her cousins had never left. She tried to imagine herself married to—and probably divorced from, given the DiFalco luck with men—a local boy, popping into Upsweep every other Saturday as much for the gossip as for maintenance. Denise, Gina, and her other cousins had all stayed put down there in South Jersey, digging their roots even deeper into familiar ground. They shopped in the stores where they had worked as teenagers, shared baby clothes and strollers, carpools and covered-dish suppers at Our Lady of Lourdes R.C. Church. Their children played together. Their husbands and ex-husbands bowled together and shouted themselves hoarse at Giants games up at the Meadowlands. They knew each other's secrets and sore points, and they understood without being told why Maddy had chosen to build a life for herself on the opposite side of the country.

What they couldn't seem to understand was why she had come home again. Who could blame them? Since leaving Seattle, Maddy had asked herself the same thing every hour on the hour.

"Look!" Denise pointed in the direction of an old Honda whizzing past them. "Isn't that Kelly in the passenger seat?"

"Couldn't be," said Claire. "Kelly usually doesn't get out of class until four."

Maddy quickly scanned her mental database. Claire had married one of the O'Malley brothers whose family owned the bar/restaurant on the pier for as long as she could remember. By all accounts Claire had enjoyed a happy marriage until her firefighter husband was killed in a warehouse collapse a few years ago.

"Your daughter?" she asked Claire.

"Don't I wish! My niece."

The image of a lovely young girl pressing a kiss against the faintly stubbled cheek of a teenage boy seemed to linger in front of the young mothers, even though the car had long since turned off Main Street.

"I think that was Kelly with Seth Mahoney," Gina said. "That's his brother's Honda."

The sound of the wind off the ocean filled the silence that suddenly surrounded the women.

"They should still be in class," Claire said after a long moment.

"It's genetic," said Fran. "O'Malleys skip classes. Always have, always will." Fran had gone to school with the O'Malleys' second son, Aidan, four years ahead of Maddy.

"Not to worry," Gina said to a frowning Claire. "Your niece is set to be valedictorian. She's National Honor So-

ciety, a scholarship winner—I think she can skip social
studies without too much of a problem."

"Besides," said Pat, "knowing Kelly, she's probably
headed to the library."

Of course they all knew it wasn't school that had them
worried. It was young love.

"I don't know about the rest of you," Denise said, "but
I'm feeling old right now."

"Nothing lasts," said Gina. "That's the one thing you
can count on. A year from now she'll be walking across
a campus somewhere with a new guy by her side."

"Right," said Claire. "And we'll still be here, waiting
for the school bus."

Maddy burst into laughter and a second later the rest
of the women were laughing, too, but Claire's remark had
struck a nerve. They had all been Kelly's age once.
Maddy had been bursting with dreams at seventeen, so
eager, so ready to meet her future that she had never once
stopped to consider that her future might not end up being
the one she'd planned. She had the feeling most of the
women standing there on the corner with her would say
the same thing. There was an almost palpable sense of
relief when the bright yellow school bus rolled to a stop
and their kids exploded back into their lives.

Gina's two little girls were first off the bus. Heather
and Saylor were five-year-old twin firecrackers, much like
their mother had been at their age. Their father, Gina's
second husband, Frank, had contributed the silky black
hair and huge brown eyes, but his quiet, calm personality
was nowhere to be found. Denise's only son, four-year-
old Peter, leaped down from the top step, then burst into
tears when Heather hit him in the head with her Barbie
backpack. Fran's son and daughter neatly stepped around
the melee while Delia's and Pat's daughters giggled and
ran to their mothers.

Hannah was the last off the bus. She stood for a moment on the top step, her enormous eyes scanning the knot
of women and children until her gaze rested on Maddy's
face. Hannah's look of relief almost broke her heart.

Smiling broadly, she waved at Hannah and struggled with the powerful urge to run over to the bus and scoop the child into her arms. This was only the beginning of Hannah's second week in preschool at Our Lady of Lourdes. Gina and Denise had convinced her that putting Hannah on the small parish school bus was the best way to help her little girl settle in, but so far it didn't look like the idea was working. Still, you couldn't expect a miracle in only six days. Unfortunately, patience didn't come naturally for her. She wanted her daughter to be happy now, right this minute. She wanted Hannah to feel safe and protected in her new hometown, surrounded by family and friends and so much love that nothing, not even her father's absence, could hurt her again.

She maintained her smile as Hannah slowly descended the metal steps.

"She'll get used to it," Claire said as her own seven-year-old son barreled up to them. "A new school is always hard, no matter how old you are."

"Ma!" Billy O'Malley tugged at his mother's sleeve. "Hurry! I gotta pee real bad."

"Emergency, ladies," Claire said with a good-natured shrug of her shoulders. "I'll see you all tomorrow morning."

"We're off!" cried Denise as she rounded up her tribe.

The rest of the women called out their goodbyes and, kids in tow, headed their separate ways.

Hannah slipped up next to Maddy the second Claire and Billy disappeared down the street. She reached up and tickled one of Priscilla's back paws. Priscilla shot her a look of regal indignation.

"So did you have fun today?" Maddy asked as she reached down for Hannah's hand.

Hannah shrugged. "I guess."

She was so small, so vulnerable. What idiot came up with the idea for preschool anyway? Her baby was barely out of diapers, and already they were telling Maddy it was time to start letting go when what she really wanted to do was hold on tight.

They turned onto Main Street and waited to cross to the other side. "Did Susan bring the butterflies to class?"

"She forgot."

"That's too bad. I know how much you wanted to tell them about the butterflies in Grandpa Bill's yard."

Hannah seemed fascinated with the workings of the traffic light swinging overhead. Maddy regrouped and tried again.

"Did Mrs. Shapiro tell you what character you'll be playing in the holiday pageant?"

That elicited a nod. It wasn't much, but it was something.

"Will you need a costume?"

"I guess."

"Did Mrs. Shapiro send home a note for me so I know what to make?"

"I forget."

She looked so small and forlorn that Maddy's impatience disappeared as quickly as it had come. "I'll call Mrs. Shapiro and ask her."

If Hannah had an opinion one way or the other, she wasn't sharing it with Maddy. Mother and daughter walked up Main Street in silence, past the Cheese Shoppe, Upsweep, the Paradise Point Savings and Loan. Maddy called out hello to Ethel Santori, who was sweeping her front porch. Ethel owned the Captain's House, the second-highest-rated B&B in town. Ethel managed a tight smile and nod of her head, but if Maddy had been expecting a display of neighborly effusion, she would have to look elsewhere.

They reached the Candlelight and walked up the driveway toward the backyard. Maddy put a squirming Priscilla down on the grass, and she and Hannah waited for the puppy to take care of business. Hannah carried the dog into the kitchen.

"That poodle has two more legs than I have," Rose observed as Maddy closed the door behind them. "Put her down, Hannah, before she forgets how to walk!" Rose's expression was pleasant; her tone, amused, but it didn't matter.

Aunt Lucy chuckled as she chopped carrot coins in half at the counter. Maybe on a different day, with a different set of characters, Maddy might have chuckled along with her, but the look in Hannah's eyes as she stepped off the school bus still tore at her heart. In her gut she knew Rose was teasing, trying to smooth over the bruised feelings of a few hours ago, but Maddy wasn't ready to let go of the bruises.

Hannah clutched the puppy close to her chest. "Mommy? Did I do something wrong?"

"Don't worry," Maddy said through clenched teeth. She thought the top of her head was going to explode. "Grandma Rose was making a joke."

Rose opened her mouth, but Maddy shot her a look that said, *One more word and we go back to Seattle*.

Rose's cheeks turned a violent shade of red, but she said nothing. Aunt Lucy concentrated on her carrot coins. Hannah hugged Priscilla tight and stared at the floor.

A victory, Maddy thought. A small one, maybe even an unfair one, but a victory just the same. Fifteen years ago it would have been cause for celebration, but today it just made her feel like crying.

Chapter Six

—

KELLY O'MALLEY BELIEVED things happened for a reason. Like when you were thinking very hard about a friend you hadn't seen in a long time and the phone rings and it's that very friend calling just to say hello. Some people might call that a coincidence, but Kelly knew better. There was a reason for everything, a pattern that you couldn't always see the first time you looked, but it was there.

Like the other day when she answered the phone at the bar and it was Grandma Irene asking for that photo of her and Grandpa Michael taken at the old restaurant just before the hurricane. It was one of those old black-and-white photos, kind of stiff-looking and unnatural the way old family photos always were, but it still brought tears to Kelly's eyes. They looked so young and happy as they stood in the lobby of the old restaurant, surrounded by Irene's collection of teapots. Beautiful English teapots, delicate French teapots, sturdy American pots with utilitarian handles and spouts, and one spectacular samovar that looked straight out of a tale from the Arabian Nights.

She'd taken the photo from the drawer under the cash

register, then headed right over to the nursing home to deliver it. Irene had been sleeping when she got there, but she'd left the photo with one of the nurses, then forgotten all about it until she was browsing through the auction site yesterday afternoon and discovered a teapot that looked an awful lot like Grandma Irene's samovar. The most perfect Christmas present Kelly could possibly find for her great-grandmother.

It was meant to be. How else could you explain it?

Just like today when her weekly meeting with the staff of *The Chanticleer,* the Paradise Point High School newspaper, was postponed until tomorrow. Seth didn't have to clock in for work at the Super Fresh until six o'clock, which gave them three hours, three blissful miraculous hours of their very own.

Meant to be.

She left her car in the school parking lot and climbed into Seth's brother's Honda and flew toward the lake where they parked at the edge of the woods, behind a stand of trees, safe from the prying eyes of family and friends who had known them all their lives.

Maybe even longer.

The lake nestled in a clearing, deep in the woods. In the summer months families with toddlers in tow vied with young lovers, retired couples, and students for a piece of emerald grass to call their own. But now, in December, with the trees stripped of their leaves and the sun moving lower in the sky they were alone, clinging to each other in a combination of terror and bliss.

"You're worried." Seth's breath was warm against her cheek.

"No, I'm not." Kelly snuggled closer to Seth. "I'm over it."

"So what if your aunt saw us. We didn't skip a class, Kel. The school canceled the newspaper meeting. We didn't."

"I know, I know." He smelled so wonderful. Did he have any idea what the smell of his skin did to her brain? She felt buoyant, weightless, as if the slightest gust of wind might send her sailing up over the lake, over the trees, through the cream-colored clouds, headed straight for the stars.

"Are you sure?" His words tickled against the curve of her throat. "Really sure?"

She kissed his neck, the sharp line of his jaw, and giggled at the faint scratch of stubble. "I'm sure," she whispered. "I love you, Seth. I've never been more sure of anything in my life."

"This isn't how I wanted our first time to be." His fingers swiftly unbuttoned her jeans and worked them down her hips. "You should have candles and flowers and—"

"I have you. That's all I've ever wanted." One day in the big unknowable future they would have flowers and candles every night, but right now they had something more important. Something rare and beautiful.

Opportunity.

"You're shaking," Seth said. "You don't have to be scared."

"I'm not scared," she said, nestling closer beneath their warm shelter of blankets. She wasn't scared at all. Her father had tried to explain it to her a few years ago, but he'd turned a brilliant shade of crimson, then asked Aunt Claire to clarify a few issues. She knew that it would hurt, maybe a little, maybe a lot. And she knew she wanted Seth so much she couldn't sleep at night and she couldn't eat and she couldn't imagine waiting one more second to take that giant step into the future they were planning together.

"I love you, Kelly," he said as he gently rolled her over onto her back. "We can stop if you want to. . . . I want you to be happy. . . ."

She opened her arms to him and whispered, "Then come here and I will be."

THE FIRST LUNCH wave blew through the door of O'Malley's a few minutes before noon. Real estate agents, storefront lawyers, med students from the hospital up the road flooded the place weekdays for a burger or bowl of chili that trashed the diet but didn't break the budget. The first wave gulped down their food, exchanged a few war stories, then cleared out in time to make room for the second wave.

The second wave included fishermen, shift workers, and guests from the local B&Bs who were looking for a bit more local color than the polished and perfumed old Victorians could provide.

But it was the third wave that formed the heart and soul of O'Malley's Bar and Grill. The retired cops, off-duty firefighters, old anglers, housepainters, and the just plain lonely who showed up midafternoon for the comfort of a bowl of chili and the warmth of friends.

"Best damn chili in the state." Frank Soriano leaned back and patted his substantial gut. "You should can this stuff and sell it. I'm tellin' you, you'd rake in the bucks."

Aidan grinned and removed the empty bowl. "Time for another brew?"

"Why not? The wife's visiting her mother. What she don't know won't hurt me, right?"

Next to him, Ed DiMaio snorted into his bowl of fish chowder. It was well known around Paradise Point that Mary Soriano wore the pants in the family. She kept a sharp eye on Frank's intake of beer, beef, and butter, the three things he loved most in the world.

"Where's Claire?" Bud Morgan called out from a table near the dartboard. "She's been riding my ass about the Giants game tonight. I want her to put some money where her mouth is."

"Dentist," Aidan said, sliding a beer toward Frank. "She'll be back any time."

Bud let out a good-natured groan. "You think I got nothin' better to do than sit around this dump?"

"That's about the size of it," Frank said.

The place erupted in laughter as Frank and Ed exchanged high fives without missing a bite.

"Y'know," said Mel Perry from the far end of the bar, "it kills me to say it, but I think Soriano's got something there. That chili you make is great stuff. It could blow the top of your head off. Why don't I hook you up with my kid the lawyer and maybe she can help get you started."

Aidan refilled a half-dozen nut dishes with salted peanuts, then reached for a bag of chips. "Next thing I know you'll have me on that cable food channel." He ripped open the bag and dumped the contents into a napkin-lined basket.

"Yeah," said Mel, sounding pleased with himself. "You could be the next Emerald."

Aidan's easy smile tightened. He reached for another bag of chips.

"Why don't you call them up?" Mel suggested. "Tell them you were a fireman. He's always cooking for firehouses, same as you. Nobody'd even notice your scars."

Silence dropped like a bag of rocks. The only sound was the clink of Ed's spoon against his empty bowl.

They're old men. They still see you the way you were. Don't ream them for taking the ball you tossed and running with it.

Across the room Mel took a swig of Heineken and popped a chip into his mouth. "Nobody's perfect. That Emerald's no Robert Redford."

"Shut the fuck up," Bud growled. "Can't you see you're making it worse?"

"How the hell am I making it worse? I think he could parlay that chili of his into something big. I said he could maybe be on TV. Is that a fucking crime?"

"Jesus H. Christ!" Bud sounded close to a meltdown. "You'd do anything to get some work for that ambulance-chaser kid of yours."

Snap! Crackle! Pop! A symphony of arthritic knees sounded as Mel and Bud jumped to their feet.

"Say that again," Mel dared, "and I'll stuff those dentures up your wrinkled old—"

"Hey, guys!" Claire and Billy Jr. breezed through the front door on a gust of winter wind. It took her maybe all of three seconds to assess the situation. "To the office with you," she said to Billy as she pointed him toward the hall. "I'll bring you milk and cookies in a few minutes." She glanced around the room. "Maybe I should bring out some milk and cookies for the rest of you children."

"Damn, you're good," Aidan said as he followed her into the kitchen. "I was afraid we were going to need a defibrillator out there."

Claire's gaze was direct. She wasn't known for her patience. "Mel and Bud looked like they were about to mix it up out there." She swung open the fridge and pulled out a container of milk. "Football, hockey, or politics?"

"Who knows." He pulled down Billy Jr.'s favorite glass from the open cabinet over the double sink. "Tomorrow it'll be something else."

She narrowed her eyes and peered up at him. "What's wrong?"

"Nothing's wrong."

"You aren't still upset about losing that teapot, are you?"

"Ask me again after I tell Kelly about it."

He knew he wasn't the most sensitive of men. Changes in the emotional landscape around him needed to be a 9 on the Richter scale before he took note, but even he couldn't miss the way Claire's expression shifted when he mentioned his daughter's name.

"What?" he asked, dumping some cookies on a plate for Billy Jr. while Claire poured the milk.

"What do you mean, what?" she countered, eyes focused on the milk container and the rapidly filling glass.

"Kelly. You looked funny when I mentioned her. What's wrong?"

Claire wiped up a spilled drop of milk with a square of paper towel. "I saw her with Seth while I was waiting for the school bus."

He did a little math. "They cut class?"

"Looks like it."

"Where were they going?"

"I don't know. They sailed by in Seth's brother's Honda."

"She was probably on the way to one of her club meetings."

"Could be," said Claire.

"You think she skipped class?" She had to be kidding. They all knew Kelly was the type of kid who loved school so much she would sleep there if they let her.

"Who knows," Claire said, sidestepping his question. "All I know is that I saw her."

From the look on her face, she obviously wished she had never told him.

"I trust her," he said, meaning every word. "If she was out there with Seth, there was a good reason." This was the kid who had lost her mother when she was three years old. This was the kid who had changed his bandages when the sight of the left side of his face had been enough to bring grown men to their knees. His little girl never flinched. She did what needed to be done and did it without fanfare or shouts of "Look at me!"

She had earned his trust. More than that, she deserved it.

"Kelly's a good kid," he said to Claire. "I don't think there's anything to worry about."

"She's seventeen," Claire retorted. "There's plenty to worry about. Believe me, I know what I'm talking about."

Kathleen, Claire's oldest, was nineteen and a sophomore at Rutgers up in New Brunswick. Her early teens had been the stuff of after-school specials and movies of the week on one of those women's cable channels. Strangely enough, her father's death two years ago had settled her down. Her grades were improving. She was staying out of trouble. It was more than most of the family had expected. No wonder Claire crossed herself every time Kathleen's name came up. Claire was a wise woman. She wasn't taking any chances.

"What time is Bernie coming over?" Claire sat down at the table next to Billy Jr. and rubbed her jaw with her right hand.

"Around six."

"Is Pete working tonight?"

Aidan snagged a chocolate chip cookie and popped it in his mouth. "He said he'd come in and man the bar while I went over the books." Pete was a retired firefighter who worked at O'Malley's a few nights a week.

She rubbed her cheek again, wincing at the touch of her own fingertips. "I took a look at the ledger," she said. "It wasn't a pretty sight."

He threw an arm around her bony shoulders and gave her a quick hug. "We'll make it work. Things will pick up, Claire. Winters are always tough."

"Where're my crayons?" Billy Jr. asked through a mouthful of cookie. "I want to color."

Claire sighed loudly. "I'm sorry, honey. I forgot to bring the toy bag with me."

Billy Jr. opened his mouth to protest, but Aidan broke in before his nephew had a chance to let go full throttle. "I have something you'll like better."

"I like my crayons," Billy Jr. said.

"More than a Game Boy?"

"You have a Game Boy?" Only seven and he sounded as suspicious as a forty-year-old.

"It was Kelly's. She said you could have it if you promise not to beat her Zelda score."

It was genetic. No O'Malley could resist a challenge. Aidan pulled Kelly's old Game Boy from the drawer near the back door and flipped the On switch. "Here you go," he said, handing it to Billy Jr. with a grin. "Let's see what you can do."

Billy Jr. settled down to play with the kind of manic concentration usually found in hockey fans and astrophysicists.

"Isn't it time for the daily chili delivery?" Claire said in her usual brusquely cheerful manner. "I want to get out of here by six so I can go home and bake cookies for Billy's class tomorrow."

"I'll be back in plenty of time."

"I didn't mean to rattle your cage about Kelly."

"You didn't rattle my cage. You told me you saw her on Main Street when she should have been in school. You did what a godmother's supposed to do." Claire saw Kelly through a different lens, one that had been shaped by her problems with Kathleen. But Kelly wasn't Kathleen, not by any stretch of the imagination.

"She might be smart, but she's still just seventeen," Claire said, "and seventeen is a dangerous age."

He remembered seventeen. The wild highs and butt-dragging lows. The nuclear-powered hormones. The explosion when desire and opportunity finally come together in a mind-blowing moment of—

Shit.

He tried to push aside the faint buzz of apprehension moving up his spine, but the memory of seventeen wouldn't let him. It sat on his shoulder as he climbed into the Jeep, and it whispered in his ear as he backed out of the driveway and headed west toward the firehouse. Seventeen lived in the now. Seventeen didn't understand that actions had consequences.

Seventeen didn't know that even love had its price.

BARNEY KURKOWSKI WAS waiting in the parking lot behind the firehouse. He looked as if he was thinking about bench-pressing a Buick.

"Whaddya got for me today?" Barney asked as Aidan unlatched the back window of the truck and lowered the tailgate. "New York strip steaks and a couple of kegs of Heineken?"

Aidan grunted as he pulled the two-gallon drums of chili out and handed them to the older firefighter. "Better quit smoking that strange tobacco, pal." He grabbed for the two enormous foil-wrapped platters that were piled high with ribs and kicked the tailgate closed with his right knee. Pain shot from knee to thigh to groin. It registered on some distant part of his brain, the part he hadn't yet figured out a way to subdue, but he kept his focus outward. Sometimes that was the best you could do.

Barney watched him closely through tired brown eyes that had seen things even Aidan couldn't imagine. Barney had taken him under his wing when Aidan first joined the company eighteen years ago, and it was Barney who had stayed with him on that long screaming ride through the hot summer night to the hospital.

And it was Barney who had helped carry his brother's casket out of Our Lady of Lourdes after the funeral when Aidan was still suspended between two levels of hell.

Neither man spoke of that time again, but it was there between them in every word they didn't say, an unbreakable bond.

They crossed the asphalt to the kitchen door. Barney slowed automatically to keep pace with Aidan's off-center gait.

"Coming in?" Barney asked casually.

"Not this time." Aidan placed the trays down on the top step. He hadn't been in there since the day of the warehouse fire. "Claire needs to leave early tonight, so I want to get back."

"Better motor then." Barney's tone was still casual. "Don't want to keep her waiting."

"Irish stew Wednesday," Aidan said as he turned to leave, "and a tray of baked mac and cheese."

"Keep 'em coming," Barney said. "Fenelli has a long way to go until he can hold a spatula to you, O'Malley."

"Save the butt kissing for the Rotary Club," Aidan said with a grin. "I'm still billing your ass for home delivery."

"Punk kid."

"Old fart."

"See you Wednesday."

"You got it."

He wondered if everyone saw the ghosts he saw around the firehouse. All the men who had come and gone over the years, the ones who died saving others, the ones who had been lucky enough to die in their own beds. He saw his brother Billy's Camaro angled in the last spot on the right, tailpipe hanging on by a thread. Aidan was the one who was good with cars, but not even he had been able to keep Billy's wheels in good repair. Billy drove the way he lived: balls-out, overdrive all the way. In the first months after the accident there had been times when Aidan would wake up from a deep sleep and for a second he was sure it was all a joke, that Billy was holed up in one of those motels on the outskirts of Atlantic City, laughing his ass off at the primo gag he'd pulled.

Then he would look in the mirror and it would all come tumbling down.

KELLY PULLED HER car into the lot behind O'Malley's at exactly eighteen minutes after six. She had waited around the corner until Aunt Claire left for the night. The last thing she wanted was to be subjected to her god-mother's endless probing questions. And she knew there was no way Aunt Claire would let the opportunity pass without a little digging around.

If only they had taken the back way to the lake. She had been so happy, so excited, that she hadn't even no-ticed the women standing on the corner until Seth said, "Isn't that your aunt Claire?" She had peered into the side mirror and there was her aunt, squinting into the fading sunlight, her face creased in permanent lines of worry. She wanted to shout out, "It isn't what you think, Aunt Claire!" but of course it was exactly what Claire thought, every bit of it.

They had been so careful, so cautious. They had thought of everything from condoms to timing to location. Driving out to the lake on a cold December afternoon—what girl in her right mind would pick such an inhospi-table spot to make love for the first time? You would have to be crazy even to think of such a thing.

At least, that's what Kelly and Seth had been banking on.

And it had been worth it. She felt like she could fly, like Seth had gathered up the clouds and the stars and laid them at her feet.

She peered at her reflection in the rearview mirror. She didn't look any different. How disappointing. She had taken a giant step into the future, but she still looked like the same schoolgirl who left for class each morning. Her father didn't suspect a thing.

And he wouldn't. Not in a million years.

She had never lied to him before, but there was no way she was going to walk into the bar and announce she had just lost her virginity. It would be easier to announce she had just robbed the Paradise Point Savings and Loan at the corner of Main and Willow. He already thought she was seeing too much of Seth, but then he had been saying that since she was six years old. Seth had been her best friend from childhood. He was the first friend she made when they moved back to Paradise Point, and the one person in the whole world she could imagine herself growing old with.

Not that she spent a lot of time thinking about things like that, because she didn't. Loving Seth was a fact of life, like her strawberry-blond hair and blue eyes. Her friends leapfrogged from boyfriend to boyfriend, falling in and out of love at the speed of light. But not Kelly. An Irish fortune-teller she'd visited at the annual Fireman's Fundraising Fair had taken one look at her cards and proclaimed her an old soul who would always choose the right path. Funny how sometimes you needed to hear a stranger tell you something you always knew before you believed it was true.

She liked that phrase. *Old soul.* It sounded right to her. She had always felt that way, settled deep down inside, as if she had come into the world with all of the important decisions already made and her roadmap clearly marked.

Even as a tiny girl she had recognized Seth as the other half of her heart. Grandma Irene used to look at the two of them playing together and laugh, but there was something in her eyes, some flicker of recognition that Kelly had understood even then. *You know, don't you, Grandma. Because it was the same for you.* The bond between Irene and Michael had been forged early and endured beyond death. Same as it would be for Kelly and Seth.

Oh, she knew better than to say something like that to anyone, but it was true just the same. They met in the schoolyard on the first day of first grade, and from that moment on their fate had been sealed. Knowing she had found the one God had meant for her to find freed Kelly to pour herself into her studies with abandon. Her life was filled with so much love—her father, her aunt, her cousins, Grandma Irene (in her own way), her beloved Seth—that she was fearless. She learned to play the piano and to dance. Her grades were the highest in the school. She was popular with students and faculty alike, and if there was even a single cloud on her horizon it was the way her father worried about her relationship with Seth.

"Why not date other boys?" he suggested every few weeks. "I worry, Kel. You're too young to tie yourself down with the first guy who comes along."

It wasn't like she had asked to fall in love so young. She didn't wake up one morning in her crib and say, "I think it's time to meet the man of my dreams." Her father seemed to see love as a limitation while she saw it as a door that opened onto the world. She still expected to graduate high school as valedictorian. She still expected to head off to Columbia on scholarship. She had as many dreams for her future as there were stars in the sky, and love wouldn't get in the way of any of them, no matter what her father thought.

She loved Seth. Being with him made her feel more completely herself, made her try harder, reach higher. This afternoon, lying there in his arms, she had believed she could do anything. Be anything. Maybe even fly.

No, that wasn't something a girl could explain to her father. Once upon a time she might have imagined going to him and telling him everything. Asking for his advice, if not his blessing. But that was a long time ago, before the Accident changed everything.

That was how she thought about it. The Accident. The day Uncle Billy died and something inside her father died right along with him. She would never forget the first time she saw him in the hospital, the day before Billy's funeral. If the doctor hadn't pointed to bed number three, she wouldn't have recognized her own father. He had always been her protector, her teacher, her source of strength. To see him like that, mangled and helpless, made her want to turn and run away as fast as she could.

Nothing seemed real to her after that. If God could take away her uncle from his family, if God could turn her strong and powerful father into a shadow, then what could she count on?

Only Seth. It was Seth who had been there for her. Seth who held her when she sobbed with fear. Seth who helped her clean the house and do the shopping and understood why she had to be home with her father when life was knocking on the door and asking her to come out and play.

Tears filled her eyes and she dragged the back of her hand across them. Life was back to normal now, or at least what passed for normal. Her father left the firehouse and took over O'Malley's with Aunt Claire. If he wasn't one hundred percent, at least he was a lot closer than anyone ever thought he'd be. And he told all who would listen that he had his daughter, Kelly, to thank.

She didn't want his thanks. She hadn't cared for him so he would sing her praises to people who didn't matter. She wanted their old life back. She wanted them to sit down at the kitchen table and talk the way they used to, back in the days when she could tell him everything.

Most girls couldn't really talk to their fathers, but Kelly had never had their problem. Aidan had been both parents wrapped up in one for as far back as she could remember. He had changed her diapers and applauded her first words. He had cheered her first steps, attended all of her school plays, taught her to ride a two-wheeler, throw a sinkerball, and make the world's best lasagna. He was the one who told her about periods and tampons when she was ten years old and scared to death at the sight of blood in her panties. He had held her close and rocked her while she cried, then told her that even though she was now a young woman, it was still okay to be his little girl.

Except that she wasn't his little girl any longer and hadn't been for a long time.

"Everything's going to be okay," she said aloud as she gathered up her things. Different but okay.

"AND TOSS SOME chopped onions on that chili, will ya?" Ron Suarez called out as Aidan headed toward the kitchen.

Three bowls of chili, one with chopped onions. Two platters of wings. A meatball hero . . . if there were any meatballs left after the first two lunch waves.

Aidan shouldered his way through the swinging door and found his daughter sitting at the big worktable with her legs curled under her. Her silky hair shone with red-gold highlights as she bent over the laptop.

"Hey, kid. How long've you been here?"

Kelly stopped what she was doing and smiled up at him. She had her mother's smile, wide open and joyous. Even after all these years the memory of Sandy could still cause his heart to ache.

"Since six-eighteen," she said. "Sorry I was late. I—I lost track of time."

She never screwed up. He knew he could cut her a little slack and not live to regret it, but he still had to ask.

"Claire said she saw you and Seth while she was waiting for the school bus."

"Yeah." She dragged her index finger across the touch pad. "She was with a whole group of DiFalco cousins."

"I thought you had club meetings between two-thirty and four."

High color flooded her cheeks and an ugly buzz of apprehension positioned itself between his shoulder blades. "We—uh, we needed some digital photos of the swans for the yearbook."

The buzz eased a little. Or at least as much as it was likely to ease between now and her fortieth birthday.

"Seth's a good kid," he said, pulling three clean iron-ware bowls from the cabinet next to the sturdy six-burner stove that had cost more than his first car. "I like him." His back was to her while he ladled steaming hot chili into the bowls. He heard the sound of a modem handshake, followed by the rapid click of the keyboard, but no comment from his kid. He tried again. "Tell him he did a great job fixing the back steps. If he feels like tackling it, the porch could use some shoring up." He pulled a pan of wings from the warming oven, then dumped them on a snowy-white oval platter. "Kel, am I talking to myself here?"

"You lost the teapot!" Her voice was filled with reproach. He turned around as she slid the tip of her index finger across the touch pad again, then tapped twice. "I can't believe it! It sold before they even reached my max bid."

"I wasn't fast enough," he said, feeling lower than whale turd. "I tried to type in your high bid, but—listen, Kel, I don't know if it was my fingers or the damn keyboard, but the next thing I knew the screen was flashing and somebody named JerseyGirl claimed the prize."

"Why didn't you type in the max bid first thing? Didn't you see the box at the top of the screen?"

"Kel, I'm sorry. What more can I do? I e-mailed JerseyGirl to see if she'd sell it to me, but it was a no-go."

Her eyes brimmed with tears. "I'm sorry," she said, sniffling. "I just wanted it so much for Grandma Irene. . . ."

"There's got to be more of those things for sale out there. You'll find another one."

She shook her head. "Never," she said mournfully. "Not in a million years."

"What's the big deal with this teapot? I still don't get it."

"I don't know!" She burst into noisy tears. "I just want her to have it!"

What the hell was going on? Drama queen theatrics weren't his kid's style. After seventeen easy years was the shit about to hit the fan?

He pulled out the chair across from her and sat down. "Do you need to talk about anything?"

She looked up at him and cried harder.

"Talk to me, Kel," he pleaded. "I can't make it better if I don't know what it is in the first place."

"It looks just like . . . all I . . . wanted . . . you to do was . . . bid on the . . . teapot and you—"

She was sobbing like he'd told her she'd been grounded until Social Security kicked in. It struck him that she had an awful lot of emotion invested in this teapot. He had never seen her like this, wild-eyed and sobbing over a rusted hunk of metal that Grandma Irene wasn't expecting, hadn't asked for, and would probably ignore if Kelly presented it to her.

They used to talk about things. Back before the accident turned their lives inside out, they used to sit down at the table and hash things out. Or at least that was the way he remembered it. They talked about their day, about school, about the firehouse, about what was going on in the family. Maybe he didn't have much in the way of paternal wisdom and advice to offer, but she had never needed any. At least not that he had ever noticed. But they were there for each other. He was part of her life same as she was part of his.

And he missed it. While he had been battling back from grief and injury, she had been growing up, and somewhere along the way she had stopped needing him.

Suddenly it hit him. The drive with Seth. Getting back late. All of this hysteria. It had nothing to do with the teapot. She and Seth had probably had themselves a whopper of a fight and had broken up and his not-so-little girl was experiencing her very first broken heart. He watched as she blew her nose into a paper towel without missing a single hiccupping sob. She was the six-year-old who had overheard the truth about Santa in her aunt Claire's kitchen. The eleven-year-old whose best friend had moved away. And somehow, mixed in with the ghosts of those familiar children, was a woman he had yet to meet. The woman she was on her way to becoming. She was trapped right there in the middle, and there wasn't a damn thing he could do to hurry up the process.

Or make it stop.

Chapter Seven

THE CANDLELIGHT INN came by its name honestly. No matter the season, each of the 147 windows boasted an electric candle that blazed to life each evening at dusk. The effect was never more magical than it was at Christmastime when the candles were joined by lush wreaths of spruce and pine that hung from each of the windows that faced Main Street. The wreaths were accentuated by plush red velvet bows and pinecones faintly dusted with silvered snow. Garlands of fragrant pine and glossy mistletoe outlined the front porch and the enormous front door, softening the sharp edges and accentuating the gingerbread swoops and curves. Rose's competitors up the street had strung thousands of tiny twinkling white lights around windows and along eaves until the stately Victorians looked like they belonged on the Vegas Strip, but not Rose. She let the candles work their magic on the house and chose, instead, to turn the two bare oak trees in the front yard into works of art. Every inch of trunk, every centimeter of branch, every millimeter of twig glittered with fairy lights.

Maddy's heart leaped as she saw the guarded look of

delight in her daughter's eyes. She and Rose exchanged glances in the winter-dark front yard, and for a moment the world felt more right than it had in a very long time. They stood together on the porch and watched quietly as Hannah told Priscilla how those magical trees would help Santa Claus find them at their new address. Maddy stiffened as her daughter talked, knowing her mother's dim view of Santa Claus, but Rose surprised her and simply smiled.

"Thanks," Maddy said as they went back into the house a few minutes later.

Rose's eyebrows lifted behind her glasses. "For what?"

She glanced toward Hannah and lowered her voice. "The Santa thing. Thanks for understanding."

"You thought I wouldn't?"

Why hadn't she been smart enough to let the moment play itself out without comment? "I know how you feel about . . . those things."

"Maddy," her mother said, "I don't think you know how I feel about anything."

Maddy watched as Rose pushed open the swinging doors and disappeared down the hallway.

"Where's Grandma?" Hannah asked, clutching Priscilla to her chest. "Is she mad?"

There were times when honesty was vastly overrated. "Grandma had something to do," she said in a lame attempt at evasion. Rose was probably searching for her Maddy Doll right now.

And a box of straight pins.

She held out her hand to Hannah. "Bathtime, kiddo."

"You said I could watch *Aladdin*."

"We watched the pretty twinkling lights instead."

"You promised!"

"You can watch *Aladdin* tomorrow."

"No! I want to watch him tonight."

She glanced at the clock. "How about you take your bath and then we'll see if there's time to watch a little *Aladdin*."

Hannah considered her words, then put her hand in Maddy's.

"Priscilla can't climb the stairs," Hannah reminded Maddy, who bent down to scoop up their extremely spoiled little dog.

"I don't see why Priscilla can't carry us upstairs," Maddy said as they made their way to the third floor.

Hannah found that idea quite funny. The sound of her giggle set off little explosions of delight inside Maddy's chest. They talked about Christmas trees and twinkly lights and how Santa managed to get so much done in one night with just a few elves to help him out. Maddy added a little lavender oil to Hannah's bath water, and the soothing scent worked its bedtime magic on the little girl. Hannah settled for an Aladdin bedtime story and the promise of the videotape tomorrow.

"Did you say your prayers?" she asked Hannah just before she turned out the light.

Hannah nodded. "I prayed for you and Daddy and Grandma Rose and Aunt Lucy and—" She stopped, her small brow furrowed. "I can't remember."

"That's okay, honey," Maddy said, kissing her daughter's forehead. "I can't remember all of the aunts, either."

Hannah's eyes fluttered closed. Her dark lashes brushed against cheeks still baby round. She was so small, so vulnerable to every decision both good and bad that Maddy made. Maddy still remembered how it felt to be a child, to be small and powerless in a world you were too young to influence or understand. Her parents' divorce had thrown her world into chaos, much the same way Tom's marriage had done to Hannah. The thought that she had contributed to her little girl's distress made her sick at heart.

Maybe she shouldn't have given up so easily. Tom's roots were in Washington State. His children and grandchildren lived in the Seattle area. His friends and colleagues were spread along the coast of the Pacific Northwest. He would never be happy in San Diego. At least not permanently. Why, he had probably already had

his fill of sunshine and sandy beaches and was beginning
to think longingly of towering pines and the Space Needle. She should have waited. She should have stayed put,
bided her time, listened to her little girl and not her
mother.

Who the hell was she kidding?

*He never lied to you, Maddy. Not once. It doesn't mat-
ter if you live in Seattle or Botswana. He's not coming
back to you. He's never going to be the father to Hannah
that you want him to be.*

There weren't enough wishing stars in the galaxy to
make that dream come true. She knew that. She had accepted it a long time ago. So why did the same ridiculous
dreams come creeping into her heart every time she let
her guard down? She didn't love Tom anymore. Not the
way she once had. She loved the memory of all they had
shared and would always share in the person of their little
girl, but the giddy, head-over-heels love she once had
for him was long gone. Still, if he knocked on her door
right now and said he was willing to give familyhood
another try, she wasn't entirely sure she wouldn't say yes.

Children didn't care about soul mates or life plans or
following your bliss. Children wanted you to be as steady
and unbending as a redwood, as sheltering, as strong.
Children wanted you to hold their hands when they
crossed the street, to hear their prayers and tuck them in
at night. Children wanted you to know without being told
about the monsters in the closet and the scary shadows
on the wall and why it's okay to have a night-light as
long as your best friend doesn't know.

But more than anything, they wanted you to stay.

August 1978

*It wasn't until Daddy took her picture down from the
mantel and stuck it in his big brown suitcase that Maddy
believed he was really going to leave them.*

*"I want to go with you!" She grabbed him by the leg
and held tight. "Take me with you!"*

He bent down and took her face between his big hands. She could see tears standing on the tips of his eyelashes, and somehow that made the whole thing more awful than ever. He gathered her in a bear hug. "You know I wish things could've been different, little girl. Your mother and I tried everything we could to make it work, but some things just aren't to be, no matter how sad it makes you feel."

And he did look sad. She had never seen Daddy look that way before, like something terrible was about to happen and he couldn't stop it.

"We could go with you," she said. "Why can't Mommy and I go live out there with you?"

Mommy had been standing near the front door, but now she stood next to Daddy and Maddy's heart began to pound super fast.

"Please, Mommy," she said. "Please can't we?"

Mommy and Daddy looked at each other for a very long time, then Mommy bent down and rested her cheek against the top of Maddy's head. "We tried, honey," she said, so softly Maddy could hardly hear the words. "Remember? We lived on Daddy's farm when you were very little, but I just—" She stopped and Maddy saw Mommy and Daddy look at each other again, longer this time, until Mommy turned away.

"Your mommy was very unhappy in Oregon," Daddy said, "and"—his voice wobbled like a broken wheel on her favorite toy car—"I'm a farmer, little girl. I need land and my animals. I can't make a living for my family here, and I won't live off—"

"It will be fun, Maddy!" Her mother's smile made Maddy cry even harder. "You can live here with me with the beach right outside our back door, and in the summers you can live with your daddy on the farm with the horses and the dogs and—"

"No!" Maddy screamed as she struggled out of her father's hug. "I want us to be together. I want Daddy to stay here!"

Her mother reached for her, but Maddy pushed her

away. "Honey, we explained it to you. Your daddy and I love you with all our hearts, and we've tried everything to keep our family together, but it didn't work."

"Why didn't it work?"

Her mother sighed. Daddy looked old and sad.

"Divorce doesn't mean we don't love you, honey," her mother said. "We both love you more than anything in the world."

"Do you love each other?"

"Yes," said Daddy, his voice loud and clear. "I loved your mother from the first day we met. Nothing's changed."

Mommy's eyes were wet, but she didn't cry. Maddy couldn't remember ever seeing her mother cry, not even when their cat Jingles ran away. "I love your daddy very much, honey, but sometimes grown-ups can't—"

Maddy ran out the door, down the front steps, across the sun-parched grass, ran as fast as her bare feet could carry her. She heard her mother calling her name, heard Daddy's voice, but that only made her run faster. If they really loved her, they would stay together forever.

No matter what.

HANNAH'S BREATHING WAS deep and even and before long the room was filled with the sweet smell of a sleeping child. They had more in common than curly hair and a stubborn streak. When Maddy looked into her daughter's eyes, she saw herself all those years ago, and the pain in her heart was fresh and new. But this time it wasn't for the little girl she once was; it was for Hannah.

She had to make things better for her. She had hoped that surrounding her daughter with family would make a difference, but so far Hannah had shown little interest in her cousins and aunts and uncles. She loved her grandma Rose, but Maddy's stomach knotted each time she left them alone together. Hannah was a fey and imaginative creature, qualities Rose found disconcerting, if not incomprehensible. The very traits Maddy sought to encourage in her daughter were the ones Rose had tried to control in her own child.

Maddy knew she would be in for another lecture on the dangers of fantasy when the samovar arrived, but she didn't care. Hannah's face, aglow with happiness on Christmas morning, would make up for it.

She slipped quietly out of Hannah's room and tiptoed down the hallway toward the stairs. She had been so busy e-mailing FireGuy that she hadn't checked for confirmation from the seller. She'd check for messages and maybe do some more work on the Web site. The door to Rose's sitting room was closed. Whispers of Verdi seeped into the hallway. Rose never locked herself away this early, and Maddy experienced a guilty burst of understanding.

I don't blame you, Mother, she thought as she moved quickly past. A few weeks into their grand experiment, and already they needed a time-out.

The only light in the office was the dark blue glow from the computer monitor. She sank into the cushy desk chair, jiggled the mouse, then waited while the screen image rearranged itself. Bless Rose's pricey fiber-optic connection. In the blink of an eye she downloaded her e-mail message, then let out a small cheer when she saw confirmation from the seller of Hannah's magic lamp. He lived one town over and would be happy to drop it off at the Inn tomorrow if she'd prefer.

If she preferred? She was over the moon with excitement! Now she wouldn't have to spend the next three days tracking the progress of the samovar as it made its way from one little Jersey shore town to another. By this time tomorrow that wonderful old teapot would be safely stashed away on the top shelf of her bedroom closet, far away from prying little eyes.

Fate, that's what it was. Lady Luck finally remembered her name and address. Not only had she won the auction, the seller was willing to hand-deliver. If she had had any lingering doubts about spending so much money on the samovar, this last bit of good fortune sent them packing.

*   *   *

JACK BERNSTEIN PUSHED his way through the kitchen door in time to see Kelly vanishing out the back door.

"Good to see you, too," he said at the sound of the door slamming shut behind her. He turned to Aidan. "Domestic disturbance?"

"I don't know what the hell it was. One second everything was cool, the next she's sobbing that I've ruined her life."

"Rachel hasn't talked to me since her bat mitzvah two years ago. Leah says she'd trade places with me, but I'm not crazy. I'll take the silent treatment any day."

"Sit down," Aidan said, pointing to the other chair. "Burger? Wings? Ribs?"

"Got any tofu?"

"Cholesterol's up?"

"Way up," Jack said. "I promised Leah I'd give it my best shot before I let the doctor put me on meds."

"Still drink coffee?"

"Bring it on."

Aidan and Jack had known each other since grade school. Jack's grandfather had kept the books for Aidan's old man, and the torch had passed from grandfather to son to grandson. He poured them each a cup of coffee, then sat down opposite his friend.

"Any changes I should know about?" Jack asked as he flipped the enormous ledger.

Aidan pulled the laptop over to his place and opened Quicken. "We're holding our own," he said. "Claire says don't tell her anything until the Fourth of July when the summer people come to town."

Most shore towns sizzled from May to September, then slumbered the rest of the year. Except for the splashy B&Bs at the sound end of Main Street, Paradise Point was no exception. The B&Bs enjoyed a steady stream of visitors but not enough to make a huge difference in the town's economy. The people who stayed at the Candlelight drove Saabs and Volvos and drank designer waters. Not exactly the clientele that called O'Malley's Bar and Grill their home away from home.

Jack made a notation in the small leatherbound notebook he always carried, then leaned back in his chair. "Ever think of opening a B and B?"

"Funny," Aidan said, "real funny. We could put them up in that room over the garage."

"Yeah," said Jack, flashing the grin that had cost his father the price of a 1967 Mustang, "maybe offer them warm beer and bagel chips for breakfast."

"One bathroom, lots of waiting."

"So it was just an idea," Jack said. "They're not all winners, but it wouldn't kill you and Claire to think about upscaling the image a little."

"O'Malley's isn't one of those eighties fern bars."

"No," said Jack, "it's more like one of those fifties places that looked outdated to our old men."

"So you're saying we have a problem."

"I'm saying you're going to have a problem if you don't start thinking ahead."

"Nothing wrong with the way things are."

"You're right," Jack said. "O'Malley's is a terrific place, but in case you haven't noticed, things are changing around here and you're gonna have to move with the times if you want to stay afloat."

Aidan slugged down some coffee. "I like the way you worked in that nautical metaphor."

"Thought you would." Jack ran a few numbers through his pocket calculator, then shook his head. "Could be better."

"Could be worse, too."

"Worse I don't want to think about. Better gives me something to look forward to."

"Jeez," said Aidan with a groan. "You're giving me your serious-accountant look."

"It's not a joke."

Aidan said nothing.

Jack took that as encouragement and forged ahead. "You and Claire have to start thinking about the future. You're getting by okay now, but that's not always going to be the case. This town is changing and you damn well better figure out a way to change with it or O'Malley's—"

"You don't have to spell it out."

"Good." Jack shut his notebook, capped his pen, and turned off his calculator. "It wouldn't kill you to start thinking a little more like Rosie DiFalco. You heard her in October at the Small Business Owners Association meeting. She got a standing O from the crowd when she said we needed to base our future on the richness of our past."

"Gimme a break," Aidan muttered. "Easy to say when you've got a ten-bedroom Victorian with ocean views tucked in your back pocket."

"You've gotta admit she seems to be putting her money where her mouth is." The transformation of her late mother's house from eyesore to showplace had been nothing short of miraculous.

Aidan wasn't willing to admit anything. There was no doubt that the town's B&Bs were doing great and that the Candlelight was doing greatest of them all. These days Rose DiFalco drove around town in a shiny new black Miata with vanity plates that read INNKEEP, and Aidan frequently found himself fighting the juvenile urge to let the air out of her Michelins. He and Rose had an adversarial relationship that had begun back when he was in high school and he'd lobbed a softball through her windshield. Rose's satin-and-lace B&B was a far cry from his gritty neighborhood bar and grill, and it was no wonder he and Rose tended to be on opposite sides of most local issues.

The success of the B&Bs had brought about a renewed interest in Paradise Point's rich history as a Gilded Age playground for wealthy families from the Main Line and Fifth Avenue. Marian Vroom, head of the Historical Society, said Web-site traffic had quadrupled since the *Star-Ledger* wrote a feature about the town's upcoming Centennial Anniversary celebration.

Needless to say the Historical Society's Web site had been Rose's idea.

Jack made a few other suggestions on how to firm up

O'Malley's bottom line. Aidan agreed with most of them and promised to pass them all on to Claire.

"Tell Claire that Leah said she'll drive them to the mall Thursday night."

Jack slipped into his heavy coat and gathered up his belongings. "Hang in there, O'Malley," he said as he stepped out onto the back porch. "Your luck's gonna change any day now."

"Yeah," said Aidan. "It could get worse."

The idea was to make his old friend laugh, but somehow his comment seemed to suck all of the oxygen out of the room. He wished he could backspace over it and start again, but life didn't come with an erase feature. Jack looked as if he was about to say something, but he shook his head instead and left without a word.

The whole thing was getting old, he thought as he threw the lock and went back to the kitchen table to power down the laptop.

MADDY WAS ABOUT to shut down the computer for the night when the familiar jingle of new mail sounded. Denise had promised to send her scans of some photos of the Candlelight that she had found tucked among some embroidered linens in Aunt Florence's very scary attic. They dated back to 1892 and would be a terrific addition to the local-history section of the Web site.

She toggled over to her e-mail screen and scanned the message headers. *Lose weight . . . Buy a Ph.D. . . . Become a private investigator in your spare time . . . Teapot.* A knot tangled itself deep in the pit of her stomach.

"Oh, damn," she muttered. What if the sale was off? FireGuy or whatever he called himself might have e-mailed the seller behind her back and made an offer he couldn't refuse. It wasn't like that sort of thing didn't happen every now and again in on-line auctions. This wasn't a big operation like eBay with all sorts of rules and regulations and safeguards. This was a little mom-and-pop fund-raiser sponsored by a regional ISP and a quartet of Chambers of Commerce. If FireGuy wanted to play dirty, who could stop him? She clicked on the header and waited, holding her breath once again while the message loaded.

TO: JerseyGirl@njshore.net
FROM: FireGuy@njshore.net
DATE: 4 December
SUBJECT: Teapot

You asked about my kid. She's seventeen, honor student, valedictorian, in all of the school clubs, no trouble. At least she wasn't until I told her I blew the auction and she started sobbing like she did the day she found out there was no Santa Claus. I don't know why she wants that teapot so badly, but she does and I feel like a rat for blowing it. Your kid hasn't seen the kettle yet. Mine has. I'll double the price you paid. You can find the world's best teapot for that kind of money.

I know I'm way out of line here, but when it comes to my kid I'll take my chances. Think about it. That's all I'm asking. Thanks.

He didn't expect her to respond. Hell, he would've sent a note like his straight to the recycle bin and chalked up the sender as a total jackass. But damned if she didn't write back.

TO: FireGuy@njshore.com
FROM: JerseyGirl@njshore.com
DATE: 4 December
SUBJECT: Re: Teapot

I wish I could help you, but I can't. You see, I'm not looking to hold a tea party here. This samovar looks like Aladdin's magic lamp, and that's not exactly something you stumble across every day in New Jersey.

I know just how you feel. I'd move heaven and earth for my daughter, too. Maybe if we hadn't just moved back here I could help you out, but things have been really tough on Hannah and I'm desperate to make her smile again. I'm hoping this samovar will do the trick. Maybe I'm crazy, but at this point I'll try anything.

Your daughter sounds like a terrific kid. You must be very proud.

TO: JerseyGirl@njshore.com
FROM: FireGuy@njshore.com
DATE: 4 December
SUBJECT: Re: Re: Teapot

Proud doesn't even come close. She's the best thing that ever happened to me. I keep thinking how proud her mother would be. Sorry your Hannah is having a tough time of it. Moving is hard on everyone, especially kids.
So what brought you back to the Garden State?

TO: FireGuy@njshore.com
FROM: JerseyGirl@njshore.com
DATE: 4 December
SUBJECT: Re: Re: Re: Teapot

Family.
I was born in a little blip of a town on the Shore (North of Cape May, south of A.C.), but I haven't lived here since I was seventeen. It's a long story so I'll spare you the gory details. Let's just say I needed a job and there was one waiting in NJ. Not very interesting but true.
I figure by your e-mail addy that you live down the Shore, too. Barnegat? Wildwood? Seaside Heights?

TO: JerseyGirl@njshore.com
FROM: FireGuy@njshore.com

DATE: 4 December
SUBJECT: Re: Re: Re: Re: Teapot

Paradise Point.
Do you know it?

Paradise Point. He lived in Paradise Point? Good grief, she'd been e-mailing her private thoughts to somebody who probably wasn't a total stranger after all. How scary was that? God help her, she might even be related to him. With a screen name like FireGuy he could be one of Rose's old boyfriends or—even worse—that hideous man Aunt Lucy had dated, the one who set small appliances on fire for amusement.

So long, FireGuy. It was fun while it lasted.

She exited the program and shut down for the night.

HE KEPT THE laptop connected while he served food, talked to customers, cheered an impromptu darts tournament, then helped Tommy close things up for the night. He didn't make a big deal of checking for messages, but every time he passed by the table he took a quick look at his in box just in case, and every damn time he was disappointed.

Enjoy your magic lamp, JerseyGirl.

He hoped her kid's wishes all came true.

Chapter Eight

THE WORKDAY BEGAN before sunrise when Lucy let herself in the back door and set about whipping up breads and rolls and sticky buns that would be served warm for the guests between eight and nine-thirty. Rose was already up and about, quietly polishing the dining room furniture, laying out fresh table linens, dishes, and silver. A few minutes before seven, the luscious smells of fresh coffee and cinnamon permeated the house from first floor to third, where Maddy was struggling to climb out of bed and go wake Hannah.

One of the unexpected benefits of the transition from boardinghouse to B&B was the attention paid to the comfort of the paying guests. That attention, to Maddy's delight, spilled over onto family as well. She remembered waking up long ago Christmas mornings at Grandma Fay's in a room so cold she could see her breath. "So put on a sweater," Grandma Fay would say when both boarders and family griped. "The boiler's older than I am, and we both take awhile to warm up in the morning."

Was it any wonder Grandma Fay's boardinghouse saw a quicker turnover than your average hot-sheet motel?

Rose had brought the ancient heating system into the twenty-first century, along with the rest of the plumbing. Moody wiring and quirky phone lines had both been replaced by state-of-the-art setups. New windows, new paint, new wallpaper, new furniture, all of which Rose had accomplished without losing the Victorian ambience or integrity of the house.

If only the day started a little bit later . . .

Hannah squeezed her eyes shut tight when Maddy entered the child's room and gently touched her shoulder.

"School day, honey," Maddy said, brushing a lock of hair off her little girl's cheek. "Time to rise and shine."

"No!" Hannah pulled the pink-and-yellow comforter over her head. "Want to sleep."

"Me too," Maddy said, "but Grandma Rose and Aunt Lucy are downstairs making breakfast." She paused a moment. "Can you smell the cinnamon rolls?"

Hannah wasn't buying it.

"Okay, kiddo." Maddy peeled the comforter down over one tiny shoulder. "You have to get up, Hannah. You're a schoolgirl now. You don't want to miss the bus."

Priscilla skidded into the room, paws sliding wildly on the polished wood floor. Hannah dived back underneath the comforter before Maddy could stop her. Priscilla barked twice, then, to Maddy's horror, a tiny puddle appeared beneath her.

Maddy swore.

Hannah burst into tears.

Priscilla's puddle grew larger.

It was going to be a long morning.

"I WOKE YOU up." Claire sounded muffled and apologetic as Aidan shifted the phone from his right ear to his left.

"It's seven forty-five," he said. "I've been up awhile."

"I need to ask Kelly a favor."

"You missed her by a half hour," he said. "She has band practice on Tuesday mornings."

Claire muttered something colorful that made Aidan

wince. "My face is blown up the size of a watermelon," she said. "I'm zonked on Tylenol with codeine. I feel like somebody stuck a cattle prod in my molar and forgot to take it out again. If you have even the slightest bit of compassion for me, your favorite sister-in-law, you'll—"

"Take Billy Jr. to the bus stop." He couldn't count the number of times Claire had filled in for him when Kelly was little and he was working twelve-hour shifts.

"Oh, thank you thank you thank you! I'm waiting for Dr. G. to call me back, and if he can squeeze me in before he starts regular office hours, I'm going to—"

She would still be talking if he hadn't reminded her to hang up so Dr. G. could get through to her.

He made some toast, gulped down some more black coffee, then hit the road. Claire said the bus came by at 8:48 sharp, which meant he'd have to haul ass if he was going to make it to physical therapy for his nine o'clock.

Billy Jr. was running circles in the front yard when he got there, while a shivering Claire watched from the door-way. She looked tired, out of sorts, and eager to say good-bye to the perpetual motion machine masquerading as her offspring.

"I owe you," she called out, then vanished into the house before Aidan could even call out a greeting.

"Got everything?" Aidan asked as he strapped his nephew in.

"Can we buy candy before school?"

"No candy."

"Can we drive through McDonald's for an Egg Mc-Muffin?"

"Not today, buddy. Gotta get you to school."

"I don't really have to go," Billy Jr. said. "I could stay with you."

"Nice try," Aidan said as he backed out of the drive-way, "but you're going to school." *You're so much like your old man . . . so damn much . . .*

"We could go to the lighthouse."

"We'll go to the lighthouse while you're on Christmas break."

"Today's better."

"Maybe for you," Aidan said, "but I have P.T. at nine o'clock."

Billy Jr. looked over at him. "What's that?"

"Physical therapy." He rolled to a stop at the corner of Summertree Road and Main Street. "A group of people at the hospital are helping me get my leg back in shape."

"So it'll work right?"

"That's what we're aiming for." No point telling the kid about the odds. O'Malleys learned all about the odds soon enough.

Billy Jr. said nothing. He swiveled his head toward the window and stared out at a gray cat sprawled on the top step of Marini's Martinizing. Billy's memory filled the truck. His laughter echoed in the space between them. The sharp bracing smell of the Altoids he popped morning, noon, and night that made their nostrils quiver. His jokes, his temper, his deep sense of loyalty, the way he loved his family (the trouble he had showing it), the wild streak that blew through him like a late summer hurricane that barreled up the shore and left behind nothing but destruction. All of the bits and pieces that had made Billy O'Malley the man he was lay deep inside the boy looking out the truck window at the old gray cat.

He reached into the console next to his seat and pulled out a Milky Way.

"Here," he said, tossing it to Billy Jr.

"Before school?" The kid's expression lurched between hope and disbelief.

"You only live once."

Billy Jr. grinned at him and tore open the wrapper. "Thanks!"

"You know," he said carefully, "your dad liked Milky Ways, too." *If you want to talk, buddy, I'm here. I'll always be here for you.*

"He did?"

"Big time. He used to hide them in the hamper with the dirty socks."

"Gross." Who knew the kid could smile that wide with all that chocolate in his mouth?

"Real gross," Aidan said. "Especially when our mom tossed them in the washer and the chocolate melted all over her favorite blouse."

"My mom would have a cow."

"Our mom sure did. She took all of his eight-track tapes away for a week." *She was your grandma Mary Ellen, Billy Jr. . . . She would've loved you.*

"His eight what?"

Talk about feeling old. "Music," he said. "She said he couldn't listen to his favorite stuff until he learned not to hide chocolate bars in with the laundry."

"Moms get real mad about stuff like that," Billy observed as he crammed the rest of the candy bar into his mouth.

"So do daughters," he said as they angled into a parking spot a half-block down from the bus stop. "Kelly was doing the wash one day and I tossed a shirt into the machine without checking my pockets."

"Uh-oh," said Billy.

"You know that fancy fountain pen I let you try?"

Billy nodded.

"You wouldn't believe how much ink that sucker holds."

Billy snorted with laughter.

"Think it's funny, do you?" Aidan pretended annoyance as he set the parking brake and turned off the engine.

"Yeah," said Billy.

"Kelly wasn't laughing when she saw what happened to the towels."

"Girls get real upset about that stuff," Billy observed with all the wisdom of his seven years. "My dad said that's why I had to try extra-hard to stay out of trouble."

"That was good advice."

"Yeah," he said. "My dad always gave good advice."

"You're right," said Aidan as they started walking toward the knot of women and children waiting at the corner. "He gave great advice."

Too bad he never took any of it.

* * *

"A SNOW SKY," Denise said as Maddy, Hannah, and Priscilla joined the group. "Bet we have a good six inches by nightfall."

"Six inches? Oh, what I could say about that if the munchkins weren't around." Gina's eyes twinkled with mischief and the other women laughed.

"Now, that's exactly what I *don't* need," Pat said, clapping her hands over her daughter's ears. "Nothing but trouble, if you ask me."

"And they're not even pretty," Joann said. "You could forgive a lot if they weren't so damn funny looking."

Maddy struggled to control her own laughter. Thank God Hannah was busy parading Priscilla in front of a cluster of cousins. Oh, the endless afternoons she and her own cousins had spent discussing the mysteries of the still undiscovered male member. *It's so . . . does it really . . . get OUT of here . . . I don't BELIEVE it . . . no way would I ever . . .*

"Wouldn't you think we'd have it all figured out by now?" she asked.

"You must be kidding," Gina said, still laughing. "It's like Big Foot or Nessie. There have been brief sightings over the years but only limited contact. You need to keep one in captivity long enough to conduct a real study."

"Only Claire's managed to—" Denise glanced around. "Where *is* Claire anyway?"

"She's late," Delia said.

Denise shot her a *Duh* look.

"Maybe Billy's ears are acting up again."

"He looked fine yesterday."

"You know how quick those things flare up. Maybe—"

"Isn't that her son?" Maddy asked as Billy Jr. bounded into view followed by a tall, broad-shouldered man. The man wore jeans, a worn-looking leather jacket that emphasized the impressive dimensions of his chest, and work boots. The standard male uniform on the Jersey Shore. He favored his right side, which gave his walk an odd, syncopated gait. His hair was thick and a little too long for

fashion, a russet brown shade that probably showed
strands of gold and red in the sunshine. Bits and pieces
of memory tugged at Maddy's sleeve. He seemed familiar,
like somebody she should know but didn't.

"Who's the guy with Billy Jr.?" she asked. Nobody had
even hinted at the existence of a new man in Claire's life,
but there he was with the woman's youngest. Her brother,
maybe? Their coloring was similar.

Denise narrowed her eyes in their general direction.
"You dope. That's her brother-in-law, Aidan. You know,
from O'Malley's Bar and Grill. I wonder why he's pulling
school bus duty."

"That's Aidan O'Malley?" Maddy asked. Aidan
O'Malley had been a star athlete at school, one of those
big strong kids whose physical presence commanded attention the second he walked into a room. "Why the
cane?"

"Shh," Gina warned. "It happened at the same warehouse fire where he lost his brother. He went back in to
try to find Billy when the roof collapsed." Gina shuddered
and wrapped her arms across her middle. "He spent a few
months in the hospital. They weren't sure he'd ever walk
again."

Billy Jr. made a beeline for Hannah and Priscilla.

Aidan seemed to be making a beeline for Gina.

Maddy lowered her voice and talked fast. "But I
thought he'd left town years ago. When did he—"

"Hey, ladies." He was one of those big men who carry
their strength lightly. He didn't ask to be the center of
attention. He simply was. It was clear to Maddy that all
he had to do was step into a room (or stand on a street
corner as it were) and all eyes were on him. Tall, broad
chest, long legs, great butt—she hadn't seen him from the
rear yet, but she'd bet money on it—what's not to like?

The fact that he had a great smile didn't hurt, either.
Wide, a little lopsided, lots of white teeth, with an ap-
pealing touch of irony around the edges. Age had done
little to diminish his appeal, but the cocky self-confidence
of youth was gone. His green-gold eyes rested for a mo-

ment on Maddy and she barely managed to hold back a
gasp at the startling sight of the long jagged white scar
that bisected the right side of his face. Suddenly the irony
made perfect sense.

"Where's Claire?" Joann demanded. "Is something
wrong?"

"She's at the dentist," Aidan said, his eyes straying
back to Maddy, as if he were riffling through his mental
Rolodex, trying to place her.

"Ouch," said Gina, rolling her eyes. "The root canal?"

Aidan nodded. "She didn't look too happy when I
swung by for Billy."

"Well, don't worry," Denise said with a friendly pat on
the man's forearm. For an instant Maddy's fingertips
seemed to register the swell of muscle beneath his sleeve.
"I'll make sure Billy Jr. gets home after school. Tell
Claire to take it easy."

Aidan thanked her, then glanced in Maddy's direction
again.

"Sorry," he said, flashing that off-balance smile. "You
look familiar, but I can't—"

"Maddy Bainbridge," she said, extending her right
hand. "I was four years behind you in school." Not that
he would remember. He had already graduated when she
began freshman year and was about to kick over the traces
of their South Jersey 'burb for college in Pennsylvania
courtesy of a big fat juicy athletic scholarship.

He had rough, callused hands and a firm grip. Strong
hands. Beautiful hands with long fingers and wide palms
that could gently cup a woman's face when he . . .

*Knock it off, Maddy. Save the fantasies for Hannah's
bedtime stories.*

Still, his hands were noteworthy and she was enough
of a connoisseur of all things beautiful to commit their
contours swiftly to memory.

Men had no idea how important hands were or of how
closely women observed them. She noted a crisscrossed
webbing of faint scars at the base of his thumb and across
the top of his wrist and wondered if he'd acquired them

at the warehouse fire or somewhere else. Sometimes the body told your story before you said a word.

"Gina's cousin?" he asked.

"One of many." That was how you identified yourself in Paradise Point. You were Gina's cousin. Lucy's niece. Fay's granddaughter. Hannah's mother. Rose's daughter. No more than two degrees separated her from every single person in town. When she was a little girl, she had dreamed about escaping to the blissful anonymity of some faraway city where she could take chances, make mistakes, even fall flat on her face a time or two without having to explain herself to a dozen concerned relatives before sundown.

The reality hadn't proved to be quite so satisfying as the dream.

He studied her face with open curiosity. "I think I see a little DiFalco in the jawline and around the eyes."

"It's mostly in the attitude," she said as her own smile (which hadn't been used all that much lately) inched across her face.

"Oh, yeah," he said, matching her smile for smile. "I know all about the DiFalco attitude."

"In this town that could mean just about anything from marriage to divorce to I'll-see-you-in-Small-Claims-Court."

Wouldn't you know it? The guy had a laugh to match the smile and the hands, one of those reluctant honey-coated rumbles that seem to erupt from deep inside a man's chest, then blossom as they work their way past his defenses. Maddy had always been a sucker for men who knew how to laugh, even if Aidan O'Malley seemed to be as out of practice as she was.

"Mommy!" Hannah's voice lifted above the din of children's chatter. "I'm stuck in 'Cilla's leash." She sounded on the verge of tears, the way she did so often these days, and in that instant Maddy's brain emptied of everything but her little girl.

The puppy had wound her way around and between Hannah's feet until not an extra inch of leash remained untangled. Maddy glanced at the gaggle of young cousins and thought they looked a tad guilty. She longed to ask a few pointed questions, but right now the important thing was minimizing Hannah's embarrassment.

"Good grief," Maddy said as she unclipped the leash from Priscilla's collar. "Priscilla, you've done quite a job." She looked over her shoulder at O'Malley, who loomed behind her. "Here." She thrust the puppy at him. "Take Priscilla while I untangle Hannah."

"Don't you look cute," Gina teased Aidan as the puppy curled up against his broad chest. "Maybe you should get one of your own."

"I think Aidan's more the Lhasa apso type," Denise chimed in.

"Whoa," he broke in with a laugh. "Isn't that one of those little—"

"Not little," Gina said. "Teeny. We're talking micro-canine. The kind of dog you name Fluffy and nobody asks you why."

"You're a cruel woman, Gina. What about the time I sent you home from O'Malley's with an extra pair of—"

"I take it back!" Gina waved her hands in the air. "Say no more! I take it all back!"

"An extra pair of what?" Joann demanded. "I was there that night and I didn't see any—"

Pat leaned over and whispered something in Joann's ear. Joann hooted, then turned bright red as the words sank in. "Gina! You didn't!"

"She did," said Aidan O'Malley. "Tommy said it took five years off his life."

"And six off mine." Gina looked up at Aidan, and Maddy swore her cousin batted her lashes at him. Was it possible Gina was in the market for a new Mr. Maybe? "You're a Great Dane kind of guy, O'Malley. I don't know what I was thinking."

"All wrong," said Denise. "I'd say he's more Irish wolfhound."

"No, no! I've got it!" cried Pat. "With those shoulders he's gotta be a cross between wolfhound and mastiff."

The fifteen years Maddy had spent away from Paradise Point suddenly felt like fifty. You had to earn the right to tease somebody that way, and the only way you could do it was by sticking around through the highs and lows and everyday sameness of life in a small town. Cousins, of course, didn't count. Cousins were family and you already knew all of their secrets, same as they thought they knew all of yours.

Which opened up a whole new area of possibilities Maddy hadn't even thought about until now.

Much easier to rescue her daughter from the tangled leash than to ponder her family's tangled lives. To her surprise, O'Malley separated himself from the pack and moved closer. She liked the easy way he held Priscilla, and judging by the blissful expression on the puppy's face, Priscilla liked it, too. If he was the slightest bit embarrassed to be seen cuddling a girlie poodle puppy against his battered leather jacket, it didn't show, and Maddy experienced another jolt of awareness in the pit of her stomach. He was comfortable in his own skin. She hadn't been comfortable in her own skin since her eighth birthday. He didn't need to prove his maleness by pretending to be too macho to show tenderness toward a small animal.

Which was, of course, reading way too much into nothing at all.

She wondered again if there was something going on between him and Gina, then, for the second time, pushed the thought from her mind. Secrets didn't stay secret very long in the DiFalco family. Not hers or anybody else's. Sooner or later everybody found out everything there was to know.

Something to keep in mind if she was ever crazy enough to consider dating anyone from the tristate area.

Hannah's lower lip was quivering and it was clear her little girl was a half-step away from a major meltdown. "Look what that crazy dog did," Maddy said as she began to unwind the leash from her daughter's ankles. "I think that animal has a very silly sense of humor, don't you?"

Hannah sniffled. Her chin trembled. Another ten seconds and she'd be sobbing and Maddy wouldn't be able to convince her to go back to school until puberty.

O'Malley hunkered down next to Hannah and looked at her with a very serious expression. "When I was your age, my cat locked me in the closet."

Hannah's blue eyes widened, but her chin continued to tremble.

"I'll bet you don't believe me," he said, supporting Priscilla's back legs with the palm of his left hand, "but it really happened."

Hannah popped her thumb into her mouth and shook her head.

"I'll bet that was some cat," Maddy said as she unwound the leash from Hannah's ankles, then her calves, and maneuvered the many turns around her plump knees. "Imagine a cat who could lock a boy in a closet!"

"She was my brother's cat," O'Malley said with great solemnity, "and she hadn't forgiven me for bringing a dog into the house." He scratched Priscilla behind her left ear with his right thumb, and the puppy practically swooned. "I was digging around in the closet for my sneakers when BAM!" Hannah jumped at his impression of a door slamming shut. "That cat kicked the door shut and locked me in."

Maddy arched a brow in his direction. "The cat knew how to use a key?" she asked, which made Hannah giggle. "Now, I can imagine Miss Priscilla figuring out how to use a key, but a cat—?"

"Don't tell anyone," O'Malley said, lowering his voice so only Maddy and Hannah could hear him, "but I'm pretty sure Spike knew how to drive."

Hannah's chin stopped trembling. Her lower lip no longer quivered. "Cats can't drive," she said in a whisper.

"Did you ever see a cat drive?" he asked.

Hannah shook her head. "Unh-uh."

"Me, neither, but that doesn't mean they can't."

Hannah's soft blond brows knotted as she cast an odd look in Priscilla's direction, as if contemplating the relative merits of dogs versus cats. Maddy unwound the rest of the leash, and Hannah ducked behind her mother the second she was freed, casting curious glances O'Malley's way.

"You're a miracle worker," Maddy said as she clipped the leash to Priscilla's collar. "We were close to total meltdown there."

"I know the signs."

They watched Hannah as she darted back to her aunt Denise, who was in charge of guarding the backpacks and lunch boxes.

"Notice that I'm not asking you about the cat and the closet door."

"Thanks," he said, maintaining the properly solemn note of gratitude. "I appreciate it."

"Although I have to admit a certain skepticism when it comes to cats and cars."

"Understandable," he said, "but it depends on the cat."

"And the car," Maddy said, getting caught up in the game.

"Goes without saying."

The rumble of the approaching school bus drowned out the chatter of the cousins and near-cousins and their kids.

Maddy grinned at O'Malley. "You can put the dog down now."

His face was transformed when he smiled. The weariness vanished and even the ugly scar that bisected his right cheek faded into insignificance. "Good idea," he said and placed Priscilla at Maddy's feet.

Priscilla evaluated the situation and found it sorely lacking. She bounced back to O'Malley and climbed onto his boots, her front paws digging at his pants leg in a blatant attempt to force him to pick her up again.

Some females had absolutely no shame.

They locked eyes, Maddy and O'Malley, and for an instant—no more than that, but entire lives were changed every day in less time—the school bus and the kids and the poodle and the cousins and the entire state of New Jersey vanished, and they saw a glimpse of how it could be if they dropped their guard, if they had the guts, if they'd met ten years earlier or five years later . . . if Priscilla hadn't picked that exact moment to pee on his foot.

"Oh, God! Oh, no!" Maddy stared in disbelief as a small puddle formed beneath Priscilla's furry bottom. "I don't believe this!"

The poor little dog cowered, and Maddy felt instantly guilty, which rendered her instantly useless. How on earth could something so tiny contain so much fluid? It boggled the mind. She just stood there and watched as the puddle spread wider, then finally achieved maximum dimensions. Priscilla wagged her tail as if to congratulate herself on a job well done while Maddy remained frozen in a combination of humiliation and disbelief. Fortunately Aidan O'Malley was made of better stuff. He calmly bent down and swooped the puppy up into his arms. He was so damn cool and unruffled that you would think poodles peed on him every day of the week.

"I am *so* sorry," Maddy said again as the school bus rolled closer. "I don't know what's with her today." She reached into the pocket of her jacket and pulled out a thick wad of Kleenex that she carried for Hannah's many emergencies, then bent down to dab at the appalling mess on his boot.

"You don't have to do that." He took the Kleenex from her, dragged them across the top of his boot, then tossed the tissues into the trash basket next to Denise.

"I'm really sorry."

"I know." Again that lopsided, wonderful smile. "I think you said it before. She's a dog. Dogs pee. End of story."

Maddy took Priscilla from him before the poodle had a chance to anoint his leather jacket. "I swear she seems to have sprung a leak this morning." *Shut up, Maddy. Let it rest. You've exceeded the pee limit for one conversation.* "I don't know what's wrong with her. First she leaves a small lake on the floor of Hannah's room and now this." *Good going, Maddy. Why don't you discuss the bladder problems of the entire DiFalco family while you're at it?*

"Why can't they make training pants for poodles?"

He looked at her for what seemed like forever, and Maddy heard every stupid comment she had ever made in her entire life in Dolby Stereo inside her head. Then he lost it. His laugh was even better than his smile. All of Maddy's embarrassment and discomfort was swallowed up inside that laugh, and she started laughing, too, huge ridiculous unself-conscious whoops the likes of which she hadn't enjoyed since pre-puberty.

Maybe if they hadn't been laughing quite so hard and so loudly, they would have noticed that everyone was watching them, everyone including Hannah and Billy Jr., Denise and Gina, Pat and Connie, Joann and their kids and friends of their kids and Sarah the school-bus driver, who had been Maddy's nemesis in Girl Scouts.

"So don't keep us in suspense," Denise said with maybe just the tiniest bit of an edge to her voice. "Who needs training pants?"

It was a perfectly reasonable question, but both Aidan and Maddy were far beyond reason and couldn't have answered if their lives depended on it.

Hannah seemed quite put out with Maddy. She made a point of kissing Priscilla goodbye but managed only a mumbled "Bye" to her mother. *It starts early,* Maddy thought as she waved at the bus. Sometimes it seemed that the whole mother-daughter relationship was built on a foundation of smoke and mirrors. One wrong word—or outsized bout of laughter—and it all came tumbling down.

Billy Jr. was immune to the whole thing. After a puzzled look at his still-laughing uncle, he shouldered his book bag and boarded the bus in an impressively macho display of indifference.

Mars and Venus.

No doubt about it.

"So tell us," Gina persisted as the bus moved away. "What was all that about training pants?"

"Training pants?" Maddy looked up at Aidan.

"Beats me," he said.

"Very funny," Gina said. "So don't tell us." She

glanced at the bank clock across the street. "Oh, damn! Lois Riordan's due for a perm and a bikini wax in six minutes and I haven't opened the shop." She grabbed her youngest, the stroller, her enormous Coach tote bag, then hurried off down the block toward Upsweep without another word.

That was the cue for the group to disperse. Goodbye, goodbye. In moments Maddy and Aidan (and Priscilla) were alone.

"I know Denise," Maddy said, shaking her head. "She won't give up until she finds out what we were laughing about."

He started to say something, stopped, then started again. "Coffee at Julie's? I think they serve poodles there."

"I'd love to. Just let me—"

"Great. We can—damn!" He looked genuinely upset. (Or was he having second thoughts?) She wasn't clairvoyant, but she was a DiFalco girl and DiFalco girls knew when a man was about to change his mind. "I hate to do this, but how about a rain check? I've got six minutes to make my PT appointment."

Maddy said all the right things. Of course he could have a rain check. No, please don't apologize. These things happen. Besides, she really should be getting home herself. She had doorknobs to polish and bathrooms to clean.

"My car's around the corner," he said. "I could—"

"No," she said. "No, thanks. I don't want to think about what Priscilla could do to your upholstery."

He hesitated.

She delayed.

Neither one knew how to make the first move so, as luck would have it, neither one made a move at all except to say goodbye.

"Your appointment," Maddy said. "You'd better—"

"You're right. I'd better get moving." It was so clear he wanted to say more, but something—reason? caution? her hair?—pulled him back from the brink. "It was good to see you again, Maddy."

"Me, too." She shook her head and laughed softly. "I mean, same here. Take care, Aidan."

Her mother and aunts and cousins would be happy to learn that Maddy hadn't let down their side. The DiFalco women's legendary bad luck with men was still going strong.

Chapter Nine

ROSE LOVED THE Candlelight Inn. She loved caring for it, living in it, cleaning it, repairing it, sharing it with an endless stream of guests. She even enjoyed preparing picnic baskets at seven in the morning for geriatric lovebirds in search of romance by the shore.

"I put a map in the basket next to the cranberry-pecan muffins," she told the Armaghs as she carried their provisions out to their car. The Loewensteins had set out a half hour earlier. "There's a thermos of decaf; a small thermos of cream; sugar; a selection of tea sandwiches; some wonderful pears; baked brie; and a few little surprises."

The Armaghs, bless their hearts, beamed with delight.

"You are the sweetest thing," Mrs. Armagh said, "doing all of this for us and you don't even charge extra."

"It's my pleasure," Rose said and she meant it. She was never happier than when she was fussing over her guests, making sure they had their maps and their picnic baskets and the chance to make a few memories. There were even times when she forgot all about the outrageous profit she made from every guest who passed through her doors.

She stowed the picnic basket in the backseat of their Chrysler, then waited while they buckled their seat belts.

"You drive carefully," she ordered them with a friendly smile. "We're having a beautiful Trout Amandine tonight that I know you'll love."

"We'll be there," Mr. Armagh said then.

She waved goodbye, then went back inside where she finished putting the kitchen to rights, checked the pantry against her dinner recipes, and called Lucy to tell her to stop at Shop Rite for cardamom on the way over. That took all of ten minutes. The house was as close to perfect as it was likely to get. There wasn't a mantel, side table, or doorway that had been neglected. Boughs of shiny holly were everywhere, laced with fairy lights and festive red velvet bows.

It occurred to Rose that there was still a half-carton of holly stowed in the mudroom, and a huge copper planter almost begging for a little Christmas cheer. Who was she to deny their mutual destiny?

Martha Stewart, eat your heart out.

Paradise Point High School

Seth was waiting for her in the parking lot behind the track. Kelly pulled into the last empty spot, and by the time she gathered up her books and papers, he was opening her door for her.

"Eleven hours, forty-six minutes," he said.

"Forty-seven," she corrected.

The hours and minutes since they had been together.

"You look tired."

She brushed the hair from her eyes. "I'm okay."

"Is something wrong?"

"Why would you think that?"

"I don't know," he said, obviously searching for the right words. "Just a feeling."

She leaned closer, breathing in the familiar smell of his skin.

"You're not sorry, are you, Kel?"

She could tell him why she was worried. He would understand. Seth wasn't the kind of guy who would run from trouble. He loved her. He would be there with her. Hadn't they spent ages talking about what they would do if the worst happened and she found herself pregnant? They didn't keep secrets from each other. That wasn't their way.

"I love you," she said. "There's nothing to be sorry about."

"Some day," he said, draping an arm across her shoulders. "Next year we'll be in college and things'll be different."

The thought both thrilled and terrified Kelly. Spreading her wings meant leaving the nest behind, leaving her father alone.

"He'll be fine," Seth said, reading her mind. "This is what he wants for you, Kel. You know he's proud of that scholarship you won."

"I know, I know. If it wasn't for the accident, I wouldn't feel so bad. He's so alone, Seth—" Her voice cracked and she paused a second, then spoke again. "I wish he had someone. I wish he wasn't so alone."

She turned and buried her face against the side of Seth's neck and cried. Lately she had been spilling over with emotion. A beautiful sunrise would start her crying. A cross look. A snippet of poetry. The thought of Grandma Irene, so old and alone. The fact that no matter what she did or said she could never make it turn out all right for her family.

"I wish we were already old," she said. "I wish I could see ahead into the future and know how everything was going to turn out."

"I know how it's going to turn out," he said, stroking her hair.

She pulled away slightly from his embrace and met his eyes. "Tell me."

"We're going to live happily ever after."

Sooner or later, somebody had to.

*   *   *

ROSE WAS ON the front porch putting the finishing touches on the planter when Maddy raced up the walk with that little dog of hers cradled against her chest. Rose's breath caught for an instant as a wave of love for her only child almost brought her to her knees. She looked so beautiful with her cheeks red with cold and her soft golden brown curls wreathing her face, so much like the old Maddy that Rose's eyes filled with unexpected tears.

Rose addressed her full attention to the holly as her daughter approached.

"I'm sorry," Maddy blurted as she climbed the porch steps. "I meant to be back here by nine to help you." She reached into the crate of holly and withdrew an armful of clippings.

"No need for apologies," Rose said, wishing she could somehow find the right tone of voice, the right words, to bridge the widening gap between them. She pointed to a bare spot on the north side of the basket and watched as Maddy filled it with luxuriant branches. "Hannah made her bus without trouble, I assume."

Her heart sank. Literally sank. She could feel it drop lower in her chest as Maddy's jaw settled into an all-too-familiar angle. Even Priscilla was looking up at her with a faint hint of scorn.

Oh, Rose, Rose ... when will you learn to keep your mouth shut?

"Of course she made her bus." Maddy met Rose's eyes over the empty carton. A crushed holly berry lay at her feet. (Rose would have to remember to wipe that up before her guests returned.) "Why wouldn't she? I'm not in the habit of making my daughter late for school."

Don't mention all the commotion this morning ... don't mention Priscilla's "accident" ... take a deep breath, Rosie, and start all over again.

"A package arrived for you while you were out." The man had shown up at her door unannounced, a pale and slender elderly gentleman who was back in his Dodge before Rose had a chance to ask his name.

The guarded, slightly sullen expression in Maddy's eyes vanished. "The samovar?"

"I didn't open it, but—"

Maddy swooped Priscilla up into her arms and raced for the front door. She lingered for a second with the door open and Rose was about to chide her gently for trying to heat the entire neighborhood when she realized Maddy was waiting for her.

Rose put her pruning shears down next to the carton of holly, brushed her hands along the sides of her tweed pants, and followed her daughter inside.

"Who delivered it?" Maddy asked over her shoulder as she made a beeline for the office.

"It wasn't UPS or the postal service," Rose said, wiping a smudge of dust from one of the hall tables as she galloped past. "Just an old man in a plaid wool jacket and a fedora."

Maddy chuckled. "A fedora?"

Rose laughed, too. "My thoughts exactly."

"Was he nice?"

"I don't know," Rose said as Maddy pounced on the package. "He handed me the parcel for you, I said thanks, he said don't mention it, and that was that."

"String!" Maddy said, fingering the twine.

"And a brown paper package." Rose leaned against the desk, struggling against the urge to straighten Maddy's stack of papers. "I feel like we should burst into song."

It took only a split second for Maddy's smile to turn into a full-fledged laugh. A current of absolute, pure delight flooded Rose's being. *Oh, baby, how I've longed to make you laugh that way! It's been so long since we laughed together. . . .*

Maddy plucked a pair of shears from the top drawer of the desk and cut the string with a flourish. "Remember when Gina and I decided we were going to stage *The Sound of Music* in Grandma Fay's front room while she was making Thanksgiving dinner?"

"I don't think I ever heard my mother use that language before in my life."

Maddy tore off the brown paper with wild abandon. "I don't think I ever heard *my* mother use that language before, either."

The years tumbled back onto themselves until Rose wasn't that much older than Maddy. It was their first Christmas without Bill, and she had felt awkward and defensive about her failure as a wife. She had been determined to be the DiFalco who would break the string of bad luck, the one who would show them how easy it was to be in love and married and happy all at the same time. Her divorce had hit her hard, much harder than she had ever admitted to anyone but Bill himself. Only he knew about the long, lonely nights. The phone calls. The declarations of love. The inability to compromise. The fact that no matter how hard they had tried, they always fell short of happily ever after.

"Oh." The sound of Maddy's disappointment snapped her back to the here and now. "You were right, Ma. Hannah's magic lamp is nothing but a rusty teapot after all."

Rose trained a critical eye on the curved lines of the samovar. The graceful swells, the slender spout, the intricately worked leaves and vines that wove their way around the handle.

"Yes, it's in terrible shape," she said, "but I have to admit it's beautiful, Maddy. Hannah's going to love it." Not that she understood the whole magic-lamp business, but there was no denying it was an attractive teapot.

Maddy trained her critical eye on Rose. "I think I like it better when you don't mince words. This is a ridiculous lump of rust. It'll give Hannah nightmares!" She gathered up the box and the tissue paper and was about to toss the teapot into the mess and haul it out to the garbage when Rose stopped her.

"Give me an hour," she said, taking the parcel from Maddy. "I bet you don't recognize the samovar when I'm finished with it."

Maddy looked confused and more than a tad suspicious. "I screwed up," she said, with perhaps less of an edge to her voice than Rose had come to expect. "I should have gone to Toys "R" Us instead of wasting my time on that on-line auction. You don't have to pretend I found a diamond-in-the-rough, Mother."

"But that's exactly what you did find," Rose protested, and she set out to prove her point.

MADDY FOLLOWED HER mother into the kitchen, where Rose ordered her to pour them each a cup of decaf while she gathered up her potions and lotions and special cleaning rags. Rose claimed she didn't believe in magic, but in Maddy's opinion nothing short of some real hocus-pocus had a snowball's chance of success.

"Why bother?" Maddy said as she slid a mug of coffee across the counter toward Rose. "It's nothing but a bucket of rust, just like you said."

"I like a challenge," Rose said as she slid her beautifully manicured hands into a pair of rubber gloves. "Why do you think I took on the Candlelight?"

"I would've thought I was enough of a challenge for you for a lifetime."

"You were that."

Maddy waited for the zinger, but none was forthcoming. Was it possible they were having a real conversation? She settled down at the kitchen table to peel some apples for that evening's individual tarts with pecans and caramel while her mother launched into the impossible task of turning a piece of junk into a well-polished piece of junk.

"What's that stuff?" she asked as Rose poured a glob of something creamy and foul-smelling onto one of the rags.

"Trade secret." Rose began applying the stuff to the side of the samovar with long, smooth strokes. "Grandma Fay's grandmother came up with it back in Ireland. She used it to clean the Squire's silverware. Fay made four bottles of it just before she died. This is the last of the lot."

"You know," said Maddy, "I've never been clear how Great-great-grandma Mary managed to meet and marry a guy from Sicily. You wouldn't think too many *paisans* wandered through County Cork in those days."

Rose's slender shoulders lifted, then fell as she reapplied the glop to her cleaning rag. "Apparently one did. The story I heard when I was growing up was that Great-great-grandpa Vincenzo saw her in church and fell in love with her at first sight."

"But what was he doing in her little Irish church?" Maddy persisted. "How did he get there?"

Rose refolded the rag, then began to buff a small portion of the samovar with short, brisk strokes. "I think he worked for a shipbuilder or something."

"And—?"

"And that's all I know."

"I wish I'd asked Grandma Fay more questions while she was alive."

"That makes two of us." Rose applied more polish to the rag. "All of those stories gone forever. It's a terrible shame."

"What about Great-aunt Louise? Do you think she might remember a few stories?"

Rose sighed deeply and brushed a lock of hair off her face with her forearm. "Lou isn't doing too well these days. She set fire to her kitchen twice back in August. Jack and Tommy and their wives decided it was time she sold the house and went into assisted living."

A shudder ran up Maddy's spine at the thought of feisty, eccentric Aunt Lou relegated to some anonymous rabbit warren of rooms where old people waited to die. "She has five kids. You're telling me not one of them could make room for her?"

"Lou said she would lie down naked in the middle of the Garden State Parkway before she moved in with any of her kids."

"Where is she now?"

"Shore View."

"Isn't that where the Bella Capri used to be?" For more generations than Maddy could count, the Bella Capri had been the place for weddings, proms, and all manner of local celebrations.

"I'm surprised you remember."

"That's where they held my senior prom."

"Six days before you packed your bags and left town."

Maddy forced herself to concentrate on the apple she was peeling and not the old resentments her mother's words called back to life. "I don't recall anyone begging me to stay in Paradise Point."

Rose's hand was a blur as she buffed a small portion of the samovar with lightning quick strokes of the cloth. "You always spent summers with your father. I knew one day you would make the Northwest your home."

"But you thought I would come back one day, didn't you?" She had to have believed that. Why else would she have let Maddy slip away from her so easily and with so little fuss?

"I hoped so," Rose said, fingers wrapped tightly around the handle of the kettle, "but I didn't think it would take fifteen years."

"Neither did I," said Maddy as she reached for another apple. *I still can't believe I came back at all*.

Shore View Home for Adults

"Mrs. O'Malley." The nurse's soft voice startled Irene as she struggled up from a dream. She dreamed a lot these days, wonderful dreams about her childhood when the world was golden and sweet as summer wine. "Jessica is here to talk to you."

"Jessica?" Oh, how she hated the crackly, dead-leaves sound of her voice. An old lady's voice. The voice of a crone or a witch from one of the folk tales from long ago. "I don't know any Jessica." The name felt foreign to her tongue, to her brain. Were any of her great-grandchildren named Jessica? She didn't think so.

Sometimes it was so hard to remember.

"Hi, Mrs. O'Malley." The girl smelled like green grass as she approached the side of Irene's bed. Her hair was sleek and blond, tucked neatly behind her small ears.

"Thanks for letting me stop by and ask you a few questions."

"You're welcome," Irene said. She liked this girl who looked and sounded like Aidan's daughter. The one who had brought her the picture. What a happy baby, so tiny and—but she wasn't a baby any longer, was she? She was a beautiful young girl whose name would come back to Irene in a second. She knew it would. The child was part of her family, after all.

The two young women who stood at the side of her bed exchanged looks. They thought Irene didn't see them, but she did. Old age was a secret society, invisible to all but the few who knew how to say goodbye and keep on living.

"Jessica is from Seton Hall." The nurse's smile was bright. She was a good woman who couldn't be blamed for wanting to be somewhere else. "She's majoring in gerontology with a specialty in the mobility problems of advanced old age."

"I'm thrilled that you're willing to give me some of your time, Mrs. O'Malley," the girl said. "I've never interviewed anyone as old as—" Her face turned bright red, and she busied herself by searching for something in the huge brown tote bag slung across her chest.

It was no secret to anyone, much less Irene, that she was the oldest resident of the Shore View Home for Adults. That alone wasn't enough to generate much notice, but the fact that she was also the only woman in the state who was old enough to have welcomed in the last century and remained sharp enough to remember it garnered her a certain notoriety. Sometimes it seemed to Irene that every medical student, journalism major, and just plain nosey individual between Manhattan and Philly had found his or her way to her bedside, eyes shining with youthful enthusiasm, notebooks bulging with questions, preconceptions firmly locked in place.

So many questions! They were so young and they knew so little about the world. The simple fact of her years embarrassed them, made them fumble for kinder ways to speak the truth of it. She had been that way once, averting her eyes from age and infirmity, secure in the knowledge that it would never happen to her while she remained safely tucked away in a world that was never meant to last.

They set up their tape recorders on the little table next to her bed, an electronic net to catch her memories before they (or she) slipped away. They fumbled with microphones and batteries, with electrical cords and balky cassettes, while Irene wondered when pencil and paper had gone out of style. They were so intent upon asking their questions, so intent upon dazzling her with their insight and their understanding, that her answers flew right over their shiny, well-shampooed heads.

"I'll be back in thirty minutes," the nurse said, lingering in the doorway. "We don't want to tire out Mrs. O'Malley."

"Mrs. O'Malley will take care of Mrs. O'Malley," Irene said firmly. Even those who should know better still believed that old and helpless went hand-in-hand.

Jessica sank down onto the upholstered chair next to Irene's bed. "You don't mind if I tape you, do you?" she asked, holding out a tiny square of metal and plastic for Irene's inspection. "My handwriting sucks and I want to make sure I quote you accurately."

It didn't matter to Irene. The questions were always the same and her answers never varied. Where were you born? How many siblings did you have? Did you go to school? Did you work? How old were your parents when they died? Children . . . grandchildren . . . great-grandchildren . . . Can you remember, Irene . . . Do you remember . . . Will you tell us . . .

And she told them what they wanted to know, told it to them in the same way she had told everyone else since the night her old life ended and her new life began.

But this time something was different. Maybe it was the questions the girl asked or the sweet lilt of her voice. Maybe it was simply the fact that there was so little time left and so many sins to be accounted for. Whatever it was, for the first time Irene wondered what would happen if she told the truth.

Once upon a time I danced with kings and princes. . . . Once upon a time I loved a boy with eyes as blue as the sky over St. Petersburg . . . and he loved me . . . oh, how he loved me. . . .

So many lifetimes ago, back when she had believed happiness could be contained in the palm of her hand like one of the Tsar's jeweled Easter eggs.

How many years had she wasted asking God why he had decreed that she would escape the carnage of those terrible days? What had she done to deserve being set adrift, alone in a land she no longer recognized? Her family slaughtered. Her friends destroyed. Running from country to country, begging for shelter, pleading for help, terrified by the danger that lurked everywhere, from everyone.

The Irishman found me sleeping in a doorway near the docks . . . more dead than alive . . . such kindness in his eyes . . . more kindness than I thought one heart could hold . . . more kindness than I could understand.

She had tried hard to deserve that kindness. When the babies came, she had prayed the sorrow inside her heart would vanish like a bird on the wing, but it never had. The years came and went more swiftly than she could count while she waited for happiness to find her, but it wasn't in God's plan. Sorrow was in her blood and in her bones, and, may the Almighty forgive her, she passed that terrible legacy on to her children and her children's children.

But through it all Michael had protected her secrets. How well he had protected their family and loved them. He kept the world from their door with the same fierceness of the warriors from her long-ago youth.

If only she had been able to love him.

If only she had been able to bestow that one simple gift upon a man who had deserved that and so much more, a man who had deserved a wife whose heart was still hers to give.

From the very beginning Aidan had been special to her. As a tiny baby he had somehow managed to find his way into the one small part of her heart that hadn't already turned to stone. *This one will break the chain of sorrow*, she had thought as she held him in her arms and met his blue-eyed gaze. *This one will finally know happiness*.

But it wasn't to be. The forces she had set into motion all those years ago were too powerful to be denied.

She had always made the selfish choice, right from the very beginning. She was one of life's survivors, and survival often exacts a terrible cost. She had buried her two sons knowing life's joys had eluded each one of them, and now it seemed as if the same fate awaited their last surviving child as well. Maybe that was her punishment then, to live long enough to see her mistakes repeated again and again in an endless chain of sorrow.

To see the sadness in a beloved grandson's eyes and know there was nothing she could do to change it.

To know in her heart that every choice she had made along the way was responsible for his pain.

There was nothing God's hell could show her that could equal that.

THEY DIDN'T TELL you about this when you were on the knife-edge between life and death. They talked about how great it would be when you were better, when the hospital and all of its incumbent horrors were a thing of the past, when you were finally able to pick up the pieces of your old life and watch them settle into their new shape.

They didn't tell you there was one more level of hell to get through before you got there, because if they did, you just might cash in your chips and call it a life.

Physical rehabilitation might not be everyone's idea of hell, but it was as close as Aidan cared to get. The first twelve months under Nina Peretti's form of tough love had damn near wiped him out. The man who had been able to bench-press a Buick and not break a sweat had been replaced by a scarred and skinny wreck on crutches.

Nina had performed a miracle.

"Relax," Nina ordered as she leaned against his right leg. "Let resistance do the work for you."

"Easy for you to say," Aidan rumbled as the familiar pain stretched and tore its way from ankle to groin and back again. "I thought this was supposed to get easier."

Nina, a tough no-nonsense woman with powerful hands and a soft spot for chocolate kisses, gave one of her ear-splitting barks of laughter. "You never heard me say that, O'Malley. It's going to get a hell of a lot tougher before you can even think about it getting easier."

Aidan inhaled sharply as she maneuvered his leg into an unnatural position and leaned her weight against it. "Whatever happened to positive reinforcement?"

"We don't have time for positive reinforcement." She rotated his foot. He was surprised it didn't come off in her hands. "You want results, you work hard. There's no other way."

He knew it. She knew that he knew it. But after almost two years of two steps forward, three steps back, he was getting tired of the routine. The only thing that kept him showing up at this torture chamber in the basement of the hospital was the glimmer of hope Nina held out that one day maybe he might be able to recover some of what he had lost. So far you couldn't prove it by his progress. The pain was still there and the instability; he still needed the goddamn cane. Three good reasons to push a little harder when reason and logic told him it was useless.

"Hey!" Nina slapped him on the back of his thigh. "You're not paying attention, O'Malley. Time for some circuit work."

"Swell." He eased his bad leg off the table and stood up. "And don't forget the whips and chains."

"Shh," said Nina, finger to her lips. "I thought the whip was our little secret."

He liked Nina. They had been through a lot together since the first time he was wheeled through the doors and handed over into her care. The anger had still run hot inside his chest, and it mingled with sorrow and the knowledge that his best hadn't been good enough. Not even close. Billy was still dead and he would carry the scars, both inside and out, for the rest of his life.

Nina heard the things he didn't say. She understood. But where others offered tea and sympathy, Nina demanded action. A full commitment to pain and humiliation and sweat and maybe, if he was lucky, some noticeable gain for his efforts. He asked himself on a daily basis if it was worth it, and each time the answer was the same.

"You're not with me," Nina said, halfway through the leg presses. "Focus, O'Malley. Concentrate on what you're doing."

Damn. How the hell did she always manage to know when he was drifting out of the moment? He'd been replaying the scene on the street corner with Maddy Bainbridge, cursing himself for not saying to hell with physical therapy and taking her for coffee. Who would have thought the formidable Rose DiFalco would have such a laid-back daughter? Maddy's hair was long and curly. Blond? Light brown? He wasn't sure. The overall effect had been a shimmer of golden light. Her eyes were a deep, almost shocking blue. She was tall, softly rounded, the kind of woman you didn't find in the pages of fashion magazines devoted to ideals of size-zero perfection.

"Too much!" Nina chided. "Back off a little and start again . . . three sets of ten . . . let's go . . ."

He grunted against the tugging sensation in his quads.

"Keep going . . . you're building muscle . . . equalize the load . . . come on . . . a couple more and you're outta here. . . ."

Pain. Mindblowing endless stretching tearing pain. He could smell his sweat above the smells of floor wax and alcohol and Nina's faint lavender soap. The muscles still remembered. That was the sad part. Down deep, hidden in the sinew, memory twitched along the nerve endings.

Before the accident he would have made it his business to see Maddy Bainbridge again. Women liked him. They always had. And he liked them right back. He didn't make promises he couldn't keep. His first priority was his daughter, and his second was his job as a firefighter. Everything else ran a distant third. Only once since Sandy's death had he believed himself in love, and that had ended badly in a hospital room six weeks after the accident that took his brother's life.

And now here he was with a daughter who'd be leaving for college next year and nothing but painful memories of his last night on the job. He had a bad leg, a bad arm, and a bad attitude to go with it. Gina and Denise had probably already filled Maddy Bainbridge in on all the gory details, and she was most likely saying a prayer of thanks to the patron saint of close calls.

Besides, he thought as he headed for the showers, she wasn't his type. She felt too much. He had seen it in her eyes, heard it in the rough velvet sound of her voice. If he had been looking for one more reason to stay away, he could quit looking right now. It was in her eyes. All of it. Every damn thing he didn't want to know about her and never would.

Chapter Ten

AIDAN SAT IN the parking lot behind the Shore View Home for Adults and nursed a cardboard container of coffee. He'd already made short work of two Egg Mc-Muffins and was trying not to think of the havoc he was wreaking on his cholesterol level. His muscles ached from Nina's prescribed torture. It seemed to him that the process should have gotten easier by now, but each session seemed to uncover new and different ways to remind him of everything he'd lost and would probably never regain.

"And aren't we off to a great start, O'Malley?" he muttered out loud. Ten-thirty in the morning and he was ready to pack it in and head for a sunny beach where they didn't know from heavy gray skies and winds that carried in them the promise of more snow.

He should have left years ago. Hell, he thought as he drained the last of the coffee, he should never have come back at all. He should have tucked his baby girl under his arm and headed out west to California or maybe south to Florida. Someplace warm and sunny. Someplace where a man's heart couldn't turn to ice even if he wanted it to.

Two nurses stepped outside the back door, shivering in their pale blue uniforms with the cheery Christmas sweaters draped over their shoulders. He watched as they both lit up cigarettes, exhaling plumes of smoke into the cold, moist air. One of the nurses caught his eye. She said something to her companion, who looked across the parking lot at him and smiled.

He had dated an X-ray technician at Shore View a year or two before the accident, a slim wiry woman with hands of steel. He had liked the woman, loved the hands, and let her go when she was ready without thinking twice. Then there was the receptionist he'd taken out to dinner. They left before dessert, so hot for each other that they didn't even make it into his car before he had her skirt up around her waist and her legs wrapped around his hips. She had ended up marrying a quiet accountant who was able to give her the one thing Aidan couldn't deliver: his heart.

The nurses' smiles grew wider and he shifted uncomfortably behind the wheel. Actions had consequences. Wasn't that what he had been trying to teach Kelly since she was old enough to know right from wrong? Every decision had the half-life of uranium in a small town. Every promise made, then broken, every promise you didn't make but should have—they were all recorded in some secret small-town ledger.

The taller of the two nurses took a long drag on her cigarette, then flipped it into the bushes. The shorter one exhaled a perfect smoke ring, then tossed her cigarette butt into the tall red can at the bottom of the steps. They flashed him one more smile, then disappeared back into the building.

He didn't have to see Irene today. Her bills were up-to-date. There hadn't been any medical emergencies that required either his signature or his attention. Irene wasn't expecting him until Friday, and that was assuming she gave a damn at all.

Still, the pull was there. The need to connect with his blood. It had sprung to life yesterday in the kitchen when

he looked at his kid and realized she wasn't a kid at all
and maybe hadn't been for a long time. It had grown
stronger when he saw that rusted teapot for sale on the
auction site and memories fell back in on him, memories
of places and people that had been long gone before he
was even born. Places and people that had been made real
for him by his parents' stories, by old photographs like
the one of the original O'Malley's that he hoped to find
hanging proudly in Room 5A, the place his grandmother
called home these days.

"MRS. O'MALLEY?" THE girl's voice found her through
the decades. "Did you hear my question? I could repeat
it for you if—"

"Of course, of course." She lifted her chin slightly in
the way Michael used to find so endearing, and pulled her
thoughts back to the here and now. "You asked me
about—?"

"These photos." The girl fanned a sheaf of newspaper
clippings and placed them on the bed table so Irene could
see them. "You were quite a successful amateur photographer years ago."

Irene's breath caught deep in her chest. The memories . . .
dear God, the memories! There was Michael, her beloved
husband, and standing next to him—not even reaching his
waist—her two sons, all three gone too soon. And there
was the house in Paradise Point, the one with the leaky
roof and the door that would never stay closed. But it was
the restaurant that made her heart ache, the place where
friends and family had gathered down through the years,
the place where she had been almost happy.

She closed her eyes as the flat black-and-white images
came to life. She saw them gathered around the dark pine
tables, heard the sound of their laughter, smelled the rich
mix of wine and bread and spices mingled with the briny
smell of the sea just beyond their door. Oh, there had been
good times along the way . . . she hadn't imagined them,
had she? *Please tell me they were real.* . . .

"I'm sorry," she heard the young girl from Seton Hall

say. "You're tired. I shouldn't have kept you so long. I'll grab these papers and—"

"No!" Irene covered the clippings with her hands, as if the memories they evoked could be absorbed through her skin. "Please stay a little longer."

The girl leaned closer. "Those pictures are great. You were a terrific photographer."

Irene smiled. "I always loved it." *Making memories, that's what Michael called it. Making memories because he knew it couldn't last forever.* How strange, more than fifty years later, that this photo should be placed in her hands twice within one week.

The girl studied a picture of the interior of O'Malley's. "I love all those teapots tucked in those tiny alcoves and hanging from the ceiling beams. Did you collect them?"

"Hundreds of them," Irene said. "We had some Wedgwood and Staffordshire, Rosenthal, Lenox—we kept those on the shelves you see running along the back of the main dining room. The rest I found in Bamberger's Basement and thrift shops, so if they broke—" She shrugged her tired shoulders. Who knew it could take so much effort to do so little? "Nobody would miss them."

"What about this one?" The girl leaned closer and pointed to a photo of the bar where guests used to spend time chatting with Irene or Michael while they waited for their tables to be ready. "I never saw anything like that before."

A slender curved spout of copper flared outward from a slightly flattened copper bowl fitted with a small round lid. The pot hung suspended from a matching stand that boasted a small burner to keep the tea or coffee warm. How many hours had she spent tracing the elegant leaves and flowers that intertwined up and down the length of the stand, drawing a soft cloth over the swells and crevices, burnishing the copper until it shone like the stars.

"That's a samovar." Irene struggled to push away the memories, but they fought hard to be acknowledged.

"Samovar?" The girl wrinkled her nose. "What's that?"

"A teapot," Irene said, running her arthritic thumb across the yellowed clipping. "A Russian teapot."

"Russian? Where'd you get it?"

"Where did I get any of them? I had a United Nations of teapots." *Michael gave it to me the year before he died. He wanted me to remember the family I left behind, to keep them in my heart. If only I had been able to push aside the memories and make room for him.*

"It's beautiful. Do you still have it?"

"No." How old she sounded. How terribly sad. How could one simple question awaken so many memories.

"How come? What happened to it? Did you give it to one of your kids?"

Bless young people. Nobody over twenty-five would ask an old woman such a personal question. "We lost everything in the Hurricane of fifty-two."

The child's eyes widened. "When you say everything, you mean like the restaurant and the teapots and—"

"Everything."

A 105-mile-per-hour gust of wind had roared across the inlet on Easter Sunday morning, taking everything in its path. The dock. The boats bobbing next to it. O'Malley's pub. The husband she had wanted so desperately to love. All of it, lost forever in the blink of an eye.

"Wow," the girl said once more and then, "I'm sorry. I don't mean wow like, 'Wow, isn't that cool.' I mean, wow like that's really terrible." She fumbled with the switch on her tiny tape recording device. "I'm really sorry."

She didn't want to think about the hurricane. She didn't want to think about the night they had told her Michael was lost forever. Her grief had roared inside her chest like the hurricane itself. She had feared it would snap her bones like branches on a brittle maple tree. Her fault. All of it. She had been so eager for his help, so hungry for his love and protection, so selfishly wildly needy that she had thought only of herself. He had offered her security in a dangerous world, and she had grabbed it with both hands, turning forever away from her old life and embracing the new one. He had loved her as she was, pregnant with another man's child, with nothing to give him that would be his alone. Not even her heart. She had given her heart to Nikolai, and he still claimed it, even after death.

If only she had loved her husband the way he had deserved to be loved. Michael had made her life possible, and she had never once thanked him for the most precious gift of all: the gift of family. There had been too many losses . . . too many mistakes . . . and she was so very tired. . . .

The girl gathered up her tape recorder and notebook, then shoved them into her huge brown tote bag. A ring of keys dangled from her right index finger.

"You bite your nails," Irene said. "One of my sons did that."

The girl grinned and the shiny gold stud through her lower lip clicked against her front teeth. "You sound like my mother."

"Your mother's grandmother would be more likely."

The girl looked at Irene's hands, which were folded neatly in her lap. Her eyes widened. "Your hands are beautiful."

Irene looked down at them, the long fingers, the faint memory of half-moons and diamonds. She had been beautiful once, as well. The pampered daughter of the privileged class in a world that was looking to destroy them and everything they stood for. She had come to understand their reasons, but she had never understood the methods they had employed. To see your parents struck down before your eyes. To watch your sisters being raped. To be torn from your dead lover's arms and be left for dead yourself but be unlucky enough to live.

She had blocked those months from her memory. Somehow she had made her way from village to village, always running, always afraid. Running with others just like her, aristocrats with jewels sewn inside their coats, with letters of introduction strapped to their legs, with only fear and desperation in their hearts and bitter memories of a world gone mad.

Once, long ago, he took my hand in his and pressed his lips against my palm. . . . We'll find a way, Irina, I promise you. . . . How beautiful he was, how young . . . so long gone . . . like all of them . . . like my heart . . . dead and gone. . . .

"I really enjoyed this," the girl was saying, her curious gaze intent upon Irene. "Your stories were great. I'd never heard about that Easter Sunday hurricane. I'll make sure I incorporate it with the other material for my dissertation." She hesitated a second. "I might even send it into the local newspaper if that's okay with you."

Irene nodded. She was starting to drift away into that cottony old-lady world where she lived much of the time.

"I'm really sorry. The nurse was right. I've tired you out." The girl's voice danced behind Irene's head . . . or was it drifting in through the window? She couldn't tell. She moved in and out of time and space these days, a girl of eighteen trapped in an old woman's body, haunted by an old woman's fears.

An old woman whose family paid the price for that young girl's dreams.

Maybe she had imagined the boy with the bright blue eyes . . . the sound of her mother's laughter . . . the child . . . dear God, the child . . .

Maybe she had imagined it all.

"I'M SORRY!" THE girl who bumped into his chest couldn't have been more than eighteen, if she was lucky. A small, round girl with shiny blond hair and serious eyes. She reminded him of his daughter. "I didn't see you standing there."

Aidan steadied her by the elbow, then smiled. "No problem," he said. "I'm Irene's grandson. I was about to knock when you—"

"Oh, no!" She looked down at the explosion of newspaper clippings at her feet. "I had them all in order, too." She bent down and a tape recorder went flying out of her gigantic tote bag. Aidan managed to catch it before it bounced, but her wallet, car keys, and notebook slid across the floor on a wave of photocopies.

He started to make a joke, meant solely to defuse her embarrassment, but he had seen that look on Kelly's face more times than he could count and stopped himself. Say the wrong thing and she would burst into a flood of tears. You would think he'd have gotten a handle on female tears by now, but they still did him in. Better to avoid them at all costs.

"Stand there," he said in his most gently paternal tone of voice. "I'll pick them up."

"You don't have to."

"Already done." He handed her the keys, the notebook, the tape recorder, and her wallet, then swept the photocopies up in one motion. He straightened the edges, and was about to hand the packet over when he realized what he was looking at.

"Jesus," he breathed. "That's O'Malley's." He grinned at the 1950 Packard angled near the entrance. His father used to tell stories about that car and a few unplanned rides down to Wildwood on hot summer nights. "Where'd you get these?"

"They're photocopies," she said. "I went to the main library in Newark and did some research."

"You're researching my grandmother?"

"It's for school," she said, shifting her gaze toward the exit as if calculating the distance between where she was and where she wanted to be. "I'm studying gerontology and—"

"Sorry," he said. "I forgot how many students like to come down here and talk with her."

"She's great!" Jessica's face broke into a wide smile. "I mean, she's the oldest person I've ever met, and she can still remember how it felt to be young."

"Did she tell you about the time they served baked clams to Ike and Mamie?"

Jessica's smile faltered. "Who?"

He felt the breath of fogeydom whispering in his ear.

"Eisenhower and his wife stopped at O'Malley's after the war," he said. "Before he ran for office. Irene had a signed photo from both of them, but she lost it in the hurricane."

"She told me all about the hurricane." She flipped quickly through the photocopies and plucked one from the stack. "She said this was probably the last picture taken with her husband before—" She paused, blushing. "Well, you know."

It wasn't exactly a shiver that ran up Aidan's spine when he saw the picture beneath that one. This ran deeper and felt a hell of a lot more unsettling, like the electrical charge your skin registers moments before a lightning strike. He reached for the photocopy, and for a second he swore he could smell the storm, hear its raging power.

"Jesus," he breathed. "I've never seen this one before." Grandma Irene, glamorous in a fancy full-skirted dress and a big picture hat, posed in the entryway of the original O'Malley's while Grandpa Mike pointed proudly toward the sign. They looked so young, so filled with excitement, that a lump formed in Aidan's throat and refused to be dislodged. And there was his father, behind the wheel of a 1950 Packard, squinting into the sun and grinning like he believed the world was his for the taking.

"I'd give it to you, but I really need it for my paper and I'm not gonna have time to go back over to Newark before—"

He barely heard her. Tucked beneath the glamorous photo of Irene and Michael and his father was another photocopy, this time of an old article from the *Jersey Shore Times*.

LOCAL EATERY SERVES GOOD FOOD AND GREAT DECOR

A few column inches were devoted to mouthwatering descriptions of Irene's famous Baked Clams Oregonata and Mike's Lobster Thermidor, then a few inches more to the satiny mahogany tables and chairs, the stained-glass lamps at every table, and Irene's eclectic collection of teapots that swung from the rafters overhead and over-flowed the many shelves lining the walls.

But it was the close-up photo of one teapot in particular that caught his attention. He read the caption:

> The Russian samovar was a Christmas gift
> from Michael O'Malley to his wife, Irene.

"Jesus," he said again. "I don't believe this."

He looked at the girl, who had backed away a few steps, just in case he was dangerous. "Okay if I make a copy?"

"Yeah," she said, "sure. Whatever." Obvious relief coupled with another quick glance toward the exit.

"A minute," he said. "That's all it'll take."

He was a man of his word. Less than two minutes later Jessica was racing for the exit while he stared down at the grainy photocopy of a photocopy of a fifty-year-old newspaper clipping and wondered if maybe he should've tried a little harder to win that auction.

ROSE BANISHED MADDY to the office. "I'll tell you when you can come back," she said firmly as she pointed toward the door.

"You're wasting your time," Maddy grumbled as she aimed a glare in the direction of that godforsaken rust bucket of a teapot. "I should e-mail FireGuy and see if he's still interested." She could recoup some of her money and take it to Toys "R" Us, where she should have gone in the first place.

"Just sit tight," Rose cautioned as she smeared another layer of gunk along the spout and along the curve of the handle. "Don't e-mail that FireGuy until I finish." She met Maddy's eyes. "Promise?"

Maddy felt herself fall backward through the years until she was eight years old and swearing on a stack of Bibles that she would do her homework before she went back to the newest Judy Blume from the library. "Cross my heart and hope to die."

Her mother winced. " 'Cross my heart' is more than enough for me."

A wave of emotion crashed into Maddy with the same force as the memory of her eight-year-old self. Her mother looked different. Less prickly, more approachable. Or could it be she was looking at her with new eyes?

"I really appreciate what you're doing, Ma. I know you have a lot to do and—"

"Scat," said Rose, all business. "Work on the Web site. I want to get that up and running by the New Year and tie it in with the print ads you were going to reserve."

The print ads. Maddy had completely forgotten about the print ads. Lately she felt as if she had left her brain back in Seattle with her old refrigerator. She took a deep breath. "I'm not moving along as fast as I'd like," she said, walking a tightrope stretched across the chasm of full disclosure. "I don't really think I can get everything in place in less than three weeks." Not with Christmas and Hannah and the ever-present Priscilla and the fact that she still felt like home would always be the place she left behind.

"You will," Rose said, applying herself to the task at hand. "I'm sure of it."

Maddy wondered what her mother had been smoking. Nobody in their right mind would believe Maddy had a snowball's chance in hell of finishing up the Web site and lining up a print-ad campaign in less than three weeks. It would take nothing less than an act of God to make all the puzzle pieces fall into place quickly enough for her to meet her mother's target date. She didn't know half as much about Flash and Bryce as she had led Rose to believe. She knew her way around the various versions of PhotoShop, but her abilities had always been more recreational than vocational.

Which was really the story of her life.

She walked slowly back to the office with Priscilla at her heels. When she was a little girl, she had dreamed about a career in show business. No matter that she couldn't sing or dance or play a musical instrument. She longed for a life in the spotlight, surrounded by people who didn't think or dress or play like anyone she knew.

Dreams didn't play well with Rose, and she demanded that Maddy secure a degree in accounting before she wasted any time pursuing a career in show business. Maddy was good with numbers. She understood the way they played off each other, the ever-shifting relationships they formed and re-formed. She sailed through college and graduated with highest honors, and those dreams of show business took a backseat to a junior executive program with a booming Seattle-based dot-com.

She had met Tom Lawlor at a conference of local businesspeople, and the attraction between them, while unlikely, had been undeniable. He was the owner and CEO of a highly successful electronics company, a key player from the early days of Apple and Microsoft who had been in the right place at the right time with the right product.

The difference in their ages was never more apparent than when it came to talk of career aspirations. Tom had achieved everything he had ever hoped for, and he was eager to put aside the eighteen-hour days, the sleepless nights, and the resident ulcers that went hand-in-hand with running a business. He wanted to kick back and enjoy the fruits of his forty years of labor, and he wanted Maddy to share it all with him.

"Quit that job and I'll take care of you," he had said to her a few weeks before he sold his company. "We'll sail to Hawaii and then see where the wind takes us." Tahiti. Bali. The Mediterranean. Anywhere her heart desired. Anything she wanted.

"What in hell are you waiting for?" her cousin Denise had e-mailed her. "Ditch the job already, Maddy! Let the future worry about itself."

He had said he loved her, that he needed her, that their five years together were only the beginning, that he wanted to show her the world, see it through her eyes, live out the rest of his life with her by his side, just the two of them.

She asked her cousins for advice. Old classmates. The Russian family down the hall with the Pomeranian. But she never asked her mother because she knew what Rose would say. Rose had encouraged her to get her degree in accounting so she would have something to fall back on if her theatrical aspirations didn't work out. From there it was an easy step to managing the finances of a little Seattle software company whose IPO had made instant millionaires of a dozen guys in sweatshirts and jeans. She had found them too late for the IPO, but even if it wasn't the job of her dreams, it enabled her to hold her own in Tom's world and that was important to her.

Now his world was changing and he wanted her to change with him, toss aside the last five years of hard work, the 401(k), the stock options, and literally sail off into the sunset with him. Ditch the furniture from IKEA, the homey bed with the old-fashioned quilt, the Mustang that wasn't quite paid off, and step out of her life and into his. She was enough of her mother's daughter to know how risky a prospect that was (and how much she might lose), but her wildly romantic heart, a gift straight from her father, was impossible to ignore.

So she said yes. Yes, she would go away with him. Yes, she would say goodbye to her job and her apartment and her friends. Yes, she was scared out of her mind, and yes, she wondered if maybe she was making a terrible mistake and yes oh yes she wanted to talk to her mother about it, wanted to spill it all in her mother's lap and let her sort it out, but her mother was living her life on the other side of the country, and besides, she knew what her mother would say and none of that really mattered because she loved him and he was leaving and what else could she do?

Two days before they were set to begin their adventure, she went to the doctor for a routine checkup, which turned out to be anything but routine when she discovered she was two months pregnant with Hannah, and everything she thought she had known about the two of them, about what they wanted from life, about what they meant to each other, collapsed like a castle made of sand.

The DiFalco luck, she thought as she took her seat in front of the computer. You could run from it, but you couldn't hide.

God knows, she'd spent the last fifteen years trying.

A MIRACLE, THAT'S what it was. A flat-out, downright miracle.

Rose stepped back and tilted her head to the right. No matter what angle she tried, the samovar took her breath away. Her shoulders ached and her wrists and fingers throbbed from the effort, but there was no denying the results were worth it.

Hannah's Christmas present positively glowed. The elegant curves and angles caught the light and reflected it back with the softness and luster that develops with time. Maddy had been right. You couldn't find something like this on the shelves at Toys "R" Us.

She tossed the soiled rags into the trash bin outside, then scrubbed her hands at the utility sink. Thank God for rubber gloves, she thought as she stepped back into the kitchen. Her mother's homemade concoctions were downright lethal to the skin.

"Maddy!" She called down the back hallway. "Come take a look."

She was buffing up a tiny portion of the spout with the sleeve of her sweater when her daughter and Priscilla appeared in the doorway. She stepped aside and gestured toward the samovar.

"So what do you think?"

"That's not the same teapot!" Maddy raced to the counter and examined it from all sides. She picked it up, turned it upside down, then held it to her ear and shook it. "Tell me this isn't the same teapot!"

"You can thank Grandma Fay for it," Rose said, inordinately pleased by the obvious joy in her daughter's eyes. "Those secret formulas of hers never fail."

Maddy ran her finger along one of the curves and started to laugh. "Eye of newt and wing of bat?"

"And a touch of mandrake root for good measure."

"Hannah's going to be so happy, Mom."

Rose nodded. "I know."

They were quiet for a moment.

"I suppose I'd better find some place to hide it so Hannah doesn't ruin her surprise."

"There's room at the back of my closet upstairs."

"Isn't that where Grandma Fay used to hide her bingo money?"

"And her Lucky Strikes. I found six cartons behind her shoe trees after she died."

"Thank you." There was a different tone to Maddy's voice, a quality Rose didn't think she had ever heard before. "Thank you so much. I was ready to give it to FireGuy before you took over."

"You don't have to thank me," Rose said. "She's my granddaughter."

And you're my daughter, she thought as Maddy went off to hide the samovar. If only one of them knew what that really meant.

Chapter Eleven

"HEY, BOSS." TOMMY rapped on the door, then stepped inside before Aidan had a chance to open his mouth. "You gonna hole up back here all day or are you gonna start the wings?"

Aidan looked up from the laptop. "Where's Claire? I thought she was taking the lunch crowd today."

Tommy whistled. "Man, I don't know what's with you today. Claire's home. Remember? Bad tooth."

Aidan leaned back in his chair and dragged a hand through his hair. "Shit. I forgot all about that." He glanced at his watch, an old Timex that Kelly had bought for him a hell of a lot of Christmases ago. "I'll get moving."

"About time," Tommy muttered. "If you ask me, it's time we got some more help around here."

"Can it, Kennedy." Aidan stood up. "I can't afford the help I've already got."

Still muttering, Tommy Kennedy went back out to tend bar and bitch about Aidan's bad mood to anyone who would listen.

Aidan couldn't deny it. He'd been in a foul temper since he got back from the nursing home. He wasn't exactly sure what started it, but something about the photo of that damn teapot sent his mood spiraling downward, and it hadn't hit bottom yet. It was more than the fact that he'd let Kelly down. After her brief explosion of tears she'd moved on to her next project without missing a beat, leaving him, as usual, with the feeling that he'd missed a chapter somewhere along the way.

He switched on the deep fryer, then pulled the highly seasoned wings from the refrigerator while the oil heated to the proper temperature. Claire had washed, dried, then trimmed three bunches of celery yesterday. She wrapped the stalks neatly in a pair of clean dishtowels and stowed them in the veggie bin so all he had to do was whip them out once the wings were cooked and drained. They were a good team most of the time. At least when they weren't butting heads about the future of O'Malley's. They were both lead sled dogs, and everyone knew what happened when two lead sled dogs vied for the only lead position.

The bar had always been Billy's domain. Even though Claire had done most of the work, it was Billy who had made it come alive. It was Billy they came to chew the fat with, Billy they wanted to make laugh.

Billy they wanted to take to bed.

"Goddamn it," he muttered as he started feeding the wings into the sizzling oil. He didn't want to think about the women. Sometimes he looked at Claire's face, the deep sorrow in her light blue eyes, and the pain in his gut would come close to bringing him down. She knew. She had always known, from the first time Billy strayed. Somehow she had found a way to keep on loving him and to hold on to some of her dignity. He had never been able to figure out how she'd managed that. Her husband was out screwing every available woman between Paradise Point and Cape May while Claire went on believing they were a match made in heaven.

And maybe they were. Who was he to say? Claire and Billy had kept their marriage together through some pretty tough times, the kind of bad times Aidan wasn't sure he and Sandy could have survived. Claire said she and Billy had been soul mates and somehow she made everyone else believe it too, as if her love for him was so strong, so all-encompassing that it wiped the slate clean. He left her a small pension and an even smaller insurance policy and O'Malley's. O'Malley's had been on the skids for at least ten years at that point, a workingclass, shorefront bar in an increasingly leisure-class town. After the accident, when it became clear firefighting was no longer an option, when it became even more clear that O'Malley's was about to go under, Aidan presented Claire with a business proposition that would keep a roof over her head and give him a reason to get up in the morning.

Sometimes it worked. Sometimes it didn't.

On days like today he wondered why he hadn't rented a bulldozer and shoved the whole damn thing into the Atlantic.

"I've got the burgers frying up front," Tommy called from the doorway, "but you better get those wings moving fast. The natives are getting restless." Wings. The requisite vat of chili with chopped onions and jack cheese on top. A mountain of ribs dripping sauce.

No wonder their customers were dying off, he thought as he poured the blue cheese dressing into six small dipping bowls. They were killing them.

Irene had always made sure their restaurant, the original O'Malley's, kept up with the times, and their bottom line had reflected that. She hadn't been afraid to retire the Lobster Thermidor, even though it was Michael's signature dish. Nobody would ever have mistaken O'Malley's menu for haute cuisine, but thanks to Irene it had managed to more than hold its own with the best restaurants in the tristate area for almost twenty years.

Obviously one tough act to follow.

When she rebuilt the place after the Hurricane of '52 that took Michael's life and destroyed the original structure, the new O'Malley's, while well received, never quite regained the same stature. The food was still superb. The menu remained varied and slightly unpredictable. The interior was homelike without being homespun. It had everything you would think a shore-town restaurant needed for success, but somehow it never regained that special place in its customers' hearts that it had held before. When Michael died, he took the magic with him.

The parallel wasn't lost on Aidan. The old-timers came to O'Malley's out of loyalty to Billy's memory. Some of them had been coming to O'Malley's back when Michael was alive and the place had been awash with laughter and good times and those ridiculous teapots of Irene's dangling from the rafters and crowding every shelf.

The lunch crowd came because it was close to the little office complex that had opened behind the grocery store. It wouldn't be long before they tired of ribs and chicken wings and found someplace else to spend the noon hour. They did a brisk business with construction crews, but a run of bad weather or a job brought in on time could blow a hole a mile wide in O'Malley's bottom line. They counted on the tourist trade between Memorial Day and Labor Day to keep them in the black, and more and more lately, Aidan had begun to sense that the changes in town would leave them behind if they didn't figure out a way to change with them before it was too late.

MADDY HAD A fat book on Flash spread across her lap and another one on Bryce balanced between her knees and the edge of her desk. She had been hunkered down over the computer since just before lunch, blind and deaf to everything but the sudden burning need to put together the world's best Web site.

And do it within the next three weeks.

She had put in a phone call to her friend Devon in Seattle with a plea for long-distance tutoring on Flash. She had e-mailed two of her old classmates, the computer nerds who went on to make big bucks following their dreams, and offered them each a weekend at the Candlelight Inn if they could help her work out her audio problems and the trouble with the mini-movie. Rose was right: people were turning to their computers for everything these days, from filling prescriptions to planning a wedding. One of her cousins had bought a house in Pennsylvania without ever setting foot on the property. Her realtor had sent her the URL of a two-story colonial, and Vicky had taken a virtual tour of every single room, including a peek inside the closets and behind the shower curtain.

If Rose was going to attract visitors from beyond New York and D.C., this was one of the ways to do it, although, after taking a look at the reservations book, Maddy wondered when Rose thought she was going to be able to accommodate more guests. The place was booked solid through the following spring, with only the month of January empty for scheduled downtime for repairs.

The thought of an endless stream of strangers wandering up and down the halls in the middle of the night made Maddy want to lie down and take a nap, but that was the nature of the B&B beast. It was clear that Rose absolutely thrived on the constant flow of visitors. Maddy couldn't remember a time when her mother looked happier or more relaxed.

Or when she had worked harder.

At a time when most women her age were moving to Florida to bake in the sun and catch the early-bird specials at the corner restaurant, Rose had not only embarked on a new career, she had made a smashing success of it. She was well respected by the community. She held a position of trust and power on the local small-business advisory board. She had been there for Grandma Fay when Grandma Fay needed her. She was there for her sisters.

And when the bottom dropped out of Maddy's life, Rose opened her arms wide and welcomed Maddy back home.

The fumes from Grandma Fay's top-secret cleaning fluid must have done something to her brain. Maybe that was how it would have happened on Walton Mountain, but Paradise Point was a whole other story. Rose presented a business opportunity to Maddy. A simple seventy-thirty split that would help Maddy regain her financial footing within a year. And when Maddy resisted the stone-cold logic of the offer, Rose pulled out the heavy artillery and aimed the maternal guilt gun her way and she was done for.

Oh, no, you don't. Don't go romanticizing Rose Di-Falco. She hadn't been one for sentimental gestures when Maddy was a little girl with a nervous stutter and a passionate need for chocolate. She hadn't morphed into a cookie-baking granny when Hannah was born. She hadn't even managed to fit a visit to Seattle to see the newborn into her busy schedule. If she'd ever wondered where she rated on Rosie's Hit Parade, that single gesture (or lack of one) told her all she needed to know. So there was no earthly reason for her to suddenly turn treacly now that Maddy was a big girl without the nervous stutter who was more passionate these days about chocolate because it was a lot easier to find (and a whole lot more reliable) than love.

AIDAN FILLED BIG earthenware bowls with chili, flipped burgers, cooked up another two batches of ribs and wings, and did it all with probably the worst display of bad humor that O'Malley's had seen since the day Claire pitched Hank Finnegan out the door for trashing the Devils.

"If you're looking to cut down on our workload," Tommy said after the early crowd dispersed, "you're on the right track." He lit a cigarette and took a long lung-filling drag. "Maybe you should think about taking a vacation."

"Shove it," Aidan said, slamming cups and bowls into the mammoth dishwasher.

"Yeah, that sweet talk'll bring in the crowds." Tommy was one of those guys who refused to be insulted.

"Don't you have a bar to tend?" He emptied a slug of detergent into the dishwasher, then flipped the door closed. The deep rumble of its motor filled the air.

"You've been acting like an asshole since you rolled in here this morning. What's the deal?" Tommy took another long drag on his cigarette. "You're worse than Adam Chandler on a bad day."

"Who the hell is Adam Chandler?"

Tommy shot him an I-don't-believe-it look. "*All My Children*," he said, as if that would explain everything.

Aidan knew better than to pursue it. One wrong question and he'd be treated to an hour-long discourse on the lives and loves of Susan Lucci. "Nothing personal," he said. "I stopped by the nursing home and—"

Tommy raised a hand. "Say no more. That could do it to the best of us. My mother-in-law was in Shore View for two years before she died. Toward the end I would've sold a kidney to keep from having to drag my ass in there." He looked carefully at Aidan's face, then apparently decided to live dangerously. "So how was she? I haven't seen Irene in—how long? A year, maybe three. She doing okay?"

"For a woman who's one hundred and one years old, she's doing great."

Tommy laughed. "That about says it all, doesn't it?"

Aidan felt the familiar stab of loneliness in the center of his chest. "That about says nothing. She spent the afternoon shooting the shit with some kid from Seton Hall, but when I showed up, she turned her head to the wall and pretended she was asleep."

"Cold," said Tommy, shaking his head. "Real cold."

"Yeah," said Aidan. "I tell Kelly all the time that it's nothing personal. Grandma's old, you've got to make allowances for her." He leaned against the table and glanced out the window. "Then I remember she wasn't always old."

"She put a roof over your heads," Tommy reminded him. "That's more than my old lady did."

Tommy's mother had abandoned her fatherless family when Tommy was six years old.

"One good thing," Aidan said, reaching into the breast pocket of his work shirt. "The kid from Seton Hall had a fistful of clippings about the original O'Malley's. She even had some photos I'd never seen before."

"Shit," said Tommy. "I forgot to tell you." His shar-pei face lit up with a smile. "I found another one of the original O's tucked away with those old-fashioned glasses we don't use anymore."

"Where is it?"

"Kelly took the one we had hanging, but I found another one in the file cabinet, so I fixed that little loop thing on the back and hung it up."

Two minutes later Aidan had the framed photo and the photocopy lined up together on the counter. They were slightly different angles taken of the same scene. The samovar, barely visible in the framed photo, was front and center in the photocopy.

Aidan booted up the laptop and connected the modem to the phone line. Moments later he was staring at the teapot Kelly had had her heart set on. The word SOLD was angled across the scan in big bold red letters, but there was no denying that rusty kettle was the long-lost twin of the one that had held pride of place at O'Malley's all those years ago.

He knew what Claire would say. *Don't be an ass. You're as bad as your daughter. Nothing short of a heart transplant will make that woman love you. If you want to waste your money, drive up to Atlantic City. At least there you've got a fighting chance.*

He loved Claire. He respected her judgment in most things. But this time she was wrong. That teapot was meant for Irene, and he was going to make it happen.

FOR A SECOND Maddy didn't recognize the name. She was so deeply engrossed in trying to back herself out of the mess she'd made with the film clip that FireGuy's message languished in her in box with the offers of barnyard frolics, work-at-home schemes, and six chain letters from one of her idiot cousins who really should know better.

She was about to reach for the phone and call her old office mate Stanley for help when FireGuy's subject line caught her eye.

"Oh, for God's sake," she said irritably as she clicked

on the message. "Give it up already. I won, you lost. It's over."

TO: JerseyGirl@njshore.com
FROM: FireGuy@njshore.com
DATE: 5 December
SUBJECT: one last shot

You probably think I'm stalking you at this point, but I'm not.
$500 for the samovar, sight unseen.
That could buy a lot of Barbies for your little girl.
Think about it. That's all I'm asking.

TO: FireGuy@njshore.net
FROM: JerseyGirl@njshore.net
DATE: 5 December
SUBJECT: Re: one last shot

No. Absolutely not. Go away. Find your own samovar.

TO: JerseyGirl@njshore.net
FROM: FireGuy@njshore.net
DATE: 5 December
SUBJECT: Re: Re: one last shot

Have you seen it yet? Maybe you'll hate it.

TO: FireGuy@njshore.net
FROM: JerseyGirl@njshore.net
DATE: 5 December
SUBJECT: Re: Re: Re: one last shot

Came, saw, polished. It's tucked away at the bottom of my mother's closet until Christmas. My kid's going to love it.

TO: JerseyGirl@njshore.net
FROM: FireGuy@njshore.net
DATE: 5 December
SUBJECT: Re: Re: Re: Re: one last shot

I found a picture today that I think you should see. It
would explain a lot. You name the place and the time
and I'll meet you there.

TO: FireGuy@njshore.net
FROM: JerseyGirl@njshore.net
DATE: 5 December
SUBJECT: Re: Re: Re: Re: Re: one last shot

Meet you? You must be kidding. Scan the photo and
send it to my e-mail address.

TO: JerseyGirl@njshore.net
FROM: FireGuy@njshore.net
DATE: 5 December
SUBJECT: Re: Re: Re: Re: Re: Re: one last shot

I don't have a scanner, and even if I did I think this
would be better in person. You don't even have to
bring the samovar with you.

TO: FireGuy@njshore.net
FROM: JerseyGirl@njshore.net
DATE: 5 December
SUBJECT: Certifiable

The last thing on the face of this earth that I would do
is a) meet you anywhere and b) bring the samovar if I
did.

On second thought, keep the scan and lose my e-mail
address.

She hit Send.

Live and learn. Another example of a nice guy morphing into a jerk without help from Industrial Light and Magic. All that talk about his perfect daughter and the hundred-year-old grandmother who just had to have that teapot under her Christmas tree, and it was just some kind of con to either snag the samovar or a quickie on the beach.

"Jerk," Maddy said, exiting her e-mail program.

And she wasn't just talking about FireGuy.

"MY KIDS DON'T know how lucky they are," Gina said as they waited for the school bus to deliver their kids to the corner of Main Street and Paradise Point Lane. "They still think they can do anything they set their minds to."

"My kid thinks all she has to do is show up for a handful of ballet lessons, and she'll be playing Clara in *The Nutcracker* next Christmas." Pat rolled her eyes skyward. "Wait until she finds out she can't dance."

The laughter was loud but not unkind. They had all seen Pat's oldest at the last recital, a girl who invariably danced right when the rest of the chorus danced left.

If you stacked their unrealized dreams one atop the other, they would reach the tip of the steeple at Our Lady of Lourdes around the corner. Gina wanted to be the next Vidal Sassoon and Denise wanted to be Picasso. Delia sang Friday nights at Franco's-by-the-Sea and dreamed of being the next Diana Krall. All but Maddy had wanted children.

"What did you want to be?" Gina asked while they shivered against the fierce wind off the ocean. Once again the smell of snow was in the air, heavy with dampness and salt and promise.

Maddy busied herself adjusting Priscilla's tiny collar. "Me? I wanted to grow up to be Madonna. Same as every other girl in South Jersey."

They laughed just the way they were supposed to, but Gina wasn't buying it.

"Really," her cousin persisted. "What did you want to

be? An actress? A dog trainer?" More laughter. Priscilla was beginning to get a reputation as a problem child. "I could tell you what every single one of us here day-dreamed about and longed for, but when it comes to you, I haven't a clue."

"Neither have I," Maddy said, and for once there was no laughter. "I always wondered what I'd be when I grew up. The trouble is, I'm grown up and I'm still wondering."

"Rose was always bragging about what a great account-ant you are," Pat offered, neatly sidestepping Denise's warning nudge.

"Nobody dreams about being a bean counter," Maddy said.

"Come on," said Denise, "admit it, Mad: you wanted to be a ballerina."

Maddy assumed fifth position, which looked fairly comical in her L. L. Bean boots. If she had a quarter for every time well-placed laughter had saved her butt, she wouldn't have to work for her mother.

Pat launched into a story about her mercifully brief ca-reer as a receptionist at the Mangano Funeral Home, whose motto was "We help your loved ones rest well," and before long nobody remembered that Maddy had never really answered Gina's question.

Give me another twenty or thirty years, Gina. I might have an answer for you by then.

Conversation rose and fell with a rhythm born of fa-miliarity. They knew each other's history. They knew who and when and how many times. They either were family, had been family, or would be family next time around. Only Maddy remained outside the circle. They loved her and she loved them, but they didn't know her. Maybe they never had. She had spent all of her summers growing up with her father and Irma in Oregon, far away from the beach parties and clambakes and sultry nights at Wildwood, sheltered from parental eyes.

And even now, they knew she wasn't here to stay, that this was just a resting place while she tried to figure out what to do next. Paradise Point was home to them in a way it never had been for Maddy and probably never could be. They never fought its hold on their hearts, while Maddy had been planning her escape almost from the day she was born.

The fifteen years she had spent on the other side of the country trying to fit in were only bits and pieces of gossip to her cousins, tidbits gleaned from scribbled postcards and conversations between their mothers and aunts. She had worked hard to lose her Jersey girl accent and her decidedly East Coast ways, but even after she had turned herself into the perfect Seattle citizen, she knew she would never really belong.

But her cousins didn't know that and neither did Rose. They thought she had fled to the West Coast, shedding her accent and outlook somewhere over the Rockies and never looking back.

She had wanted to love Seattle. She had wanted to settle in and feel her roots growing deep and long. She was her father's daughter, after all, and Bill was a man who couldn't be happy anywhere east of the Rockies. She had friends, a good job, a nice apartment. And for a long time she had Tom. A man whose history was happily entangled with the explosive growth of the Seattle economy and outlook. He opened doors to a Seattle Maddy hadn't known existed. She met the right people, some of the wrong people, and everyone in between, and still she felt as if she was only passing through.

Puget Sound was beautiful, but it wasn't the Jersey shore. The harbors and seaside towns were quaint and picturesque, but they couldn't compare to the scrappy little survivor of a town where she had grown up. She missed the briny smell of the ocean creeping through her windows on sunny autumn mornings. When Hannah was still nursing, Maddy used to sit in a rocking chair near her bedroom window and watch the play of lights against the darkness of the water, and she would find herself longing for Paradise Point. By that time she knew that she would be raising Hannah alone, that once again the mystery of a happy family life had managed to give her the slip.

It wasn't as easy as she had believed it would be. If the one you loved didn't love you in the same way, with the same depth of emotion, if that person didn't share your hopes and dreams, you might as well get used to the fact that you were in it alone even if you kept right on believing in happy endings until he went off and found one of his own.

"Is Claire coming to pick up Billy Jr.?" Denise asked nobody in particular.

"Doesn't look like it." Delia inclined her head toward the opposite side of the street. "Looks like Aidan's on school-bus duty again."

He had just turned the corner from Church to Main, limping slightly but without the cane Maddy had seen him with that morning. He had a large brown envelope tucked under his arm.

"So he doesn't need his cane all the time," she said to Denise as she untangled Priscilla's leash from around her ankles.

"No," said Denise, her gaze assessing as she looked from Aidan across the street to Maddy. "It's been a long haul for him. He's lucky he can walk at all."

Maddy watched him as he paused for a moment in front of the print shop, then disappeared inside. What would he be doing in a fancy print shop that specialized in frou-frou invitations and personalized stationery heavy on pink and fuchsia? Sure they had faxes and copy machines and scanners, but—

Wait a minute! Was it possible? Could Aidan O'Malley be *FireGuy*?

Chapter Twelve

"WHAT'S WRONG?" DENISE asked.

"Did that dog of yours bite you?" Pat usually gave Priscilla a wide berth.

Maddy picked up Priscilla and thrust her at Denise. "Watch her," she said. "And watch Hannah, too, if I'm not right back."

She dashed across the street, dodging an oncoming Chrysler driven by an old lady who obviously didn't believe in stop signs. She hadn't grown up on Nancy Drews for nothing. The clues were all there. The one wonder was that it had taken her so long to add them all up.

He had a daughter who was both saint and scholar. He lived in Paradise Point. He even had an ancient grandmother.

She'd told FireGuy to scan the photo and e-mail it to her, and, less than an hour later, there was Aidan O'Malley leaning across the flower-strewn counter of Le Papier, talking to the lovely Olivia Wentworth, who had bought the shop—a former insurance office—with her divorce settlement. Olivia's dark eyes twinkled with amusement as she spoke with Aidan. Maddy couldn't see what

Aidan's eyes were doing, but if body language was any indication, he was doing a fair bit of twinkling himself.

Not that it was any of Maddy's business.

The brown envelope she'd spied tucked under his arm was clutched to Olivia's voluptuous chest. The woman could make a manila envelope look like it held Victoria's secret.

Not that that was any of Maddy's business, either.

Olivia had moved down the shore from New Hope, Pennsylvania. She had sold her half of a thriving antique shop to her ex-husband, then plowed the proceeds into this high-priced paper boutique. Maddy had met Olivia last week at the December meeting of the Paradise Point Women Business Owners Association. Rose had insisted Maddy attend in her place and get to know some of the other entrepreneurs in town. Rose believed in the sisterhood of businesswomen, that together they could accomplish ten times more than they ever could toiling in isolation.

It seemed to Maddy that there was precious little isolation in Paradise Point and even less in the way of privacy, but, when it came to business, Rose was rarely wrong. Olivia was a dark-haired, dark-eyed woman of about forty who had apparently ignited an unprecedented explosion of interest in personalized stationery among the men in town.

Olivia glanced up and caught Maddy's eye. She actually looked happy to see Maddy, which meant that either there was nothing romantic going on between Olivia and Aidan or Olivia was one great tradeswoman.

"Hi, Maddy." Olivia's smile was wide and bright. Gina claimed the divorce settlement had included a new smile and a boob job, but so far there was no proof of either. Olivia might just have been born lucky. "I'm afraid Rose's thank-you cards won't be ready until tomorrow afternoon." She shrugged her shoulders and Maddy had to struggle to keep from staring as the shock waves animated her cleavage.

Aidan turned around and he smiled at Maddy. "How much longer until the bus pulls in?"

"Six minutes," she said. "How's Claire?"

"Swollen like a chipmunk," he said, blowing out his right cheek to illustrate. "She's zonked on Percoset."

Olivia, who had been watching the two of them closely, cleared her throat. "Give me a minute," she said to Aidan with a warm but businesslike smile. "This should scan beautifully."

Maddy felt like high-fiving herself. She waited until Olivia disappeared into the rear office.

"I knew it," she said.

"Knew what?"

"FireGuy."

It took him a second but not much longer. "JerseyGirl?"

She didn't know whether to laugh or hit him over the head with a bar mitzvah invitation. "You're scanning the photo of the teapot."

His shoulders were so wide they blocked her view of the artful arrangement of baby announcement cards on the counter. He hadn't seemed quite this huge outside.

"You said you wouldn't meet me for coffee."

"I thought you were turning into one of those Internet perverts you hear about."

He winced. "Now, that hurts . . . and after all we meant to each other."

She couldn't help it. He had a way about him that undercut all of her defenses and made her laugh. "Those heartfelt e-mails," she said, "those declarations of doubling my purchase price . . . I'm bitterly disappointed."

"I was going to e-mail the scans to you when I got home."

"I wouldn't have opened the attachment," she said, grinning. "I never open attachments from men I barely know."

"The cautious type?"

"A girl can't be too careful." *Girl? Don't push it, Maddy. You left* girl *behind a long time ago.*

It didn't seem to bother Aidan O'Malley. He seemed

to get both her text and subtext, and the power of meeting someone who actually laughed at her jokes made Maddy downright giddy with pleasure.

His nose had obviously been broken on more than one occasion. A jagged scar ran down the right side of his face. His hair was shaggy and windblown and he needed a shave. The Irish fisherman's sweater boasted a few sorrowful moth holes on his left sleeve and the faded jeans fit the way jeans were meant to fit a man's body—

"You won't believe your eyes," he said, and it took her a second to realize he was talking about the samovar.

"Two rusted wrecks in one day," she said with a shake of her head. "You're right. I probably won't."

"Did it clean up well?"

"Better than I do. I don't know what was in that concoction my mother used, but it performed a minor miracle."

Olivia wafted out from the back room with the brown envelope dangling from her beautifully manicured hand. "I scanned it and e-mailed the image to you," she said, handing Aidan the envelope. Again her glance quickly moved from Aidan to Maddy, then back to Aidan.

Don't worry, Olivia. There's absolutely nothing going on here.

Aidan pulled a five-dollar bill from his back pocket and handed it to Olivia.

"I'll make out a receipt."

Aidan made a *don't bother* motion with his hand, but Maddy shook her head. "Always get a receipt," she said. "You never know when it might come in handy."

Olivia's merry peal of laughter rang out. "Spoken like a true accountant."

"You're an accountant?" Aidan asked.

"I'm lazy," Maddy said. "I was always good with numbers, so I followed the path of least resistance."

"I would've figured you for something a little less—" He stopped, fumbling for the right word.

"Boring?"

He grinned. "Practical."

"I'm unemployed," she offered with an answering grin. "Does that help?"

"Gina told me you were doing voice-over work in Seattle."

"Did she tell you I was the voice of a talking Volkswagen?"

He laughed. "She skipped that part."

"Wise choice." She lowered her voice to a sultry pitch, placed her right hand on her hip, then said, "Name your price, baby."

His laughter stopped. "You're kidding."

She made an X over her heart. "Swear to God."

"I hope they paid you big bucks for it."

"Don't I wish. They planned a whole series of them, but sales plummeted." She shrugged her shoulders. "They canned the ad manager and the entire team."

"It was a lousy concept, but you sounded terrific."

"Unfortunately most people remembered the lousy concept and forgot about who was terrific."

"You have a great voice," he said while Olivia soaked up every word and nuance of their conversation. "You should get out there and audition for more voice-overs."

Pale skin: the Irish curse, even if you were half Di-Falco. Her cheeks flooded with heat at his compliment until she was sure she looked like a boiled lobster.

"Not much call for voice-overs in Paradise Point," she said.

"Yeah, but you're flanked by New York and Philadelphia."

"Maybe some day," she said, feeling vaguely uncomfortable with his enthusiasm. "Right now I have my hands full with Hannah and helping out around the Inn."

"Are you back in town to stay?"

"For a while. Hannah's had a very rough year and I thought being surrounded by family might help." She rolled her eyes. "I might've been wrong."

He started to say something, but Olivia broke in. "Listen, you two, I hate to interrupt, but see that big yellow thing rolling past the window? I think it's called a school bus."

They were out of the store in a flash. Maddy darted into the street, but Aidan caught her by the arm and drew her back to the curb as a black SUV with heavily tinted windows roared by.

"My God!" She placed her hand over her heart. "I didn't see it coming until you pulled me out of the way." She touched his hand lightly. "Thank you!"

"Look both ways next time," he said. "I won't always be here to pull you back."

Their eyes met and once again everything else fell away. The street. The traffic. The big yellow bus. The curious friends and relatives watching them from the opposite curb.

"You forgot to show me the newspaper clipping," Maddy said when she found her voice.

"We could take the kids for some hot chocolate at Julie's. I'll show you there."

"Great idea, but that would ruin Hannah's surprise." She hesitated. "Tomorrow morning, after the bus leaves? That is, if you're still subbing for Claire."

"Sounds great." They started across the street and just before they reached the other side, he bent down and whispered something in her ear and she burst into laughter.

Aidan looked sly and pleased with himself.

Maddy simply looked delighted.

"Not in a million years," she said, loud enough for her cousins to hear. "Not a chance in the world."

He didn't say anything at all. He just smiled that killer smile, the one she felt all the way down to her toes, then headed home with Billy Jr.

"You're going to tell us," Gina said as soon as he and Billy Jr. were out of earshot. "Every. Single. Word."

"Why did you follow him into Olivia's shop?" Denise demanded, shushing her kids, who were dancing in front of her for attention.

"Spill," Delia said.

"Or else," Gina added.

Hannah clutched Priscilla and watched her mother with big eyes.

"There's nothing much to tell," Maddy said, which was literally true but substantively false. A perfect combination when dealing with nosy family and friends. "He was scanning an old newspaper photo of the original O'Malley's, and I wanted to see a copy of it." She bent down and kissed Hannah on the top of her head. Her baby girl leaned against her hip, and a wave of love strong enough to bring her to her knees washed over Maddy.

They seemed to accept her answer, but then Pat piped up with, "How did you know he had it before you went into Olivia's shop?"

She angled her eyes down toward Hannah and shook her head. *Little pitchers*, her look said, and every mother there understood.

"Lucky guess," she said, ignoring Gina's snort of derision.

"I'll bet old Olivia almost popped out of her Wonderbra when you followed him into the shop."

"How the mighty have fallen," Denise said with a mock sigh. "Aidan was the last holdout. Next thing you know O'Malley's will be sporting lace-edged menus all done up with fancy calligraphy."

Even Maddy had to laugh out loud at the thought. It had been years since she'd been in O'Malley's, but she had the feeling little about the dockside bar and grill had changed.

"Mom-meee!" Hannah thrust Priscilla against Maddy's stomach. "Too heavy."

"Too heavy?" Gina said to her little second cousin. "My hair extensions weigh more than that pooch."

Hannah looked at Gina, then buried her face against Maddy's hip.

"Was it something I said?"

Yes, Gina, actually it was. "She's shy," Maddy explained for what seemed like the hundredth time since she returned home. Shyness wasn't one of the usual DiFalco family traits. Nosiness. Pushiness. A tendency toward cellulite. Now, those were family traits to be proud of. "It comes over her sometimes and we just have to wait it out."

"She wasn't like that when we visited you guys last year," Denise observed. "She's changed a lot."

"Listen, guys, this really isn't the best time to have this discussion." Her cousins had more children than Maddy could keep track of without a scorecard. You would think they would know better than to talk about a child as if she wasn't there. "I think Hannah and I better get Miss Priss home."

"Wait!" Gina called out. "You still didn't tell us what Aidan said to you."

That's right, Maddy thought as she took her daughter's hand. *I didn't.*

"I HAVE NO idea what you're talking about," Rose said to her sister Toni a few hours later. "Maddy isn't seeing anyone and certainly not Aidan O'Malley."

"All I know is what I heard," Toni said in that supercilious way that set Rose's teeth on edge. "My Gina said the sparks were flying this morning and again this afternoon. Your Maddy even chased after him into that Wentworth woman's paper store."

Rose counted to ten and reminded herself that blood was thicker than water. God knew, it was certainly more annoying. "Olivia Wentworth doesn't own a paper store, Toni. Sy Gardstein owns a paper store. Olivia runs a gift shop that specializes in fine stationery."

"It's a store and she sells paper," Toni said. "Here I thought Maddy was walking around with a broken heart, and Gina tells me she's cozying up with Aidan to beat the band."

Rose balanced the cordless between her ear and her shoulder and rummaged through the catchall drawer for Advil or Tylenol or a rubber hammer. Anything to put her out of her misery. Next thing you knew Toni would have them flinging off their clothes and having at it in front of the Super Fresh.

She popped two Advil and washed them down with Hannah's leftover glass of milk.

"And what difference would it make to you if Maddy *was* cozying up with Aidan O'Malley? I don't see how it's any of your business."

Toni drew in a very audible breath, and Rose smiled at the image of her sister puffing up like a toad. "She's family," Toni said indignantly. "I'm worried about her. I don't think she needs to get dumped by another man so soon after the last one."

This from a woman who had been married four times and engaged six and still thought of herself as great wife material. It was more than Rose could handle. "Toni," she said in as calm and cool a voice as she could muster, "you're a horse's ass."

And with that she—still calm, still cool—hung up the phone.

Now Toni would have another scandalous tidbit to offer up to the rest of the family. She could just imagine her sister hitting that speed-dial key for all it was worth.

The thought did more to ease her headache than an entire bottle of Advil could.

Right on cue the telephone rang. Toni, most likely, determined to get the last word.

She picked up the receiver. "Unless you're calling to apologize, I don't want to talk to you."

"Apologize for what?" the familiar voice questioned. "I've kept this old nose clean long as you've known me."

How was it possible that the sound of a man's voice could carry you back through the years to a time when happiness sat on your doorstep, waiting to be invited in?

"Bill," she said, curling the phone closer to her ear, "is everything all right? You don't usually call until Wednesday."

Bill Bainbridge, her ex-husband and the love of her life, chuckled. "Does something have to be wrong for me to call you? You've been on my mind all day, Rosie. Instead of worrying, I figured I'd make a call."

A delicious feeling of peace flowed through her body as she sank into Grandma Fay's old rocking chair in the corner of the kitchen. "Everything's fine here," she said, closing her eyes so she could conjure up his image. His body was still tall and strong. Skin tanned nut brown from years of outdoor work. Thick white hair that was always a bit too long for Rose's taste. Hannah had his eyes, bright blue and questioning. Sailor's eyes even though Bill Bainbridge had no love for the sea. "Maddy's working on something in the office. Hannah's in there, too, playing with Priscilla."

Our family, Bill. Our blood. Proof that once upon a time we loved each other and shared a life together.

He was quiet for a moment and she knew he was thinking the same thing.

"Any improvement?" he asked after a bit.

"We had a battle over a rusted teapot," she said, then launched into the story of the samovar, ending with the miracle of Fay's cleaning formula.

"So you admitted the teapot had some merit," Bill said.

"I did," Rose said. "And Maddy seemed very pleased with the results."

"Our girl can do better than that," Bill said.

"She was pleased," Rose said again. "She thanked me. That's enough."

"You're not talking to Lucy," Bill said. "You're talking to me."

"We're making progress," she said. She thought about the look in Maddy's eyes when she saw the restored samovar, the tone of her voice. "Definite progress."

They spent the rest of the phone call talking about Hannah. The changes in their beloved granddaughter's personality upset both of them deeply. To see a happy, lively child turn inward the way Hannah had after her father's marriage reminded them both of how their own daughter had grieved when Bill returned to Oregon after the divorce.

"We did the best we knew how, Rosie. It wasn't good enough, but maybe it never is."

"We loved each other," Rose said, choking back embarrassing tears. "We loved our baby. Why couldn't we make it work?"

"I don't know," Bill said softly. "Damned if I've ever been able to figure it out."

"Oh, God," Rose said, wiping her eyes with a tea towel. "It's the damn holidays. They make me too sentimental."

"I like you this way," Bill said, "and I think our girl would, too. This is as good a time as any to open up your heart, Rosie. We never know when the chance will come 'round again."

Which, of course, was Bill's way of getting to the real reason for the frequent phone calls.

"I feel just fine," she said.

"I wasn't going to ask."

"And I love you dearly for that, but we both know that's why you called."

"When do you go in for the blood work?"

"Next week."

"And the CT scan?"

"Bill, you asked me this on Saturday and on the Wednesday before and the Wednesday before that. If the appointment changes, I promise I'll tell you. The CT scan is the end of January and knock wood we're not expecting anything unusual."

"I could fly in, Rosie."

"Don't you dare! We'll see you on Christmas. That's quite enough."

"Maddy and Hannah still don't know, do they?"

"Of course not. If there's one thing I can do, it's keep a secret."

"I'd better push off," Bill said. "I want to make it to K.C. by nightfall."

"Don't overdo," Rose warned him. "You're not as young as you used to be."

"The day comes I can't get behind the wheel, I'll pull

off to the side of the road and let the buzzards pick my bones."

She laughed despite the gruesome image. "Just take care," she said. "That's all I ask."

"Same with you," he said, his voice gruffly tender. "God bless."

"God bless," she whispered as she hung up the phone. God bless every stubborn bone in his stubborn body, every hair on his head, every beat of his loving heart.

HANNAH WAS VERY subdued all evening. She picked at her hamburger and only managed to eat a few pieces of bun, one forkful of beans, and absolutely none of her salad. Both Rose and Maddy tried to engage her in conversation, but the little girl's contribution was limited to a few shrugs of her tiny shoulders and a muttered "No" when asked if she was feeling any happier at school.

Maddy and her mother exchanged a glance across the table.

"Do I have something wonderful for dessert!" Rose exclaimed as they cleared the table. "In fact, I think it's someone's favorite."

Maddy ruffled her daughter's hair and smiled down at her. "Hannah, do you think that maybe Grandma made brownies for you?"

Hannah's eyes remained focused on the midpoint of the kitchen table. "Dunno," she muttered. Her eyelids drooped as if she were about to fall asleep in her chair.

"Brownies with pecans," Rose said, placing the platter down in front of the little girl. "All gooey in the middle, just the way you like them."

A year ago Hannah would have been bouncing up and down in her chair, begging to be allowed to grab a piece and smoosh it into her mouth. Now there she was today, acting as if fried grasshopper would be every bit as tasty.

Rose placed a slice on a small plate and handed it to Hannah. "I'll get you some milk."

Maddy waited a moment, then prodded, "Say thank you, sweetheart."

"Thank you."

Rose beamed at her granddaughter, but the worry lines between her brows cut deeper than ever. She turned away to load the dishwasher.

Maddy pressed a kiss to her daughter's forehead, then placed the back of her hand against her cheek. Hannah squirmed away from Maddy's touch but not before Maddy was able to ascertain that the child didn't have a fever. Not that she had expected anything else. There was nothing physically wrong with her daughter. The only thing wrong with her was that she missed her father, and there was nothing on earth Maddy could do to change that.

"I'd give anything to see her old smile," Rose said after Maddy put Hannah to bed for the night. "It hurts to see her looking so sad."

Maddy's eyes welled with tears. "I know," she said. "I thought a change of scene might help, but . . ." Her words trailed off. She had been that little girl once herself, many years ago, a little girl who missed her daddy so much she thought her heart would break. A little girl who blamed her mother for breaking up her perfect family.

"It takes time," Rose said, placing a hand on Maddy's hand and giving a gentle squeeze. "There's nothing for it but time."

Maddy nodded, then withdrew her hand. "I'm going to do a little more work on the Web site before I turn in. Do you mind?"

"No." Rose took a step backward. "Of course not."

"Leave the pots. I'll do them in the morning."

"Go," Rose said. "Work on your Web site."

Maddy hesitated. All she had to do was take a step forward. Place her hand on Rose's or her arm about her mother's shoulders. Kiss her cheek. The slightest gesture could take them so very far.

But she waited too long and the moment for such gestures slipped away. Rose's eyes met hers and Maddy saw pain in them and resignation, but there was nothing she could do about either. A deep gnawing sadness burrowed deeper into her gut and spread outward. That feeling had been with her since she wasn't much older than Hannah, and it had never quite gone away.

She doubted it ever would.

"I CLOSED OUT the register," Tommy said from the doorway. "If you want, boss, I'll make the night drop on my way to pick up the wife at her sister's house."

"Great," Aidan said, looking up from his laptop. "I appreciate it."

"No sweat." Tommy lingered, casting a curious eye in Aidan's direction. "Touring the *Starship Enterprise* again?"

"Wiseass," Aidan said, shooting him a grin. "I'm e-mailing a scan of that newspaper clipping I showed you."

"Since when do you know how to do all that fancy shit on the computer?"

"Kelly could do that fancy shit when she was ten years old. It's taken me awhile to catch up."

"And since when do you got a scanner?"

"Olivia Wentworth has one," he said, then braced himself for a barrage of smart cracks.

Tommy inscribed a womanly figure in the air. "Now, that is what I call a woman with a capital W."

"Get in line," Aidan said. "Every man on the town council has ordered new business cards from her."

"That's not the business I'd be looking for from that dame."

"I thought you were a one-woman guy, Tommy."

"I am," Tommy said, "but that doesn't mean I don't have eyes in my head. You can't tell me you haven't noticed she's got a great set of—"

"I noticed," Aidan broke in. He'd taken great strides in sensitivity since Kelly reached puberty. Nothing like the sight of some old goat ogling your daughter to make you rethink the way you viewed the opposite sex. "She's a nice woman but not my type."

"You gotta be kidding."

Aidan let it slide with a noncommittal shrug. Tommy

had lived vicariously through Aidan for a long time, right up until the accident, when Aidan's life did a 180.

Tommy shifted his weight, then cracked his knuckles.

"Something you want to say?" Aidan asked.

"Mel said he saw you looking pretty cozy this afternoon with Rosie DiFalco's kid, the one who moved away as soon as she was old enough to drive."

"Oh, yeah?"

"Said you two were laughing together in front of Olivia's fancy paper store like you had a secret joke."

"Sounds like old Mel has a lot of time on his hands."

"Nah," said Tommy, who never was one for irony. "His wife sent him out to pick up a bottle of red for some family dinner they were having tonight, and he saw you when he was pulling out of the parking lot."

"Nothing's going on."

He wasn't sure if that was relief on Tommy's face or disappointment. "You haven't been out with anyone since—"

"Back off, Kennedy. I don't need the advice."

"Ya know, I was thinking. My niece Susan and her husband split up about a year ago. She's in real estate up in Paramus. Not that big a drive if you leave early on a Saturday. Maybe—"

The look he gave Tommy must have been a good one, because the older man stopped mid-sentence.

"Or maybe not." Tommy grabbed his jacket from the coatrack near the door. "See you in the morning."

He heard the door slam shut behind Tommy, then the sound of the locks tumbling into place. He thought about ducking out the back door and calling the old guy back in, maybe sharing a cup of joe together, something to smooth away the feeling that sharp edges seemed to be sticking out all around him, but Tommy's Ford was already crunching across the gravel parking lot.

Tomorrow, Aidan thought. He turned back to the laptop.

*   *   *

MAYBE HE WASN'T going to send her the scan after all. If you stopped and thought about it, why should he? They were going to see each other the next morning, and they would compare the newspaper clipping and the samovar in person. It wasn't like he had any other reason to e-mail her.

Wait. Where did that come from? How long had that e-mail from FireGuy been languishing in her in box anyway? And an attachment, too! He remembered. She could feel her smile tugging from one ear to the other as she clicked on the envelope icon.

TO: JerseyGirl@njshore.net
FROM: FireGuy@njshore.net
DATE: 5 December
SUBJECT: scan

Sorry I took so long, but we had a full house tonight and they didn't feel like leaving. I'm sending out the scan for you to see. It's not great, but you get the idea.

Anyway you'll see the real thing tomorrow.
Aidan

PS: Are you bringing that dog??

Hmm. Maybe he was right. Priscilla might not be a great addition to Julie's Coffee Shop. She had sworn to herself that she wouldn't ask her mother to pick up the slack for her, but her aunt Lucy was on baking duty tomorrow morning, and Lucy would do anything if she thought it would help the situation between Maddy and Rose.

Oh, God. What was she going to wear? She was sick of jeans. It was too cold for a skirt. Maybe those stretchy black pants with her soft old leather boots and the charcoal-gray sweater, the soft one with the faintest hints of peach and cream. Maybe she would set the clock a few minutes earlier than usual. Not because she was going to do anything fancy—of course not! Still, it wouldn't hurt to make sure she had a chance to put the samovar into a tote bag or something before Hannah woke up and got all curious.

And if she could dig up her blow-dryer from the back of the closet, that wouldn't be a bad idea, either.

She was about to shut down the computer and head upstairs to look for the peach lipstick she hadn't worn since at least 1997 when she realized she hadn't opened the attachment yet. It was late and she had a million things to do and what difference did it make anyway when she'd see the original clipping in not that many hours from now, but she couldn't resist.

Double-click.

Wait a second while the machine chugged and clunked and then—

Oh, God.

She sank back down into her desk chair and leaned closer to the monitor.

Oh. My. God.

The samovar in the clipping was a dead ringer for the one in her mother's closet.

Chapter Thirteen

"LOOK AT YOU!" Lucy said when Maddy entered the kitchen the next morning. "Don't you look gorgeous!"

Maddy's glance darted quickly to Rose, who was busy snipping chives near the stove. "Thanks, Lucy." She pressed a kiss to her aunt's cheek. "You're looking pretty spiffy yourself."

"This old thing?" Lucy tossed her head, making her signature dangly earrings tinkle. Clothes were her passion, and while her figure might not fit haute couture, she always looked stylish and wonderful. "I'm going to have to ask Frankie to come over and build on a new closet. Now that I've discovered on-line-shopping, there's no stopping me."

"There wasn't any stopping you when you used to drive all the way to Freehold," Rose observed, her kitchen shears making soft little noises as she snipped. "I still think you divorced Joe because he took up too much closet space."

"You may have a point there," Lucy said, eyes twinkling with amusement. "In the long run I've found clothes give me a lot more pleasure and require a lot less upkeep than your average husband."

Maddy poured herself a mug of strong coffee while the two sisters bantered between themselves. She was enjoying their lighthearted byplay, and she was grateful that it took some of the attention away from the fact that she wasn't wearing her usual early-morning jeans-and-sweatshirt combo that Rose abhorred.

"Something special on tap?" Rose asked as Maddy finished her coffee, then popped the mug into the industrial-strength dishwasher. "You really do look lovely."

A burst of pleasure flooded Maddy at her mother's words. "Thanks," she said. The truth was, she hadn't taken a lot of care with her appearance in quite awhile. It was a relief to discover she remembered how.

"Something special?" Rose repeated.

"Sort of," Maddy said, opting unexpectedly for the truth. "I'm meeting Aidan O'Malley at the coffee shop. It turns out he's the one who was trying to buy the samovar I bought for Maddy on that auction, and he says he has a picture of something his grandmother used to own and—"

You're rambling, Maddy. You sound like you're making it up as you go along.

"Anyway, we're going to compare the samovar and the clipping at the coffee shop. I would've shown it to him yesterday afternoon, but with Hannah around and—"

"You could bring him back here for coffee," Rose said. "God knows we always have enough."

"No," Maddy said, a trifle sharply, then caught herself. "I mean, thanks, but this isn't a big deal or anything. We'll just duck across the street after the school bus leaves and compare the teapot to the clipping."

"And then what?" Lucy piped up. "What do you expect to find?"

Maddy stared at her aunt as if seeing her for the first time. "I don't actually know," she admitted. "It all made sense yesterday. Now I'm not quite sure what the point is."

"Curiosity," Rose said. "Just so long as you don't let him talk you out of Hannah's Christmas present."

"Your mother's right," Lucy said. "Those O'Malley men can be extremely convincing when they set their minds to it."

"I don't think I'm in any danger," Maddy drawled. "He can look all he wants, but he can't touch."

Her mother and aunt burst into laughter and were still chuckling when Maddy and Hannah left for the bus stop.

"Why can't Priscilla come?" Hannah asked as they walked slowly down the ice-frosted street. "She always goes to the bus with us."

"I had to leave her home with Aunt Lucy today," Maddy said, "because I'm going someplace where dogs aren't allowed."

"Where's that?" Hannah asked. "You're not going away?"

"Remember Julie's, the coffee shop across the street from the bus stop?" Hannah shook her head. "Grandma Rose and I took you there for a hot chocolate when we first moved here. Remember now?"

"I dunno." Hannah wrinkled her nose. "Maybe sort of."

"I'm meeting Billy's uncle Aidan there for a cup of coffee."

"Why are you meeting him?" Hannah asked. "Is he your boyfriend?"

"You know I don't have a boyfriend, Hannah." Maddy's cheeks reddened—the brisk wind, most likely—and she thanked God they were still a block away from the bus stop. Her cousins would have a field day with that question. "He wants to show me a photograph of his grandma's old restaurant."

"Is that why you're carrying that bag? Are you going to show him pictures of my grandma's restaurant?"

"Yes." Maddy winced inwardly. She could almost hear the ghost of Dr. Spock telling her that good mothers never take the easy way out. They always answer a simple question with the longest, most convoluted, too-much-information answer possible, all in the interest of being honest with their kids.

Too bad, Maddy thought. *It's Christmastime.* Any mother of a young child could tell you that all bets were off in December, at least until your kids were old enough to know who Santa really was. The samovar was going to be Hannah's big surprise or she'd know the reason why.

"You know, Hannah, Grandma Rose doesn't really own a restaurant."

"People eat food there."

"Yes, but that's because they're guests in Grandma Rose's house."

"Grandma says they pay her money to stay there."

"That's right and for their money Grandma Rose gives them a beautiful room and some delicious meals."

"I thought that's a rest'rant."

"You don't sleep in a restaurant, Hannah."

"Lisa says Grandma doesn't like you." Hannah looked up at Maddy, her blue eyes wide with curiosity. "I hear you fighting sometimes."

I need a road map, God, and fast. Something to point out where the land mines were hidden before she stepped on one. Who knew the mother-daughter dance began so early?

"Grandma Rose loves me very much," Maddy said, "same as she loves you. It's just that we don't see eye-to-eye on a lot of things."

"Lisa's mommy says you ran away from home when you were little."

The *National Enquirer* had nothing on Paradise Point, where gossip was an art form cultivated in the cradle.

Maddy smiled at her daughter. "I think I must have run away a thousand times."

"Really?"

"Really. I had a little Barbie lunchbox—"

"You had a Barbie?"

"I had two Barbies," she said, enjoying the look of astonishment on her daughter's face. "And I used to grab

my Barbie lunchbox and my crayons and my *Grease* coloring book and storm out of the house."

"They had Barbies when you were little?"

"Barbie's been around a long time."

"Did Grandma get mad at you?"

"Sure she did, but I didn't care. I was going to run far
away where she'd never find me."

Hannah fell silent and Maddy's heart felt ready to burst
through her rib cage with love. Hannah was seeing Maddy
as a little girl for the first time, a little girl who maybe
felt just like Hannah was feeling.

"Did you run far away?"

Maddy laughed. "Remember that spot on the beach that
I showed you?"

"The spot near the fence where Priscilla—"

"That's the one. When I was little there was a big boulder there, and I'd tuck myself between the boulder and
the dunes and pretend I was invisible."

"But you weren't."

"Nope, I wasn't invisible at all." Grandma Fay and
Rose and all of her sisters had been watching her every
step along the way. She learned later that the telephones
rang off the hook every time she ran away from home as
a posse of aunts and cousins kept their collective eye on
her.

"Were you scared?"

"A little."

"But being in your secret place was good."

"Yes, it was."

Hannah considered that idea for a few moments. "I
have a secret place."

"Behind the curtains in my bedroom."

Hannah made a face. "That was in the old place."

"I could hear you giggling back there." Was there really
a time when her little girl had been so filled with happiness that there was laughter to spare?

Hannah looked up at her, and for an instant Maddy
didn't quite recognize the look in her daughter's eyes.
Hannah looked older and sadder. More knowing. She

looked the way Maddy had looked after her father went
back to Oregon.

"Do you have a new hiding place, honey?" she asked.
"I could show you—"

But Hannah's eyes were no longer dancing with curiosity. She had withdrawn into sadness once again and
Maddy knew all she could do was wait for her daughter
to reach out again.

No matter how easy you tried to make it for them, no
matter how you tried to cushion the blows, there was
nothing you could do to keep your child's heart from
breaking when her home was split in two. All the Satur-
days in the park, all the Sunday brunches—they couldn't
begin to equal going to sleep each night, knowing that
both of your parents were right outside your door.

"YOU DON'T HAVE to do this," Claire said as they
waited while Billy Jr. ran back upstairs for his homework.
"I can make it to the bus stop."

"How much sleep did you get last night?" Aidan asked,
taking note of the dark circles under her eyes and her
swollen right jaw.

"I don't know," she said, stifling a yawn. "An hour . . .
maybe two. Percocet puts everyone else on earth to sleep.
On me it works like six cups of espresso."

"So go back to bed after we leave. Take it easy. Root
canal's a bitch."

His sister-in-law might be sleepy, but she wasn't stupid.
"Okay, spill," she said, giving him a variation of the look
she used to shoot at Billy. "What's with all of this brotherly concern? The last time you treated me this nice was
when I went into labor during Midnight Mass."

"You were the one bitching about squeezing twenty-
five hours into twenty-four. I thought I'd cut you some
slack. Give you a chance to veg out one more day."

"Yeah? And who's going to do my work at the bar?"

"We can go another day. It'll be rough, but we'll manage."

"Wiseass." She popped him in the forearm with a softly

clenched fist. "Just tell me what the deal is with doing school-bus duty and I'll leave you alone."

It wasn't like ten other people wouldn't tell her before he and Maddy Bainbridge ordered their first cup of coffee.

"I don't get it," Claire said, shaking her head. "She's not your type."

"She doesn't have to be," Aidan said, suddenly irritated. And what the hell was *his type* anyway. "We're having coffee at Julie's, not a three-way at the No-Tell."

Claire's eyes almost popped from her head. "A three-way? Sweet Jesus! Did you ever—"

"No," he said, grinning. Then, "Did you?"

She started laughing, then placed a hand over her swollen jaw. "You bastard. Don't make me laugh when I'm in pain." She met his eyes. "So why are you having coffee with Maddy? Are you looking for some of her mother's secrets to success?"

"Remember that rusty teapot I was bidding on?" He told her the whole story, about the auction, Maddy's win, Kelly's annoyance, his visit to Grandma Irene, then his discovery.

"So you really think it might be the same teapot?"

"Probably not, but it's possible."

Claire shrugged. "Hope you don't mind me asking, but so the hell what?"

"You don't think it would be pretty damn incredible to find something you lost almost fifty years ago?"

"That's what I was afraid of." Claire's expression darkened. "What is wrong with you anyway? When are you going to get it through your fat skull that nothing short of a visit from God Himself will change that old bat?"

"It's part of our family history."

"Bullshit. Since when did she ever share any of her family history with any of you? I've been around this crew a long time, brother-in-law, and I know that old bat hangs on to her secrets the same way she hangs on to her bank books."

"She had a tough life."

Claire's tone was fierce. "Don't start that crap again,

please. I love you too much to fight over that bitch. I just wish she would die already and leave us all the hell alone."

"I didn't want to get into this, Claire," he said as calmly as he could manage. "You asked what was up and I told you."

Billy Jr. bounded into the room before she could respond. "I'm gonna be late," he said, fidgeting like an over-caffeinated hummingbird with a buzz cut. "We better go."

Claire ran a hand over his shorn head, then pulled him close and kissed him. "Did you pee?" she asked.

"Ma-a-a."

"Did you?"

The kid flung down his book bag, then ran for the downstairs john off the laundry room.

"Forgot how it used to be, didn't you?" Claire said with a sly look.

"Jesus," Aidan said, remembering the early days. "How did any of us survive?"

"At least Kelly's almost on her own. I still have a good twelve years ahead of me."

Aidan knew what she was going through. He knew it in his bones. There was a reason it took two to make a baby. Once the fun was over and the baby was actually there, it took at least that many hearts and hands to get the job done.

His brother and Claire had been there for him from the start. After Sandy died, they had driven up to Pennsylvania where he sat, shocked into numbness, into immobility, into a grief so far beyond tears that it scared the hell out of everyone except for Kelly, his beautiful baby girl who depended on him for everything but the air she breathed.

Billy and Claire cleaned them both, fed them, then bundled them up into their station wagon and drove them back down to New Jersey. When sorrow had him so deep in its grip that he couldn't come up with a reason to face another day, it was Claire who had listened to him, held him, then finally told him it was time to get a grip because his baby girl needed him.

And it was Claire who had picked up the slack when he was working double-shifts at the firehouse, taking Kelly to school and picking her up in the afternoon, helping her with her homework, listening to her prayers. He could never repay her for all she had done for them. The debt was incalculable.

"*Now* can I go?" Billy Jr. demanded as he raced into the room for a second time.

Claire helped him into his sweater, jacket, scarf, and mittens. He looked like one of those Teletubbies that had been popular a few years ago, but Aidan wisely kept that observation to himself. He hadn't survived Kelly's childhood without learning a few lessons.

His sister-in-law turned to him and made a show of checking for scarf and mittens, much to Billy Jr.'s amusement. "New sweater?"

He ignored the glint of mischief in her eyes. "Last Christmas," he said. "You gave it to me."

She grinned. "Say hi to Maddy for me."

If Billy Jr. hadn't been standing there, watching them like they were the Williams sisters and the front hallway was center court at Wimbledon, he might have said something memorable. As it was, he placed his hand on his nephew's shoulder and said, "Let's shove off, pal," and pretended he didn't hear Claire laughing.

"FOR CRYING OUT loud," Maddy protested after Denise feigned a swoon at the sight of her sleek black trousers and high-heeled boots. "Would you guys stop acting like you've never seen me out of jeans before? You'd think I showed up here in a prom dress, the way you're all carrying on."

Gina pretended to wave smelling salts under Denise's nose. "You clean up well, cuz," she said with her usual wry delivery. She turned toward the other women huddled together on the street corner for warmth against the coming snowstorm. "Lipstick," she stage-whispered. "And mascara."

"Mascara before eight in the morning?" Pat rolled her eyes as she gathered her coat tighter around her. "The last time I had mascara on at eight in the morning it was because I didn't wash it off the night before."

Her remark was met with whoops of laughter.

"If the kids weren't around, I could tell you a few stories about—"

"Shh!" Pat poked Delia in the ribs. "They're listening."

The same children who had been happily annoying each other a few feet away were now solemnly—and quietly—listening to every word their mothers were saying.

"So how about those Jets," Gina said. "Think they'll make it to the playoffs this year?"

"You have to be so careful," Maddy said. "The one thing you don't want them to overhear—"

"Yeah," said Pat, "and what they don't overhear, they make up and tell your mother."

Another outburst of early morning laughter.

"Have you guys always had this much fun waiting for the school bus?" Maddy asked, trying not to let on that she'd noticed Aidan's truck pulling into a spot half a block down from where they were standing.

"Last year was terrible," Gina said bluntly. "Maria Segretti and her mother were here every morning and every afternoon waiting for Maria's spawn of Satan. I swear to God they carried tape recorders in the pockets of their stretch pants."

"I said three rosaries in thanks when they moved to Cherry Hill," Delia said. "I thought we were going to have to start speaking in code."

"I remember Maria," Maddy said with a grimace. "She'd break that code in three minutes, then publish the text in the *Paradise Point Weekly Shopper*."

"Honey, you don't know the half of it," Gina said. "When I was dating Aidan, I—"

Another loud "Shh!" from Pat, who gestured over her shoulder.

Maddy tried hard not to stare at her cousin. *When I was dating Aidan . . .*

"Hoo boy!" Gina said with a loud wolf whistle. "Lookin' good, O'Malley."

"I'll say!" Pat agreed. "You're not half bad."

If there was anything still happening between her cousin and Aidan, they were pretty good at hiding it. Maddy didn't detect any sexual current flowing between them. He bantered with Gina the same way he bantered with Pat and Denise and the other women waiting at the corner for the school bus. And Gina flirted with everyone. Men. Women. Small children. House pets.

Whatever they'd had going between them had apparently been downgraded to a comfortable friendship.

Unless, of course, they had spent the night together.

Which, needless to say, wasn't any business of Maddy's. Her cousin was informally separated, and as far as she knew, Aidan O'Malley had never remarried.

"Maddy." Gina snapped her fingers in front of Maddy's nose. "The man is talking to you."

She looked up at him. "You were?"

"Yeah." He was smiling, but uncertainty twitched at the corner of his mouth. Hmm. This was getting interesting, and interesting was the last thing she'd been expecting. He gestured toward the Macy's shopping bag at her feet. "Is that it?"

"Yep." She inclined her head in the direction of Hannah. "Pictures."

He looked over at Hannah, then nodded. "I know the drill."

They locked eyes and it happened again. Everything else, her cousins, the kids, the wet and icy wind, it all dropped away as if it didn't exist, and there was only the two of them standing there on the corner, smiling at each other as if they shared a big juicy secret.

Which in a way they did, but it certainly wasn't half as big or one-tenth as juicy as Gina, Denise, and the others were starting to think.

"Don't mean to interrupt," Denise said, eyes twinkling

with mischief, "but there's a school bus about to run your asses over if you don't move in the next ten seconds."

"Didn't Maddy almost get run over yesterday afternoon?" Pat asked, eyes wide with feigned innocence. "I think it was when she followed Aidan into the paper store."

"You're right," Gina said. She didn't do as good a job with innocence, feigned or otherwise. "You'd think she had her mind on something else, wouldn't you?"

Maddy mumbled something in high school Spanish that made Aidan laugh out loud.

The school bus rolled to a stop and pandemonium broke out as book bags, lunches, backpacks, permission slips, mittens, gloves, hats, scarves, and runaway caps were handed over, retrieved, signed, tucked into pockets, slung over tiny shoulders, pulled down over frozen ears. Except for Billy they were all still young enough to kiss goodbye in public without causing permanent damage to their reputations.

"Be good," Maddy whispered in Hannah's ear. "Make sure you drink your milk. Don't swap lunches with Greta. Grandma Rose made you peanut butter with chopped raisins and celery on that bread you liked so much last time."

Hannah's eyes swam with tears, and Maddy was afraid her own eyes were welling up, too. "You'll be home before you know it, honey."

Hannah nodded, then boarded the bus.

"It gets easier," Aidan said as the bus inched away from the curb. "I used to want to grab Kelly off the bus and take her back home with me."

"Am I that obvious?"

He shrugged. "I know the signs."

"You mean I'm going to make it to first grade?"

He pretended to study her intently. "You might even make it to third."

"I'm going to hold you to that."

"Well," said Gina with a toss of her silky dark head, "I don't know about the rest of you, but I have to get to work."

"Same here," said Denise. "Four loads of laundry, the kitchen to clean, and a trip to the pediatrician."

"Add a post office run to your list and you'll see how my day's shaping up," Pat chimed in.

"Not me," said Maddy, reaching for the shopping bag that held the samovar. "I think I'll spend the morning drinking coffee at Julie's."

"Sounds good," said Aidan. "Let's go."

Chapter Fourteen

"SIT ANYWHERE, YOU guys," Julie called out from behind the counter. "I'll bring your coffees."

Two of Maddy's former schoolmates were seated at the counter, perusing what looked like architectural diagrams. Kris and Jill looked up to see the identity of the new arrivals. Kris whispered something to Jill, who whispered something back.

"Hey, Maddy!" Kris said. "Hey, Aidan!"

"How's it going?" Jill asked, her gaze darting from Aidan to Maddy and back again.

Maddy waved hello. Aidan asked how the plans for the new house were going and laughed when the two women mimed sticking their heads in a matching pair of nooses.

"They're building a house?" Maddy asked as they made their way to the only empty booth.

"Over by the lake," he said.

"Together?"

"You didn't know they were a couple?"

"I'm really out of the loop, aren't I?"

"Spend a little more time with your cousins. They'll get you caught up."

Aidan knew everyone in the place. Hello. Hey. How ya doing. A litany of greetings. And it was the same for Maddy. She knew almost everyone by sight or lucky guess, and the ones she didn't know knew her through Rose.

"Now you know why I moved to Seattle," she said as she folded up her coat and placed it on the bench seat next to her. The shopping bag rested at her feet. "No such thing as a private moment in this town."

Aidan tossed his jacket on his seat and slid in opposite her. "I started dreaming about escape when I was six years old." He placed the envelope containing the scanned photocopy on the table between them. "Almost made it, too."

Maddy flipped through the bits and pieces of information she remembered about the younger O'Malley brother. "You went to school in Pennsylvania. Football scholarship, I think."

"You have a good memory."

"You and your brother were prime topics of conversation when I was growing up." She grinned across the table at him. "Like you didn't know." The O'Malley boys had been great-looking, a little wild, and utterly irresistible to the girls of Paradise Point.

"One of the reasons my grandmother was glad about that scholarship. Anything to get rid of me before I did something to blacken the O'Malley name."

"When did you move back here?"

"A few weeks short of Kelly's third birthday. Claire and Billy drove up to see how we were doing and ended up taking us back home with them."

Maddy sighed. "Sounds familiar."

"The word was you were having a tough time back there in Portland."

"Seattle," she corrected him, "and it's my daughter who's having the tough time. Her father decided to marry and move down to San Diego to be near his wife's family and—" She shrugged and turned her hands palms up. "That turned Hannah's life upside down."

"How about yours?"

"Tom and I parted a few months after Hannah was born. This—" She paused for a moment. Did she really want to answer this question? "Okay," she said, throwing caution to the wind. "The truth won't kill me, will it? Yeah, it turned my life upside down. I didn't think it would, but it did."

"You still loved him?"

"That's a personal question."

"Yeah," he said. "It is. You don't have to answer it."

"I want to answer it. I loved him as Hannah's father. I loved him for what we'd shared. But we hadn't been lovers for a lot of years when he met Lisa."

And you know what? I would have taken him back in a heartbeat if he'd asked me to.

Anything to make Hannah smile again. Anything to give Hannah a family she could depend on.

"I heard he was a lot older than you."

She leaned forward on her elbows and met his eyes. "Why don't you tell me exactly what you've heard, and I'll tell you if it's true or not."

"You're angry."

"No, I'm not angry at all. You asked a question. I countered with another question."

"Fair enough."

"So tell me what you've heard about me."

"You're putting me on the spot."

"Think about how I feel." She flashed a quick smile. "It's not like I don't know Gina has a big mouth."

Okay, O'Malley. Let's see how you react to that.

"You're right," he said as Julie approached. "The woman's plugged into every source of gossip from here to Atlantic City."

Julie Corbin was somewhere in her late fifties. She had purchased the coffee shop twenty years ago with the money she had made on the sale of her old house. She had plunged all of the profits into the coffee shop. She had even slept in the back room for the first two years until she could afford to rent a place within walking distance. Paradise Point had been at the start of its transition from run-down seaside resort to charming seaside village when Julie began her own renovations, and in many ways her success paralleled that of the town.

"You two don't need menus, do you?" she asked. "It's not like you don't have it memorized."

"Toasted blueberry," Maddy said. "No butter."

"I'll take a short stack, sausage well done, and one egg over easy." He thought for a second. "And some OJ."

Julie shook her head as she scribbled in her order pad. "If I ate like that I'd be the size of a double-wide." She looked up at them, then her eyes widened as if she had suddenly realized that this was a brand-new combination. "I'll get your coffees."

"Did you know that Julie's son was married to my cousin Denise years ago?"

"Roger?"

"No, Alex. The one who sells Mazdas in Ocean City."

"Alex married a flight attendant and has four kids."

"Yeah, well, it's three kids, and before that he was married to Denise."

He shook his head. "I don't know how that one slipped by me."

"You think I can keep track? I've given up sending wedding presents. I wait six months and if they're still together, then I start shopping."

Julie deposited two huge mugs of coffee, a pitcher of cream, then hurried away.

Maddy watched as he tore into two packets of sugar, then dumped them into his coffee. He didn't add cream. He didn't stir.

She poured a small measure of cream into her coffee, stirred once, then wrapped her hands around the warm mug and breathed deeply.

"Heaven," she said. "Plain ordinary coffee. You have no idea how much I've missed it."

"Oh, yeah," he said. "I forgot you were living in Latte Land."

"Took me three years to learn how to order, and then they claimed they couldn't understand my Jersey accent."

"You don't have a Jersey accent."

"In Seattle I do."

"Actually you have a great speaking voice."

Don't fight him, Maddy. For once in your life accept a compliment like an adult.

"Thanks," she said, amazed at how difficult that single word could be. "After I lost my accounting job, I kind of fell into doing voice-overs for a used-car lot in Bellevue."

"You told me. Did you enjoy it?"

She laughed. "I loved it! I was a deejay in college, and for awhile I'd thought about ditching accounting and going into broadcasting."

"Why didn't you?"

"I don't really know. I'm not a terribly ambitious woman. It feels like I blinked my eyes and found myself in a navy blue suit and carrying a briefcase."

"Can't imagine you in a navy blue suit."

"I had three of them," she said, shaking her head at the memory. "Plus one charcoal and one black. What the well-dressed accountant will wear."

"You're not my idea of an accountant."

"I was one," she said, "and I was damn good."

"Why'd you leave?"

"I didn't," she said. "The company was a dot-com telecommunications company and—" She did a first-rate impression of an exploding bomb. "Took our 401(k)s, our severance pay, everything. And the worst part was we weren't the only ones. We went from a thriving industry to nothing overnight. I cried for three days straight, and then when I finished crying, I realized there was no place to go. So I decided to switch gears. I went on a few auditions after that, but nothing much came out of it beyond the car dealership gig." She gave a self-deprecating laugh. "Although I'm proud to say I was the official voice of Hartz Electronics in the Pine Brook Shopping Center."

"Another commercial?"

"Well, not exactly. I taped their voice-mail messages for them."

He laughed out loud, drawing curious glances from the

other patrons. "Are you going to look for voice-over work here?"

"Doing what?" she countered. "Voice-mail messages for my mother?"

"You're midway between New York and Philadelphia. There has to be something out there."

"I'm supposed to be working with my mother," she reminded him. "And besides, I'll be moving on before too long. No sense starting something I won't be around to finish."

"Gina said you were given a fifty-fifty share of the Candlelight."

"Gina's been listening to her mother. Rose and I have nothing formal set up. Right now I'd say we're both trying to decide if we'll make it to the end of the year without killing each other." Considering it was only December 6, it was anybody's guess.

"So you're not staying."

"Given my track record with my mother, it's not very likely. Besides, I can't see spending the rest of my life sharing the bathroom with total strangers." She told him about her midnight encounter with Mr. Loewenstein in the upstairs hallway and had him laughing so hard he couldn't speak.

She wondered if Gina had ever rendered him speechless. Then she recalled some of Gina's stories about her sexual exploits, and she found herself wishing she hadn't demanded every single juicy detail, details that were so hot she half-expected the authorities to confiscate her computer before her e-mails went up in flames. Gina had probably rendered Aidan O'Malley speechless or unconscious. Take your pick.

Julie popped up again, this time with a huge platter of pancakes and the trimmings for Aidan and a toasted blueberry muffin for Maddy.

"No butter," Julie said as she slid the plate in front of Maddy.

"Thanks."

"Lots of butter," Julie said to Aidan as she deposited his plate.

"Syrup?"

"I'm way ahead of you." She plucked three plastic tubs of imitation maple syrup from the depths of her apron pocket and put them down on the table. "Enjoy, guys."

Maddy took a bite of her muffin, chewed, then swallowed. "It needs butter."

He gestured toward the mountain of butter melting atop his stack of pancakes. "Help yourself."

Normally Maddy wasn't a *help yourself* kind of woman. She had never so much as grabbed a French fry from Tom's plate in all those years they were together. Then again Tom wasn't exactly a diner-and-French-fries kind of man. Still she felt surprisingly comfortable with Aidan, despite the definite surge of cascading hormones every time their eyes locked over the salt and pepper shakers. The cascading hormones were a definite bonus. Not that his were likely cascading in return. That would have been too good to be true. He was probably just waiting for her to whip out the samovar so they could compare notes.

Too bad, she thought as she dipped the delicately browned edge of her muffin into his golden pool of butter. She could easily get used to the butter, the blueberries, and the man.

THE SECOND SHE sank her perfect teeth into a juicy blueberry and sighed with delight, he knew he was a goner. Up until that moment he had been able to explain away the commotion inside his chest as a combination of hunger and sleep deprivation, but now he knew it for what it was.

One of the DiFalco cousins. The one who had taken off for Seattle right after high school and never looked back. The one with the wild mane of caramel-colored hair, eyes the color of a stormy sea, and a body that made clothes a crime against nature. She was tall, voluptuous, and opinionated. She had the kind of laugh that made you want to take a pratfall just so you could hear the sound. Her sense of humor was still intact even if those stormy eyes never quite caught up.

She was as direct in person as she was in e-mail. She loved her kid the way a kid deserved to be loved. Hell, she gave up the life she had built in Seattle to move back to New Jersey just to try and make her daughter happy again. He had watched her with Hannah at the bus stop and the calendar flipped back a dozen years and it was Kelly with the weepy eyes as he told her the day would be over before she knew it and he would be right there waiting for her in the afternoon. He had grown up with his feet planted firmly on shifting sands, taking his cues from his mother's moods, his father's sorrows, his grandmother's distance, and never quite getting it right. He swore the home he built for his daughter would have a solid and steady foundation.

You did what you had to do. You put your kid and her needs first and worked backward from there. And when you saw the beautiful young woman she had suddenly become, you knew it was all worthwhile.

He wanted to tell Maddy all of that and more, but he'd be damned if he knew why. She would learn it for herself soon enough. He had heard stories about why Maddy and Hannah's father had split up, that the guy already had grandchildren older than Hannah and wasn't looking to start over again and nothing Maddy could say or do could convince him to stick around.

It seemed to Aidan that the kid always paid the price for his parents' mistakes. You paid for it with loneliness and the sense that there was something you could have said or done that might have made a difference. If only you had brushed your teeth before bed, put your toys away, done your homework without being asked ten times, maybe then you would have a family.

He had the feeling Maddy knew that, too.

He busied himself with his pancakes while she finished up her blueberry muffin and flagged Julie down for more coffee for Maddy.

"You?" Julie asked, the coffeepot hovering over his mug.

He shook his head. "I'm at my limit."

"Wimp," Julie muttered as she walked away.

Maddy checked her watch. She didn't make a show of it, but he took note. It was pushing nine. He had to start two pots of steak soup, a mega meatloaf, and a dozen shepherd's pies. And then whip up a vat of Irish stew and mac and cheese for the guys at the firehouse. She probably had even more to do.

He reached for the manila envelope next to his empty coffee mug.

MADDY WANTED TO crawl under the table and stay there for the rest of the morning. Checking her watch was a nervous habit she had developed as a kid. She hadn't even realized she'd done it until she saw his eyes zero in on her wrist and she sensed a change in the atmosphere between them. He probably thought she was counting the minutes until breakfast was over when nothing could be further from the truth.

"So let's see the magic lamp," he said, sliding the photocopy of the newspaper clipping across the table to her.

She took a sip of coffee, then wiped her mouth with the edge of her paper napkin. "Good idea," she said, then reached down into the Macy's shopping bag and pulled out the samovar. She placed it on the table between them, then pulled off the tissue-paper covering. "So what do you think?"

At first he didn't say anything. His eyes narrowed slightly and he reached out with his right forefinger to trace the curve of the handle. She tried to keep her expression impassive, but it was impossible.

"What do you think?" she asked again, unable to mask her excitement.

He met her eyes. "You see it, too?"

"I couldn't believe it when your scan arrived. I thought it was some kind of joke."

"No joke," he said. "It's a flat-out dead ringer for the one in the picture."

"I think so, too." She willed herself to stay cool. "Do you think it could be the same one your grandmother had in her restaurant?"

"Hard to imagine two of them showing up in Paradise Point, isn't it?"

"I can't sell it to you," Maddy said, "if that's what this is all about. I told you that from the start."

"Who asked you to sell it?" He looked annoyed, which annoyed her. What right did he have to get testy about *her* samovar? "I just want to know if it's the same one my grandmother had back in 1952."

"You think the hurricane swept the samovar out to sea in 1952, then a magic wave swept it back into shore more than fifty years later?"

"Yeah," he said. "That's exactly what I'm thinking."

She couldn't help it. She burst out laughing. "I think you're nuts."

"Right," he said, his annoyance fading into a half-smile. "And you're the one who thinks it's a magic lamp."

"If I thought it was a magic lamp, do you think I'd be sitting here at a diner in New Jersey in *December*? I'd be in Hawaii and I'd have much better legs."

He pretended to peer under the table. "Nothing wrong with your legs."

"I'm wearing pants," she said, laughing again. "You can't even see my legs."

"We could—" He stopped dead. "Sorry," he said with a rueful grin. "Force of habit."

"You asked me a few personal questions before," Maddy said. "Now it's my turn."

"You can ask," he said, "but I'm not guaranteeing I'll answer."

"Fair enough." She leaned back in her bench seat and looked him straight in the eye. "Was it serious between you and Gina?"

"You know about Gina and me?"

"I don't know anything," she said. "That's why I'm asking."

"We went out a few times about six or seven years ago. She was looking to get married. I was looking not to get married. No surprise when it didn't work out."

"That's it?"

"That's all I know about." He frowned. "Why? What did she say?"

"She didn't say anything. Somebody mentioned something at the bus stop this morning, and I wondered if you two were still seeing each other."

"Gina's married."

"Listen," Maddy said, "I love her like a sister, but I'm not blind to her faults."

"I took Denise out a few times, too," he said.

Maddy struggled to keep her jaw from bouncing off the tabletop. "Denise was never single for more than four weeks between husbands."

"I never said it was a long-term relationship."

"Who else did you see?"

He named three of her cousins and at least a dozen of her old classmates.

"You're kidding."

"Nope."

"You slept with all of them?" The question was out there before she had a chance to censor herself.

"No," he said, looking a little annoyed. "Not a smart thing to do these days."

"Maybe it never was a smart thing to do." Another rapid-fire response before she had the chance to get her brain in gear.

"No argument there."

"Gina?"

He didn't answer.

"Denise?"

He still didn't answer.

"Pat?"

Silence.

"You're not going to tell me, are you?"

"Nope."

"That's not fair."

"It is to them."

If she had liked him a little before, she liked him a whole lot more now.

"How do you find time for a social life?" she asked him. "Since Hannah, I have trouble finding time to wash my hair."

"My family," he said, as if that explained it all. "They figured watching Kelly was a small price to pay to find a new mother for her. They kicked my ass back out there before I knew what hit me."

"And now that your daughter's almost grown and you don't have to worry about who's watching her anymore—"

"I don't go out anymore."

"At all?"

"At all."

"You probably dated everyone in Paradise Point."

"Damn close. It gets old pretty fast."

She hoped the look she shot him reflected her deep skepticism. "I met Tom on the first day of my first job after I graduated." She reached for her coffee and took a sip. "And that concludes the Dating History segment of my program."

"Nobody since?"

"Nope." She took another sip. "And not many before, either. I didn't inherit the mantrap genes that run rampant through the rest of my family."

"That could be a good thing."

"Are you being sarcastic?"

"No. I loved my wife," he said. "If she'd lived, I'd be telling you a very different story."

"I loved Tom." How easy it was to say the words. How amazing that they didn't have the power to hurt her any longer. "I was a good partner and I think I would have been a good wife, even if the DiFalco women are better at getting married than they are at staying married."

"Don't go grabbing for all the glory, Bainbridge. The

O'Malleys could give you a run for your money in the dysfunctional family sweepstakes."

She wanted to press for details, but Julie swept down on them again, waving a check.

"I almost forgot about you two." She dropped it next to Aidan's plate. "You can pay Terry up front. I'm going on break."

"Do you think that was a hint?" Maddy asked as Julie disappeared into the kitchen.

"Could be."

Maddy reached for the samovar.

"Wait," he said. "Can I take one more look at it?"

She pushed it toward him. He lifted it up, then flipped it over to inspect the base.

"Initials," he said, peering closely at some writing scratched into the metal. "Can you tell what they are?"

Maddy took the samovar from him and looked. "K.R.?" She looked again. "Or maybe it's E.S."

"You wouldn't happen to have a magnifying glass in that suitcase of yours, would you?"

"Everything but," she said with a nod toward the seventy-five-pound tote bag she carried around.

She began to rewrap the samovar in tissue paper, carefully tucking it around the spout and handle.

"No chance I could convince you to sell it."

She laughed. "Not a chance in the world."

"Your kid's going to love it."

"That's the plan."

"What if she doesn't?"

"Can't happen."

"You know kids. They love something Christmas morning, but by New Year's they've forgotten it existed."

"I'll make a deal," Maddy said. "If Hannah doesn't like it, you can have it for what I paid for it."

"Add another fifty and it's a deal."

"Nope. What I paid for it or nothing."

"You drive a hard bargain," he said, extending his right hand. "Shake on it?"

Big mistake.

Enormous mistake.

Beware human contact when you're feeling lonely and vulnerable and you've already shared more secrets than you knew you had. Beware the warmth of skin against skin when it's been so long you can't even remember being touched by a man. Beware the Christmas season when even the hardest of hearts cracks open just wide enough to let a miracle or two slip in.

But most of all beware a man who knows how to keep his own counsel. There was nothing more dangerous than a big gorgeous man who was straight, single, loved his kid, and who didn't kiss and tell.

A woman just might do anything with a man like that.

Chapter Fifteen

THERE WAS NOTHING a DiFalco liked better than juicy gossip about another DiFalco. Five minutes after Maddy and Aidan stepped through the door of Julie's for that cup of coffee, Rose's phone started ringing off the hook.

"You won't believe what Maddy's doing. I was on my way home from Mass and I saw her—" That was her sister Toni, the one who somehow didn't recognize her own daughter when she saw her tumbling out of the Rusty Schooner with a sailor on each arm.

"Am I always going to be the last to know?" Her sister Connie claimed her status as youngest of the sisters relegated her to the bottom of the food chain when it came to family news. "I don't like it." Connie never liked much of anything if it didn't reflect back on herself and her own multi-married daughters. "Maddy should be worrying about Hannah, not playing footsie in public with Aidan O'Malley."

"Footsie?" Rose hung up the receiver and turned to Lucy, who was kneading dough for homemade onion rye. "What century is this?"

"I think Connie needs therapy." Lucy gave the elastic dough an extra-hard push with the heels of her hands. "Somebody should tell her to spend a little more time trying to straighten out Gina's and Denise's lives and a little less poking her nose into Maddy's."

"Well said." Rose pointed toward the wall phone. "I'll dial if you'll talk."

"Do I look crazy?"

The sisters burst into laughter at the thought of confronting the slightly manic Connie.

"So what do you think is going on with Maddy and Aidan?" Lucy asked as she divided the ball of dough into two pieces, then covered each with a lightly floured tea towel.

"Nothing." Rose soaped her hands at the sink, rinsed them, then soaped them again. "As far as I know, she was going to show him the samovar and that was that."

They worked in silence for a few minutes.

"I've always liked Aidan O'Malley," Lucy said as she began to mix corn-bread batter.

"He's certainly had his share of bad luck," Rose said. She was topping and tailing string beans for her guests' farewell dinner.

"He's done a wonderful job with Kelly."

"Did I tell you she's going to be helping us out around here?"

"You hired her!" Lucy sounded positively delighted. "I was hoping you would."

"She'll be a godsend when we open back up in February." They were growing more quickly than even Rose had anticipated. Kelly O'Malley would be helping out in the dining room and wherever else she might be needed.

"Such a lovely girl," Lucy said. "And such beautiful manners."

"There's no doubt Aidan did a wonderful job with her."

"Oh, go ahead," Lucy said with a chuckle. "You know you have one of those huge maternal sighs just dying to bust loose. It's just me. I won't tell."

"You know me too well." The sigh wasn't half as im-

pressive as it might have been, but there was no denying
the fact that she felt better with it out of her system. "I
wish I'd done as well with Maddy."

Lucy concentrated on her corn-bread batter.

"You're not going to tell me I did just fine?" Rose
asked.

"Nope." Lucy added a touch more corn meal to the
mix. "You did the best you could at the time, but we both
know it wasn't all that Maddy needed."

"Spoken like a woman without children."

"You asked."

"I did, didn't I," Rose said, yanking the top off a bean
and tossing it into the growing pile. "Remind me not to
do that again."

Lucy poured the batter into a prepared pan, then wiped
her hands on her apron. "And what about the time you
went shopping with me for a dress for one of Gina's weddings? Remember what you said to me when I asked how
I looked in that blue suit?" Lucy didn't wait for Rose to
respond. "You said I looked like Aunt Frankie."

"Aunt Frankie was a good-looking woman."

"Aunt Frankie's butt was the size of a Chrysler."

"Lucia." Tears were alien to Rose, but suddenly she
felt like crying. "I'm sorry if I hurt your feelings. I wanted
you to look your most gorgeous for the wedding, and you
seemed so intent upon that suit."

"I know," Lucy said. "I'm just pointing out that we
both can be a bit blunt."

"Point taken."

Lucy slid the corn bread into the oven and set the timer.
"So do you think something might develop between
Maddy and Aidan?"

"Not likely," Rose said. "When it comes to being unlucky in love, the O'Malleys are the only family in town
that can hold a candle to us. I think it'll be a cup of coffee,
a few comments about the samovar, then they'll go their
separate ways."

"Maybe," Lucy said as she reached for a pile of string
beans. "But then again maybe not."

*   *   *

"SNOW!" MADDY EXCLAIMED as they stepped out of the fragrant warmth of Julie's coffee shop. "I thought the storm was expected tonight."

"Welcome back to the Jersey Shore," Aidan said. "If you don't like the weather now, wait ten minutes."

"I hope we have a blizzard," she said, tilting her face up so the icy flakes melted on her warm cheek.

"I hope you have four-wheel drive."

"Men are so literal."

He glanced around. "Where's your car?"

"Back at the Candlelight. I walk Hannah to the bus stop most days."

"Why don't I drive you back?"

She shook her head. "That's okay. I love walking in the snow."

"Then why don't I walk back with you?"

She blinked in surprise. "Because it's snowing," she said. "And it's out of your way."

"I like the snow."

"So do I."

He took the shopping bag from her, and they started toward the Candlelight. The sidewalk was glazed with a mix of snow and ice, and after a half block she wished she had accepted the ride. His gait was syncopated. He favored his right leg, and she walked a little slower than she normally would have in order to keep pace. She wished he had his cane with him. Not only were the sidewalks icy, they were also devilishly uneven. If she started to fall, she would be sure to fall away from him because the last thing on earth he needed was another broken bone.

And if he started to fall—oh, God, she didn't want to think about it. He outweighed her by maybe seventy pounds. The chances of being able to stop his fall were less than zero.

She reached for the shopping bag. "I'll carry it."

He pulled away. "I promise I'm not going to take off with it."

"There's no reason why you should lug my stuff around."

"I asked you to bring it."

"So?"

"Help me out here. I'm being polite."

"I'm impressed. Now give me the bag." *I don't want to be responsible for you ending up on crutches.*

She made a lunge for the bag and just as her fingers were about to close over the handle, her feet slid out from under her and she started to fall. Why was it that the most embarrassing events of her life always seemed to happen in slow motion? Her fifth birthday when she threw up on the Carvel cake. The senior prom when her strapless dress lost its will to live. Why did humiliation take so long? A piece of chocolate was gone in the blink of an eye, but falling? Good grief, it was taking forever. She was bent in the middle like a boomerang. Feet pointing toward the sky, arms flailing, butt answering the call of gravity, the whole thing taking longer than *The English Patient*—

"Gotcha!"

A pair of strong hands grabbed her by the jacket and caught her just before she hit the concrete. Her booted feet hit the ground hard and she felt shockwaves right up to her molars, but she didn't fall. Aidan O'Malley had seen to that.

"You okay?" His eyes were beautiful, a clear shade of blue rimmed with navy and framed by thick lashes. Kind eyes. Beyond their beauty, beyond the fences he'd erected around himself, there was nothing but kindness.

"Fine," she said. "Humiliated, but fine."

"You slipped. No big deal about that."

"I was a jerk," she said. "I should've taken no for an answer."

"It's your bag," he said. "I shouldn't have pulled the macho crap on you."

"Okay," she said, "you convinced me. You're a jerk, too."

Concern turned to surprise and then slid right into that grin she was becoming way too fond of. "You want the bag?" he asked. It was on the ground next to his feet.

"Not on your life," she said.

"I'll take that as a no."

She kept her eyes fastened on the sidewalk, which was quickly vanishing beneath the onslaught. "If you don't mind, I'd like you to carry the bag."

She could sense his smile, but she didn't look up to verify it.

"Hold on to my arm," he said.

"No, thanks." That would be all they needed. She'd slip and take them both down.

"Don't be so goddamn stubborn. Hold on to my arm or would you rather break a leg?"

"I'd rather break a leg," she muttered.

His bark of laughter stopped her in her tracks.

"I'm not trying to be funny."

"I know," he said. "That's the beauty part."

"Listen," she said, growing exasperated, "I didn't want to spell it out for you, but you're not giving me any choice. You're still recovering from your injuries. You go to physical therapy a few times a week. I really don't want to be the one who puts you back in traction."

NOBODY BUT NINA, his physical therapist, had ever spoken to him that way before, with the same mixture of blunt truthfulness and exasperation. Everyone else tiptoed around the truth, around his limp, his limitations, his scars, as if not speaking about them would make them go away.

Now here was a woman who saw him as he was and wasn't afraid to deal with it.

He wasn't sure if he liked it, hated it, or wanted to pull her into his arms and kiss her hard, right there on Main Street with the snow swirling around them and her shopping bag on the ground next to their feet.

He settled for walking her home.

"IT'S ME, AUNT Rose. Is she back yet?"

Rose rolled her eyes until they almost fell out the back

of her head. "Denise, don't you have a job? This is the fourth time you've called in the last hour."

"I know but—"

"When Maddy gets home, I'll tell her to call you. Unless you want me to send out a search party, that's the best I can do."

"You don't have to get huffy with me, Aunt Rose. I'm concerned, that's all."

"You've been talking to your mother, haven't you? There's nothing to be concerned about. Maddy and Aidan are inspecting a teapot Maddy bought at an on-line auction. That's all."

"You weren't there. You didn't see the way they were looking at each other."

"Goodbye, Denise." She hung up the phone.

Two seconds later it rang again.

"Denise, this is ridiculous. If you don't stop—"

"This is Jim Kennedy at WNJI, the Shore's Hottest Station. I'm trying to reach Madelyn Bainbridge. If it's a bad time, I'll—"

"No! No!" Rose struggled to recover her professional demeanor. "I thought you were one of my nieces."

"Is this Ms. Bainbridge?" His voice was low and mellow, like melted chocolates. A perfect radio voice.

"This is Rose DiFalco. I'm her mother." Her heart was pounding so fast she had to lean against the side of the counter for support.

"Rose DiFalco who owns the Candlelight?"

"The same."

"I got your letter, Ms. DiFalco, and I have a proposition for you and your daughter that I think you're going to like . . ."

"OH, NO." MADDY groaned as they neared the Candlelight. "Please don't tell me she's sweeping the porch in a snowstorm."

Aidan shielded his eyes and peered into the swirling snow. "Your mother?"

"Who else. I swear she can hear a leaf hit the ground from a hundred yards away."

"Don't knock it," he said. "She must be doing something right. The Candlelight is the most successful B&B in all of South Jersey."

Rose stood on the top step in her heavy dark green storm coat and waved excitedly as Maddy and Aidan approached. Priscilla, looking impossibly tiny and cute, barked wildly at her feet. Maddy had to stifle the urge to turn around and see who was behind her.

"Do you always get that kind of welcome?" Aidan asked.

"Not since I was three years old." Had Rose finally inhaled too much furniture polish and gone around the bend?

Rose favored them with a wide smile, the kind that not only showed all of her very white teeth, but actually reached her eyes as well.

Maddy's heart started a slow, but cautious, melt.

"Good to see you, Aidan," Rose said. "I missed you at last month's meeting."

It was clear that wasn't the greeting Aidan had expected.

"I—uh—Tommy couldn't watch the bar and Claire was visiting her mother so I—"

"You don't have to explain," Maddy snapped as the melt reversed itself.

Rose's cheeks reddened just enough for Maddy to notice.

"Of course you don't," Rose said to Aidan, her manner easy and cordial. "I meant what I said. I missed your input at the meeting."

Aidan's eyes lost the guarded quality they had assumed moments ago. "Those meetings can get a little rowdy."

"They can," Rose agreed, "but sometimes that's the only way you can get things done."

Rose turned to Maddy, who was struggling to absorb the byplay between her mother and Aidan. "Maddy, there was a phone call for you. I left the message on the kitchen table. You might want to see to it now."

"Hannah's okay?" She couldn't keep the note of apprehension from her voice.

"Hannah's fine." Rose patted her arm. "I'm sorry. I should have said that up front."

"Dad? Tom?"

"I'm sure they're both fine. Go inside," Rose urged. "I said you would be back any minute. He's waiting for your call."

"I'd better shove off," Aidan said, looking uncomfortable. He handed the shopping bag with the samovar in it to Maddy. "Great breakfast."

Maddy beamed at him. "It was. Next one's on me."

Oh, damn. There she went again, spilling words all over the place without thinking first. The only reason they had had coffee together was so she could show him the samovar. When she found a Japanese tea service, maybe then she would give him a call.

"Sounds good."

"Really?"

"Yeah," he said. "Julie's pancakes are the best in three states."

So much for romance.

Rose watched them with a combination of interest and impatience.

"Maddy," she said in a mild tone of voice. "The phone call—?"

Maddy nodded in her mother's direction, but her attention was on Aidan. "Why don't you wait a minute," she said to him, "and I'll drive you back to your car." The sidewalk was treacherously slippery, and the thought of him taking a header with no one around to help him didn't sit well with her. Not at all.

Rose looked like she was about to say something but wisely kept her own counsel.

"I'd better get moving," he said. "Tommy's probably there setting up, and I need to—"

"Maddy's right," Rose said to her daughter's profound

shock. "Why don't you come in and have some coffee while Maddy makes her phone call. The sidewalk crews should be out any minute."

It was clear Aidan was torn between wanting to get to O'Malley's and wanting to stay there at the Candlelight. He locked eyes with Maddy, then they both quickly looked away.

"Guess I could call Tommy and let him know I'm delayed."

"Good idea," Rose said, then turned to Maddy.

"Okay, okay." Maddy threw her hands up in defeat. "I'll make the phone call." She looked at Aidan. "Promise you won't leave."

"I won't let him," Rose said.

Welcome to the Twilight Zone.

Chapter Sixteen

"YOU NEED SOMETHING, Irene?"

The nurse hovered over the bed like a bird of prey. These days Irene's imagery tended toward the vivid and frightening.

Irene cleared her throat. So dry . . . like parchment paper. Her hair, her skin, even her eyelids. So dry and thin that light passed through them like sun through an open window. The years take their toll. They demand their price.

"A picture," Irene managed, wishing she could reach the tumbler of water on her nightstand. "The one my—" What was she? A granddaughter? Great-granddaughter? And what was her name? "I think it's on the wheelchair seat in the corner."

The nurse rooted around here and there, then sighed. "I don't see anything."

"The wheelchair," Irene said. Once upon a time people had jumped at her commands. "In the corner."

"Honey, there is no wheelchair in the corner." The nurse leaned closer so Irene could see her face. "Jimmy took it for Mrs. Weber. Don't you remember?"

She didn't. She wasn't sure who Jimmy and Mrs. Weber were.

"I need that picture," she said in her most imperious voice. "You must find it."

The nurse patted her forearm with cool smooth fingers. "I'll do my best, Irene." She straightened the covers, brushed a strand of hair from Irene's forehead, then turned to leave.

"Water," Irene said. "I need some water."

"Right there on your nightstand, honey."

Irene wanted to cry with frustration. Of course it was right there. She *knew* that. Didn't they understand she couldn't reach through the metal rails on the bed in order to reach the glass? They set up situations where it was impossible for you to help yourself, and then they huffed and puffed when you called for assistance.

"Useless," Irene muttered. "Every single last one of them."

Her time was running out. Each morning when she awoke it was with the sense that her sunrises were limited. Thousands and thousands of sunrises had slipped by unnoticed, and now she wanted to slow down the spinning earth just long enough for her to set her private world to rights. She was a useless, pointless old woman whose life rolled on and on, sapping up time and space and money, while younger people died far too early. Her son. His wife. A granddaughter-in-law. A grandson. An endless chain of sorrow with roots buried deep inside her wicked heart.

Seeing those photos again had made up her mind. The Almighty was clearly sending her a message, and if age begat wisdom, then she was at long last wise enough to know this was a job only she could do, and it must be done now while she still had a few sunrises left.

She needed to see the photo again. She needed to see Michael's face, see the old O'Malley, touch that golden moment that had been hers for the blink of an eye. That nurse was wrong. The picture was there. She knew it was. She could see it in front of her, as clear as a bell. That

Jimmy person probably tucked it under an extra blanket on the chest of drawers or maybe put it on the top shelf of the closet for safekeeping. Yes, that's what any intelligent person would do. Put it away for safekeeping.

She fumbled beneath her pillow for the proper button. No, no. Not the buzzer. The button that released the railing. Some things never changed. If you wanted something done, you had to do it yourself. . . .

AIDAN HADN'T BEEN inside the Candlelight since Rose's July Fourth Open House Clambake three years ago. The place had looked good then, but that was nothing compared to the way it looked now.

"You did a hell of a job," he said, shaking his head in amazement. "No wonder you're booked a year in advance."

Rose nodded in thanks. "It took a long time to get it to this point, but it was worth it."

He ran his hand along a satiny expanse of wood that served as a hall table and whistled. "Antique?"

Rose laughed. "Yard sale up in Bricktown."

She led him through the parlor, down a long hallway, to the kitchen in the rear of the house.

"Coffee?" she asked.

"If it's no trouble."

"One thing we always have is coffee." She poured the fragrant brew into a pure white cup. She placed the cup on a saucer and handed it to him. "Take a seat at the table. The cream and sugar are both there."

She poured herself a cup, then sat down opposite him.

Suddenly he felt twelve years old and about to be grounded.

He leaned forward and reached for the cream. Maddy's supple voice floated toward them from somewhere nearby. He couldn't make out her words, but she sounded very happy.

"So," said Rose, fixing him with the type of look she usually reserved for the last half hour of the Small Business Owners Association meetings, "how are things at O'Malley's?"

"We've been better," he said. No point dodging the truth. There were few business secrets in Paradise Point.

"Still having trouble with your septic system?"

"No," he said. "I called the plumber you recommended. Saved me a bundle. Thanks for putting me on to him."

"That's the whole point of the Association," she said, still looking at him with those knowing eyes. "If we share our resources, everyone benefits."

"You really believe that?"

"For the most part, yes."

The coffee was so good it could be a sacrament.

"Kona blend," Rose said, reading his mind. "Incredible, isn't it?"

They looked at each other, coffee cups drawn and ready.

"So what is it, Rose?" he asked. "You don't have to entertain me while I wait for Maddy to finish up." *I won't break any windows.*

For a moment he thought he saw her queen-of-the-world demeanor slip. She looked softer, younger, more like her daughter, and then he blinked and the resemblance was gone.

"I was going to phone you about this, but since you're here—"

"If it's about the resolution to add streetlamps near the proposed park site, I—"

"It's about Kelly."

She had his attention.

"Since she is just seventeen, I feel she should have your permission."

"Permission?" He polished off the rest of his coffee. "For what?"

"To work here."

The kitchen fell into one of those uncomfortable silences.

"I take it she hasn't told you yet."

"This is the first I've heard of it."

Rose smoothed the sleeves of her soft gray sweater and adjusted the clasp on her smooth gold bracelet. "I ran a help wanted ad in the *Paradise Point Shopper*. Kelly came in Saturday to apply for the job and, to be honest, nobody else came close." Her smile was warm and genuine. "She's a wonderful girl, Aidan. You must be very proud."

"She works hard enough," he said. "I don't think she can handle another job."

"I asked her about her other commitments," Rose said, "and she seemed positive she could handle it."

"What exactly is her job?"

"Mainly table service," Rose said. "Friday and Saturday evenings beginning in February."

"Anything else?"

"Nothing defined," Rose said with surprising candor, "but there might be some light housekeeping duties depending on how many guests I have and what my staffing needs are at the moment."

"And Kelly thinks she can handle this?"

"She seemed quite sure."

He nodded.

"You're comfortable with the arrangement?" Rose probed.

"No," he said honestly, "but if she is, I'll back her up. So far my kid hasn't steered me wrong."

Rose smiled and he saw traces of Maddy in the way her eyes crinkled at the outer corners. "I'm sure I'm not telling you something you don't already know, Aidan, but Kelly is a very special young woman. She's going to go far."

"Billy used to say she was a changeling," Aidan said, smiling at the memory. "We couldn't figure how an ambitious O'Malley managed to sneak into our slacker family."

"I think her parenting had a lot to do with it."

"Don't get me wrong. I'd like to take credit for the way she turned out, but sometimes I think she raised me."

There was a sadness in Rose's expression. She didn't

explain—and he certainly didn't ask—but it was there and it didn't go away, and for a minute he actually liked her.

JIM KENNEDY HAD one of those voices that great radio was built on. If he had been born thirty years earlier, he could have ruled the airwaves, but Jim had had the misfortune of being born right in the middle of the television generation, a time when movie-star good looks were more important than genuine talent.

He had been with WNJI for six years, slowly building a Jersey Shore audience that might not be the biggest on the East Coast but was definitely among the most loyal. Maddy hadn't expected to hear his entire curriculum vitae, but once Jim started he was hard to stop. Clearly his fans weren't the only ones who enjoyed the sound of his voice.

"So Friday it is," Maddy finally interrupted as she glanced at her watch. Poor Aidan. She really had to get moving. "I'll be at the station by one-thirty for the sound check."

"Make it one-fifteen," Jim said, neatly changing gears. "If news is light, we'll start the interview early."

"I'm looking forward to it."

"No more than I am," he said. "You're going to be great. You'll need to build on more rooms to catch the overflow."

What was a little hyperbole between friends? He meant well, that was the main thing. And free radio publicity certainly couldn't hurt. But how had it ended up with Maddy giving the interview instead of her mother? Rose was the one who brought the Candlelight to life. She had chosen every curtain, every drape, every roll of wallpaper, every can of paint, the furniture, the dishes, the menu— every last detail had Rose's stamp all over it. From top to bottom, the Candlelight was her creation, and certainly she was the one who should be basking in the limelight.

Maddy hung up the phone and took a second to smooth down her hair by her reflection in the computer monitor. She frowned at the halo of frizz and curls clearly visible.

Maybe a blow-dryer . . . or a whip and a chair. No matter. Unlike the Candlelight, this was as good as it got.

Her footsteps sounded loud as she ran down the hallway. She stopped for a second to glance into the mirror, then quickly looked away. A buzz cut. There was no other cure for the last thirty-two years of bad hair days.

She was about to dash into the kitchen when she remembered the samovar. Good grief, where had she put the bag? The foyer? The kitchen? Oh, wait! She'd carried it with her to the office and tucked it under the desk. Now all she had to do was remember to slip it back into its hiding place in Rose's closet before Hannah came home from school.

She pushed open the kitchen door and stopped dead in her tracks. It looked like a scene from *The Waltons*. Soup simmering on the stove. The smell of bread baking wafting through the air. A fire crackling away in the small stone fireplace near the table where Aidan and Rose sat together, thumbing through an old copy of *This Old House*. All the picture needed was a shawl for Rose and a pipe for Aidan, and it could have been entitled "Domestic Tranquillity." And to make the scene even cozier, there was Lucy, a new arrival, shaking snow from her boots in the mudroom near the back door. Priscilla—didn't every lovely scene of domestic tranquillity have a puppy?—sniffed at the snow, sneezed, and backed away as quickly as her tiny legs could carry her.

"I don't know how you did it, Ma," Maddy announced, "but I'm going to be on *Weekdays with Kennedy* this Friday afternoon. A one-hour interview about the Candlelight."

Rose leaped to her feet, pure joy radiating from every pore of her body. "I'm so happy!" she cried, then wrapped her arms around her daughter. "How wonderful!"

Maddy stiffened. She didn't mean to do it. She didn't want to do it. But she did it just the same. Rose quickly ended her embrace and stepped back, still smiling.

"You're going to be wonderful," Rose said.

"Tell me the time and I'll make sure I catch the show,"

Aidan said, beaming at her. "He gets pretty good numbers for the station. You'll be famous."

"Why would he ask for me?" Maddy asked her mother. "I mean, how would he even know I exist?" She paused. "Unless—"

"I wrote him a note," Rose said, lifting her chin. "I told him about the Candlelight, a little bit about us, and suggested he consider us for an interview for his 'Down the Shore' segment."

"Then you should be the one he speaks with."

"No, Maddy. I've been front and center for four years now. I'd like to concentrate on taking the Candlelight to the next level and let someone else handle promotion."

"Someone like me?" Maddy asked.

"If you're going to be part of the team, I'm going to need you to take over different aspects of running the place." She stood up and reflexively smoothed the front of her perfectly tailored trousers. "You and I can discuss this later, Maddy. Right now I need to help Lucy with the soup and you need to take Aidan back to his car."

"Fine," Maddy said, face flaming like an embarrassed teenager. "Whatever." She grabbed her jacket from the hook near the door and met Aidan's eyes. "I'll start the car."

THE DOOR SLAMMED behind Maddy and the kitchen fell silent.

Lucy DiFalco busied herself with the dog's water dish while Rose regained her composure.

Time to go.

"Thanks for the coffee," he said to Rose.

She smiled. "And thanks for letting Kelly take the job."

"She's been pretty much calling her own shots since she was ten years old," he said, "and she hasn't been wrong yet. I'll trust her judgment."

"You're a lucky man," Rose said softly. "Very lucky."

He said goodbye to Lucy, kept his feet out from under Priscilla, then almost slid down the back steps in his haste to get out of there.

And here he'd thought the O'Malley clan had the market cornered on tension and subtext. The DiFalcos made them look like amateurs. The tension between Maddy and Rose was so real he almost asked it to pull up a chair and sit down.

Maddy was parked off to the side, near the garage. Her Mustang idled roughly, kicking out puffs of dark smoke that would probably cause her to flunk her state inspection. She was drumming the steering wheel with the heels of her hands, and, judging by her profile, her mood hadn't improved.

"I was going to send in a search party," she said as he settled into the passenger seat and closed the door. "I thought they might be holding you for ransom."

"You embarrassed her," he said. He had meant to say, *If you need a good mechanic while you're here, I have a few names.* Clearly it would have been the wiser choice.

Maddy swiveled in her seat and stared him in the eyes. "What did you say?"

Was it too late to pretend he didn't speak English?

"I said, you embarrassed her."

"You couldn't embarrass her if you caught her in bed with Martha Stewart and Jackie Chan."

He didn't want to laugh, but that didn't stop him. "She didn't want to discuss family issues in front of a stranger."

Maddy made a face. "If she knew you were on her side, she would have."

"I'm not on anyone's side."

"Tell me about it."

"You were pretty rough on her."

Maddy looked away. "It was a lot easier when we had the entire continent between us."

"She's probably thinking the same thing right about now."

"Listen," she said as she started to inch the car down the icy driveway, "blood may be thicker than water, but it doesn't mean every family is going to live happily ever after. Not even fairy tales can manage to pull that one off every time."

He raised his hands in surrender. "Listen," he said, "forget I said anything. I don't know jack about what's going on between you and Rose. I should've kept my big mouth shut."

"Yes, you should have," Maddy said. "But I'm glad you didn't."

"Is that a shot?"

"No," Maddy said. "I mean it. I'm surrounded by family and every single one of them has her own agenda going. I needed a non-DiFalco perspective."

She eased out onto the street, keeping the Mustang in first until she had gained enough traction, then shifting smoothly up to second. She knew how to handle a clutch. He liked that in a woman.

"You might find this surprising, but I'm not usually your mother's greatest supporter."

"Could've fooled me. You two seemed to be forming a mutual-admiration society in there."

"We're usually on opposite sides of every issue in town."

They rolled to a stop at the corner and slipped a few inches into the intersection.

"Join the club. We've been on opposite sides since the day I was born."

"She loves you."

"She told you that?"

"She didn't have to. Anyone could see it."

Tears, ridiculous, inappropriate tears, welled up, and she turned her head. "I always said men were the true romantics."

Icy pellets pinged off the windshield and bounced across the hood of her aged Mustang. Main Street was a sheet of ice overlaid with enough fresh snow to make driving treacherous.

"Pull over," he said after they'd gone another fifty feet.

"What's wrong?"

"You don't need to be out in this. I'll walk."

"No."

"Pull over."

"The hell I will. I said I'd drive you back to your car, and that's what I'm going to do."

"It's too dangerous."

She ignored him and kept her attention focused on the road ahead.

"You know, there's a lot of your mother in you," he said when she slid to a stop a few feet away from where he'd left his car parked.

She looked at him as she applied the parking brake. "Which is it? Stubborn? Pigheaded? Won't take suggestions from anybody?"

"Gutsy," he said. "Independent." *And bright and funny and beautiful . . .*

Her breath caught for a split second, then released. "I try," she said, then grinned at him. "Thanks."

"Don't mention it."

She smelled faintly of perfume and shampoo, womanly smells that made him lean closer. Snow was quickly piling up on the windows as they idled there at the curb, shielding them in a world of their own. It was a heady combination: the storm outside; the warmth inside. If it had been any other woman but Maddy, he would have leaned across the console and kissed her goodbye and not thought twice about it. The moment demanded its due and he would have been happy to oblige. Instead he had to remind himself this wasn't a date. He was interested in her samovar. She was interested in his interest.

That was as far as it went, as far as he had any intention of letting it go. Probably further than she wanted it to go.

Looking for a losing combination? Try O'Malley and DiFalco. A train wreck would have a better chance at a happy ending.

"If I sit here any longer, you'll need a tow truck to get back to the Candlelight," he said, unsnapping his seat belt and reaching for the door handle. "Thanks for the lift."

"No problem. Thanks for the breakfast."

"Remember what I said about the teapot? If your kid doesn't want it, I do."

"I won't forget."

She leaned over to pick up her glove, and for an instant he considered bridging the distance between them and kissing her goodbye, but she was too quick or maybe he was too slow, and the moment, like all moments, vanished forever.

Chapter Seventeen

MADDY SAT PERFECTLY still while he trudged through the snow and ice to his car. She watched while he knocked snow off the windows with his hand and forearm, unlocked the door, then climbed into the truck. It took maybe two minutes tops, and in that span of time she relived the kiss-that-wasn't at least fifty times.

He had wanted to kiss her. She was as sure of that as she had ever been of anything in her life. When she leaned over to get the glove that had fallen off the dashboard, something had happened. Their eyes locked and he leaned closer and she held her breath and you could almost hear those great tectonic plates of destiny getting ready to slam together and set off an earthquake of monumental proportions.

Or something like that.

She held her breath. His eyes drifted to her mouth. Her mouth parted. His pupils dilated.

And then he said, "See you," and opened the door.

Nothing like a slap of wind and snow to bring a girl back down to earth. The inside of the Mustang still hummed with disappointment.

His parking lights switched on and the rear windshield wiper started slapping left then right, left then right, cutting through the relentless snow. He shimmied back a few inches, cut the wheel, then pulled forward and out. With a quick double-beep of his horn he disappeared into the storm.

A metaphor for her life if ever there was one.

She released the parking brake, shifted into first, and headed back to the Candlelight, where romance had its price, but satisfaction was guaranteed.

THE LOEWENSTEINS AND the Armaghs had planned to spend their last afternoon at Caesar's in Atlantic City, trying their hands at the slot machines. Rose had arranged for a limo, complete with bar and TV, to take the two couples up, but the second they saw the weather they begged off.

Mrs. Loewenstein was devastated by the turn of events. She had heard that Caesar and Cleo regularly paraded through the casino and posed for photos with day-trippers and high rollers, and she had had her heart set on pictures of herself in Caesar's arms.

"We coulda gone anyway," Mr. Loewenstein said. "So what if it's snowing. We'd be in a big safe car. What's gonna happen?"

"Half those limo drivers drive with their eyes closed," Mr. Armagh said. "They work around the clock, most of them. Asleep on their feet. Better you should stay put in weather like this."

"Amen to that," said Mrs. Armagh. "I broke my right hip last year in that big snowstorm. I'm not breaking my left hip for nobody."

Mrs. Loewenstein sighed deeply, then turned to Rose and Lucy, who were standing in the archway to the public living room.

"We have something wonderful planned for lunch," Rose said in her cheeriest innkeeper's voice. "Lucy and I are going to light a fire in both of the fireplaces for you. We have some of our fabulous special-blend hot cocoa in the carafes on the table to keep you warm." *Help!* she silently pleaded with her sister. *Magic tricks! Puppet shows! Anything!*

"There's a selection of great movies in the basket over there by the bookshelf," Lucy said with her usual display of grace under fire. "And we have CDs of your favorite music, a chessboard all set up for you, and if you'll look on the bottom bookshelf, you'll find an assortment of popular board games. Please help yourselves."

The two sisters barely made it into the kitchen before they collapsed in belly laughs that they muffled by pressing dishtowels to their faces.

Lucy sank into one of the chairs. "Twenty-four more hours," she said longingly. "Then you can say goodbye to innkeeping for six glorious weeks."

"I never thought I'd say this, but I need a break." Rose poured them each some hot chocolate and sat down next to her sister. "How on earth are we going to keep them occupied? Anything short of a Lucky Seven machine and a seafood buffet is going to be a disappointment."

"Tough toenails," Lucy said, making Rose laugh again. "That's why they stayed here instead of the Hilton, isn't it? They wanted to live in a real home, and that's what they got."

"I think Mr. Loewenstein will get huffy if I offer them tomato soup and grilled-cheese sandwiches for lunch," Rose said. "I wasn't planning on this."

"Oh, don't worry, Rosie." Lucy stood up and smoothed her skirt over her plump hips. "You have eggs. You have cream. You have Swiss cheese and Gruyère. I'll whip up a quiche in nothing flat if you'll make your famous salad with walnut dressing. If we add some of Maddy's home-made cookies for dessert, they should all be happy as fat little clams."

There was no time to debate the menu. They tied on their aprons and got to work.

IT TOOK MADDY fifteen minutes to drive four blocks. She had forgotten what winter in New Jersey was like and her snow-driving skills were sorely lacking. By the time she slid into position next to the Loewensteins' monster car, beads of sweat were trickling down her forehead and into her eyes. She had fought the good fight, but it looked as if she just might end up having to buy a vehicle with four-wheel drive.

She half-walked, half-slid her way to the back steps, then clung to the railing for support as she negotiated her way into the kitchen.

"Uh-oh," said Lucy, taking in Maddy's ice-encrusted hair and jacket. "How bad is it out there?"

"Gruesome," Maddy said, slipping out of her wet coat and hanging it in the mudroom to dry. "You could practice for the Olympic speed-skating team on Main Street."

Rose had her back to Maddy. She was painstakingly rinsing greens at one of the kitchen sinks, dipping them into a bowl of clear water, lifting them up, then dipping them back in again until every last grain of sand was washed away. Then she rinsed them under running water, popped them into her bright red salad spinner, and spun them until they were bone dry. At home Maddy usually gave her iceberg a quick pass under the faucet, then mopped it dry with a handful of paper towels. It was clear her technique needed some improvement.

"Mom," she said, approaching Rose. "I want to say something."

"Can it wait?" Rose didn't turn around to look at her. "The Loewensteins and the Armaghs canceled out on their day trip to Caesar's. We have to put together lunch for them."

Maddy reached for an apron and tied it around her waist. "Just point me in the right direction," she said to her mother.

Rose opened her mouth to say something, then closed it again.

Maddy looked at her. "That was quite a straight line I handed you just now, wasn't it?"

Rose tore dry lettuce leaves into bite-sized pieces, then

tossed them into the glass salad bowl. "I thought I showed admirable restraint."

"You did," Maddy said. She drew in a deep breath. "I wish I'd showed a little before."

Rose's right eyebrow arched just enough for a daughter to notice, but she said nothing.

"I'm sorry," Maddy said. She cleared her throat and drew in another, shakier gulp of air. "I overreacted. I don't know why and I'm not making excuses." She placed a tentative hand on her mother's delicate shoulder. "But I am sorry."

"Apology accepted." Rose neatly tore another stack of lettuce leaves into bite-sized pieces. "I need the tomatoes from the windowsill and some of that wonderful basil." She added the pieces to the bowl. "Can you chiffonade?"

"No, but if you hum a few bars . . ."

Rose sighed, but there was affection in the sound. "Always the wiseguy. Lucy, show your niece how to chiffonade. I think she's old enough."

"I don't know," Lucy said, feigning doubt. "I was forty before I even thought about attempting chiffonade."

"Very funny," Maddy said. "I watch the Food Network, too. I can learn."

"Come here," said Rose, pushing aside the lettuce. "Your aunt is busy. I'll show you."

ROSE'S DAUGHTER HAD many skills, but her knife work was not among them.

"No, no, honey," Rose said, placing her hand atop Maddy's. "You angle the tip like this and use it to pivot."

Maddy rolled her eyes. "Why does it look so easy when you do it?"

"Because I've been doing it for years. You need a little practice, that's all."

"I need a stunt double is what I need."

Rose laughed out loud. "You know, you're going to be wonderful with Jim Kennedy."

"You think?" She sounded doubtful.

"Do you really believe I would have suggested you if I didn't know you'd do yourself proud?"

"So when you said you suggested 'us' earlier, you weren't telling the whole truth."

"I didn't think I needed to, but your reaction was so—"

"Crazed?"

"I was going to say 'emotional.' " She smiled and to her blessed relief her daughter actually smiled back. "I'm not perfect by a long shot, but when it comes to what's best for my business, I won't take a backseat to anyone. That interview is going to be a turning point for the Candlelight. Just you wait and see."

And maybe, if we're very lucky, it might be a turning point for us as well.

"WHERE THE HELL have you been?" Claire demanded as soon as Aidan stepped into the yeasty warmth of O'Malley's. "And why the hell didn't you have your cell phone on?"

Damn.

He reached into his pocket and pulled out the cold dead body of his Motorola. "Out of juice," he said. "Sorry."

"Irene fell," she said. "I tried to call and tell you so I could save you the trip back here in the snow, but—"

"Fell? What are you talking about?"

"The nurse said she must have been trying to climb over the bed rails and she took a header. They need your permission to ship her over to Good Sam for X rays."

"Is she okay?"

Claire's face hardened. "To tell you the truth, I didn't ask. The old bag is still alive. That's all I know."

"Claire—"

She raised her hand. "Don't start. Just get your ass back here as fast as you can. I'm not in the mood for Tommy today."

He was out the door and on his way to Shore Haven before she finished the sentence. There was nothing grandmotherly about Irene. Not in the storybook sense of cookies fresh from the oven served by an apple-cheeked woman in a gingham dress. But she was his blood, the only remaining link to his parents and Grandpa Michael. When she died the stories would die with her before he had even had a chance to hear them.

Since when do you give a shit about family stories, O'Malley? You've never been big on nostalgia.

Hell, he'd spent most of his life trying to forget.

Irene O'Malley wasn't a storyteller. The idea of his grandmother sitting down and weaving spellbinding tales about her early life was enough to make him laugh. Grandpa Michael died before Aidan was born, and most of the clues to O'Malley family history died with him. All anyone knew about Irene was that she had been sick and down on her luck when she met Michael at a seaside village in northern Italy. Michael was an Irish seaman who went wherever the seas beckoned, and Irene—well, there you had him. His father told him that he thought Irene had been a lady's maid to an English noblewoman summering on the Mediterranean. Claire said that Billy told her that Irene had been orphaned as a young child and that she had gone from pillar to post in search of a roof over her head and food in her belly. Irene had been in her early fifties when Michael died, still young enough to build a new life for herself, but she never remarried. "It's so romantic," Kelly had said, sounding much like her mother Sandy before her. "A true forever kind of love."

Yeah. Right.

He was with Claire on this. Irene wasn't a forever kind of woman. She might live forever, that seemed like a real possibility, but he had never sensed that she had a deep attachment to anything but life itself.

And even that was only an educated guess.

What O'Malleys did best was keep secrets. Every damn one of them lived behind a shield of smoke and mirrors designed to keep other O'Malleys away. The fact that it also kept the rest of the world away was a bonus. He had tried to break that chain of solitude with Kelly. How well he'd succeeded was anyone's guess, but nobody could say it was for lack of trying.

He and Billy used to lie awake nights when they were very little and listen to their parents fight. They couldn't understand the meaning behind the ugly words, but the anger came through loud and clear, and the sound of it still lingered in his ears.

And always there was Irene on the sidelines, watching her family splinter apart the same way she would watch an old movie whose outcome had been determined a long time ago.

It was done. Finished. Why the hell was he wasting time thinking about any of it? Grandpa Michael was long gone. His parents. His wife.

Billy.

Every time, after every loss, he'd struggled to pull himself back up to the surface, and each time it got a little harder, took a little longer. Nobody ever tells you the truth about loss. You don't only lose someone you love, you lose a part of yourself as well. Your heart. Your humanity. Maybe even your soul.

It was the samovar, he thought as he skimmed across the icy roads. It had triggered something deep inside his memory banks, something that pulled him closer while staying just out of reach. And then bumping into that student and seeing the photos of Irene and Michael and his father and the original O'Malley in its heyday. A series of coincidences, nothing more than that, but potent just the same.

Kelly was young enough to believe it all meant something, that the forces of Destiny or whatever they were calling it these days were pointing him toward a certain path and that he should pay attention. He was old enough to know he didn't need to. Life kept coming at you just the same.

"SHE'S LUCKY." DR. Harris made a notation on Irene's chart, then looked up at Aidan. "It looks like she didn't break any bones. At her age that's nothing short of a miracle."

"But you still think the X rays are a good idea."

"Absolutely. There could be a hairline fracture we're not aware of."

"She's pretty frail," Aidan said. "How do you think she'll handle the ambulance ride?"

"She's tougher than you think." Dr. Harris allowed herself the faintest hint of a smile.

"If she was that tough, she wouldn't be going to the hospital."

"Touché, Mr. O'Malley. What I mean is, she's a survivor and she'll continue to survive until she decides it's no longer worth the fight."

He couldn't help smiling at the serious-faced young woman who stood before him in her white lab coat and no-nonsense shoes. "Does the AMA know about your radical views?"

She didn't so much as blink. "There's more to death than dying," she said, and he was surprised when she didn't add "Grasshopper."

"Can I see her?"

"She won't know you're there. We gave her some meds to keep her comfortable."

He nodded. "Will she be at Good Sam overnight?"

"Depends on what they find, how long it takes, how she handles the trip."

"In other words, you don't know."

"I don't know."

He thanked Dr. Harris, then navigated the corridors until he found Irene's room at the end of the dogleg. The door was wide open, and he could hear voices talking quietly within.

"Only family," said a nurse he didn't recognize.

"I am family," he said, stepping into the room. "Her grandson."

The nurse looked doubtful, but the aide standing next to her nodded. "Her grandson," she said. "I saw him around the other day."

Irene looked younger somehow. Asleep her face lost the tightly controlled look of a woman used to guarding her secrets. The worry lines softened. The downward curve of her mouth seemed less severe. Her soft white hair fanned out on the pale blue pillow, and for a moment he thought she was smiling at him.

Of course she wasn't. She was floating out there in a Valium-induced haze.

Claire was right. His being there was of no consequence to Irene. He had done what he needed to do, signed the permission papers, and now they were free to take her off to Good Sam for tests or treatment or whatever else her situation warranted.

He could have phoned it in or faxed it.

He looked down at his grandmother, his link to almost everyone he had ever loved and lost, and for the first time he felt pity.

She would never know how much she missed.

He wished he could say the same.

THE NURSE AND her assistant exchanged glances when the grandson left the room.

"Not much on sentiment, was he?" the nurse said with a roll of her eyes. She had seen all kinds come through Shore View. There weren't many who could find something to love in a very elderly relative. Most of them paid the bills, easing their troubled consciences with the fact that Granny was getting three squares a day (even if the three squares were fed directly into her gut) and somebody else was changing her diaper.

"Listen." The assistant motioned for her to be quiet. "I think she said something."

The nurse chuckled. "Honey, she's zonked on Valium. She won't be saying anything until tomorrow the earliest."

"No, really." She bent her head closer to the old lady, almost pressing her ear up against the wrinkled mouth. "Ay-dah. She said it again. Ay-dah."

"Ada?" The nurse wrinkled her nose. "Nobody by that

name around here." She reached for the blankets. "Let's get her ready. The drivers will be here any minute, and Harris will have my head on a platter if we don't have the patient ready to go."

Chapter Eighteen

MADDY STAGGERED THROUGH the kitchen doorway and pretended to collapse onto a chair opposite her aunt and her mother.

"I hope that soup is ready soon," she said, "because Mrs. Loewenstein is bored and wants to know if we get the *Playboy* channel."

"Don't you dare!" Rose warned her sister as Lucy started to laugh. "If they're looking for romance, that means we're doing our job."

"Romance?" Lucy said through her laughter. "Next thing they'll be looking for is Viagra. Maybe you should toss some free samples in the gift baskets you have in the guest rooms."

Maddy, who was on the brink of wild whoops of laughter herself, struggled to hang on to her composure, but she saw the gleeful twinkle in her mother's eyes and the way her mouth was twitching and it was all over. She buried her face in her hands and howled with laughter at the thought of the Loewensteins swinging from the chandeliers.

"It's a good thing we're going on hiatus," Rose said

when the worst of their hilarity abated. "Another day like today and I'd be drummed out of the Innkeepers Association."

"Wh-what should I tell Mrs. Loewenstein?" Maddy asked, dissolving once more into helpless giggles.

"You can tell Mrs. Loewenstein that we have some wonderful classic romantic comedies she might enjoy."

"She's not looking for *Pillow Talk*," Maddy said. "She wants *I Am Curious Gray*."

Rose looked at her and started to laugh again herself. "You really are going to be a smash on Friday, honey. You're a natural." She reached toward Maddy, then pulled her hand back as if afraid she might offend.

Maddy hesitated. This was all so new for both of them, the moment so fragile, the wounds so deep and wide.

She slid her hand forward. Just a tiny bit. Just enough so her mother would notice.

Rose didn't say anything and she didn't meet Maddy's eyes. But she slid her own hand forward another tiny bit herself until her hand covered Maddy's.

The moment was over almost before it began, but what a flood of emotion it roused in Maddy. She felt, by turns, overwhelmed, thrilled, puzzled, confused, angry, and knocked flat by the sheer force of the love she had for her mother. Love she hadn't believed existed except in memory. They had connected, really connected for what felt like the first time. She glanced across the room at her aunt Lucy, who was watching them with her heart on her beautifully tailored sleeve, and she felt another sharp jolt of recognition.

Maybe she belonged there after all. That was her beach beyond the window, her ocean. That was where she had played as a little girl, where she had spent her teens, dreaming about the day she would be old enough to grab her books, her pictures, her future and get as far away as possible.

These women were her family. She wondered if she had ever truly understood the meaning of the word before. If something happened to her tomorrow, the years of estrangement, the fights, the differences—all of it would disappear as if it had never happened. Rose would open her arms to Hannah, and her aunts and cousins would gather round and help keep the child from harm.

She knew this without being told. She knew it in the deepest part of her soul, the part where she was four years old and the world was still a good place, a place where little girls could go to sleep at night secure in the knowledge that the world would still be the same safe place when she woke up the next morning.

They fed the Loewensteins and the Armaghs a lovely noon lunch. They made them laugh with stories of Grandma Fay and the boarders who had drifted in and out of the old Victorian before Rose waved her magic wand. Rose added more wood to the fireplaces. Lucy found a DVD copy of *An Affair to Remember*, and Maddy made sure the coffee and hot chocolate pots were warm and filled to the brim.

Outside the winds whipped up off the water, blasted the beach, then slammed into the Candlelight. Pellets of ice clattered against the windows while the worst kind of damaging snow piled up against doors and steps and obliterated the roads and sidewalks.

Inside the air was warm and fragrant with chocolate and fresh bread and pine. The intoxicating sound of Cary Grant's voice mingled with commentary from the Armaghs. Priscilla slept soundly in her basket near the stove while Rose and Lucy worked on the accompaniments to the evening's farewell meal. Maddy stood by the window and watched her breath turn frosty against the pane. When she was a little girl she had dreamed of a cozy kitchen with a mother who sang softly while she made cookies, a puppy with a red bow on her collar, a family who would always be there to keep her safe from harm.

Twenty-five years later, in her mother's kitchen, she finally had the feeling she might be on the right track.

ONLY THE STALWARTS showed up at O'Malley's that afternoon. The usual lunch crowd of doctors and nurses and attorneys wisely decided not to risk the treacherous roads for a bowl of chili and a blast of icy ocean air. By one o'clock the only people in the place were Aidan, Tommy, Claire, and the crew of retirees who would brave an F-5 tornado for O'Malley's Manhattan clam.

"You guys are freaking nuts," Tommy said as he doused a half-dozen coffees with a glug of Bailey's. "Wouldn't catch me here on a day like this."

"Earth to Kennedy," Soriano said, laughing into his steaming bowl of chowder. "You're here, buddy."

Nothing much bothered Tommy. He shrugged his brawny shoulders and said, "Yeah, but I wouldn't be if he wasn't paying me."

"I think we should close up," Claire said to Aidan as she turned away from the front window. "It's pretty bad out there."

"Go home," he said with a glance toward the window himself. "If it keeps up like this, I just might close up around six."

Her face still had a touch of the post–root canal chipmunk to it. He would never tell her because she would probably do him bodily harm, but he found her slightly swollen state endearing. Over the years Claire had built up layer after layer of defenses until it was almost impossible to dig down to the woman Billy had brought home more than twenty years ago. She had been so young—hadn't they all?—so wide-eyed and filled with dreams of a golden future where good things happened to good people and nobody ever got sick and nobody ever got injured and sure as hell nobody you loved ever died.

"Leave the car here," he said, draping a brotherly arm over her shoulder. "I'll drive you."

"Gotta get Billy Jr.," she said, casting another worried glance toward the window, "and pick up my prescription at Shoprite."

"I'll do it."

She eyed him with friendly suspicion. "What's with you? Why so nice?"

"You don't like nice?"

"Oh, I think I remember it somewhere way back in the mists of time, but it's been awhile."

He opted for the truth even though it would most likely piss her off. "I'm thinking about Irene."

She pulled away and glared up at him. "Fuck Irene. What the hell did she ever do to deserve this concern?"

"This could be it, Claire. She's over one hundred years old. Sooner or later—"

"If you ask me, it couldn't be soon enough."

"Goddamnit, Claire, she's my blood. She's the last link I have to my family. I don't give a rat's ass if you like her. Hell, *I* don't like her. But she's all I have."

To his surprise Claire's blue eyes welled with tears. "What about Kelly? And what about my crew? I suppose you think we're chopped liver."

"You know what I'm talking about. The kids are the future. Irene is the last link with Grandpa Michael and my folks and—"

"Not Billy," she whispered fiercely. "Don't even think of saying Billy."

He hadn't been going to say Billy, but he was glad she stopped him. Claire had no patience with nostalgia. As far as she was concerned she had enough relatives as it was. The thought of pawing through a stack of papers or interviewing a group of old people just to find out that Aunt Sadie went to her reward in August 1872 made her laugh.

Hell, maybe if he had a sprawling, loud loving family like Claire's, he wouldn't be looking for connections that might not even be there. But he didn't. The past was a murky soup of whispers and silences and grudges held way too long. He grew up learning about families from television. Reruns of *Leave It to Beaver* and *Father Knows Best*. Fantasies that Greg would wreck his car and Aidan could step into *The Brady Bunch* without a ripple.

Big surprise that he had married young. From the first moment they met, Sandy had been his anchor, the home he had always longed for. She had seen through the tough-guy exterior and straight into his heart in a way that nobody before or since ever had. They had fallen in love in the ninth grade and stayed that way until the day she died, three months short of Kelly's second birthday.

At least he had known it once. At least he knew he was capable of love and happiness and all the other things the rest of the O'Malley clan found so damn hard to come by. It helped on days like this when he found himself wanting to know how it was his whole family always ended up on the outside of happiness looking in.

There had to be a reason, some cataclysmic incident that had sent them all into solitary orbits, but damned if he knew what it was. The only thing he was sure of was that if anyone had the answer, it was Grandma Irene.

"I'm going," Claire said as she shrugged into her puffy black storm coat. "And if you were smart, you'll go, too, before it gets any worse."

"Sure you don't want me to drive you?"

She slung her bag over her shoulder, grabbed her scarf and her car keys. "For what it's worth, Aidan," she said from the doorway, "I'll say a rosary for Irene. But not for her sake. I'll say it for yours."

THE SCHOOL CALLED Maddy to inform her they were letting the kids out thirty minutes early because of the storm, which sent Maddy tearing out of the house to warm up her Mustang.

She needn't have bothered. The Mustang wasn't going anywhere. She turned the key once, twice, three times and was rewarded with a couple of puny clicks and then total silence. There wasn't time to call AAA and ask them to send out somebody to help her. Hannah's school bus would be at the corner in less than fifteen minutes. She could have borrowed either Rose's car or Lucy's if it weren't for the small fact that she had cleverly parked in such a way that the two vehicles were blocked in.

She whipped out her cell phone and punched in Gina's code.

Her cousin answered on the second ring.

"This better be good," Gina said in her smoky tones, "because I'm about to skid into a snowdrift."

Maddy quickly told her what had happened. "I know it's a big favor on a day like this, but could you pick up Hannah and bring her home?"

Gina might not have made the world's best wife, but she was definitely in the running for best cousin. If you had a problem, Gina was the one you wanted on your side. She was blunt at times, painfully honest, the one most likely to say exactly the things you didn't want to hear at the exact moment you least wanted to hear them, but when she gave you her word, you really had something.

"You're gonna owe me," Gina said. "Make sure the coffeepot's on and there's a plate of Aunt Lucy's mini chocolate cheesecakes."

"Will you settle for freshly made chocolate chunk cookies with macadamia nuts?"

Gina moaned. "Settle? We'll be there if I have to pull the car with my teeth."

Maddy tossed the cell phone back into her bag, then steeled herself to get out of the car. The snow was heavy and blowing in from the water, which meant huge snowdrifts were forming all over town. God only knew what it would be like come evening. Rose was going to hit the roof. Her mother was a stickler for thinking ahead, trying to imagine all possibilities before choosing a course of action. You could bet she wouldn't have parked her old car sideways across the driveway and blocked two other vehicles. And, if for some unthinkable reason she had, her battery wouldn't have dared to drop dead on her. Some things simply wouldn't happen.

Rose looked up from the cookbook she was thumbing through as Maddy stepped into the kitchen. "Do you need me to move my car?" she asked.

"It's the other way around," Maddy said as she slipped out of her coat and tossed it in the mudroom to dry. She braced herself for the eruption and explained about the dead battery and its repercussions.

"Not to worry," Rose said. "It isn't like we're going anywhere tonight in this weather."

"What about Aunt Lucy?" She could hear her aunt laughing with the guests in the front room.

"She can stay in one of the empty rooms or grab a ride with Gina."

That's it? Maddy looked at her mother closely, searching for signs of hidden anger or impatience, and found nothing but good cheer.

"Is something wrong?" Rose asked pleasantly.

"You're taking this awfully well," Maddy said. "I thought you'd be annoyed."

Rose shook her head. "As long as we can get the Loewensteins and the Armaghs on the road tomorrow, I don't care if we're snowed in for a month."

Maddy managed to suppress a shudder. A month might be taxing their newfound rapport to the breaking point, but her mother's easygoing acceptance of the unexpected was still amazing.

She poured herself some coffee. "We do still have some of those macadamia nut cookies, don't we? Gina demands them in payment for picking up Hannah at the bus stop."

"Gina has the eating habits of a ten-year-old," Rose said with a shake of her head.

"Yeah," said Maddy, thinking of her sexy and curvaceous cousin. "It's really done her a lot of harm, hasn't it?"

Rose took off her reading glasses and placed them on the table next to the stack of cookbooks. "I used to feel the same way about Lucia and Toni. The boys were like bees buzzing around them. I was lucky if one of their castoffs bothered to look my way."

Maddy's eyes widened. "You're joking. To hear Lucy tell it, you were beating them off with a stick."

"Nothing of the sort." Rose laughed, but it held a hint of irony. "Lucy was by far the prettiest of us all." She looked over at Maddy. "Same as you're the prettiest of the cousins."

Maddy's bark of laughter sent Priscilla yapping. She crouched down to pet the sleepy puppy.

She was grateful for the distraction. The prettiest of the

cousins? Where on earth was that coming from? She had grown up with nothing but criticism from her mother. *Too fat . . . too thin . . . Stand up straight . . . Do something with that head of hair . . . Why on earth are you wearing all that eye makeup . . . Pink just isn't your color, Madelyn. . . .*

She was the bookworm, the loner, the one who would use her spending money on a new boxed set of *Lord of the Rings* instead of the latest double-lash mascara and iridescent eye shadow. In a family of divas, there was always someone eager for the spotlight, and in one of her first acts of rebellion, Maddy decided to opt out of the competition.

"You can more than hold your own with Gina," Rose was saying. "Don't tell me you didn't know that."

"No, Mom," Maddy said in a surprisingly steady voice. "I didn't know it at all."

ROSE REGRETTED THE words the moment she uttered them. They felt strange on her tongue, unfamiliar. No wonder. How could Maddy know how lovely she was when her own mother had taken thirty-two years to tell her? A child gained her first sense of self from her parents, and how Rose had failed her. Bill had doted upon his daughter, and when they divorced the change in Maddy had been alarming. Her happy child had turned moody and quiet, much like dear Hannah was today, and nothing Rose said or did seemed to reach her. But a word of praise from Bill, a note of encouragement, and Maddy walked on air for days.

Guilt and shame nipped at the back of Rose's neck as she remembered the times she withheld praise for fear of spoiling her child, when she criticized rather than encouraged because criticism had spurred her on to greater achievement while encouragement turned into nothing but white noise.

But Maddy isn't you, Rosie. Bill had said it many times over the years, and Lucy, too. Why was it so hard to understand that her daughter was a separate being with needs Rose didn't have to share in order to respect?

Her daughter's eyes were filled with tears as she busied herself doing something or other to Priscilla's collar. She looked as vulnerable as Hannah at that moment, and almost as young. This was the time when Maddy usually fled the scene, leaving Rose feeling simultaneously relieved and frustrated and more than a little bit angry. But this time, to Rose's surprise, her daughter didn't run. She stayed, bent low over the poodle puppy, her back arched in a line so graceful it almost brought Rose herself to tears.

She could see the years rolling back until they were in the kitchen of the house on Lighthouse Lane. Rose and Bill had fallen in love with the place the first second they saw it. Small, cozy, with a view of the beach, and a manageable monthly rent. They would be happy there. Bill would forget about his farm and the life he had left behind in Oregon, and Rose—well, no point thinking about it. All the things that had been wrong between them were every bit as wrong in the sweet house on Lighthouse Lane as they had been in Oregon before that.

The marriage ended not long after they moved in, but the love was still going strong almost thirty years later. No man had ever loved her more than Bill Bainbridge had. No man ever could. She had given him her heart, and nothing, not divorce or distance or their very separate lives, had changed her feelings for him.

Had she ever told Maddy any of that? She wasn't sure. Sometimes it seemed as if life had swept them along in its raging current, and they had been too busy keeping their heads above water to take time to get to know each other. An odd thought, that love required time to grow, but it was true. She could see it right now in her daughter's face. They had grown closer in this single afternoon than in the ten years that had come before.

You fell in love with your child the first moment she was placed in your arms, still slick with birth fluids, squalling at the indignity of the process, cold and hungry and yours. Oh, pride of ownership was a dangerous thing in the land of mothers and daughters. You fed her and dressed her, you bathed her and played with her. You were her morning sun and evening star, and then one day you look at her and see a stranger looking back. A woman who doesn't like you. A woman you don't understand. A woman who wants to get as far away from you as possible just as fast as she can.

In a way you don't blame her. There had been times when you were grateful for every mile that separated you, every river and mountain.

But through it all, through the distance and the anger and the years, the bond remained strong and the love, even stronger.

Even if you couldn't find the words to tell her so.

GINA EXPLODED INTO the kitchen a few minutes after three o'clock. "Cookies!" she cried, to the delight of her brood and Hannah. "Cookies before I die!"

She feigned a swoon at the entrance to the mudroom, which sent Priscilla into a frenzy of yipping and tail-wagging.

Rose, laughing, looked at Maddy. "Has Priscilla—?"

"Oh, no!" Maddy leaped over a prone Gina and grabbed for her coat and the dog's leash. "C'mon with us," she said, kissing her daughter soundly on the cheek. "I'll show you how to make a perfect snowball while Miss Pris does her thing."

Hannah didn't seem to think very much of the idea, but she was a good girl and she went with her mother, ignoring the smoochy, butt-kissing noises her cousins were making.

"Boys are stupid," she said as she clung to Maddy's hand on the slippery steps.

"Not all the time," Maddy said, praying they wouldn't fall on their heads. "I think the snow makes them stupid."

Hannah giggled at the idea. "They're stupid when it rains, too."

"Sometimes," Maddy agreed, "but I think they're quite smart when it's cloudy."

Hannah considered the idea. "No," she said firmly, a

tiny spark of her old self peeking through. "They're only smart when it's sunshiny outside."

Maddy cleared a huge circle in the snow and placed Priscilla down in the middle of it. "Go ahead," she urged the shivering puppy. "We're freezing, too."

Priscilla sniffed the pristine white surface, then sniffed again. She looked up at Maddy and Hannah with a puzzled expression in her big brown eyes.

"She can't find the smell," Hannah said. "She needs to go where others dogs go."

Maddy almost toppled over into a drift in surprise. "How do you know about that, honey?"

"Billy O'Malley told us on the bus," she said, dragging her toe through a pile of snow. "That's why they sniff each other's bottoms."

Am I really having this conversation? Maddy stared down at her cherubic daughter and wondered if the next thing on the agenda was a lesson in sex education.

"Actually, honey, one of the reasons they sniff each other is so they can identify their friends and family."

"Why can't they just look?"

"I guess because lots of dogs look alike."

"Why can't they ask each other?"

"Because dogs can't talk."

"Yes, they can," Hannah said with great certainty. "But they speak dog so we can't understand them."

"Did Billy tell you that?"

"I told me."

Maddy was delighted to see a glimmer of Hannah's wonderful imagination after so long. "You might not want to tell Grandma Rose that dogs talk to each other."

"I already did."

Maddy's stomach did a double-twist. "You did?"

"Yes."

"What did she say?"

"She said she already knew."

Literal-minded Rose DiFalco, who had declared her entire life a No-Whimsey Zone? "Did she say how she knew?"

"Yes," said Hannah. "She said Priscilla told her."

Chapter Nineteen

"YOU LIE!" GINA popped another piece of chocolate chunk–macadamia nut cookie into her mouth. "Aunt Rose actually said that?"

Maddy grinned at her cousin and poured herself another cup of tea. "Your aunt, *my* mother, the redoubtable Rose DiFalco, actually said Priscilla talked to her."

Gina whooped with laughter. "Aunt Rose speaks dog! I can't believe it!"

"Not just dog," Maddy corrected her. "Poodle."

"Well, la-di-da." Gina wiped her mouth with the Christmas napkin next to her plate. "You know I don't believe a word you're saying."

Maddy crossed her heart with a teaspoon. "I swear on Priscilla it's true."

"I'd ask if Hell froze over, but it's cold enough out there to do it without Rose's help." Gina looked toward the kitchen door. "Any munchkins around?"

"They're up in the attic with Rose and Lucy looking for the Christmas stockings."

"Remember when Grandma Fay was alive? How many hours did we spend up there looking for those stockings?

I was pissed when I turned fourteen and she told me I was too old to pretend I still believed in Santa."

Maddy laughed. "Remember the gingerbread men she used to hide exactly where she knew we'd find them?" Perfect gingerbread men with bow ties and big buttons and a grandchild's name written across each one in royal frosting.

"I miss Fay," Gina said. "I don't think the family's been the same since she died."

"I know," Maddy said. "I keep expecting to see her coming down the stairs in that red dress she loved."

Gina's face lit up. "The one with the shoes she had dyed to match."

"And her hair! Who else in Paradise Point had a grandmother who dyed her hair to match her outfits?"

Gina peered over her shoulder and lowered her voice. "I think our Rosie is on her way. That Light Auburn number forty-three is getting real close to Lucy Ricardo territory."

Maddy laughed and poked her cousin in the arm. "Shh! You know she loves your colorist. As soon as Mamie—"

"Dies?"

Maddy poked her again. "—retires, she'll be back with you on a weekly basis."

"And not a moment too soon," Gina murmured. "What worked for Grandma Fay doesn't exactly work for Aunt Rose."

There was no doubt in anyone's mind that Fay DiFalco had been an original. Her daughters had flown in the face of convention and buried their mother in the red dress, with a copy of *The Racing Times* and her Caesar's Atlantic City slots card.

Gina broke off another piece of cookie, then popped it in her mouth. "So how was the big breakfast?"

"What big breakfast?" No sense making it too easy for Gina.

"You and Aidan. Julie said you two were in there until lunchtime."

"Julie needs to learn to tell time."

"So how was it?"

"Fine. I had a blueberry muffin. He had a short stack. We both agreed the samovar was pretty damn nice. End of story."

"This is me you're talking to, Madelyn. You mean to tell me there weren't any sparks?"

"No sparks," Maddy said. "I doubt if either one of us is looking for sparks right now."

"I think you're kidding yourself."

"You think wrong."

"We all saw the way the two of you were looking at each other. Even the kids could see something was going on."

"Nothing was going on."

"Maybe not now," Gina said knowingly, "but it's only a matter of time."

Maddy searched Gina's face for signs of jealousy or worry. "He's a nice guy, but that's as far as it goes."

"He's also easy on the eyes." Gina's own eyes were dancing with merriment. "I think the scars actually give him a devil-may-care quality. Very Harrison Ford."

"Gina," Maddy said, leaning across the table, "you don't have to do this. I *know*."

"Of course you know. All you have to do is look at him to see the resemblance. A young Harrison Ford."

"That's not what I mean. I mean, I *know*."

"If this is some kind of puzzle, I left my decoder ring at home."

Okay, Gina, you asked for it. "I know you've been sleeping with Aidan."

Who knew such a tiny woman could spit coffee so far? After they wiped up the spray from the tabletop and Maddy's left cheek, Gina leaned back in her chair and fixed Maddy with a look she had never seen her cousin give before.

"I'm not sleeping with Aidan O'Malley."

"You dated him."

"A few times. But we were friends, not lovers. We were

both lonely and we liked hanging out together." Gina shifted position in the chair. Maddy's unflappable cousin had obviously been flapped by the question. "Why are you asking?"

"Denise said something at the bus stop that made me think—"

"Aidan didn't say anything, did he?" There was an odd look in Gina's eyes, an almost frantic worry.

"Aidan was silent as the grave."

"Level with me," Gina said. "You like him, don't you?"

"I already told you I think he's a nice guy."

The sound of laughter and running footsteps grew louder. Any minute the kids would burst into the kitchen with their Christmas stockings and the moment would be lost.

"Let me take a wild guess here: You think he's a nice guy, but you're going to keep your distance because you think he and I . . ." She finished her sentence with a wave of her hand. "Right?"

"Right." She met her cousin's gaze. "Denise seemed pretty clear on it."

"Because that's what I wanted her to think."

"I'm not following you."

Gina broke their eye contact and glanced over at Priscilla asleep in her basket. "Aidan wasn't the O'Malley I was sleeping with."

It took a few moments before Gina's meaning sank in. "Billy?"

The sorrow in her cousin's eyes was all the answer she needed.

"Oh, God, Gina! He and Claire—"

"I know." Gina lifted her chin and met Maddy's eyes. "You don't think I hate myself every time I see Claire and Billy Jr.?"

"But why? How could you—"

"Why?" Gina's voice rose with her distress. "Why the hell do you think? I love him." She caught herself. "Loved him."

"When? How on earth—"

Gina buried her face in her hands. A strangled laugh broke through. "It started almost twelve years ago. I broke it off for a few years, then—" Her shoulders lifted, then slumped in despair. "We couldn't stay away from each other."

"Oh, Gina." Maddy's emotions were torn every which way. Shock. Compassion. Sorrow. Understanding. Anger. "Did you think he was going to leave Claire?"

"Yes." Her hands fell to her lap and she blinked away tears. "I know what you're thinking. He never led me on."

"Give me a break," Maddy snapped. "He was cheating on his wife for more than half of their marriage. I doubt if he was above leading you on."

"It wasn't like that. *He* wasn't like that. We loved each other."

"I don't doubt your feelings, but I'm afraid I'm not quite as certain about his."

"You didn't know him. He was so wild, so free—"

"You make him sound like a Chincoteague pony."

"Not funny." Gina's temper flashed to life. "There was nobody like him. Nobody ever—"

They both started at the sounds of children's laughter and footsteps on one of the upper staircases.

Gina started to speak again, but Maddy lifted her hand to stop her. She didn't want to hear the litany of Billy O'Malley's virtues. Right then she would have found it very difficult to restrain herself from telling Gina exactly what she thought of the story.

"I still don't see where Aidan figures into this," she said. "You were sleeping with his brother, but you were dating him?"

"We were friends. I needed a friend and he became one. Nothing more than that."

"There has to be something more. The pieces aren't adding up for me."

"Welcome to the real world," Gina said bitterly. "The pieces usually don't add up, or haven't you noticed that yet?"

*   *   *

THE LIGHTS ALONG the shore clicked on around four o'clock. They were activated by an automatic sensor system that had been installed with great fanfare by the town officials as part of a beautification project designed to inch Paradise Point higher up the tourism ladder.

Aidan stood by the window and watched as the sweep of snow-covered shoreline came to life beneath the murky twinkle of artificial light. Somebody had decided that each lamppost deserved a swag of red velvet and a candy cane, but that same somebody hadn't factored in the water-repellant qualities of velvet.

All in all, it had been one strange mother of a day. He had shut down O'Malley's a little before three o'clock, sending the regulars home and telling Tommy he might as well get going, too. He had a few repairs to make to one of the windows that opened up onto the water, and once he finished, he intended to shove off as well. Kelly would be heading over to Claire's after school to help her aunt with preparations for the South Jersey Firefighters Fund Drive. Claire had spearheaded the drive every year since Billy's death, but it required a hell of a lot of emotional energy to pull herself through the process. Helping out was Kelly's idea, and he appreciated the timing. If the roads got much worse, she could bunk there overnight.

He turned away from the window. In fact, if it got much worse than it already was, he'd be bunking at O'Malley's for the night. The thought didn't thrill him. The thing to do was fix the busted window, then get his ass on out of there while he still had the chance.

He was heading for the storage room in the back when the phone rang.

"This is Dr. Lipman from Good Samaritan Hospital. I'm calling to speak with"—the sound of rustling papers—"Aidan O'Malley."

"Speaking. How's my grandmother?"

"That's why I'm calling, Mr. O'Malley. I'm afraid the news isn't good."

While they were preparing Irene for an MRI, she had slipped unexpectedly into unconsciousness.

"Are you saying she's in a coma?"

" 'Coma' has certain connotations I'm not willing to embrace yet," said Dr. Lipman. "At the moment she is unconscious and unresponsive, but her vital signs are rock solid."

"Sounds like a coma to me," Aidan said.

Silence from Dr. Lipman.

"Is she going to stay at Good Sam or are you sending her back home to Shore View?"

"That's why I'm calling, Mr. O'Malley. You realize, I'm sure, that your grandmother signed a Living Will form some time back and is DNR."

" 'Do not resuscitate,' " Aidan said. "I know."

"Since she seems to be in good health in other ways and there is little we would be permitted to do to help her if she were not, I feel she should stay with us overnight and then, weather permitting, be returned to Shore View sometime tomorrow afternoon."

Lipman said there was no indication whatsoever of any broken bones, but he would perform an MRI on Irene if Aidan insisted.

"No," said Aidan. "All I want is that you make sure she's not in any pain."

"I assure you she isn't," the doctor said.

"How would you know for sure?" Aidan persisted. "She's unconscious."

Lipman went on about physiologic responses and what they represented, but Aidan was no longer listening.

"How long do you think she'll be unconscious?" he interrupted.

Another long silence from the good doctor. "There is no way I can predict that for you, Mr. O'Malley. She may be coming out of it while we're speaking or she may—"

"Never come out of it."

"At her age, that's a distinct possibility."

They were talking about the end of a person's life and it sounded abstract and clinical. Devoid of anything resembling human emotion.

Aidan hung up the phone and went into the storage

room to grab what he needed to repair the window. No doubt about it: one strange mother of a day.

KELLY WASN'T SURE why she burst into tears after supper when Aunt Claire told her about Grandma Irene. It wasn't as if she didn't already know about the accident. Her father had called her on her cell phone during lunch and told her what had happened, about the fall and the trip to the hospital and the fact that she was now unconscious.

"Grandma Irene is over one hundred years old," he had reminded her gently. "We shouldn't be surprised if—"

"I know," she had said, trying not to cry. "I'm prepared."

But she wasn't prepared at all. The second Claire told her about Grandma Irene being unconscious, it was like all the sadness and fear she had contained inside her heart came flooding out and she couldn't stop it. Good thing Billy Jr. was in the family room watching one of those crocodile-hunter shows he loved. His teasing would be more than she could handle.

"I'm sorry," she kept saying over and over again like a parrot. "I'm really, really sorry." And then she would start blubbering all over again.

Aunt Claire had never made any secret of how she felt about Grandma Irene. Claire hadn't even allowed Grandma to attend Uncle Billy's funeral, which had caused a big rift in what was left of the family. Kelly's father was still in Intensive Care at the time and didn't know what was going on, but the fighting and name-calling had been pretty awful. She didn't think she would ever forget the sight of Claire, eyes nearly swollen shut from crying, as she stood on the church steps and refused to let the health-care aide wheel Irene into the chapel.

"You didn't give a rat's ass about him when he was alive," Claire had roared at the old woman, "and I'll be damned if I let you pretend you care now that he's dead!"

But Claire wasn't roaring at anyone right now. She

placed her hand on Kelly's shoulder and gave it an affectionate squeeze.

"PMS," Claire said with a nod of her head. "I recognize the signs."

Kelly managed a smile. "You think?"

"Is your period due next week?"

"Yeah, actually it is."

"And you're weepy and tired and thinking about chocolate day and night?"

She laughed. "Oh, definitely!"

Claire cut them each a humongous slice of chocolate cake with thick dark chocolate frosting. "Coffee, tea, or milk?"

"Milk," Kelly said. "Definitely milk with chocolate cake."

"Smart girl."

Claire placed the container down on the kitchen table, then pulled two clean glasses from the dishwasher.

"So," she said in that fake kind of cheerful voice parents liked to use when they were about to nail you to the wall, "I saw you and Seth the other afternoon."

Kelly, whose mouth was filled with cake, shrugged. *Please, God, one bolt of lightning . . . a small earthquake . . . anything!*

"It was around two-ish. I was on the corner waiting for Billy Jr.'s school bus." Claire took a bite of cake and chewed it quickly. "You were in his brother's Honda."

Oh, great. She loved her aunt, but really. Why couldn't Claire worry about her own kids and leave her alone?

"We had to take some pictures out at the lake for the yearbook."

"Before school ended."

"They canceled last period."

"I didn't know you were a photographer."

"Yes, you did," Kelly said. If there wasn't eight feet of snow out there, she would jump into the Tercel and take her chances. "Remember you gave me Uncle Billy's old Pentax."

Claire looked down at her hands for a second. Kelly

hated sometimes even mentioning Billy's name because it seemed to hurt Claire so much to remember.

"Your father already asked you about this, didn't he?"

Kelly nodded. "He said you told him that you saw us."

"I'm not trying to pry into your life, Kel, but I've seen what happens when a girl makes mistakes. I don't want what happened to Kathleen to happen to you."

"I don't do drugs, Aunt Claire." *And I don't sleep around. There's only Seth.*

"I know you don't and I never said you did. It's just that it's so easy for a girl—what I'm trying to say is all it takes is one mistake, one tiny little slip, and your whole life is changed forever."

Kelly counted to three before she spoke, the way Grandma Laura had taught her when she was a little girl. "I'm going to Columbia in the fall," she said. "Nothing can change that."

"Life can change all of your plans," Claire said. "You have to be careful."

Kelly felt the noose around her neck drawing tighter. Did Claire actually suspect something or was this just that freaky maternal radar system at work?

"I'm always careful," she said. "You know that."

"I hope so, honey." Claire finished off the last of her slice of cake. "You have a wonderful future ahead of you. I'd hate to see you lose out."

"I won't lose out," she said in a confident tone of voice. Much more confident than she was actually feeling. "You'll see."

"I hope so." Claire sounded dubious, but it was clear she wanted to believe Kelly was right.

"I will," Kelly promised. "You can count on it."

Claire's face lit up with a gigantic smile.

"Here," she said. "Have another piece of cake."

GINA AND THE kids left at a little after five. Rose and Lucy invited them to stay for supper, but Gina said if they didn't hit the road that second, the Candlelight would have more overnight guests than they had bargained on. Kisses all around and they were gone.

"What are the paying guests up to?" Maddy asked as Lucy poured coffee for her and Rose. "They're awfully quiet in there, aren't they?"

"They're napping," Lucy said.

"Poor dears." Rose drizzled a tiny bit of sugar into her cup. "It won't be long before you and I are dozing our afternoons away in front of the fire, too, Lucia."

"That's not what I meant," Lucy said with a devilish smile. "They're napping . . . upstairs."

Maddy sighed as she put cake plates and cups into the dishwasher. "Whatever it is about this place, you ought to bottle it and sell it on the open market. A quartet of octogenarians has a better love life than I do!"

Her mother and aunt laughed with her. She had been around long enough to appreciate the difference.

"You know the old expression," Lucy said. "If you can't do, then teach."

"I know an even older expression," Rose said dryly, "but Maddy's still too young."

Maddy closed the dishwasher door with her hip. "Speaking of quiet, where's Hannah?"

"I don't know," Lucy said. "I haven't seen her since Gina left."

Rose thought for a second. "I think I saw her heading down the hallway a few minutes ago."

"Please don't tell me she was heading for the office," Maddy pleaded.

"Actually I think that's exactly where she was going."

Maddy was out of there in a flash. She sprinted down the hallway, praying she wouldn't be too late. If only she had taken that extra second to stow the samovar back in Rose's closet. What kind of idiot mother would think a shopping bag stuffed under her desk was any kind of hiding place for a Christmas present? You would think she had no experience being a kid. When she was Hannah's age, she would have thrown herself into a Dumpster if she thought that was where Rose had hidden the latest

Barbie. Her childhood Decembers were a blur of Advent calendars, Christmas carols, and a systematic search of every closet, drawer, cubbyhole, and cupboard within reach.

She burst into the office on a wave of crazed maternal holiday adrenaline only to find her offspring curled up with Priscilla on the window seat. They were watching the snow swirl down from the night sky, drifting into soft pillows against the deck railing out back. With the porch lights on, the snow dazzled like falling diamonds.

Maddy cast a quick look under the desk and almost wept with relief. The shopping bag was still under there, and it didn't look as if it had been disturbed. She wanted to fling herself on the bag as if it were a live hand grenade, covering it with her body so Hannah wouldn't find the samovar. Of course, there was just the slightest chance that such behavior might pique her daughter's curiosity, so she opted for the casual, more nonchalant approach.

Priscilla yipped happily when she saw Maddy, and Maddy couldn't help but grin at the wriggling puppy who leaped from Hannah's arms and pranced her way.

"You brushed her!" Maddy said as she scooped up Priscilla and sat down next to Hannah on the window seat. "Look how pretty she looks!"

Hannah nodded, but didn't take her eyes off the shimmering snow.

"You even fixed her ribbon."

Hannah nodded again.

She placed Priscilla down on the floor, much to the poodle's indignation.

"Time to wash your hands for supper," Maddy said, standing up. "Why don't you go take care of that and I'll meet you in the kitchen."

"Already did it," Hannah said, holding her hands up in front of her.

"Oh, no," Maddy said, laughing. "You were up to your elbows in puppy dog. Off to the bathroom with you, young lady."

"You were up to your elbows, too," Hannah said.

"And I'm going to wash my hands, too." Maddy stole another glance at the shopping bag tucked in the kneehole of her desk. "I just want to do one thing first."

"I can help."

What on earth was going on here? The way Hannah was acting, you would think the 9-by-12-foot office was an offshoot of Disney World.

"Wash your hands," Maddy repeated. "I'll meet you in the kitchen before Grandma Rose serves your favorite steak soup."

"I don't like that soup."

"Sure you do. Remember how Grandma Rose served it in your very own little loaf of bread?"

"It's stupid soup," Hannah said.

"Well, let's keep that our secret, Hannah, because Grandma Rose and Aunt Lucy worked very hard to make it for us, and we don't want to make them feel bad."

Hannah didn't look particularly thrilled, and, maybe it was Maddy's nerves, but it seemed her daughter cast a longing glance toward the general area of the desk.

"Scoot," she said as Priscilla wove between her ankles. "Last one there is a rotten egg."

Hannah finally left the room, but her entire demeanor screamed that she was only doing it because she was four and Maddy was thirty-two.

The second Hannah disappeared down the hall, Maddy leaped on the shopping bag and yanked it from its hiding place. She had maybe three or four minutes to race the samovar upstairs to the safety of Rose's closet before the best Christmas secret of all time was ruined. She tiptoed past the bathroom door, which was slightly ajar, then took the back steps two at a time. Why on earth did they have to have hallways the length of your average bowling alley? Whatever happened to the cramped and crowded Victorian houses Steve and Norm liked to prowl around in on *This Old House*?

She flicked on the switch, flooding Rose's room with soft pink light. The huge closet was set between the bedroom itself and the small dressing room Rose had had

installed when she remade Grandma Fay's boardinghouse
into the Candlelight. Every aspect of the room was breath-
takingly lovely, but Maddy didn't have time to waste admiring the antique quilt on the quilt stand or the
four-poster bed or the smell of Chanel No. 5 that wafted
from the closet the second she opened the door.

She even tried not to notice the fact that her mother's
closet showed a greater sense of organization than
Maddy's entire life, but it wasn't easy. She would have
had to rent a backhoe to shovel through her own closet
to make room for the shopping bag. All she had to do in
Rose's closet was gently move aside a long silk robe
hanging from a padded hanger and slide the bag into—

"Mommy, why are you in Grandma's closet?"

Busted.

Chapter Twenty

"TELL ME YOU'RE joking, Madelyn," Rose whispered as they stacked the guests' dirty dishes near the pantry. "She didn't!"

"She did," Maddy said. "There I was with my butt sticking out of the closet, and she's there watching from the doorway. I swear I almost needed CPR."

"Did she see the—"

"Shh!" Maddy hissed. "Don't say it! Don't even think it!"

"But did she—"

"No—thank God a million times—she didn't. But it was close."

"Where did you put it?"

"Same place it was before, hidden by that gorgeous teal silk robe."

"It's lovely, isn't it?"

"Scrumptious. A present?"

Rose laughed. "You can put your eyeballs back in your head, miss. A present from me to me."

Maddy hesitated, then decided what the heck. "Nobody tall and handsome on the horizon?"

Rose shook her head. "Not unless he shows up at the Candlelight with an AmEx in one hand and a reservation in the other."

A wave of sadness washed over Maddy. When had those random strands of silver, impervious to Clairol, first appeared in her mother's impeccably coiffed hair? Were they new arrivals or was Maddy simply looking at her for the first time? Rose was a beautiful woman but she wasn't immortal. There were lines at the outer corners of her eyes, a faint downward pulling of her mouth. Small things when taken separately, but together they sent a faint chill up Maddy's spine. Her mother was growing old, and to Maddy it seemed that it happened overnight.

"She's wonderful with her." Rose inclined her head toward the kitchen where Lucy and Hannah were finishing their supper. The sound of Lucy's robust laugh made both women smile.

"She would have been a wonderful mother," Maddy said, leaning against the doorjamb. "It's a shame things didn't work out that way for her."

Rose adjusted the ties on her apron while she watched her sister and granddaughter playfully vie for a piece of buttered homemade rye bread. "Life doesn't always work out the way we'd like it to."

"Especially if you're a DiFalco," Maddy said. "Just once I'd like to see a DiFalco woman waltz off with Mr. Right."

"Oh, we've found our share of Mr. Rights," Rose said. "We just can't seem to figure out how to hold on to them."

"You've all done pretty well without a long-term liaison," Maddy said. "Maybe being alone isn't such a bad thing."

Rose said nothing, which, of course, spoke volumes. Was it possible her mother longed for more than she had? Before tonight Maddy wouldn't have believed it could be true, but standing there in the warm pantry with the snow and wind beating against the house and the ocean roaring beyond the windows, anything seemed possible. Maybe it was an illusion, this feeling of closeness Maddy was experiencing, but she wished it never had to end.

"Are you lonely?" She had never asked her mother a question like that. It would never have occurred to her that Rose would allow herself to feel lonely.

Rose looked at her. "Sometimes."

"Do you ever wish—"

"Sometimes."

"You didn't give me a chance to ask my question."

"I didn't need to. I know what it was."

"Daddy."

Rose nodded. "Like I said, sometimes."

Maddy's heart seemed to expand, crowding her lungs until she could barely draw in a full breath.

"Look how beautiful Hannah looks," Rose said after a moment.

"I wish I could make things perfect for her," Maddy whispered. "I wish I could make it all better."

"We all wish that, honey," said Rose. "Every single one of us, starting with Eve."

AIDAN CLOSED UP around seven. The broken window was fixed. The boiler would hold on through the night. There was nothing keeping him at O'Malley's except for a general reluctance to head home. He thought about calling Kelly to tell her that he'd swing by Claire's to drive her home, but thought twice about it. Kelly hadn't seen much of her godmother or her cousins lately. A little enforced familial togetherness might not be a bad thing. Besides, he knew Claire had the bit between her teeth about Seth and would probably deliver the kind of lecture Aidan tried to avoid.

Walking across the snowy parking lot to his truck required a hell of a lot more effort than he had expected. The snow was over eight inches deep in places, drifting two and three feet higher than that in others, and it showed no signs of stopping. Despite the general pain-in-the-ass nature of it, the beauty was staggering. How was it he forgot from year to year the magical, almost mystical beauty of a winter snowstorm? Through the veil of falling

snow he saw the street lights curving along the boardwalk
that lined the shore, shimmering like ghostly apparitions.

What really struck him, though, was the silence. There
was a hushed quality to the world, as if all the bits and
pieces of everyday life had been put aside in the face of
nature's majesty. No engine noise. No horns. No buzz of
conversation. No birdsong. No music drifting from an
open car window. Only smaller, simpler sounds unique to
the moment. The shattered-glass sound his boot made as
it broke through the glittering layer of ice, followed by
the soft sigh as the snow gave way. Even the ocean was
subdued; its ever-present roar sounding muffled, more like
a gentle murmur than crashing thunder.

He'd build a fire when he got home. Maybe pop a
movie into the VCR, one of the old films he liked and
Kelly rolled her eyes over. Maybe he would even open a
bottle of red and nuke some leftover pizza. Hell, might as
well make a night of it if he was going to be home alone.

Strange to see where the day had taken him. The breakfast at Julie's with Maddy Bainbridge seemed light-years
ago. Walking through the early snow with her, talking
about things in a way he hadn't talked with anyone in
years. He had had a sense of connection with her, something that went beyond his appreciation of her lovely face
and form. They shared a hometown, an outlook, a situation. The two hours they had spent together had been two
of the best hours he had enjoyed in a very long time, and
if he had one regret about that morning, it was that he
hadn't followed his heart and kissed her.

Before the accident he wouldn't have hesitated. He
would have leaned across the console and claimed her
mouth. He would have left no doubt about what he was
feeling or where he wanted it to lead.

But that man had died in the fire with Billy. That man
had died in a hospital room while the rest of the town
buried his brother. The swaggering confidence that had
once been part of him had been replaced with a brooding
sense of isolation that had always been there, unacknow-
ledged, but growing stronger with each year that passed.

He wondered what she was doing right now. One thing was sure: She wasn't alone, thinking about him. The Candlelight was probably buzzing with energy, guests gathered around the table, Rose ordering everyone around, Maddy's little girl watching it all with big blue eyes that reminded him painfully of Kelly at that age. He tried to imagine the kind of man who could walk away from a new family but came up short. He understood about wanting something different, a life free of encumbrances (he'd be lying if he said he had never once fantasized about chucking it all, heading out on his boat, just him and the wind and the sea), but the distance between understanding it and actually doing it was a distance he'd never wanted to bridge.

"You're almost there," Claire had said to him one afternoon a few months back. "This time next year Kelly will be away at school and you'll be able to start a new life."

Trouble was he didn't want a new life. He wanted to hang on to the one he had for as long as he could. He liked being a father. Bringing up a daughter alone had been a scary proposition, but Kelly had made it easy for him. The thought of not seeing her face at the breakfast table every morning made him feel old and very alone. Old he couldn't do much about, but alone bothered him. The choices he had made over the years no longer seemed rock solid. Kelly was his first priority. She had been from the start and he had never met a woman he believed could step into his late wife's shoes.

And maybe, if he was being honest, he hadn't wanted anyone to.

He had loved once and deeply, but it was a young man's love, built on the foundation of a young man's dream of what romance should be. They had had so little time together, not even close to enough to begin to build that foundation into something meant to last a lifetime.

He liked to think they would have made it this far. He needed to believe that he had what it took to go the dis-

tance. It helped ease the bitter taste of regret that they
would never get that chance.

It was slow going as he gently steered his truck through
the unplowed streets leading away from the docks. He
rolled silently past houses he had known since childhood,
houses that had changed hands five, six, seven times in
the last thirty years but somehow always stayed within
the same extended family. Father to son, mother to daughter, aunt to nephew, sister to sister, cousin to cousin, every
combination you could imagine. He wondered what the
secret was. What did those families know about happiness
that his family couldn't seem to grasp, and where the hell
did you go to take lessons?

He was running out of time with Kelly. He had done
his best for seventeen years, but in the grand scheme of
things he wasn't sure that was anywhere close to being
enough. The world turned faster these days. The problems
were thornier and the risks, greater than anyone could
have imagined. She was every good thing a parent could
ask for in a child, but when she stepped out there into the
world, would any of that be enough to keep her safe from
harm?

Like today. Who would be there to tell her to stay off
the road during a snowstorm? Who would even know if
she got where she was going or was missing somewhere
and—

This was the storm talking. The whisper of icy road
slipping away beneath the wheels of his four-wheel drive
and the snow lashing against his window until he was
lucky he could see the end of his hood. If he wasn't such
a stupid SOB, he would've been home two hours ago and
not slogging his way through a blizzard toward an empty
house that didn't care if he came home or not.

Normally the drive from O'Malley's to the small bridge
that spanned the canal took less than four minutes. That
night it took thirty. As he slowly approached he noted the
glare of red lights and a police car blocking the way. He
braked carefully, slowing to a cautious stop a few feet
away.

"Hey, O'Malley." It was Jim Wagner, an old-timer. "Hate to break it to you, but looks like you're not getting home tonight."

"Shit," Aidan muttered. "What happened?"

"It's a solid sheet of ice. After the fifth accident, we had to shut it down."

"I've got four-wheel drive. I'll put it in neutral and slide down to Main Street."

"Good try, but no dice. We have a spare room now that Kimberly's in college. If you want, I'll call Doreen and tell her you're coming."

"Thanks, buddy," Aidan said, "but I can bunk for the night at the bar."

"Got heat and light still?"

"I did when I left."

"Not a night to take chances," Jim warned. "You sure I can't call Doreen and have her make the bed up for you?"

"Positive," Aidan said, "but thanks. I might take you up on it some other time."

Turning around was going to be a bitch and a half, both men agreed, as Aidan began the slow process of making his way back down to the docks and O'Malley's.

HANNAH YAWNED AS Maddy helped her slip into her warmest pair of pajamas.

"How about a pair of socks?" Maddy asked as she looked down at her little girl's tiny bare feet. "It's freezing tonight!"

"No socks," Hannah said.

"Not even your Christmas socks with the picture of Santa Claus on them?"

"No socks."

"Can I wear your Christmas socks?" Maddy asked as she finished buttoning the last button on Hannah's pj jacket.

Hannah shook her head. "They're mine."

"But you're not wearing them."

"Yes, I am." Hannah grabbed them from the top of the

nightstand and sat down on the floor to pull them on her feet.

The method probably wouldn't win Maddy any medals for parental technique, but it got the job done. She flipped down the covers. As soon as Hannah climbed in, she tucked the sheet and down comforter snugly around the child, then kissed her twice.

"Did you say your prayers?" Maddy asked.

Hannah shook her head. "I—"

"Phone, Maddy!" Rose's voice sounded softly through the intercom system she had installed in the family portion of the Candlelight. "Please come down."

"Don't you go away," Maddy teased her daughter. "I'll be back before you know I'm gone."

She dashed downstairs, wondering why Rose hadn't suggested she pick up the cordless or one of the many extensions.

Rose and Lucy were waiting for her in the kitchen. Lucy mouthed the words "It's Tom" to Maddy when she entered the room.

"Here she is now, Tom," Rose said cordially. "It was wonderful to hear your voice as well."

Maddy tucked a lock of hair behind her ears, then took the phone from her mother. A year or two ago the sound of his voice would have been enough to send her into a week-long tailspin of longing and loneliness that invariably ended up in another tearful weekend where she tried to convince him they should try just once more, if only for Hannah's sake.

Thank God those days were over. Now the sound of his voice only awakened a bittersweet affection and curiosity.

"Rose said you already put our girl to bed," Tom said after they dispensed with the amenities.

"Almost," Maddy said, "but not quite. We haven't dealt with prayers yet or tonight's episode in the ongoing saga of Aladdin and Jasmine move to New Jersey."

Tom's rich laughter made her smile. He loved Hannah.

Of that there was no doubt. "So Aladdin followed her to Jersey, did he?"

"Oh, yes," Maddy said. "He's still number one on her hit parade." She thought of telling him about the samovar, then decided against it. With her luck she would turn around and find Hannah standing behind her, soaking up every word. "So where are you calling from?"

"Lisa and I are in Maui," he said. "I flipped on CNN and heard about your blizzard. They're saying a foot of snow, maybe more, from D.C. up to Maine."

Maddy peered out the kitchen window into a swirling snowy sky. "Sounds about right. I'm going to have to shovel a path for Priscilla or we'll lose her!"

"You have your digital camera, right?"

"Of course," Maddy said. "And you want photos of Hannah playing in the snow."

"If you wouldn't mind."

"I don't mind. In fact I took one of her with Priscilla and my cousin's kids earlier. I'll download it and send it to you before I go to bed."

"I miss her."

"Good," Maddy said. "She misses you, too."

"Think I could speak to her for a minute before lights out?"

"Hang on," she said. "I'll pick up on the extension in her room."

She handed the phone to Rose, who launched into conversation without missing a beat. Maddy dashed up the back stairs, down the hallway, and into Hannah's room.

"Honey, you're going to be so happy. It's—" She stared at the empty bed. "Hannah! Where are you?" She peeked under the bed, behind the rocking chair, in the closet. Maybe she had gone to answer nature's call one last time. They were on fairly solid ground with that issue, but sometimes Hannah fretted about wetting the bed and tended toward hypervigilance.

She walked over to the nightstand and picked up the receiver. "I know this is costing you an arm and a leg," she said to Tom after Rose made her goodbyes again, "but she's in the bathroom. Let me go tell her you're on the phone."

She placed the receiver on the bed and was midway between Hannah's room and the bathroom they shared when she heard her daughter's soft voice behind her.

"Mommy," she said, "where are you going?"

Maddy spun around to see her little girl standing in the middle of the hall, halfway between Rose's room and the bathroom. Hannah couldn't possibly have been snooping in Rose's closet, could she? She had only been downstairs for a few moments. The odds that Hannah would have chosen that opportunity to race down the hall and into her grandmother's room to poke around in search of Christmas presents was far-fetched at best.

"Guess who's on the phone wanting to talk to you, Miss Hannah Bainbridge Lawlor."

Hannah's blue eyes widened. "Daddy?"

"You bet! He wants to know if you had fun in the snow today and—"

Hannah didn't hear a word Maddy said. She turned and ran barefoot back to her bedroom, leaped up on the bed, and clutched the phone as if it were one of her favorite stuffed toys.

"Daddy, it's snowing!" The sound of her voice made Maddy happy and sad at the same time. She was thrilled to hear the joy in her little girl's voice and equally thrilled that Tom had decided to call on the spur of the moment to see how their daughter was faring. Would she sound that way every single day if they had been able to turn themselves into the twenty-four-hours-a-day, seven-days-a-week kind of family Hannah so desperately wanted them to be? Once again Maddy was pierced with a longing that cut straight through to the bone, only it wasn't for Tom himself; it was for the kind of family she had never had. The same kind her little girl longed for, too.

Maybe that was how it was meant to be, she thought as she listened to Hannah chirp to Tom about Priscilla and the gingerbread men up in the attic and the snow drifting against the windows. Children had the right to be loved by their parents, no matter if those parents couldn't find a way to love each other anymore. You could be a world-class single parent who did school-bus duty, baked brownies, attended every soccer game, every glee club practice, every school play, but it would never be enough. Your child would always long for the one who wasn't there. They didn't care if you fought. They didn't care if you rarely spoke to each other. They didn't care about quality time or weekend visitations or blissful summers in Oregon. All they cared about was that the two parents who tucked them into bed at night were there at the break-fast table each morning when they woke up.

Unfortunately Rose and Bill hadn't been able to sum-mon up that miracle for Maddy when she was a little girl, and, in the finest tradition of the DiFalco women, Maddy hadn't been able to conjure up a miracle for Hannah more than twenty years later.

That was a family tradition she could live without.

AIDAN FISHTAILED TO a stop in front of O'Malley's around nine o'clock. The snow had slowed down and the moonglow, combined with the shore lights illuminating the boardwalk, added to the otherworldly feel. Snow turned prosaic objects—a bare tree, a mailbox, a parking lot—into objects of incalculable beauty. Tomorrow after the plows came through and the sun came out all of this pristine whiteness would turn to gray slush and the world would be back to normal. But right now it seemed filled with magic and possibilities.

He deactivated the alarm system, then let himself into the bar. So far the electricity was holding, but if it didn't he had a stack of wood covered on the back step that he could toss into the old fireplace in the main room. He pulled himself a Guinness, then grabbed a container of chili from the freezer to nuke for supper.

He checked in with Kelly, who sounded as if her high-decibel cousins were wearing her out. "Just stay put," he told her, trying not to laugh. "I'll rescue you tomorrow."

The microwave dinged and he pulled out the nuked

chili. No point dirtying a bowl, so he grabbed a clean spoon and carted his makeshift supper out into the main room. The cable was out, but he managed to find a weak signal coming from Philadelphia. Some guy with a helmet of hair spewed endless factoids about the storm—The biggest! The longest! The earliest!—and the requisite warnings about the dangers of shoveling snow.

He finished the last of the chili, then turned off the television. He was a Jets fan, a dying breed on the Jersey shore. A Philly station wasn't likely to waste any airtime analyzing Gang Green's chances on Sunday against the Dolphins. If he wanted an update, he'd be better off booting up the desktop in the office and logging onto their Web site.

And maybe, since the computer would be on anyway, he'd zap off an e-mail to JerseyGirl.

"ALTHOUGH THE COMPANY is wonderful, ladies, I'm going to call it a night." Lucy rose from the easy chair next to the fire and stretched. "This has been quite a day."

"And then some," said Rose. "I'm glad you stayed with us, Lucia. I don't think I could have handled the Loewensteins *and* the Armaghs today without you."

Lucy brushed off her thanks. "I don't think Patton could have handled them alone today." She walked over to the window and peered out through the curtains. "Do you think the roads will be passable tomorrow?"

"Oh, God," Rose moaned, "I hope so."

Lucy and Maddy burst into laughter, and, a moment later, Rose joined in.

"You know I don't mean you, Lucy," she said. "I was talking about—"

"I know." Lucy pecked her on the cheek. "Besides, my sensibilities aren't so fragile that I can't take a joke."

Mine are, Maddy thought as she watched the byplay between the sisters. A tiny misstep like the one Rose just made would have been enough to drive her away in a snit.

Maddy and her aunt exchanged good nights, and Lucy left the room.

It was Maddy's turn to stand up and stretch. "I suppose I should call it a night myself."

Rose looked up from her magazine. "So early?"

"I've been waiting for a response on a Web site question from one of my old friends back in Seattle. He doesn't usually get around to answering his e-mails until around ten or eleven our time."

"It's only ten-thirty," Rose said with a quick glance at the neat little tank watch on her left wrist. "Have a little more hot chocolate before you go."

"You realize the food here is too delicious," Maddy said as she settled down again with a fresh cup of cocoa. "I think I've gained five pounds since we moved back."

"You could use it," Rose said.

Maddy grabbed the sides of her chair to keep from falling to the floor in shock. "I thought you said I was getting fat."

"I never said that!"

"When I wore that dark gold outfit to the township meeting," she reminded her mother, "you said I looked hippy."

"That's right," Rose agreed. "You did look hippy in it. But I didn't say you *were* hippy."

"I don't see the difference."

Rose removed her reading glasses and massaged the bridge of her small, straight nose. "You have a lovely figure. That outfit didn't do you justice."

"Why didn't you just say that?"

"I thought I did."

"Maybe you did, but that's not the way it sounded to me."

"I know," Rose said with a touch of a smile. "That's our problem in a nutshell, isn't it? Neither one of us hears exactly what the other is saying."

Maddy took a sip of cocoa, letting the deep rich aroma of chocolate fill her senses before she spoke. "Today was wonderful," she said. "The Armaghs and Loewensteins notwithstanding."

The lines of tension on Rose's face visibly relaxed, and it occurred to Maddy that she had as much power over Rose's moods as Rose had over hers. The realization made her feel sad.

"We did laugh a lot today, didn't we?" Rose said. "You seemed to feel like one of the team."

"I did," Maddy admitted. "For the first time I began to see where I might fit in around here."

They were silent for a few moments. The only sounds in the room were the crackling of the logs in the fireplace, the whistle of wind beyond the windows, and Priscilla's soft snore.

"I have ideas," Rose said after a while. "They're not quite ready to present to you, but after Christmas, they should be."

"I'm intrigued," Maddy said. "Any hints?"

Rose shook her head. "Not right now. But when the time comes, I want you to be honest."

"That's never been a problem between us, has it," Maddy said, then laughed. Their relationship had been built upon blunt observations and painful truth-telling, and look where it had gotten them. Thirty-two years locked in the mother-daughter dance, and they were still learning how to speak to each other, still struggling to understand how to listen.

Maddy finished her cocoa, then stood up once more. "I'll shut down the office," she said, gathering up her cup and spoon and latest mystery novel.

"I thought you were waiting for some e-mail."

"I'll use my laptop. All I want to do is crawl between the covers and listen to the wind."

"That's what you used to do when you were little," Rose said, a faraway look in her eyes. "Bill and I—" She stopped and returned her gaze to her magazine. "No matter."

"Don't stop!" Maddy sat on the arm of her chair and looked at her closely. "You and Daddy what?"

"I was going to say that your father and I used to stand in the doorway and listen to you talk to the wind."

Maddy grinned. "I talked to the wind?"

"All the time," Rose said, smiling at the memory. "You were crazy about kites. You used to tell stories about how one day the wind was going to lift you and your kite high up into the air and take you away on an adventure."

"I sound like Hannah."

"I know."

Maddy gathered up her nerve and pushed forward. "Is that why you don't think I should encourage Hannah's imagination?" *Because she'll end up an unemployed single mother just like me?*

"I never said you shouldn't encourage Hannah's imagination."

"Of course you did." Maddy stood up, wishing she had ended this conversation five minutes earlier, when things were still going well. "Remember what you said about the samovar? You felt I was encouraging Hannah to live in a dream world."

Rose's expression seemed to close in on itself and the old familiar feeling of dread settled itself in the pit of Maddy's stomach. They had come so far today—and so unexpectedly. She hated to see it all vanish so soon.

Rose met her eyes. "I was wrong."

"What?"

"I was wrong. I had no business trying to mold Hannah's personality into something it isn't. She's very much like you. I see it more with every day."

Maddy's own expression must have undergone a metamorphosis, because Rose reached over to touch her hand.

"That isn't a criticism," she said. "I meant it as a compliment."

"I was hoping," Maddy said, "but considering the fact that I'm an out-of-work, thirty-two-year-old single mother with no prospects, I wasn't too sure."

"You'll find your way," Rose said. "We all do, sooner or later."

"You never seemed to have any trouble."

Rose arched a brow but said nothing.

"I'm serious, Mom. You've always been so goal-oriented, so sure of yourself and what you wanted."

"Is that how I seemed to you?"

"Yes," Maddy said. *Why else would you have worked seventy- and eighty-hour weeks instead of spending time with your kid?*

"I had goals," Rose said slowly, "but they weren't necessarily the ones I achieved."

"You seem happy enough now," Maddy said, painfully aware that she had never once considered her mother's happiness—or lack of it—before that very moment. "Don't take this the wrong way, but you've changed a lot." *For the better.*

"I am happy now," Rose said with conviction. "It was a long time coming, but well worth the wait."

"I always wondered why you decided to bag your career and start over. I mean, it wasn't like you had any guarantee that the Candlelight would be even half the success it is."

"I know," Rose said, a half-smile tugging at the corner of her mouth. "That was exactly what I needed at that moment."

"But why?" Maddy persisted. "That was right around the time when I was pregnant with Hannah and—"

Rose raised her hand between them. "Not my finest hour," she said with a shake of her head.

Maddy thought about the harsh words that had met her announcement of Hannah's impending birth and the prolonged and icy silence that had followed. "No," she said, "it wasn't."

Rose winced. "I suppose I deserved that."

Maddy sighed. "And I suppose I've waited over four years to say it."

"I'd like it very much if we could put that episode behind us and try again."

Maddy reached out and took her hand. "Isn't that exactly what we've been doing?"

*   *   *

AT LEAST ROSE didn't cry until Maddy left the room.

"Tell her," Lucy had been urging her sister. "Tell her before it goes on any longer." But Rose hadn't been able to find the opportunity. Too many people. Too much work. Too much distance between them.

And then tonight, out of nowhere, the perfect opportunity, the once-in-a-lifetime chance to explain away so many things dropped into Rose's lap, and in that very instant her courage took a hike.

There was no easy way to say to your daughter, "I had breast cancer." She needed to tell her. Maddy deserved to know. For many reasons. But she had chosen to fight her battle privately, and now that it seemed she was finally in the clear, that maybe the rest of her life was going to be much longer than she had dared hope for, her resolve failed her.

Funny thing. She had had the guts to fight cancer, but when it came to telling her daughter, she found herself weak and spineless. Afraid to open up her heart completely to the child who had always held the key right there in the palm of her hand and never known it was there.

Chapter Twenty-one

MADDY HAD TO hand it to her mother: Rose had gone first-class when she decorated the Candlelight. Even the family rooms had been blessed with the same attention to comfort and detail as the guest rooms and public areas. Her bed was an acre of pillowy comfort topped with sheets with a four-digit thread count and a pair of down comforters that could keep a girl warm in the middle of the Arctic. Outside the wind howled and the snow fell and the ocean did whatever it was the ocean did during a blizzard, but inside Maddy felt like the cosseted princess in a fairy story.

Of course the flip side to all of this luxury was the fact that the princess also doubled as scullery maid, sous chef, and office worker, but it was a small price to pay. In fact, she was beginning to see what her mother liked about innkeeping. There had been something endearingly goofy about the process today, a certain structured sense of chaos that appealed to the part of her that had been buried during her bean-counter years. From the moment you opened your eyes in the morning, you were playing it by ear. Human beings were unpredictable creatures, and it was that unpredictability that made running a B&B more of an adventure than Maddy had anticipated.

Wait a second! What a perfect topic for the interview on Friday with Jim Kennedy. She had decided to forego her laptop for a good mystery novel and an early lights-out, but she was old enough to know that the brilliant idea you dream up at bedtime is usually the brilliant idea you've forgotten by morning. She hated the thought of climbing out of her cozy dream of a bed to fetch the computer resting atop her dresser, but needs must and all that.

Next time she would remember to stow a notepad and pen in the drawer of her nightstand or keep the laptop on the extra pillow. She hit the On button, waited while Windows loaded, then opened the file marked Ideas.

And why not do a little multitasking and check for e-mail while she typed?

WHY THE HELL was he fighting it? He'd practically memorized the Jets Web site and was rereading the Jets archive on the *Newsday* site, all because he couldn't get it through his fat skull that she wasn't going to answer his e-mail.

You blame her, hotshot? She probably thought he was sleeping with Gina or Denise or maybe both of them, for all the hell he knew. Hey, what could be better than a scarred and crippled bar owner who's been fucking his way through your family? There weren't enough cheap breakfasts in the entire state to make up for that.

So when the new-mail bell chimed, he figured it was another note from Kelly, complaining about the noise level at Claire's house. When he saw the name JerseyGirl, he broke out in one of those goofy wall-to-wall smiles that make you look like you're fifteen and still waiting for your voice to change.

TO: FireGuy@njshore.net
FROM: JerseyGirl@njshore.net

DATE: 6 December
SUBJECT: Great minds

You're not going to believe this, but I was just about to
send YOU a note about breakfast. It really was fun,
wasn't it? But next time it's on me.

Hannah almost uncovered the samovar this afternoon.
I'll spare you the details, but I swear the experience
took ten years off my life. I need remedial present-
hiding instructions ASAP.
Isn't the snow BEAUTIFUL?
Maddy

Hard to believe it was possible, but Aidan's smile grew
wider. It was in danger of taking over the kitchen, the
pantry, and the back porch. If it grew any bigger, he
would need a building permit from the town.

She said "next time."

*She's being polite, moron. There's not going to be a
next time.*

She hadn't struck him as the polite-to-be-polite type.
She was too direct for that, too straightforward.

*Yeah, and you're a real expert on women. That's one
hell of a track record you've got going for you.*

Just shut up and answer her, dammit, before the power
goes out.

IF THE INTERNET had existed when Maddy was a teenager, she never would have left the house. Think of all
the embarrassing Friday night dances she could have
avoided, the miserable evenings spent praying somebody
she wasn't related to would ask her to dance.

There she was curled up in her gorgeous Martha-
Stewart-Meets-Madame-Pompadour bed, typing witty
missives to a dangerously sexy man who hadn't the
faintest idea she was wearing flannel pajamas and woolly
socks instead of a few wisps of satin and lace.

Okay, so maybe it was hard to find a suitably languorous position when you were wedged between a toy poodle and your laptop, but in her mind's eye she was draped voluptuously across the pillows while kind indirect lighting turned her pale skin to pure alabaster and her—

Mail!

TO: JerseyGirl@njshore.net
FROM: FireGuy@njshore.net
DATE: 6 December
SUBJECT: Re: Great minds

You wouldn't think the snow was beautiful if you'd
been turned around at the bridge. Solid ice. I'm bunking at O'Malley's tonight. But I know what you mean—
I stood out on the dock for a few minutes and I felt like
I was in a cathedral.

At Christmas the one sure thing with kids is that if you
hide it, they'll find it. The only thing to do is ask one of
your friends to hide the samovar and don't let Hannah
visit their house until after Christmas.
I'd be happy to take it off your hands.

He wanted to take it off her hands? What did that mean? He had probably only answered her note because he still wanted to wrap his grubby paws around that samovar.

And look. He didn't respond to her breakfast invitation. That wasn't a good sign. She'd bet Gina never had to ask him twice to . . .

Oh, wait. Gina said they'd never slept together.

This was getting very confusing.

WHY THE HELL did he type that stupid line about taking the samovar off her hands? What kind of dumbass wiseguy garbage was that anyway? It made him sound like he was chatting her up in e-mail so he could snag the teapot away from her.

She was taking a long time to answer. Maybe she'd turned away from the screen in disgust, then logged off.

No, there she was. JerseyGirl, right there in his in box, waiting to tell him where to get off.

TO: FireGuy@njshore.net
FROM: JerseyGirl@njshore.net
DATE: 6 December
SUBJECT: Re: Re: Great minds

LOL! Nice try, but no cigar. It's stashed in the back of Rose's closet right now. Believe me, nobody in her right mind would EVER try snooping around in Rose's closet without a search warrant and an armed guard.

Where is Kelly while you're stuck at O'Malley's? If you don't want her to be alone, God knows we have plenty of extra rooms. I'd be glad to walk over and get her.

Let me know, okay?
Maddy

She seemed to feel he could fend for himself (which rankled a little), but her concern for Kelly touched him more deeply than he might care to admit under normal, non-blizzard circumstances. So he hadn't been kidding himself. They had connected that morning in some way that went beyond teapots and breakfast at Julie's.

He'd been around too long—and seen too much—to be wrong about that.

TAP. TAP. TAP. Maddy almost jackknifed off the bed at the sound of the knock at her door.

"Madelyn, are you awake?"

Rose's voice, soft and curious, floated through the closed door.

Maddy waited for her usual Pavlov's dog reaction to the sound. Normally her stomach would clench, her shoulders would lift up to ear level, and her adrenaline would surge in a fight-or-flight wave of readiness.

Nothing. No stomach pains. No adrenaline. Just an odd little ripple of familial warmth.

"Come in," she said, just loud enough to be heard. Hannah was a light sleeper who seemed to hear through walls.

Rose opened the door and stepped into the room.

"Did you notice that power outage a few minutes ago?" Rose had washed off her makeup, brushed her hair back into a no-nonsense nighttime look, and changed into a nightgown and robe. She looked twenty years younger than she had any right to look.

"You couldn't miss it," Maddy said. "I think we'd better make sure the flashlights are all working."

"Not to worry," Rose said. She reminded Maddy that there were flashlights with fresh batteries in both nightstands. "And don't worry about Hannah's room. The night-lights are battery-operated. I change them the first of every month, so we're in good shape."

Priscilla awoke from her deep sleep, noticed Rose standing near the foot of the bed, and began to thump her tail against the mattress in greeting.

Rose's left eyebrow shot up, but her smile was warm as she scratched the puppy under her tiny chin. "You let her sleep in the bed with you."

"Of course not," Maddy said, making her eyes all wide and innocent. "Where would you get that idea?"

Rose settled lightly on the edge of the mattress as she stroked Priscilla. "There's a B&B near Kennebunkport in Maine for pet lovers only. Each room comes with a dog or cat of your choice to cuddle with."

Maddy laughed. "I like that idea. I don't know how we functioned before we found Priscilla."

"You always wanted a puppy when you were little."

"And you always said no."

"I wonder why," Rose mused. "For the life of me I don't know what my reason was."

The chime announcing new mail sounded. Rose tilted

her head in the direction of the laptop. "One of your West Coast friends?"

It would be so easy to say yes and let it go at that. "No," she said. "It's from Aidan O'Malley."

If Rose was surprised she didn't let on. "You two seemed to get along quite well today."

"I like him," Maddy said. "What I mean is, we had a common interest in the samovar."

"It's all right to like him," Rose said. "He's a very likable man."

Maddy waited for the punch line, but there didn't seem to be one. "He said the bridge is down. He's stuck at the bar overnight." She paused a moment. "I said that his daughter is welcome to one of our rooms if he doesn't want her to be alone tonight."

"Of course," Rose said. "But how would she get here?"

"I guess I'd walk over to their house to get her."

"In a blizzard?"

"I don't think it will come to that," Maddy said, "but it might."

"That was an impulsive gesture," Rose observed.

"I know." As usual, she had blurted out her first thoughts without considering whether or not she could even open the front door against the drifts piling up out there.

"You have a kind heart," Rose said. "I've always admired that about you. You reach out to people spontaneously, without weighing the pros and cons of a gesture."

"Right," Maddy said, turning quickly so Rose wouldn't see her wipe away the tears balanced on the tips of her lashes. "Before I even know if we can open the front door against the snowdrifts."

"I know you well enough, Madelyn, to know you'd find a way if you had to."

Is that how you see me, Mother? You almost sound proud!

"I wasn't sure you liked Aidan O'Malley," Maddy said, steering the conversation away from herself.

"He's not one of my biggest admirers," Rose said with a small, self-deprecating laugh, "but I think he felt a tad more relaxed with me today."

"You can be a little intimidating," Maddy said. "Especially to someone who's in competition with you."

"Competition? He runs a bar, Maddy, not a B&B. Our clientele is different." She paused for a moment, lost in thought. "Of course, it needn't be quite so different as it is."

"Meaning what?"

"An idea," Rose said, drifting toward the door. "One I've been toying with for a while. I'm going to go make a few notes while it's still fresh. Sleep well, both of you. I'll see you in the morning."

Maddy was astonished to realize she hated to see her mother leave. "Do you think the roads will be open tomorrow?" She didn't really care, but she wanted to delay Rose a second more.

"Oh, God, please!" Rose said with a theatrical gesture of her hands. "One more night with our four friends, and I'll clear the roads with my bare hands."

Maddy was still chuckling after Rose closed the door behind her. Things were changing between them. There was no doubt in her mind about that. She wasn't sure if Rose had become softer or she had become less defensive, but they were communicating with each other in a way they hadn't since Maddy came out of the womb thirty-two years earlier.

No doubt about it. From start to finish, this had been an amazing day. And it wasn't over yet.

She settled back against her mountain of pillows, kissed the top of Priscilla's fluffy head, then opened the e-mail from Aidan.

TO: JerseyGirl@njshore.net
FROM: FireGuy@njshore.net
DATE: 6 December
SUBJECT: Re: Re: Re: Great minds

Good thing Kelly doesn't know about your offer. She'd
be at your door right now. She's staying at Claire's tonight and the noise level is getting to her.

Besides, you'll be seeing a lot of her once she starts
working over there at the Candlelight.

But thanks for thinking of her.
A

Was that a polite kiss-off or an opening for more conversation? She wasn't exactly sure, but her fingers were
flying too quickly across the keyboard for it to be much
of a problem.

TO: FireGuy@njshore.net
FROM: JerseyGirl@njshore.net
DATE: 6 December
SUBJECT: Re: Re: Re: Re: Great minds

You mean that smart and pretty blond my mother
hired is YOUR DAUGHTER? No wonder you're so
proud of her! What a great kid she is. If I'd been half
as together as your Kelly when I was her age, I
wouldn't be back in Paradise Point working for my
mother!

What's your secret? Can you bottle it? When I look at
Hannah and think of the future, it scares me so much
sometimes that I want to hide under the bed and not
come out until she's married with kids of her own.

Advice gratefully accepted.
Maddy

He found himself liking her more with each e-mail. She
was warm, funny, and straightforward, three attributes you
didn't often find in the same person. And she liked his
kid. That didn't hurt, either. She didn't take herself too

seriously, but she understood what was—or should be—
important in life.

If the power ever came back on, he'd answer her e-
mail.

TO: JerseyGirl@njshore.net
FROM: FireGuy@njshore.net
DATE: 6 December
SUBJECT: Luck (was Great minds)

Wish I had some advice for you, but I just got lucky.
Unlike her old man

"Oh, no!"

The battery alarm buzzed a "2% remaining" warning
and Maddy leaped from bed to grab for the A/C cord. She
scrabbled around on the floor, snaked her hand under the
bed, and grabbed for the power brick, then managed to
plug the whole shebang in a split second before the room
went black, taking Aidan's message with it.

"Come on, you can't do this to me!"

She peered out her bedroom window. The entire street
was dark. When was she going to learn to keep her laptop's battery properly charged? She couldn't begin to
count the times she'd managed to get herself in trouble
with a drained battery and a misplaced A/C cord or, like
tonight, a power outage.

Hannah's voice seeped through the wall that separated
their rooms and Maddy hurried out into the hall. She
inched Hannah's door open a tiny bit and peeked inside.
Bless Rose and the battery-operated night-lights that
bathed the room in a soft pink glow. Hannah's curls were
barely over her beloved Aladdin blanket. How Rose must
have mourned when she saw Aladdin featured promi-
nently at the center of her Victorian decorating scheme,
but she never said a word.

Maddy tiptoed closer to the bed. Hannah's soft, gentle
breathing filled her heart with joy. She leaned over and

pressed a kiss to her daughter's cheek and was about to
return to her room when Hannah spoke.

"Go back to sleep, sweetie," Maddy whispered. "Everything's all right."

Hannah mumbled something, but Maddy couldn't de-
cipher the words. She leaned closer. The rhythm was familiar—rise and fall and rise and fall—and it reminded
her of the Russian family who had lived next door to them
in Seattle. The condo walls were very thin, and the Grin-
kovs' conversations came through loud and clear. Apparently Hannah had absorbed the sounds and made them
part of her rich fantasy life.

For nine months Hannah had been a part of her, flesh
of her flesh. Now the tiny baby who had depended upon
Maddy for her every need had a secret inner life she could
never penetrate. It thrilled and dismayed her at the same
time. She wanted to nurture Hannah's individuality, but
oh, how she longed for the days when she knew all the
curves and shadows of her daughter's heart.

She returned to her room as the lights flickered on,
dipped, then came back to life. She didn't waste a second
and within minutes she was back on-line, picking up
where she had left off.

> Kelly has been making the right decisions since she
> was Hannah's age. All I've ever done is watch and lis-
> ten and be there for her.
> You're right to be scared. It's a hell of a job, especially
> when you're in it alone.
> A.

Another power hit like the last one and the desktop
would be toast. Aidan fumbled around for the flashlight
and set it upright in a beer mug. It cast a wide arc of light
across the ceiling beams of the stockroom-turned-office
and spilled down the walls like pale malt. Too bad he
couldn't come up with an easy fix for the computer.

He dug a worn pack of cards from his desk drawer and
dealt out a hand of solitaire. He was about to top the five

of spades with a four of hearts when the lights came on
and he was back in business.

TO: FireGuy@njshore.net
FROM: JerseyGirl@njshore.net
DATE: 6 December
SUBJECT: Re: Luck (was Great minds)

Hope you're still there. We lost power and then I heard
a noise from Hannah's room, so I went in to investi-
gate. (Yes, I was afraid she'd gone on a samovar
search!)

Turns out she was talking in her sleep! And not only
talking, but I swear she was speaking with some kind
of accent. Don't laugh but do you remember Boris &
Natasha? Hannah sounded like a baby Natasha!

Maybe Rose is right and cartoons really are a brain
drain.
Did you let Kelly watch a lot of TV?
Maddy

TO: JerseyGirl@njshore.net
FROM: FireGuy@njshore.net
DATE: 6 December
SUBJECT: Cartoons

Guilty. Scooby-Doo. Josie and the Pussycats. And
those Saturday mornings didn't seem to hurt her any.
(And I got some extra ZZZZs.)
A.

TO: FireGuy@njshore.net
FROM: JerseyGirl@njshore.net
DATE: 6 December
SUBJECT: Re: Cartoons

You mean I don't have to feel guilty for letting Hannah
believe Aladdin and Jasmine are part of the family??
Maddy

TO: JerseyGirl@njshore.net
FROM: FireGuy@njshore.net
DATE: 6 December
SUBJECT: power outage

Hey, sorry I disappeared. The lights blew (third time)
and then the phone went out for a couple minutes
right after. This storm is worse than I figured. Are you
still there?
A.

TO: FireGuy@njshore.net
FROM: JerseyGirl@njshore.net
DATE: 6 December
SUBJECT: Blizzard??

Same thing happened here. Hannah's curled up next
to me now. (So is Priscilla. She sends her regards to
your right shoe.) I think we're on borrowed time.

Hannah asked me if tomorrow will be a Snow Day.
Remember them? Gina and I used to sneak down to
the beach and build anatomically correct snow mermaids.

Whoops! The lights just flickered. Better send this off
before the power goes out again. If I can't connect
again, this has been fun.
Maddy

TO: JerseyGirl@njshore.net
FROM: FireGuy@njshore.net

DATE: 6 December
SUBJECT: snowmaids?

Snow Days were like Christmas, Halloween, and your birthday all rolled into one.

(Anatomically correct snow mermaids?? Where was I when this was going on?)
A.

TO: FireGuy@njshore.net
FROM: JerseyGirl@njshore.net
DATE: 6 December
SUBJECT: Re: snowmaids?

I don't know where you were, O'Malley. We didn't exactly run with the same crowd, did we? But if you can make your way down here tomorrow, I just might show you how it's done.
Maddy

TO: JerseyGirl@njshore.net
FROM: FireGuy@njshore.net
DATE: 6 December
SUBJECT: Re: Re: snowmaids?

It's a deal.
Sleep well, Maddy Bainbridge.
Aidan
PS: Breakfast sounds great. How about Friday?

Chapter Twenty-two

"HANNAH WANTS TEA," Rose said when Maddy walked into the kitchen the next morning. "I didn't know she drank tea."

"She doesn't," Maddy said, casting a curious glance in the direction of her daughter. "Do you really want tea?"

Hannah nodded. "In a glass, please."

Rose, Maddy, and Lucy exchanged looks.

"A glass?" Lucy said, then started to laugh. "Of course! You want iced tea, right, Hannah?"

"No," said Hannah primly. "Hot tea in a glass with a lump of sugar."

"Don't look at me," Maddy said to her mother and aunt. "I have no idea where this is coming from."

"Where did you learn about hot tea in a glass?" Rose asked as she slathered sweet butter on a freshly baked cranberry-pecan muffin.

Hannah looked puzzled for a second, then brightened. "I just know, that's all."

"We could use one of those nice heavy glass beer mugs," Lucy said. "That should be able to withstand the heat."

"And a lot of milk, I would think." Rose added the buttered muffin to the basket of other buttered muffins.

"Oh, why not?" Maddy pulled a pair of clean glass mugs from the top shelf of the cabinet over the fridge. "It's a glorious day out there. I think we should celebrate!"

Lemony winter sun bounced off the snowy yard and splashed through the wide windows, bathing the kitchen in crystal-clear light that took your breath away. The storm had washed the world clean and returned it all sparkling and new.

"Isn't she in a wonderful mood," Lucy said as Maddy added a tea bag to each of the mugs.

"Indeed she is," Rose said with a smile for Maddy.

She poured hot water carefully into each of the mugs. Hannah watched, enchanted, as the water began to turn darker shades of amber.

"It's a beautiful day," Maddy said. "Who wouldn't be in a wonderful mood on a day like this?"

Rose started to laugh. "We're snowbound. The phones are out. The plows haven't been through yet. We might end up welcoming in the New Year with the Loewensteins and the Armaghs, and you look like you won the lottery."

"It's been a long time since I saw a bona fide blizzard. Look!" she said, gesturing toward the window and the shimmering vista beyond. "Have you ever seen anything more glorious in your entire life?"

"Yes," said Lucy. "A snowplow with my name on it."

Teasing words flew about the kitchen, but they were gentle words meant to remind you that you were part of something bigger than yourself. A family. Had the words themselves suddenly lost their cutting edge, or was Maddy hearing them through new ears? She hadn't a clue. All she knew was that the words felt like hugs.

She added milk and sugar to Hannah's tea, stirred it, then tasted it to make sure it wasn't too hot for her. Assured that it was a safe temperature, she placed the mug down in front of her little girl.

"Well, there you go, Hannah," she said, milking and

sugaring her own mug of tea. "Hot tea in a glass, just like you ordered."

Hannah wrapped her tiny hands around the glass and smiled up at Maddy. *"Spasibo,"* she said.

"She speaks Russian?" Lucy said. "I thought you said she was crazy about Aladdin."

Maddy made a fierce face at Lucy. That was all she needed, for her aunt to ruin Hannah's Christmas surprise.

Rose waved away the comment. "Maddy had Russian neighbors back in Seattle. Children are sponges. Remember when Denise's youngest spent the night with Julia Gonzalez and her family? She came home sounding like Antonio Banderas." She untied her apron and hung it on the hook behind the kitchen door, then picked up the basket of muffins. "Time to say good morning to our guests. Pray for the snowplows, ladies."

Hannah was happily enjoying her glass of tea and a bowl of maple-drizzled oatmeal. Maddy popped two slices of homemade white into the toaster and gazed longingly at the jar of homemade raspberry jam on the table.

Lucy piled mountains of fluffy yellow scrambled eggs into the chafing dish. "So things are going well for you two," she said with one of her patented Lucy smiles. "It does my heart good to see the change."

The DiFalco women were nothing if not direct. No point pretending she didn't know what Lucy was talking about.

"We have a lot of history between us," Maddy said carefully. "The last few days have been amazing but—"

"I know," Lucy said. "But humor me. I think this could be a fresh start for both of you."

Maddy walked over to where her aunt stood near the sink and pressed a kiss to her soft, smooth cheek. "You always did believe in miracles, Aunt Lucy. That's one of the reasons I love you so much."

"I know what I know," Lucy said with a toss of her head. "And I know that you and Rosie are more alike than either of you realizes."

Maddy made a face. "I wouldn't go that far."

"There! That's exactly what I mean. You both hide your feelings with a few funny words and a laugh, but that doesn't mean they aren't there."

"Rose always told me I was too free with my emotions."

"Anger definitely," Lucy said, "but until Hannah came along, I don't think I ever really saw you open your heart."

"Lucy!" Maddy stared at her aunt. "I thought I was the one who wore her heart on her sleeve."

"Oh, that's what you wanted us all to think," Lucy said. "But one look in your eyes told the real story. Your heart was hiding in plain sight."

"Motherhood changes you."

Lucy looked as if she had been about to say something, but thought better of it.

"What?" Maddy asked. "Go ahead. We've never held back with each other, Lucy."

Lucy shook her head, her dangly earrings dancing in the sunlight.

"Rose *is* different these days," Maddy said, "and I don't think it's a delayed response to motherhood."

"You're right," Lucy said. "She is different."

Was it her imagination, or were Lucy's eyes wet with tears?

"I've never really understood why she left her old career the way she did and poured everything into the Candlelight. It seemed to come from nowhere." It had all happened around the time when she was so deeply involved in pregnancy and childbirth and the upheaval in her relationship with Tom Lawlor that her mother's decision never really registered on Maddy the way it might have at another time. "Do you know why she did it?"

"You should ask her," Lucy said, looking somewhat uncomfortable.

"I have," Maddy said. "The most I get is some vague New Age-y kind of answer about changing lifestyles and following your bliss."

Lucy started to laugh. "Your mother never said she followed her bliss."

"No, but that's what she meant. It just doesn't sound much like the Rose I grew up with."

"She isn't the Rose you grew up with. She's changed and so have you."

"I want to know why."

"It's not my place," Lucy said. "This is between you and your mother."

"Wonderful, Lucy. After all these years, you pick today to become diplomatic."

"I had to start sometime," Lucy said.

"Come on, Lucy, what is it? Did she have a bad hair day? Did one of her boyfriends break up with her? Did she just get sick and tired of the old nine-to-five routine and decide to hang up her realtor's license? Give me a hint, please, Lucy. Just a little hint."

But for the first time in DiFalco history, Aunt Lucy's lips were sealed.

KELLY WAS WAITING in the front yard when Aidan arrived. Claire's street had been cleared, but the plows had managed to block every driveway with a mountain of snow that would take the homeowners hours to dig their way through.

Her Tercel was stuck in the driveway for the duration—he recognized it under the heavy blanket of snow—but there wasn't a blizzard on earth that could hold his daughter in the same house with her younger cousin for one minute longer.

"You took forever!" she said as she leaped into the truck, spraying snow everywhere. "Billy was driving me completely crazy with that stupid Game Boy you gave him."

"Good morning to you, too," he said, sounding like every father of every teenage daughter in the country.

"Oh, Daddy!" She leaned over and gave him a quick peck on the cheek. "Good morning." She unwrapped the heavy green scarf that was looped around her neck and sighed. "You don't know how great quiet sounds."

He grinned. "Gives you new respect for your aunt Claire, doesn't it?"

"How does she stand it?" Kelly said. "It's like living in the middle of a tornado."

"It's called parenthood."

She shot him a funny look, one he couldn't read. Then again, that might have been a trick of the light. "I wasn't like that."

"Really?" He started to laugh. "You were a great kid, Kel, but you weren't quiet."

They rode a few blocks in silence until he turned south on Main Street.

"Wrong way," she said.

"I'm swinging by the Candlelight." He kept his eyes on the road. "Thought we'd say hello to your new employer."

She groaned. "I was going to tell you, Daddy."

"When?" he asked. "Your first day on the job?"

"It was kind of a spur-of-the-moment thing. I saw the ad and—" She shrugged her shoulders. "I figure the more I can save before college, the better. Then I won't have to look for work the second I get to Columbia."

"Anything else you forgot to tell me?"

There it was again. A look that came and went so quickly he wasn't sure it had been there at all.

"I'm serious, Kel. Something on your mind?"

"What could be on my mind?"

"School. Work." He paused a moment, debating. "Seth."

"No, everything's fine."

They glided to a stop at a traffic light, and he turned to look at her more closely. "You look tired."

"You'd look tired too if you spent the night under the same roof with that little maniac."

"You've looked tired for the last week or so," he said. She was working too hard, asking too much of herself. Why hadn't he been paying attention? "You don't have to push yourself so hard, Kel. We're not broke. I can help you out with expenses when you're at Columbia."

Her face was turned away from him as she watched Sara Minelli shoveling her front walk at the corner of Bay Breeze Circle and Main Street. When was the last time they had had a heart-to-heart? Damned if he could remember. For a long time after the accident, the focus had been on his needs, his recovery. His strong and competent daughter had stepped into the breach and held them together with the sheer force of her will. Two years had come and gone since the accident that took Billy's life. His little girl had gone from child to woman when he wasn't looking, and he found himself wondering what he had missed along the way and how he could get it back.

Was this how it was supposed to be? One day you wake up and discover that your child has a life of her own, one that doesn't involve you. One you don't even know about.

"I'm okay."

"You don't sound it."

"There's a lot going on at school right now," she said. "Yearbook meetings, the newspaper, band." She shrugged but didn't turn away from the window. "You know."

"And you want to add another job to the mix. Doesn't sound like a great idea to me."

She was silent as they moved forward again. "So maybe I'll quit one of my other jobs."

"Good idea. You work hard enough as it is."

"I like to try different things," she said. "I thought it might be fun to see how a B&B works from the inside."

"It's housekeeping," he said, "just on a bigger scale."

"Are you going to tell me I can't take the job?"

"No," he said, "but I'm going to ask you to evaluate how much is too much." He glanced at her and they locked eyes. "Can you do that?"

"Yes, I can do that." She adjusted the zipper on her down jacket. "If you're not asking me to quit the job, why are we going to the Candlelight?"

"Mermaids," he said. "We're going to meet a mermaid."

*   *   *

"COME WITH US, Grandma," Hannah said as Maddy zipped her into her bright blue parka. "Mommy's going to make a snowman."

"A mermaid," Maddy corrected her daughter. "We're making snow mermaids."

Rose threw back her head and started to laugh. "Not the infamous snow mermaids again!"

Maddy winked at her over Hannah's head. "A G-rated version this time around." She adjusted Hannah's cap, then handed her the red mittens Lucy knitted for her. "Why don't you join us?"

"Lucy's going home soon and we still have guests." *One more day. Please, God, just one more day.*

"I think they're all taking a siesta," Maddy said. "You're allowed to enjoy the fresh air, aren't you?"

"We'll see," Rose said. She reached out and adjusted Maddy's collar. "Don't forget your camera. Hannah's first snowmaid is a very special occasion."

They hurried out the back door, across the plowed driveway, then down the snowy slope to the boardwalk. The B&B owners on the south end of Main Street paid dearly for special services, and it was on days like this when they were grateful for every penny spent. Driveways were clear. Paths. Steps. The parking lot. Sand had been scattered liberally. It would take another twenty-four hours for the rest of the township to catch up with them.

She heard footsteps behind her followed by the scent of her sister's gardenia-scented perfume.

"I thought you'd be down on the beach with them," Lucy said, joining her at the window.

"I made a decision." Rose turned to face her sister. "You're not going to like it."

"I was afraid of this." Lucy headed straight for the coffeepot. "You're not going to tell her about the breast cancer, are you?"

"That's right," Rose said, preparing for battle. "I thought about it long and hard last night. I had the perfect opportunity to tell her the truth and I didn't."

"You couldn't."

"Couldn't. Didn't. What's the difference? Things are better between us, Lucia. For the first time since—well, maybe the first time ever, we're enjoying each other's company. She laughs at my jokes! Do you know how wonderful it feels to see my daughter laugh at my jokes? I wouldn't jeopardize that for the world."

"Just because she laughs at your jokes, don't think she's forgiven you for not being there when she needed you. That's not the kind of hurt a daughter forgets, honey. Not without one damn fine reason."

"It doesn't have to be perfect," Rose said, wishing Lucy would try to see things her way just this once. "If things stayed exactly the way they were today, I could be happy."

"What about Maddy?"

"What about her? She's moving ahead with her life. We're rebuilding our relationship. Why belabor old griev-ances?"

"If you don't understand, Rose, there's no point to this conversation."

"If it's the family medical history you're concerned with, she's still young. I know she does a monthly self-exam. She goes to the doctor. I'm not worried."

"You should be and not because of the cancer."

"She's my daughter, Lucia. This is my decision."

"Same old Rose," Lucy said, shaking her head. "I thought you were making progress the last few years, but I was kidding myself."

"And what's that supposed to mean?"

"It's always about you. It's always about what you want, what you think, what you need."

Rose's temper started to simmer. "It's called self-sufficiency, Lucia. I think we all subscribe to the theory."

"It's called selfishness," Lucy shot back. "You're so busy planning how you're going to handle things, how you're going to cope, that it never occurs to you that maybe part of the process is letting yourself ask for help."

The statement caught Rose by surprise. "I don't under-stand."

"Let's put the rest of the family aside for the time being and just talk about Madelyn. You denied her the opportunity to help you, Rosie. You didn't give her a chance to step up to the plate and be there for you. Being needed is one of life's joys."

Angry tears welled up from nowhere and spilled down Rose's cheeks, but she refused to acknowledge their existence.

"Go ahead, Rosie," Lucy urged. "Say it. I can take it. Say whatever you need to say. Get it out in the open."

The words ripped their way up from the center of Rose's gut. "Damn you, Lucia, I didn't tell her because I didn't think she would care." Better to be alone by choice than have to face the fact that your only child can't stand to be in the same time zone with you.

"She would have been here."

"You don't know that."

"I think I do. That girl loves you. Maybe more than you deserve. And she's been looking for your approval since the day she was born."

All of Rose's energy seemed to vanish at once, and she sank into one of the kitchen chairs and rested her elbows on the table. She closed her eyes against the glare of reflected sunlight crashing through the window.

"I could override you, Rosie. I could walk down to the beach and tell her everything."

"But you won't."

"I should."

"But you won't," Rose repeated. "Give me the chance to get to know my child again. Maybe in a few months I'll feel differently, but I've waited over thirty years for this. Let me enjoy it, please."

"What do you think she'll do when you tell her? Turn away forever? Rosie, if she didn't turn away from you forever after you blew off the birth of your granddaughter, she'll never turn away. When are you going to understand how much she loves you? How much we all love you."

"I wouldn't have told you if you hadn't been with me when I got the news."

"And I thank God every night I was there. We're not meant to go through things like that alone, Rosie. That's why we're a family."

They had been down that road a thousand times before and would never agree on the matter. Lucy believed a burden shared was a burden halved. Rose believed burdens grew heavier with each pronouncement. How much easier it had been to go through the lumpectomy and the months of treatment afterward keeping the truth a tightly held secret. No sad eyes watching your every move. No endless "But how are you *really?*" refrains coming at you ten times a day. No counting you out before you had a chance to be counted in.

At least she had spared Maddy that. She hadn't tarnished the joy of pregnancy and childbirth with the harsh reality of cancer. Maddy had been joyous those nine months. Astonishment had turned to wonder and wonder to joy, and there she had stayed. Rose wouldn't have changed any of it, not for the world. No matter how badly she yearned to be with her daughter when she gave birth to a daughter of her own.

What was done was done. She had no regrets.

And if she did, she would never admit it, not even to herself.

THE BEACH BEHIND the Candlelight was crowded with kids and parents. At least a dozen snowmen were in progress and at least twice as many snowball fights. An impressive pair of snow forts were being erected at the south side of the shoveled pathway by a group of Kelly's classmates. She quickly chose sides and set to work.

His daughter was laughing with her friends, perched atop the snow fort next to a stack of snowballs. Her hair glowed in the sunlight like golden fire. She was her mother all over again, filled with energy and enthusiasm and more love for life than anyone he had ever known. She was breaking free of the connection. That was what she was supposed to do. And he would have to let go because that was what he was supposed to do. But he had never understood how hard it would be until that moment. One more blink of the eye and she would be gone, launched into the future with all of his hopes and dreams for her tucked inside her heart.

Seth stepped away from the knot of teenagers, and Kelly launched herself at him, flying across the snow and into his arms. He swung her around, and the sound of his daughter's laugh was her mother's laugh before her when Aidan caught Sandy in his arms on their wedding day and spun her around on the top step of the County Court House.

Full circle, O'Malley. They're in love and there isn't a damn thing on earth you can do about it.

That was when he saw Maddy and Hannah, not more than twenty feet away from where he stood. Mother and daughter. Snow-covered. Bathed in sunshine. Laughing.

Maddy caught sight of him and she waved her arm in a wide arc. "Join us!" she called. "I promised you a snow-maid and I'm a woman of my word."

He couldn't move. Couldn't breathe. Couldn't think. He felt his heart crack open as sorrow, joy, regret, passion—every emotion under the sun—broke free, crashing against his chest with the force of last night's storm. It was like waking up after a long sleep and discovering that the world was still there waiting for you and you hadn't lost your place in line.

It was a little like falling in love.

Good Samaritan Hospital

"Look!" the nurse said. "She's smiling. I think she's coming back to us."

"Reflex," said the other nurse. "Doesn't mean a thing."

"She's dreaming," the first nurse said. "Can't tell me she isn't thinking happy thoughts right now."

NIKOLAI DANCED HER through the ballroom, past her parents, who were whispering together near the ice sculptures, past her sisters and their boring beaux, past the

*other handsome soldiers wooing the prettiest girls in St.
Petersburg. He danced her out into the garden, into the
shadows.*

*The night air was chill, but she didn't care. He was so
tall and handsome in his uniform with his golden hair
shimmering in the moonlight, his blue eyes blazing with
desire.*

*They were young and in love and they believed the
future was theirs for the taking.*

"I love you, Kolya," she said.

*He murmured sweet words against the curve of her
throat, the creamy pillows of her breasts, hot breath
against cool skin until she thought she would die of the
love she felt for him.*

*Deeper into the shadows . . . past the ice house . . . past
the pond . . . until no one could see them.*

*She was afraid, but because she loved him she gave
herself to him. "Nothing will ever part us," he told her
as she trembled in his arms. "No matter what happens,
we'll always be together."*

Kolya . . . her sweet Kolya . . .

"KOLYA," HANNAH SAID. "I love you, Kolya."

Maddy looked up from the mermaid's torso. "What was
that, honey?"

Hannah looked dreamy, different in a way Maddy
couldn't define.

"Hannah," Maddy said again. "What did you say?"

"Nothing, Mommy. I was talking to my friend." She
patted snow along the mermaid's right hip.

Maddy sighed and looked over at Aidan, who was busy
working on the mermaid's snowy flippers. "Did Kelly
have *friends*, too, when she was Hannah's age?"

Aidan grinned at her. "A pocket horse named Ivor who
lived in Barbie's Dream House."

Maddy burst into laughter. "And what did you think
about that?"

He shrugged. "I left a cup of shredded wheat 'hay' on

her nightstand every Saturday until Ivor went off to join the circus."

"The first time I brought home one of those friends, Rose took us all off to family therapy."

It was his turn to burst into laughter. "Somehow that doesn't surprise me."

Hannah was having trouble making the mermaid's scales, so Aidan gently guided her hands until she caught on. Within minutes she was beaming from ear to ear, proud of every scale that appeared beneath her fingers. Most men hadn't a clue what to do with a four-year-old girl. They either talked over her head or treated her like a tiny doll. Aidan did neither of those things. He saw Hannah as Hannah, an individual child with likes and dislikes and quirks all her own, and Hannah responded in kind.

You're a good father, she thought. She had assumed so by virtue of his daughter's many accomplishments, but now she had the proof. He seemed to effortlessly hit just the right note with Hannah and soon had her giggling the way she used to do before grown-up problems turned her life upside down.

"Hi," said a young woman's voice behind her. "Okay if I join you guys?"

Maddy squinted up into the bright sunshine and saw Kelly smiling down at her. "Grab a flipper," she said, smiling back. "I think your father's having some trouble."

Hannah peered over at Kelly. "Who're you?"

"I'm Kelly." She pointed a thumb toward Aidan. "He's my dad."

"You have Kolya's eyes," Hannah said.

Kelly looked over at Maddy for an explanation.

"Kolya is Hannah's new friend," she said carefully, not wanting to burst Hannah's imaginative bubble. "None of us has met him yet because he's very shy."

"Well," said Kelly, taking it all in stride, "I guess Kolya has blue eyes. Right, Hannah?"

But four-year-olds have no attention span at all. Hannah had already abandoned both the conversation and her mermaid's scales for another project.

A teapot made of snow.

Chapter Twenty-three

THEY SAID NECESSITY was the mother of invention, and that night at the Candlelight, Rose proved the truth of the axiom. Maddy couldn't remember ever being more delighted to be Rose DiFalco's daughter than she was that night as they all gathered around the huge dining room table and feasted on a meal of leftovers and fellowship.

Rose, her face pink from the heat of the stove and maybe from pleasure as well, sat at her accustomed place at the head of the table. She gestured for Maddy to take her place at the other end of the table, in the position of second-in-command of the Good Ship Romance. She noted that Rose had made sure Aidan was seated to her right while Maddy was flanked by Mr. Armagh and Aidan's daughter, Kelly. Rose had asked Maddy if Hannah could sit next to her in a special place of honor. Maddy was delighted, not only by the offer but by the fact that Rose had run it by her first.

Mrs. Armagh and Mrs. Loewenstein carried on a lively debate about which casino had the best buffet while Lucy and Mr. Loewenstein managed to plow through four large wedges of Rose's homemade focaccia between them, laughing together like co-conspirators.

Conversations overlapped as people talked over each other, under each other, and around each other. Verbal volleys flew from one side of the table to the other, and if you missed a comment the first time around, not to worry. Sooner or later somebody would bring you up to speed.

"So tell me about O'Malley's," Mr. Armagh said when he caught Aidan's attention. "Is it one of those swell Irish bars with singing and darts?"

"And Guinness," Mr. Loewenstein added. "Gotta have Guinness or it's no kind of bar I want to know about."

Everyone laughed, Aidan most of all.

"Yeah, we have darts," he said, catching Maddy's eye and grinning. "Our team took first place in Atlantic County three years running." Whoops and hollers from the assembled diners. He raised his hand in a display of fake modesty that made everyone laugh. "The singing and the Guinness seem to go hand-in-hand."

"Maybe we should stay another day," Mrs. Loewenstein said. Maddy could almost hear Rose's groan clear across the table. "I'd like to see that place. I never knew a tavern owner before."

"It's not much of a tavern," Aidan said as Kelly rolled her eyes. "My brother and sister-in-law took it over years ago from our grandmother."

Mrs. Armagh's brows shot toward the ceiling. "Your grandmother ran a bar?" She looked as if the idea had plenty of appeal.

Aidan explained about the original O'Malley's and the Hurricane of '52 and how what was once a restaurant renowned in four states evolved over time into a down-on-its-luck Irish tavern on the south side of Paradise Point. "We're pretty much back to basics these days," he said. "Guinness, darts, and buffalo wings."

"That selection ultimately limits your customer base," Rose said. "I know your menu. You offer more than buffalo wings, but the list is still pretty basic."

"I'm not a chef," Aidan said, an edge slicing through his voice. "I learned to cook in a firehouse."

"And some of the best cooks in the country are firefighters," Rose said, not rising to the bait. "Did you ever think of hiring on another retired firefighter to help you out in the kitchen? All you'd have to do for the moment is add a few health-conscious salads and sandwiches to the mix, and I guarantee you'd bring in more business."

"Maybe if I had your profit margin I could branch out, but we're barely hanging on."

"There are still things you can do and stay within budget. Salads and sandwiches won't break the budget, Aidan."

Suddenly Aidan looked interested. "What else?"

Rose hesitated. "Listen, what do I know? You know better than I how to run a bar. O'Malley's is an institution."

"Yeah," said Aidan, "and you know as well as I do that we've been running on history for a hell of a long time now. I'd appreciate your help, Rose."

They were off and running. Everyone at the table had an opinion, and nobody was shy about expressing it. Maddy felt a strange combination of envy and pride at the sight of her mother and Aidan engrossed in animated conversation.

"She's something, isn't she?" Lucy almost sounded like a proud mother hen. "It's like she was born to run a business of her own."

Maddy nodded. Truth was, she didn't trust herself to speak. Rose's openness and generosity were what really surprised her. Again she was left wondering if there had indeed been a sea change or if her own agenda had made her blind to her mother's many attributes.

"What do you think, Maddy?" Rose turned the force of her attentions down the table to her daughter. "You grew up here. You know the town as well as anyone."

"I grew up here," Maddy said, "but I haven't lived here in fifteen years. It's a whole different ball game."

"That's even better," Aidan said. "You have perspective but a fresh eye."

"I haven't been inside O'Malley's in years," she said. "All I remember are dark walls and a lot of old men playing darts in the corner."

Aidan's grin was rueful. "That pretty much sums it up."

"That's how a tavern's supposed to be," Mr. Armagh piped up. "Bring in too much daylight and you ruin the magic."

"There's some truth to what Mr. Armagh says," Rose admitted, "but there are still ways you can offer customers something new and fresh and still stay within your operating budget."

"The dock!" Maddy could see it right there in front of her.

Rose looked down the table toward Maddy. She positively beamed. "A few tables and chairs—"

"—a few umbrellas," said Maddy, "and you're in business."

"Like mother, like daughter," Lucy said as everyone laughed. "It's in the blood."

They peppered poor Aidan with a barrage of questions. What condition was the dock in? How much frontage did he have around back? How many slips could O'Malley's accommodate?

"Boat traffic?" he asked.

"Why not?" Rose countered. "And how about take-out for boaters? They fax ahead their orders and you have their chili or ribs or steamers ready for them when they arrive. Hire a few cute-looking college kids, both sexes, to deliver directly to the boats."

Maddy saw it happen. A big smile spread across Aidan's face as Rose's ideas began to sink in and spawn ideas of his own. It turned out the Armaghs had run a small luncheonette up in Morristown for thirty years, and they had a lot to offer on the subject. The Loewensteins were both retired CPAs who could crunch numbers in their heads and never miss a beat of conversation. Mr. Loewenstein asked Aidan a few direct questions, then wrote down a few numbers on a sheet of paper provided by his wife. He handed it to Aidan.

"That'll give you some idea of what you'd need to start renovating. What you need is an exhaustive profit-and-loss statement to take with you to the bank when you go for financing."

"Financing?" Aidan shook his head. "We do it on our own or we don't do it."

It was Maddy's turn to jump in. "Financing makes perfect sense," she said, donning her accountant's hat for a moment. "You don't want to invest all of your capital in a new venture."

"What capital?" Aidan tossed back at her. "By the time we pay for goods and services, employee wages, and utilities, we're a half-step away from closing the door for good."

"All the more reason for you to give some thought to broadening your scope," Rose said, undaunted by reality. "It sounds to me like you don't have anything to lose."

ROSE'S WORDS HIT Aidan hard. *You don't have anything to lose*. Maybe that wasn't such a bad thing after all. Jack Bernstein had warned him that O'Malley's was approaching the point of no return. Maybe they could eke out another five years the way things were, but then what? He was too young to think about retirement, and how the hell would Claire manage without the income, however small, that the bar provided?

Why not take a chance on expanding O'Malley's horizons? Why not kick open a few doors and windows and let the sun shine in? Rose DiFalco knew what she was talking about. One look at what she'd accomplished at the Candlelight would tell you that. And, to his everlasting surprise, he had the gut feeling she was playing straight with him. That she even liked him and wanted him to succeed.

Had she always been like this, or was he finally pushing aside the green-eyed monster and seeing her as a colleague and not as competition?

Besides, O'Malley's wasn't competition for the Candlelight and never would be, although why it had taken him so long to figure that out was anybody's guess.

There was something almost magical about the Candlelight. It wasn't hard to see what drew guests back time and time again. Rose had managed to create an atmosphere that was more homey than home itself, a world of soft lighting and rounded edges and good food and great conversation.

"Rose here told me that your grandmother is Irene O'Malley," Mr. Armagh said, leaning across the table to be heard.

Aidan nodded. "She and my grandpa Michael ran a few restaurants down here."

"I knew her," Mr. Armagh said. "It was a heck of a long time ago, but I used to see her around the trade shows up in New York. Fine-looking woman in her day. I'm sorry to hear she's in the hospital."

"You knew Grandma Irene?" Kelly almost leaped from her seat with excitement. "Did you know her well?"

"Sorry to say I didn't," Mr. Armagh replied. "I was just starting out. Had two pushcarts near the courthouse in Newark, which was a far cry from what the O'Malleys were doing down here in Paradise Point. But I remember how she looked just like a movie star, all dolled up in a blue dress with a big blue"—he turned to his wife—"what do they call those hats?"

"Picture."

"Picture hats with her blond hair brushing her shoulders." He sighed audibly. "A fine-looking woman, that's for sure."

"Did you ever talk to her?" Kelly pressed.

"A few times. She was real polite, don't get me wrong, but you got the feeling her mind was somewhere else."

"You mean she was like that even then?"

"Like I said," Mr. Armagh went on, "I didn't really know her. Just what I noticed about her from year to year."

"I thought it was just because she was old." Kelly swiv-

eled in her chair to look at Aidan. "Was she like that when
you were growing up?"

He nodded. "Your uncle Billy called it her dead-fish
stare. She aimed it at Claire the day Billy introduced her
as his fiancée. I don't think Claire ever forgave her for
it."

Rose quietly rose from the table and started to clear
away the dishes. Maddy rose to her feet to help. He had
the feeling the women were trying to create a zone of
privacy for him by leaving the room, and the gesture
touched him deeply.

"I worked at O'Malley's for a few years when I was
in high school," Lucy offered, "and I have a completely
different take on Irene."

All heads swiveled in her direction. Even Maddy lingered a moment in the kitchen doorway before returning
to the dishes.

Lots of Paradise Pointers got their first job at the original O'Malley's, but most of them had died or moved
away. No wonder Kelly was almost climbing across the
dining room table with excitement.

"You knew Michael?" Aidan asked.

"I sure did. A nicer, kinder man you'd never meet."
She smiled at both Aidan and Kelly. "Kelly has his blue
eyes."

"What was he like?" Aidan asked. "He died before
Billy and I were born, and Irene wouldn't talk about him."

"A broken heart," Kelly said, suddenly sounding like
the teenage girl she was. "He was her true love."

"Funny thing," Lucy said as she began to stack dishes
for busing, "but there was always a tragic feeling about
Irene even before the hurricane."

Kelly stared at her wide-eyed. "Like a tragic love affair?"

"Listen, I'm just an old woman rambling on. What do
I know? I'm just saying there was always a feeling of
sadness around Irene, right from the first. The most successful and lovely woman in town, and you always
walked away thinking, 'Boy, am I glad I'm not Irene

O'Malley.' It didn't make sense, but that's how I remember it."

Hannah, who had been listening to them with greater interest than you'd expect from a four-year-old, got up and whispered something in Kelly's ear, then tugged at her hand.

"Hannah," said Lucy, "I know your mommy told you yesterday that whispering at the table is bad manners. If you have something to say to Kelly, you should say it loud enough so we can all hear."

Again, that older-than-her-years look, followed by a voice that was pure post-toddler. "I want to show Kelly my toys."

Aidan had to bite the inside of his lip to keep from laughing. How many times had he gone down the same road with Kelly when she was Hannah's age?

"Kelly was having a conversation, honey. You shouldn't interrupt."

"It's okay," Kelly said, ruffling Hannah's hair with an affectionate gesture. "I'd like to see Hannah's toys, if it's okay."

He knew his daughter too well. Kelly couldn't wait to see the Candlelight's family quarters. She had her mother's looks and curiosity.

"Please," Hannah said.

He could see Lucy was a goner. "Go ahead," she said. "I'll tell your mother where you are."

"They could pass for sisters," Lucy said as the sound of their footsteps receded up the stairs. "Same coloring."

"I noticed," Aidan said. "Kelly was the same way when she was Hannah's age. She could manage to sit still while we were eating, but the second it was over, she wanted to be on to something else."

"It's called youth," Lucy said with a sigh. "A distant memory." She polished off the last of the wine in her glass, then looked over at Aidan again. "I'm sorry if I said too much before. It's not like Irene and I were friends or anything. It's just that the other waitresses and I were in awe of her, and I guess we romanticized things just a little bit."

"You don't believe that, do you?" he asked.

"No," Lucy said after a moment, "actually I don't. Something broke Irene's heart, and it was long before she lost Michael. I'm sorry if that upsets you, but I believed it then and I believe it now."

"Something did break her heart before the hurricane," Aidan said, "but it wasn't the way you think. She lost her oldest son in the Second World War. From what I was told, she never got over it."

Lucy buried her face in her hands. "Forgive me, Aidan. I completely forgot that Irene had two sons. I'm so sorry."

"No need to be," he said. "No reason you should remember. There were a lot of tragedies during the war."

"I probably have no business saying this, Aidan, but I'm still not convinced there wasn't something else."

"Or someone."

"Listen, I know she's your grandmother and I'm certainly not implying she didn't love Michael, but you have to admit there's always been something . . . mysterious about Irene."

He started to laugh. "I'm not going to argue with you, Lucy. You're right. 'Mysterious' is a good way to put it." He and Billy had grown up knowing chapter and verse about Grandpa Michael's life before he returned to America with Irene by his side. But it had often seemed to Aidan that Irene sprang to life at the moment she sailed into New York Harbor with her young husband. Nothing that came before seemed to matter. His mother told him that when she first met Irene, she asked how she had managed to lose her brogue; Irene had greeted the innocent question with icy silence that lasted until Billy was born. O'Malley family members quickly learned to stay away from certain topics. Irene's life before Michael was at the top of the list.

"I heard about her fall," Lucy said. "I hope she's doing well."

Aidan gave a noncommittal shrug of his shoulders.

"She didn't break anything, but she's not doing well."

"She's lived a long and remarkable life, Aidan. All you can do is hope that when she goes, she goes in peace and comfort."

He agreed. It was what everyone hoped for when the end was near.

But in some ways he was just like his seventeen-year-old daughter. He wanted the impossible, too. He wanted to know that in some way, some small insignificant way, they had really been a family and not just survivors who happened to board the same lifeboat.

Just once before Irene died, he wanted to hear her say she loved them.

HANNAH HAD TO use the bathroom, so Kelly sat on a cute little upholstered chair near the top of the stairs, pulled out her cell, and called Seth. He was going to drive around with his father for a while and see if they could make a few extra bucks plowing driveways for homeowners who had been plowed in by the township's trucks earlier in the day. He said he would be home by seven, and since it was quarter after, she figured there was a good chance she could reach him.

He answered on the first ring and they had made their arrangements before Hannah finished washing her hands. He would pick her up at the Candlelight in fifteen minutes. Her father would probably blow a fuse when she told him she wouldn't be driving home with him, but it would be too late for her to call Seth and cancel.

One of the few good things about loving a guy who didn't have a cell phone.

"So where is this special toy you've been telling me about?" she asked when Hannah came out of the bathroom. "I hope it's Barbie. I loved Barbie when I was your age." In fact she probably still had some of the Barbie doll clothes Aunt Claire had made for her up in the attic. They would make a nice surprise for Hannah, if she could find them.

"It's not Barbie," Hannah said, slipping her hand into Kelly's. "It's a secret."

"A secret?" She chuckled. "I had lots of secrets when I was your age."

"But this is a real secret," Hannah said in that serious little voice of hers. "You can't tell anyone."

"Not anyone at all?"

"No." Hannah looked up at her. "Promise?"

"Okay," said Kelly. "I promise."

Hannah pushed open the door to the last room on the left and pulled Kelly inside.

Kelly gasped when she saw the acres of silk and satin on the walls, draped over the bed, the plush chaise longue, the soft throws, the outrageously fluffy pillows, the scented candles, the beautiful oil paintings, the sense of absolute contentment that seemed to radiate from every corner of the room.

"Wow!" Kelly managed, as she drank it all in. "This isn't your room, is it, Hannah?" If it was, she wanted to be adopted and fast.

"Nope. It's Grandma Rose's."

"Maybe we shouldn't be in here," Kelly said, reluctantly inching toward the door.

" 's okay," Hannah said, grabbing Kelly's hand and tugging her back inside. "This is where I keep my toy."

Had she been such a little drama queen when she was Hannah's age?

She watched as Hannah slid open the door to Rose's closet and revealed a rainbow of color organized with the precision of a drill team. Working for Rose was going to be a trip. Growing up without a mother, she had never learned all of these secret female things that her friends seemed to understand without even trying. Aunt Claire had tried her best to fill in the gap, but once the troubles with Kathleen started and then the accident that killed Uncle Billy—well, there wasn't a whole lot of time or energy left over to teach her niece how to organize her closet.

At least Hannah had Maddy and Rose to help her figure

out how to be a girl. Not that her father hadn't done a terrific job, because he had, but the last few years since the accident had been hard on both of them. She didn't blame him for it. He didn't go looking to be in a terrible accident, and he sure didn't go looking to lose his brother. But that didn't change the fact that just when Kelly had needed him most, he hadn't been there for her to turn to, and deep down inside, in a place she never let anyone see, she felt very small.

And very alone.

Hannah carefully pushed aside the bottom of a gorgeous teal silk robe that almost screamed out to be touched. She reached deep into the closet and pulled out a Macy's shopping bag.

"Hannah," she warned, "it's just a few weeks before Christmas. You'd better not go snooping around. You might find one of your presents and ruin your surprise."

"Santa doesn't leave presents in Grandma's closet."

Oops. Kelly quickly regrouped. "You're right. Of course he doesn't." She bent down near Hannah. "So what have you got?"

"Close your eyes."

"Hannah, that's silly."

"Close your eyes. That's how my mommy always does it."

"Okay, okay. I'll close my eyes." Kids really took their toys seriously.

"Put out your hands."

She put out her hands.

"What—?" The weight surprised her. The chill of metal against her skin surprised her even more. But what she saw when she opened her eyes was the biggest surprise of all.

Grandma Irene's samovar.

Good Samaritan Hospital

The nurse leaned over Irene's bed and smoothed the seafoam-green blanket over her chest. "I heard the snowplows a little while ago, Irene. We should be able get you back to Shore View in the morning."

Please call my grandson. I need to talk to him before it's too late.

"Is that blanket too scratchy against your skin, Irene? Here. Let me see what I can do."

The nurse folded back the blanket, then spread a well-washed sheet over Irene. "There," she said, repositioning the blanket. "That's better."

The bed swayed gently beneath Irene as she rode the swells. The sea was calm tonight. The black sky overhead was spangled with stars. She was sailing away from what remained of her world, trusting her future—and her baby's life—to a man she barely knew.

THEY WERE MARRIED as Nikolai lay dying, married in the burned-out shell of a once great house near St. Petersburg. Irina's knees sank into the blood-soaked ground as she knelt beside the father of her child and prayed for a miracle.

Her cousin Seriozha, a priest, heard their vows, made before God, and united them moments before Kolya drew in his last breath. Irina had seen terrible things in the weeks before that moment, the murder of her parents and her sisters and brothers, the destruction of her home and the world she knew, but nothing had prepared her for the enormity of this moment. Nothing. She felt as if someone had torn her heart from her chest.

When you steal a woman's dreams, you have taken everything of value.

Seriozha reached across Irina and gently closed Kolya's eyes. He murmured familiar prayers of comfort and eternal life, but she felt nothing beyond a yawning emptiness that seemed to suck the air from her lungs. "You must go," he said. "There isn't much time." He had escaped the first onslaught against the church and the nobility, but that would soon change, for he had vowed to avenge the murder of their family and her beloved Kolya, whose only sin had been to love her.

"Go," he said. *"There are others like you headed for the sea. Join them. Leave this place behind. It is your only salvation."*

Go where? This was her world. Her life. She knew nothing of the world beyond. There was nothing left but fear.

And the baby inside her belly.

"THERE'S A PROBLEM?" The doctor's shoes squeaked as he stepped into Irene's tiny cubicle. "Vital signs seem to be holding steady. She's not spiking a fever. No pain. So what's wrong?"

"I'm not sure," the nurse said. "I think she's trying to talk."

There was a prolonged silence. Irene struggled to form the words, but only a whistle of air passed her lips.

"I'm on break," the doctor said in a clipped tone of voice. "Don't call me again unless it's important. I want to get out of here on time tonight."

His shoes squeaked against the floor tiles as he stormed away.

"Bastard," the nurse muttered, then laughed softly. "If you can hear me, Irene, I'll bet you'd agree. Men are all bastards, aren't they?"

HE WAS THE kindest man she had ever known, and he had deserved so much more than she had been able to give him.

Michael O'Malley fell in love with Irina the first moment he saw her sleeping in a doorway near the docks in Trelleborg, Sweden. She was terrified when he approached, all frail bones in dirty clothing with a belly beginning to grow big with another man's child. She was the most beautiful thing he had ever seen in his life, more beautiful than the sea or the stars.

What began as a gesture of kindness from a seaman to a stranger swiftly became much more. Within days he had offered her his name and his love, with the promise that he would care for her child as if it were his own.

"I will never love you," she told him in a voice as dead as her dreams. In that same measured voice she told him her story. All of it. She would never tell it again to anyone. The risks were too great. She had heard tales of reprisals against the Russian nobility that extended far beyond the borders of her homeland. Better to bury the past the same way she had buried everyone and everything she had ever loved.

She would care only for the child.

But Michael O'Malley was an optimist, and he believed that in a world filled with sorrow, love could work miracles. He believed that his love was strong enough for both of them and that sooner or later her heart would open up to its magic. He took her back to Ireland with him, where his beautiful young wife gave birth to a golden-haired son with eyes as blue as the sea.

She loved that boy, and even after a second son was born years later in America, it was the blue-eyed boy who claimed her heart. When that boy died on the beach at Normandy, something in Irene died on that beach with him, and there was nothing Michael O'Malley could do to set things right.

He died eight years later knowing that the wife he worshiped had never loved him in return.

"MICHAEL!"

Kelly was so engrossed in inspecting every inch of the samovar that the sound of Hannah's voice took a moment to register.

"Oh, Hannah!" She put the teapot down on the floor next to her. "Did you hurt yourself? What's wrong?"

The child's tiny face was the picture of profound sorrow. Kelly felt a shiver run up her spine. No four-year-old should look so grief-stricken. In a perfect world she would never have reason.

"Tell me what's wrong, Hannah. Please!" Should she call downstairs for Maddy or Rose? You could almost feel waves of sorrow spilling over both of them, flooding the room.

Maybe it was the samovar that was upsetting her. Kids could be really weird about the strangest things. Dolls took on lives of their own. Monsters hid under beds and in closets. Who knew what a child's imagination could make of an exotic teapot with swirls and squiggles and strange markings on the bottom? Maybe she was afraid Aladdin himself would come swirling out of the spout and take her away on his magic carpet.

Reluctantly Kelly slid the samovar back into the shopping bag, then stowed the whole thing in Rose's closet. Touching that samovar had almost been like touching a bit of her family's past. So much of their history had been shrouded in half-truths. *Don't ask. You don't want to know. It's over. What difference does it make*. Only her father shared her need to understand why the O'Malleys were the way they were, and so far he hadn't had any more luck than she had at uncovering the truth.

It probably sounded crazy—and she wasn't about to tell anyone, not even Seth—but when Hannah placed the samovar in her hands, she had felt Grandma Irene's presence in the room with them. If only Hannah hadn't got so upset. She would have loved to see where that sense of connection led.

Hannah's tears began to subside, and Kelly felt a surge of relief. She had done some baby-sitting in the past but not enough that she felt confident in her ability to calm a little girl's fears. Another two seconds and she would have been forced to bring in the reinforcements. On impulse she reached over and hugged the child close.

"Why don't we go back downstairs," she suggested. "I'll bet your Grandma Rose has something wonderful ready for dessert."

"You promised," Hannah said. More of the little girl was beginning to peek through the cloud of adult sadness that had descended over her.

"Promised what?"

"You said you wouldn't tell."

So it was the samovar that had upset Hannah.

"You promised," Hannah said again, her blue eyes blazing up at Kelly. "You said it was a secret."

"You're right," Kelly said, relaxing again now that she knew what the problem had been. "It's our secret."

"I'll let you play with it again," Hannah said, putting her hand in Kelly's as they started downstairs to rejoin the others.

"I'm glad," Kelly said. She wanted to take some photographs of the markings and see if she could solve the puzzle. Not that it mattered to anyone in her family but her. Still, it would be nice to know that something of her family's history, besides bitterness and secrets, had managed to find its way home again.

Then again maybe it wasn't Grandma Irene's samovar after all. Maybe it was just another fancy teapot that had found its way onto the auction site. Just some strange coincidence that puzzled you for a while, then faded away.

She wasn't buying that for a minute. She didn't need an expert to tell her what she knew deep down in her bones. That was the samovar Grandpa Michael had bought for Irene over fifty years ago, the same one that had graced the lobby of the original O'Malley's, the same one that was featured in newspaper articles and the photo that hung over the cash register at the bar. Somehow it had found its way back to Paradise Point and into the hands of a little girl who seemed to understand, same as Kelly did, that it wasn't blind luck that had brought them all together.

It was fate.

Chapter Twenty-four

"YOU DON'T HAVE to be out here," Maddy said to Aidan as Priscilla sniffed delicately at a mound of pristine white snow. "A sane person would be inside by the fire."

"You looked like you could use some help controlling the beast."

"I'm not sure Priscilla would appreciate being called a beast." She smiled as she said it. The thought of a two-pound poodle being considered unmanageable delighted her.

He grinned. "Just an observation."

It was one of those crystal-clear winter nights whose beauty took your breath away. The sky was a canopy of black silk studded with diamonds, an artist's rendition of what a winter sky should be. A slender crescent of moon rose high overhead, adding its silvery luster to the world below.

They watched in silence for a while as Priscilla scrabbled around on her canine reconnaissance mission. Her paws crunched their way through the fragile mantle of ice, and she yelped as she sank deep into the snow.

Maddy rescued the puppy, then placed her back on a

cleared portion of the driveway. Seconds later the sound of laughter drifted toward them from the front of the house, followed by the roar of a car engine with something to prove.

"He needs a new muffler," Aidan said as he looked up at the stars. "He's not going to pass inspection with that load of rust."

"Kelly's boyfriend?"

"Feels more like one of the family. He's at our house more often than I am."

"I got the feeling you were surprised to see him at the door."

" 'Surprised' is one way to put it."

"He seems like a nice kid."

"He is a nice kid," Aidan said. "I just wish—" He caught himself. "Forget it."

"You wish they weren't so serious?"

"It shows?"

"A little." She paused. "Okay, a lot, at least it did this evening." She tried to project Hannah a dozen years into the future, but only managed to conjure up a four-year-old in a prom dress.

"The whole thing goes by faster than you can imagine," he said, bending down to pick up a shivering Priscilla. "When I was where you are now, it felt like things would always be the way they were at that moment. I'd always know where she was and who she was with." He laughed softly at his folly. "I always figured her life would fit neatly into mine for safekeeping. Then it seems like I turned away for a minute and she grew up while I wasn't looking."

"You did a great job with Kelly."

"I only followed her lead."

"You keep saying she did all the work, but I don't buy it. Kids like Kelly don't just happen. I'd say you must've done something right along the way."

"I've pretty much been missing in action the last couple of years," he said with a matter-of-fact honesty that caught her attention. "The fire at the warehouse forced her to grow up a hell of a lot faster than I would have liked. She took care of the house, of me, kept up with her school-work, and somewhere along the way my little girl turned into a young woman I don't really know anymore."

"You know what scares me?" Maddy said. "What if Hannah and I end up the way Rose and I did—" The words caught in her throat. "What if she can't wait to put three thousand miles between us?"

"You'd do everything you could to bridge that gap."

"And if I failed?"

"You'd try harder."

"You make it sound easy."

"It isn't. And it doesn't always work. But what choice do you have if you love her?"

She thought of Rose, of the dozens of phone calls last summer and early fall, of the letters and e-mails. She thought of the gates and fences, the high walls and slammed doors she had put in Rose's way. Nothing had stopped her. Rose had been relentless in her drive to somehow bring them together.

She had been cold with Rose, downright hostile and rude at times, but that only made her mother try harder. Was that love? She wasn't sure. When she was a little girl, she had believed love was a mother who was there when you got home from school each day, a mother who never missed a school play because she was closing on a condo down in Cape May or showing a town house near Absecon. A child couldn't possibly understand the re-sponsibilities shouldered by a single mother. Maddy was in the same position now as Rose had been, and slowly she was beginning to recognize all that Rose had accom-plished.

But that was years ago when Maddy was little and Rose was struggling to make ends meet. Where was Rose when Maddy was pregnant with Hannah, when things were fall-ing apart with Tom, when her baby was born? Business commitments seemed a sorry excuse for missing one of the biggest events in a woman's life: the day her daughter gave birth to a daughter of her own.

You were the one who left, Maddy. You were the one who picked up her marbles and walked away.

Fifteen years was a long time to be apart from your family. The people you loved and left behind didn't stay preserved in amber while you were gone. They grew up. They grew old. Marriages waxed and waned. Babies were born. People died. Alliances were formed and old grudges continued. And all of it happened while you were searching everywhere for a place to call home. For a family who would love you no matter what.

"If you feel like talking, I'm a good listener." The sound of Aidan's voice felt like a warm caress.

"It's a funny thing," she said. "I've spent the last fifteen years trying to make sense of my mother, and you managed to explain her to me in three sentences."

He touched her cheek with the tip of his index finger, and she was astonished the snow around her didn't melt away. The warmth of the gesture, the slow-hand eroticism of his touch, her own sweet tangle of emotions—who could say what magic really was or why it suddenly decided to visit itself upon two unsuspecting people?

But there it was, shimmering between them like captive stars, the kind of magic that happened when two people, who hadn't been looking for love, found it right in their own backyard.

Neither of them moved. Neither broke eye contact. He dipped his head forward and brushed his mouth against hers, and in that instant the entire world, and everyone in it, disappeared. She moved closer to his warmth. He moved nearer to her softness.

Her breath caught. Or maybe it was his. His mouth brushed hers again, warmer this time, more urgent. Her lips parted at the first touch of his tongue.

They melted into each other as if they had waited all of their lives for that moment. Their hearts, their souls, their dreams—they held nothing back.

"Wow," he said when they broke apart to catch their breath.

"Definitely wow," she said.

They looked at each other and started to laugh with the
pure simple wonder of finding each other at the exact
point when they had given up looking for happiness.

"Is this real?" Maddy whispered. "I never—"

"I didn't think—"

"Do you feel—"

"Come here."

Who knew so much could be said, so many promises
made in the span of a kiss. He tasted a little like coffee
and cinnamon. His nearness, his taste, his smell—it all
swirled together inside her skull until she was light-
headed with desire. He cupped her face in his big strong
hands, fingertips pressing gently against the pulse beating
at her temples, and she opened her eyes during the kiss
to find him looking at her with an expression of such
tenderness, such yearning that she swayed on her feet and
would have fallen if his strong arms hadn't been holding
her tight.

Nobody had ever looked at her that way. Nobody had
ever managed to fill the cold and empty places inside her
heart with so much love. She felt loved. Of course it was
too soon. You couldn't fall in love this fast and expect it
to last. Sane women knew that. Cautious women lived by
that rule. But she felt neither sane nor cautious.

She felt like shouting her joy up to the stars. She
wanted to run her fingers along the planes of his face,
along the shiny length of his scars. She wanted to mem-
orize every angle, every curve. She wanted to ease the
pain inside his body and the pain inside his heart until
there was room for nothing but joy.

Priscilla tugged at the leash, straining toward the
warmth of the house.

"I don't want to go back inside," Maddy said. "I could
stay out here forever."

Another kiss. He was a man of few words.

"Breakfast tomorrow," he said. "Julie's at eight-thirty."

"I have the radio interview in the afternoon."

"I'll drive you."

"What about O'Malley's? You have a bar to run."

"Let Claire worry about it."

She raised up on her toes and kissed him soundly. "Claire might have something to say about that."

He said something wicked and very flattering, and she laughed despite herself. Priscilla threw back her head and started to yowl.

"You'd better get her inside," Aidan said. "She's turning into a pupsicle."

They had been outside for less than thirty minutes, and in that time everything had changed. They made their way up to the back door with Priscilla neatly tucked under Aidan's left arm. They held hands until they reached the porch landing, where, by unspoken consent, they reluctantly broke apart. They wanted to keep their secret just a little bit longer.

THEY NEEDN'T HAVE bothered.

Rose registered the change in the atmosphere the second they strolled oh-so-casually into the kitchen. She had suspected an attraction between them during dinner, but the looks on their faces (and the stars in their eyes) as they shrugged out of their coats and dried Priscilla's paws were unmistakable.

And unless she missed her guess, wasn't that a smudge of Maddy's apricot lipstick at the left corner of Aidan's mouth?

She glanced toward Lucy, who was fixing herself a cup of decaf. Lucy's head was slightly turned away, but even at that angle, Rose could see a definite smile on her sister's face.

How self-consciously casual Maddy and Aidan were being. How sweetly obvious. And they hadn't a clue that their every gesture, every unreturned glance, every withheld sigh told the story in letters two feet high.

It brought it all rushing back to Rose. All of the wildly improbable dreams, the staggering highs and crushing lows, the feeling that you could spread your wings and fly because you loved and were loved in return.

She had never seen that look in her daughter's eyes

before, not even when she was living with Tom and expecting their child. With Tom, Maddy had often looked unsure of herself, like a child wearing her mother's clothing. Like a visitor in her own home.

Maddy had always been a pretty woman, but her prettiness had been muted, as if she were afraid to let herself shine the way she was meant to. Ah, but tonight! Tonight she glowed with unmistakable happiness, the special beauty of a woman who was finally coming into her own.

Aidan O'Malley was a good man and a great father. Kelly was the kind of girl who made you believe there was hope for the future, and there was little doubt in Rose's mind that Aidan was mainly responsible. Yes, he was rough around the edges, and yes, he had cut a wide swath through the ladies of Paradise Point. There were those who might say Rose had her own rough edges . . . as well as an interesting past. But Aidan was kindhearted and loyal and fair, three attributes you rarely found in a man that good-looking.

Or one who had known as much heartache.

She studied his face from across the room. What did he see when he looked at Maddy? Did he see her fierce intelligence? Her quick temper? Her loneliness? Her devotion to Hannah? Did he have any idea how deeply she had been hurt when Tom ended their relationship or how long she grieved for what might have been?

If only she could sit him down at the kitchen table and tell him everything he needed to know to make her daughter happy.

Too bad she hadn't a clue.

Good Samaritan Hospital

"I know it's late," Kelly said to the nurse guarding Grandma Irene's room, "but I just have to see her."

"Honey, it's not the time that's the problem. How much do you know about Mrs. O'Malley's condition?"

"I know she's in a coma," Kelly said, "and I know her chances aren't good."

"She probably won't even know you're here."

"But she might. I did a lot of reading about comas, and some people hear everything that's going on around them."

"I'll let you sit with her for a few minutes," the nurse said, "but don't be disappointed when you don't get a response."

Grandma Irene looked so small and frail that tears filled Kelly's eyes and she had to blink very fast in order to find her way to the chair next to the bed. The old woman's eyes were closed. Her lids were paper thin and criss-crossed with fine blue veins. An ugly purple bruise dominated her left cheek. She looked so terribly old, as if the slightest breeze would carry her away like fallen leaves.

Kelly glanced at the clock hanging over the bed. Seth was downstairs in the parking lot. He didn't like hospitals. She'd had to drag him in when his own sister had her first baby. She didn't want to keep him waiting forever out there.

"Grandma, it's Kelly. I don't know if you can hear me or not . . . I mean, I'm not sure if I'm just talking to myself, but there's something I really have to tell you. Remember that teapot you had in the lobby of the old O'Malley's? That fancy Russian one with all the curlicues on the spout? Well, you won't believe what I found on the Internet. . . ."

THERE WAS SOMETHING unfathomable about Nicky's death, something so deeply unknowable that Irene was never truly able to make sense of it. The thought of her beloved son mowed down on some faraway beach, his blood staining the sand beneath him, blue eyes staring sightlessly up at the sky—it was more than her mother's heart could deal with.

The nightmares began soon after. The blood-soaked ground, the screams of terror. But it wasn't her son on a Normandy beach, it was his father, her Kolya, her love, on the frozen ground, blood spilling everywhere, his beautiful eyes staring up at the moonless sky.

*Michael O'Malley grieved with Irene. He was a good
man with a big heart, and he had loved Nicholas the same
as he loved the child of his blood. He longed to gather
Irene in his arms and weep with her, but she remained,
as always, beyond his reach. How she wished things could
be different. Michael's longing tore at her heart, but there
was nothing she could do to change things. The deep and
abiding love he deserved wasn't hers to give and never
would be.*

*As the months after Nicky's death passed, and then the
years, Michael began to fear she was going to leave him
and that fear settled deep inside his heart and wouldn't
be dislodged. He lavished her with time and attention, but
still she remained locked away in her grief, so distant that
her second son, Michael Jr., was all but invisible to her.*

*Michael continued to search for the key to her heart,
the one thing he alone could give to her that nobody else
on earth could. He was the one who kept her secrets, the
only one who looked at her and saw Irina and not the
woman she had become.*

And that was when he found the samovar.

*One of his suppliers told him about a bankruptcy sale
being held up in Brooklyn, a fine old restaurant that
hadn't been able to make the transition into the post–
World War II economy. The owner had fled Russia during
the Bolshevik uprising, barely escaping with his life. His
restaurant had been an homage to the world he left behind, a world of opulence and privilege, of handsome soldiers in uniform and beautiful women in silk gowns, of
jeweled Easter eggs and hot tea in tall glasses.*

*The samovar had been brought to New York from St.
Petersburg in 1918, the year he and Irene married, an
ornately decorated and exotic glorified teapot to join the
collection of china teapots that were an O'Malley's trade-
mark. He wanted to give her something that represented
the home she had left behind, the family and way of life
that had been torn from her in the most violent way imag-
inable.*

He gave her the samovar at Christmastime in 1951, and

for the first time in many years Irene was moved to tears. Michael O'Malley had finally found the key to what remained of her heart, but she couldn't break out of her sorrow to tell him.

When Michael died four months later during the Hurricane of '52, Irene was left with profound grief and the terrible knowledge that he had died not knowing that she had finally learned to love him in her fashion.

MADDY WOKE UP at 3:12 A.M. to the sound of Hannah's bare feet shuffling across the carpet.

"Hey, sweetie," she said, switching on her bedside light. "What are you doing up?"

"My throat hurts."

Maddy was instantly wide awake, her full maternal warning system shifting into gear. She reached out her arms. "Come here. Let me see."

Hannah's skin was cool, thank God, but the slightest bit clammy. A faint sheen of perspiration glistened on her forehead and the palms of her tiny hands.

"Does your tummy hurt?" she asked, drawing the little girl into the bed with her.

"I don't know."

"Do you feel like you have to throw up?"

"Sort of." She leaned her head against Maddy's shoulder. "Maybe."

"But nothing hurts?"

"My head."

Could be the flu, Maddy thought, or maybe nothing more than the beginnings of a head cold. Still, it didn't hurt to be careful. She swung her legs out of the bed and tucked her little girl in among the fluffy pillows and lovely down comforters. Hannah was one of those lucky children who seemed immune to the various bugs that floated about schools and daycare centers. Knock on wood, Hannah had never experienced anything more than the occasional run-in with sniffles that quickly passed before the day was out.

There was no reason to be so anxious, Maddy scolded

herself as she went in search of a thermometer. Absolutely no reason at all.

"I THINK YOU'RE reading too much into a sore throat," Rose said a few hours later as she started the morning coffee. "Keep her home from school, but don't cancel your breakfast with Aidan."

"Your mother's right," Aunt Lucy chimed in. "No reason you should miss your breakfast. We're here to watch Hannah."

Maddy knew they meant well, but their advice grated on her nerves. "Hannah never gets sick," she said for what felt like the tenth time in thirty minutes. "I think it's best if I stayed here and kept an eye on her."

"Your decision, of course," Rose said, pouring filtered water into the machine, "but it seems unnecessary to me."

"I'm not surprised," Maddy said.

Her mother turned away from the counter and faced her. "And what exactly does that statement mean?"

"It doesn't mean anything in particular."

"I think it does."

"Then tell me what you think it means."

"I'd rather you tell me."

"Who's on first?" Lucy murmured, then laughed in a vain attempt at defusing the situation before things went too far.

Neither woman acknowledged her comment.

"You weren't exactly June Cleaver," Maddy pointed out. "I don't remember you ever staying home from work when I was sick."

"You were a very healthy child."

"What about when I had chicken pox?" Maddy asked. "Or the tonsillectomy? Where were you then, Rose? Out showing a four-bedroom with two full baths?"

"Employers weren't as understanding about childcare difficulties back then, Madelyn. If you had a job, you were expected to be there no matter what was going on in your personal life. It was a different world, but I always made sure you were with family if I couldn't be there with you."

"Like when Hannah was born?"

She hadn't meant to say that, but the words had a life of their own and they exploded into the room with the force of a guided missile aimed straight at Rose's heart.

Rose, however, said nothing. She turned back to the coffeemaker and carefully measured freshly ground beans into the filter.

That was Maddy's cue to throw her hands in the air and storm out of the room, all adolescent anger and high dudgeon. But she didn't want to play that game anymore.

"Don't do this, Mom," she said, hands gripping the edge of the kitchen table. "Don't turn away. Let's talk it through once and for all."

She was only vaguely aware of Aunt Lucy's retreating footsteps as she slipped out the back door with Priscilla.

Rose remained silent.

"I want to know why," she persisted, praying her voice wouldn't break under the weight of emotion. "I'm grown now. I can make myself understand why you did things the way you did them when I was a little girl, but I can't for the life of me figure out why you weren't there when Hannah was born." She moved a step closer and willed Rose to turn around and face her. "I've come up with every possible reason, but not one of them is good enough to explain why you weren't there with me." She couldn't bring herself to say the last few words. *When I needed you.* "Please tell me, Rose. I want to understand." *Do you love me enough to turn around and tell me the truth?*

But the moment for answers had come and gone.

"It's getting late," Rose finally said. "If you're not going to breakfast, you'd better phone Aidan and let him know."

Chapter Twenty-five

MADDY SOUNDED WORRIED as she told him about Hannah's head cold. Aidan remembered those early days when every sneeze, every sniffle signified a terrifying descent into major illness instead of something as benign, if uncomfortable, as the common cold. He reassured her that it was probably nothing—being careful not to take Rose's side in their latest battle—then said he'd call in a few hours to see how Hannah was feeling.

And to hear the sound of your voice, he thought as he hung up the phone. He was tempted to jump into the truck and drive over to the Candlelight, but good sense kept him from making a fool of himself. Hannah was her first priority right now, which was the way it should be.

The phone rang again and a big stupid grin spread across his face.

"You changed your mind," he said instead of hello. "Hannah's made a quick recovery and you can't stand the thought that—"

"Mr. O'Malley?" A man's voice. Not the voice he had been expecting.

It was Irene's doctor and the news wasn't good.

He went upstairs and woke Kelly to tell her that Grandma Irene wasn't expected to live out the day. Kelly began to weep softly, pressing her face against her pillow. He sat down on the edge of the bed and patted her shoulder.

"We knew this was coming, Kel," he said softly while she cried. "She's old and she's very tired. It's her time."

But he knew that wasn't why she was crying. She wasn't crying for what they were about to lose; she was crying for what they'd never had.

"She always called me Kelly Ann," she said through her tears. "My full name. When I was little, I hated that sooo much."

"She called me her 'blue-eyed boy,' " he said. "Do you know the grief I got from Billy over that?"

Grandma loves her blue-eyed boy. She had said that to him when he was little more than a baby. He remembered the words and how they made him feel.

Did those words exist only in his imagination? There had to have been some good times along the way. He refused to believe otherwise.

"You'd better phone Aunt Claire," Kelly said, wiping away the tears with the back of her hand. "She won't care, but still . . ."

"You're right," he said. If Claire didn't care, maybe one of her kids might. At the least, they were family and they had the right to know.

Claire greeted the news with her usual blunt candor. "If you're looking for tea and sympathy, you dialed the wrong number."

"I'm not looking for anything, Claire. I'm just passing on the information."

"Consider it passed on."

"You'll tell Kathleen and the others."

"Of course." She paused and he could hear the sound of cigarette smoke being exhaled. "So do we open up as usual today or wait until all the roads are cleared?"

"Your call," he said. "I'm going over to the hospital."

"Right," she said. "Of course you are. So Tommy and I will open. You get there when you can."

"I can't make any guarantees, Claire. I don't know how the day's going to play out."

Claire's laugh held more than a hint of bitterness. "Nobody does, Aidan. That's the hell of it all."

"YOU'RE BEING VERY quiet," Rose said to Lucy over breakfast.

"Am I?"

"I know what you're thinking. You're thinking I waited too long to tell Maddy about the cancer."

"So you've added mind reading to your list of accomplishments now?"

Rose's cheeks flushed at Lucy's pointed words. "If you have something to say, Lucia, please say it."

"Fine." Lucy put down her coffee cup. "Let's put your gigantic mistake about your cancer aside for right now and deal with the slightly less gigantic mistake you made this morning. Maddy was right, you know. You never were one for fussing over a sickbed or making cookies for the school bazaar."

"And that's a crime? We're not all Florence Nightingale or June Cleaver. You, of all people, should understand that."

"And I do. What I'm saying, Rosie, is that I always had the feeling you loved Maddy but found motherhood itself an uncomfortable fit. And no, that's not a crime. I like to believe I would love being completely responsible for another human being's life, but the distance between theory and reality is very wide. I know what your life was like when she was growing up. I know how hard you worked to secure the future for the two of you, the sacrifices you made, but sometimes I think you felt staying home would have been the bigger sacrifice." She hesitated, searching Rose's eyes for encouragement. "Help me out here, Rosie, will you?"

Rose sighed and reached out for her sister's hand. "Life is funny, isn't it, Lucia? Somehow it always gets the last laugh." Lucy had wanted to be a mother from the time she cradled her first doll in her arms while Rose never gave it a thought until they handed her a squalling baby girl named Maddy and said "Good luck."

"You're right. They weren't all sacrifices," Rose said. "I enjoyed being out there in the world much more than I enjoyed being home watching *Sesame Street*." How many times had she ditched a recital or a PTA meeting— she couldn't count that high. A heavy workload . . . unexpected meeting . . . a closing three towns over that couldn't be postponed. Oh, there was always some handy-dandy excuse she could pull out of her Filofax, always someplace she needed to be.

"I love her," Rose said with a touch of defiance. "I have from the first moment."

"She knows that," Lucy said. "But she has Hannah now and she's trying to make sense of things. She's trying to find her own way, but to do that she needs to understand yours."

"She knows I loved my work. I'm proud of my accomplishments. I tried to instill that in her from the very beginning." That a woman could take care of herself. That work was a good thing. That you didn't have to be afraid of being alone. "I did a good job," Rose said angrily. "I raised a good woman."

"So tell her."

"I have told her."

"Tell her again."

"That's ridiculous."

"Is it?"

Rose pushed back her chair and stood up. "I'm going to see how Hannah is doing."

MADDY WAS IN the office saying goodbye to Jim Kennedy when her mother walked into the room.

"So how much of that did you hear?" Maddy asked as she hung up the receiver.

"I wasn't eavesdropping, Maddy."

"I canceled the radio interview."

"Oh, Maddy! You didn't."

"I can't leave Hannah."

"But the interview—"

"I understand and applaud your devotion to business," Maddy said, "but my first responsibility is to my daughter."

"You don't understand how important that interview was."

"You're already booked solid for the next two years."

"I'm thinking of the future," Rose said.

"And I'm thinking of Hannah." She moved past her mother into the hallway and headed toward her daughter's room. "She's feeling worse, by the way," she said over her shoulder.

"That's what I intended to ask you about." Rose sounded both angry and embarrassed. "We got sidetracked."

Maddy was proud of herself for letting the twenty or thirty biting retorts that presented themselves remain unspoken.

Hannah was sleeping when they entered the room. Her hands were outside the covers. Her fingers worried the Aladdin blanket, twisting a portion, then releasing it. Over and over again.

"Does she have a fever?" Rose asked in a whisper.

"Not to speak of." Maddy placed the palm of her hand against her daughter's forehead and frowned. "She still feels clammy." She met Rose's eyes. "What do you think?"

Rose placed her lips against her granddaughter's cheek, then her forehead. "She's cool enough, but I agree. She's a little clammy."

A sudden surge of terror rose up inside Maddy and a small sound escaped her lips. Rose reached out and placed a hand on her arm.

"I don't think it's anything to worry about," Rose said, "but why don't you give the pediatrician a call just to put your mind at rest."

Good Samaritan Hospital

The red-haired nurse smiled at Aidan as she finished entering data into the computer terminal adjacent to Irene's bed. "Your grandmother has beautiful hands," she said, with a rueful shake of her head. "They put mine to shame."

"My daughter has the same hands," he said, grateful for the small talk.

"Lucky girl. So far that's the one thing you can't buy at your local surgeon's office."

Aidan watched as Irene's fingers tugged repeatedly at the blankets, the railing, the paper-thin skin of her wrists and forearms. "Is she in pain?" he asked. "She keeps plucking at things."

A shadow passed across the nurse's face. "She's not in any pain," she assured him. "That restlessness is one of the signs we see as a patient moves through the process of letting go."

Which was, they both knew, a euphemism for death.

"We have some very informative booklets on the shelf near the nurses' station," she went on. "You might want to browse through the one on this subject."

Kelly had come with him to the hospital, but after five minutes she had run from the room crying. He had never fully understood why Kelly loved Grandma Irene the way she did. He would be the first one to admit Irene had given the girl next to nothing in return for her affection, but that didn't seem to matter to his daughter. She loved unconditionally. No strings. No expectations. The way she loved her mother's memory. Her cousins. Claire. Himself. And now Seth. He wished he could take credit for her kind heart, but he couldn't. Her kind heart was a gift from her mother, but in every other way she was her own miracle.

The Candlelight

"Maddy's upstairs with Hannah," Rose said as she ushered Kelly O'Malley into the warm kitchen and sat her down at the table. "Is there something I can do to help?"

How lovely she was with her strawberry blond hair curling around her face and her cheeks so bright with color. And those blue eyes! They reminded Rose of Hannah's, and for the first time all day the tiniest bud of fear began to blossom inside her chest.

It was clear the girl was in a highly emotional state.

"It's all right if you'd rather talk with Maddy," Rose said. "I understand."

"No, it's not that." Kelly made an effort to pull herself together. "It's just—" Her eyes filled with tears she didn't blink away. "Grandma Irene is dying, and I was wondering if maybe I could borrow that samovar just for an hour or two. I'd like to take it to the hospital and let her see it."

"Are you talking about the samovar Maddy won at the auction?"

Kelly nodded. "It's exactly like the one Grandpa Michael gave Irene the year before he died. I thought maybe if she—" More tears spilled from her big blue eyes, and Rose's heart was quite simply undone.

She went upstairs to fetch the samovar.

THE PEDIATRICIAN CALLED back a little after two o'clock. She listened to Maddy's description of Hannah's symptoms, then chuckled kindly.

"I'd say we have a common head cold building. I'm a little concerned about the clamminess, but that could simply be her body's way of dissipating a fever before it sets in. Continue doing what you're doing and call me again around six o'clock and let me know how—"

"Something's wrong," Maddy said. "I know the symptoms don't add up to much, but—"

"You have a feeling. I know all about those feelings, Maddy. I'm a parent myself. I respect those feelings. But in this instance I believe we really don't have anything more than a cold to be concerned about."

"You don't think I should bring her into the office?"

"No, I don't. Not at this point. Let's talk again at six."

Click.

She supposed she should feel grateful for the privilege of speaking to the doctor and not one of a squad of "health-care professionals" hired to take the burden of actually dealing with patients off the shoulders of the poor beleaguered MDs, but at the moment she didn't feel anything but worried. She couldn't help feeling that this was one of those times when the whole was truly greater—and maybe more serious—than the sum of its parts.

Good Samaritan Hospital

Aidan stepped out into the corridor and flagged down a passing technician. "Did you happen to see a pretty, blond-haired girl in the lounge?"

"Just a couple of old men with hearing problems," the technician said and kept on walking.

Damn. It wasn't like Kelly to just take off like that. The Jeep wasn't in the parking lot, which meant she wasn't out there taking a walk around the block. Where the hell had she gone?

He checked the cafeteria, the lounge, and the gift shop, and was on his way back to Irene's room when he saw a door marked *Chapel*. On a hunch he stepped inside.

The small room featured a raised altar with a crucifix on one side and a menorah on the other. An open Bible rested on a small wooden stand on the left. A guest book and pen rested on the right. A nondenominational stained-glass panel dominated the room, fierce reds and yellows, tranquil blues and greens.

Kelly was sitting in the first pew on the right. A shopping bag rested next to her. Her head was lowered, and if she heard him approach, she gave no indication. He slid into the pew next to her.

"You okay?" he asked.

She shrugged. "I guess so."

"Feel like telling me where you were?"

She met his eyes. "I went to the Candlelight and got the samovar."

"You *stole* the samovar?"

"I asked Mrs. DiFalco and she gave it to me."

"Rose doesn't own the samovar. Maddy does."

"Maddy was upstairs taking care of Hannah."

He registered the information about Hannah and Maddy and tucked it away for later.

Kelly grabbed the shopping bag and put it on her lap. "You're not going to say I can't do it, are you?"

"No," he said, "but I'm going to remind you that she probably doesn't even know we're in the room with her, much less recognize an old teapot."

"But I have to try," she whispered. "You know that, right?"

"I know," he said, "and I'm not going to try and stop you."

Her shoulders began to shake and she lowered her head. Seventeen years and Aidan still didn't have a handle on tears. He placed an arm around her and gave her a hug.

"I just want Grandma to know she's not alone." She rested her head against his shoulder. "It seems like the least we can do for her."

"You make me proud, Kel." His voice was choked with emotion. "Your mother would have been proud, too."

"I love you, Daddy." For a moment he thought he saw the little girl she used to be, but then he blinked and she was almost grown.

The Candlelight

Aidan called a little after three o'clock to see how Hannah was faring.

"There's still no fever," she said, "but I can't shake the feeling something's very wrong."

"What did the doctor say?"

" 'Wait until six o'clock, then call me back.' She was polite and kind and all of that, but I think she has me pegged as a hysterical single mother of an only child."

"Call her back now."

"She told me to wait until six."

"Go with your gut," he said. "Nobody loves Hannah more than you do, and nobody knows her better."

"I don't want to alienate her pediatrician."

"Screw the pediatrician. There are other doctors out there, but there's only one Hannah."

She was silent, thinking about his words. Rocking the boat had never been one of her favorite pastimes.

"I'm right on this," he persisted. "You know you won't rest until the doctor sees Hannah, and she won't see her unless you push hard."

He was right and she knew it. She promised to call him back with the outcome, then hung up and dialed Hannah's doctor.

THANK GOD FOR cell phones.

Rose almost cried with relief when Bill's booming voice leaped through the wires into her heart.

"Talk to me, Rosie," he said. "Is something wrong?"

"No . . . yes—oh, God, Bill, I just don't know. It's just a feeling I have that—" She stopped. There were some fears that were better off remaining unspoken.

"It's not your cancer, is it?" Bless him for not beating around the bush.

"No," she said, although she would rather bear anything than see Maddy or Hannah unwell. "It's the little one."

She tried to explain the situation to him, but it sounded so ridiculous in the telling that she ended up apologizing.

"I sound crazy, don't I? No fever. No nausea. Nothing I can point to and say, 'Aha! That's the culprit!' But something's wrong, Bill, I can feel it in my gut." She told him how Maddy had been the first to suspect something wasn't right and how her suspicions had seemed more and more on target as the day progressed.

"What did the doctor say?"

"She's going to drive over on her way home and take a look at Hannah." Which must be the first house call made in Paradise Point since the Korean War.

"I'm on my way," he said.

"Bill, that's not necessary. You'll be here for Christmas. Don't cut your—"

"Rosie, don't you know by now there's no point to arguing with me when it comes to family? Sit tight. I'll be there before long."

She hung up the phone, then lowered her head and started to cry.

TO: tlawlor@nomads.org
FROM: JerseyGirl@njshore.net
DATE: 8 December
SUBJECT: Hannah

I'm not sure there's any reason for you to worry, but Hannah isn't feeling very well and I can't pinpoint why. It started around three A.M.—she's not feverish or vomiting, but she's also not very responsive, either. Everyone thinks it's a head cold, but where are the sneezes? The sniffles? Just a sore throat. She's been asleep most of the day; no appetite, no conversation. And you know that's not at all like our daughter. I called the pediatrician twice—finally got her to agree to stop by and see Hannah. Like I said, there doesn't seem to be any reason for worry, but I'd be lying if I said I wasn't feeling very uneasy about this.
Hence this e-mail.
I'll keep you posted.
Maddy

PS: I'm attaching two photos taken last night of H. playing in the snow with Priscilla. God, how I wish I'd kept her inside watching TV.—M.

Good Samaritan Hospital

It came as no surprise when Irene failed to respond to the samovar. Aidan had tried his best to prepare Kelly for the total lack of response, but nothing could prepare her for the sight of her great-grandmother lying still as a corpse in the hospital bed.

They rested the samovar on the bed next to Irene and lifted her hand to touch its sleek and shiny surface, but there wasn't so much as a flicker of recognition or even curiosity from the old woman.

"You tried, Kel," he said as they slid the samovar back into the shopping bag and placed it on the chair in the corner of the room. "That's more than most people would have done."

"She doesn't even know we're here," Kelly said, her voice breaking. "It's like we're in different worlds."

Pretty much the way it's always been.

But he didn't say it. His kid had made it this far without cynicism and bitterness. He'd like to see her stay that way a little longer.

"It's part of the process," he said softly, turning away from Irene. "I read one of those booklets they have near the nurses' station, and it explained the stages a person goes through in a natural death."

The O'Malleys knew a lot about death, but none of it had ever been natural. The gift of old age, of dying in your sleep, had been denied to them. Grandpa Michael. His first son. Aidan's wife, Sandy. His parents. Billy. A long, sad list of lives cut short for no good reason other than the fates were bored and needed something to amuse themselves with.

Only Irene had lived out her span and more, and he wondered if maybe that wasn't her own taste of hell.

Irene stirred and both he and Kelly turned to look at her. The old woman's eyelids fluttered, and for a moment he thought they might open wide and she would see them, really see them, for the first time. *Those poor O'Malleys. What terrible luck they have.* Those words had followed him like the tail on a kite throughout his life. Irene had caught him staring at his face in the mirror once not long after his parents were killed in the accident. *There's nothing to see,* she had told him, understanding instantly what he was all about, *but it's there just the same.*

Which, if you thought about it, was a hell of a thing to lay on a fourteen-year-old boy who had just buried his parents.

She had always viewed the world through the darkest lens. At least in the years he'd known her she had. But how could he blame her? By the time Aidan and Billy were born, Irene had already lost her firstborn to war and her husband to the sea. She had earned the right to be bitter, but how much happier their lives might have been if she had been able to offer them the hope of something better.

Kelly left the room to make a phone call. He sat down on the edge of Irene's bed and took her hand in his, a gesture he would have been unable to make if she were conscious, and held it tight. She wasn't a toucher, not at all the cuddly, cookie-baking grandparent immortalized in movies and TV shows. She had always been distant, quick to criticize, steadfast in her belief in family, but loyalty seemed to matter more to her than love.

He wished he knew how she had come to be that way. It wasn't as if her past was shrouded in some deep, dark mystery that the family had been trying for years to un-ravel; it was more that her past didn't exist at all. Who had she been before she married Michael O'Malley? She had been born in a time when birth certificates were often afterthoughts, if they were thought of at all. Born on the other side of the ocean, of that he was sure. Irene Taylor O'Malley. Carved in granite, immutable, unknowable.

He had known old people like her before, met them in the crazed aftermath of a fire or false alarm. Some spilled their histories at your feet before the flames were extinguished. Others claimed no history at all; they simply sprang to life at eighty-five or eighty-six with arthritis, no teeth, and a subscription to *Modern Maturity*.

The booklet he'd found near the nurses' station talked about the stages a patient went through in the hours or days before death. The restless picking at the bedcovers. The deep, almost drugged sleep. The occasional nonsense syllables Irene muttered without opening her eyes. Names he had never heard her mention before. The booklet called it "The Life Journey," where the dying man or woman somersaulted back into his or her own life and relived events at random, met up with old friends and foes and family, maybe worked through issues or redefined them as sand spilled through that metaphorical hourglass at an alarming rate.

Was that what was happening with Irene right now? Was she standing in front of the original O'Malley's with Grandpa Michael by her side and her youngest son beaming into the camera? Or maybe it was in those days between the worst of the Depression and the start of World War II, back when she had two healthy, strapping sons and a popular restaurant and a husband who adored her.

"Were you ever happy?" he asked his sleeping grandmother. "Did any of it ever make you happy?"

She didn't answer him. He hadn't expected her to. Why should today be any different than a thousand other days?

He leaned closer. "We love you." He had never said it that way to her before. She wouldn't have allowed it. "You took Billy and me in when nobody else would." He swallowed hard against the memories. "Kelly tries so hard to—" No more. He'd gone as far as thirty-five years of conditioning would let him go.

Tell me how to make it better for Kelly. Tell me how to put an end to all the years of unhappiness and build something fine for at least one of the O'Malleys.

Irene, as usual, had nothing to say.

The Candlelight

The pediatrician didn't mince words. "We're taking her to Good Sam," Dr. Romanelli said as she washed her hands at the bathroom sink.

"Oh, God." Maddy felt her legs slip out from under her. She grabbed her mother's arm for support. "What is it? What did you find?"

Dr. Romanelli dried her hands on a guest towel. "I don't know what it is," she said bluntly, "but I don't like what I'm seeing. I think we'd all rest easier if we get Hannah admitted so we can run some tests."

"Good Sam," Rose said, sounding as terrified as Maddy felt. "Isn't that out of the way? Especially with the roads the way they are."

"Good Sam has the best diagnostic facilities in South Jersey," the doctor said, eyeing Rose with fleeting curiosity. "No question that's where Hannah should go."

"Of course," Maddy said with a quick glance at her mother. Rose had aged ten years in the last five minutes. "Wherever you think she'll get the best care."

The doctor nodded, then pulled a cell phone from the pocket of her jacket. She punched in a number, waited, then fired off a rapid series of instructions, only some of which penetrated the icy burst of terror in Maddy's brain.

"An ambulance?" Maddy started to shake. "She needs an ambulance?"

"You have medical, don't you?"

Maddy nodded. Thank God she had kept it up on her own after losing her job. "I don't care about the money. Is Hannah that sick?"

"I'm being cautious," the doctor said. "The roads are bad . . . why not take advantage of what's available, right?"

She wanted to cry. She wanted to throw herself in her mother's arms and sob until she woke up and found out this was only a bad dream.

"She'll be fine," Rose said as they walked back down the hall toward Hannah's room. "This is all precautionary."

"Of course it is," Maddy said. "They think they can make a few extra bucks by calling for an ambulance."

"It's all about money," Rose agreed. "Isn't that always the case?"

But it wasn't. Not this time. And they both knew it.

Chapter Twenty-six

KELLY HAD JUST tossed her empty plastic coffee cup into the trash when she saw them.

At first she thought she was hallucinating. That couldn't be Rose DiFalco and Maddy Bainbridge standing near the admin desk at the entrance to the emergency room. She blinked her eyes. It couldn't possibly be. She'd just seen them a few hours ago.

Her glance drifted toward a tiny figure on a stretcher who was being hustled quickly through the double doors and into the great unknowable bowels of the ER.

Hannah.

"Oh, God," she whispered, then crossed herself. Hannah was only four years old.

She lingered in the hallway between the cafeteria and the entrance to the ER, watching Maddy and Rose fill out the endless reams of paperwork. She wanted to walk over to them and say something comforting, but she couldn't think of anything that wouldn't sound trite and insincere. She'd only met Hannah last night, after all, and how much of a connection could you forge with a four-year-old over supper and a teapot?

Still, there had been a connection between them, a very real one. *Click.* Like the sound of a door being unlocked. Once, when Hannah was pouring water from Rose's bedside pitcher into the samovar to serve pretend tea, Kelly had experienced the sensation that Hannah was somehow taking her in hand, teaching her things she needed to know.

None of which made the slightest bit of sense, no matter how you looked at it.

But then, who would have imagined that the little girl with the sad blue eyes would be rushed by ambulance to Good Sam less than twenty-four hours later?

She forced herself into the corridor and toward the waiting area. Rose disappeared into the ladies' room while Maddy leaned against the doorway to the office with her eyes closed.

Her eyes fluttered open at the sound of Kelly's footsteps.

"Kelly." Her eyes widened. "What are you doing here?"

"It's my grandmother," she said, determined not to get weepy. "They think she's—" She couldn't say the word, so she shrugged instead, a big up-and-down motion of her shoulders.

"Oh, honey." There was nothing but compassion in Maddy's eyes as she reached out to touch her hand. "I'm so sorry."

Click. Another connection she didn't understand.

"I saw you and Mrs. DiFalco and—" She forced herself to take a deep breath. "Is Hannah very sick?" *Stupid question. How could you ask such a stupid question?*

Maddy's eyes welled with tears, but there was still nothing but kindness in her expression. "I don't know, Kelly. She's restless, yet we can't seem to rouse her from sleep. She keeps pulling at her pajamas, the sheet, the blanket—Rose heard her mumbling something, but we couldn't understand her."

Dread washed over Kelly and she struggled to keep the fear from her eyes. Maddy's description of Hannah's condition sounded exactly like the way Grandma Irene had been acting all day.

No.

She refused to let her mind move in that direction. She tried to will the thought into extinction. Suddenly she longed to see Seth, to see her father, to hold Grandma Irene's hand. Terrible things happened every moment of every day. You could be walking down the street one morning, young and healthy and happy, and a car could jump the curb and your life, your future, your hopes—everything, gone in an instant.

"Ms. Bainbridge?" A nurse popped out of the admissions office. "Your daughter's in Room 2. I'll bring the rest of the paperwork back there for you to sign."

Maddy thanked the woman, then turned again to Kelly.

"I'd better get back before my dad wonders where I've disappeared to," she said.

"Thanks," Maddy said, kissing her swiftly on the cheek. "I'll say a prayer for your grandma."

ROSE LEANED AGAINST the narrow sink in the closet-sized rest room and took a deep breath. The air barely made it into her lungs. She closed her eyes and tried again. *Breathe*, they all say. Just breathe deeply and your anxieties will melt away like snow in spring.

Of all the hospitals in South Jersey, why did it have to be Good Samaritan? If she wasn't feeling so fragile right now, she would appreciate the irony. She had been diagnosed here at Good Sam, had surgery at Good Sam, endured chemo and radiation at Good Sam. And all because it was the one hospital her family and friends rarely used.

Secrets required planning, and Rose had always been good with details. Of course it was inconvenient—Good Sam was a longer drive—but blessed anonymity was well worth it.

And now there she was, selfishly wrestling with her own ridiculous fears while her beloved granddaughter lay sick in the ER and her prickly and equally beloved daughter struggled to hold it all together.

You should be out there helping her, Rosie, not cowering in the bathroom.

"Tell her," she said to the terrified old woman in the mirror. "Tell her while it's still your choice."

Before someone else took matters into their own hands and told Maddy for her.

"IRINA! YOU'RE NOT to tease your sister like that. You are late for your studies, and Monsieur LeGrand says your grammar is most appalling. Come along! Come along!" It is most important that the girls learn to speak perfect French as befits their position in Russian society.

Natalya, the governess, stands in the doorway to the nursery-turned-schoolroom and looks most sternly at her young charges. Irina can't stop giggling. She tries to hide her mirth behind her hand, but Natalya isn't easily fooled.

"She pulled my hair!" her little sister cries out. Maria is six years old but still a baby. "She must be punished!"

But Irina knows Natalya will not punish her. The big house is filled with love, each floor, every room, and she knows it will always be that way. . . .

IRENE CONTINUED TO hover in some sort of half-world. A feeling of sorrow permeated the room, almost visible like fog rolling across the snowy beach. Aidan had finally gotten it through his head that there wasn't going to be a happy ending this time. Irene was dying. Each shaky inhalation of breath moved her closer to that moment when respiration would slow, her heart would stop, her life would end.

Nurses came and went. They checked Irene's bedclothes, wiped her brow with a damp cloth, swabbed her mouth with what looked like a cotton lollipop, tried to offer her sips of water, which she refused to take. Each step toward the end choreographed with the tight precision of a ballet.

*   *   *

*"IRINA! IRINA! STAND still or I shall not be able to
fasten this last button."*

*Irina laughs and playfully bats away Mila's faltering
hands. "Oh, do stop, Mila!" she says as she dances out
of her maid's reach. "You are just teasing me. Let me see
myself in the glass or I shall go mad."*

*Mila pretends great annoyance, but Irina sees the way
her tired old eyes dance with delight as Irina pirouettes
before the mirror.*

*"I look like Mamma, don't I?" she asks as she admires
her reflection. "I have waited all my life, and finally I
look like Mamma."*

*"You are lovely," Mila says, but her words dance right
past Irina's reflection.*

*She is thinking of Nikolai, her beloved Kolya, and the
look in his beautiful blue eyes when he sees her in this
lovely dress. . . .*

THEY HAD STOPPED suggesting that he might like to
go home for a while, that there was little point to being
there. She didn't know. She didn't see. She didn't care.
"It could be hours, it could be days," the doctor said.
"You might as well go home for a while and come back
later."

He told them he was staying put. Irene wasn't going to
die alone.

It was toughest on Kelly. She couldn't stay in the room
more than ten minutes at a time. Irene would make a
sound or start plucking at the bedclothes, and his daughter's face would turn white, and next thing he knew she
was off to make another phone call or buy another cup
of coffee.

He glanced at his watch and saw it was almost seven
o'clock. She'd been gone quite awhile. He wondered if
this time she'd bailed for good. No matter how many
times you'd been in its company, no matter how old you
were, death was never easy.

"Daddy." Kelly stood in the doorway. She looked
stricken.

"What's wrong?"

She stepped closer and he could see she had been crying. "They brought Rose DiFalco's granddaughter into the
emergency room."

"Jesus." He felt like he'd been sucker punched. "How
bad?"

"I don't know," Kelly said. "Maddy looks pretty
scared."

He was on his feet. "You mind being alone here for a
while?"

Kelly shook her head. "I'll be okay."

He saw the fear in her eyes and the resolve. This young
woman who had seen too much of death already.

"If anything happens—"

"I know," she said. "I'll find you."

He had the sense of being trapped in a bad and familiar
dream, the one where everything that matters is slipping
through his fingers and washing out to sea. Last night he
had almost believed the bad times were coming to an end,
that maybe there was a chance to turn the O'Malleys' long
run of lousy luck around and start over again. Figure out
happy. Get a lock on optimistic. Maybe even snag one of
those fairy-tale endings he had stopped believing in a long
time ago.

*SHE HEARS HIM leave the room. She tries to call out to
him, but her words are a tumble of that long-ago language, of sounds that seem to begin somewhere beyond
this shell of a body that lies dying on the white bed. She
senses the girl, that lovely child whose name is so hard
for her to remember, crying softly from somewhere close
by. Is that love? She wonders. It has been a very long
time. . . .*

*Her beloved parents stand near the foot of the bed . . .
how beautiful Mamma looks and how strong and tall
Pappa stands in his elegant uniform . . . her sisters . . .
and oh, how her heart leaps when Kolya steps forward,
smiling, always smiling, and reaches for her hand. . . .*

*But it is only the girl with the soft hands and sweet
voice who touches her, whispering in Irina's ear. . . .*

"I KNOW YOU can hear me," Kelly said to Grandma
Irene. "You may not be able to answer me, but I know
you're listening to every word."

She squeezed Irene's hand gently, and for a moment
thought she felt the slightest pressure in response. The
doctors would say it was only a reflex action, some in-
voluntary motion that hopeful relatives invariably misin-
terpreted the way they misinterpret a newborn's grimace
for a smile.

"I'll bet Grandpa Michael's waiting for you," she said.
"And Billy, too. You were the first one to explain heaven
to me . . . do you remember? I was just a little girl, and
you took the time to explain it all in a way I could understand. . . ."

She talked softly, drifting from subject to subject, trying
to ignore the odd sounds Irene made from time to time.
They sounded like words, but certainly not English words.
Gaelic maybe? They almost sounded Russian, but that
was ridiculous. Where would Irene learn Russian?

Click.

Another connection made.

The samovar was resting on the chair in the corner of
the room. She imagined she could see it shimmering and
bright inside the shopping bag. A second later it was on
her lap, almost on the edge of Irene's bed.

"I wish you could see this samovar, Grandma," she
said. "It's almost an exact duplicate of the one you and
Grandpa Michael displayed at O'Malley's."

She gently lifted Irene's hand and placed it on the curve
of the handle.

"See? I was told it was in terrible shape, but Rose
DiFalco polished it up. It's for her granddaughter . . . Hannah's four years old and she thinks it looks like Aladdin's
lamp from the Disney movie. Hannah's in the hospital,
too, right down the hall. They don't—"

Was she imagining it, or did a smile swiftly move

across her grandmother's face as she touched the base of the samovar?

"I wish I'd known Grandpa Michael. He loved you so much. Everybody says so. I hope that Seth and I can be as happy as you and Grandpa were."

She held her breath. Irene's long, beautiful fingers were tracing the leaves and vines entwined on the handle.

"They had dozens of samovars at the Russian Tea Room," she babbled on. "You would have loved them. Our debating coach treated us to lunch there the day we won the Tristate Gold Medal."

On and on she went, talking about everything that popped into her head while her grandmother's fingers inspected every inch of the samovar. It was a little unsettling. Irene's eyes remained closed, and the rest of her body remained perfectly still. Only those beautiful hands were in motion.

"Why a Russian samovar, Grandma? Why did Grandpa Michael buy you a samovar?" In a restaurant that had been filled with shamrocks and shillelaghs, it was definitely a strange choice.

Did he buy it because it was beautiful? Because it filled an empty space in the front lobby? Because it was the only type of teapot she didn't have?

Or maybe he bought it because it meant something that only the two of them understood.

Click.

Irene began to whimper, and then the whimpers became loud sobs that brought a floor nurse running.

"What's wrong?" the nurse asked as she checked the IV line. "Did she try to get up?"

"She was running her hand along this teapot," Kelly said, "and the next second she was crying."

"Poor thing." The nurse adjusted the drip, then stepped over to the computer terminal to key in the information. "I promise we'll find the right balance. We want to keep her as comfortable as possible." She inclined her head in the direction of the samovar. "You might want to stow that. No use upsetting her any more."

*   *   *

HOW NERVOUS MICHAEL is! Like a bridegroom, the way he fusses around Irene that night, so attentive and loving.

How lucky she is to have a husband like that. Thirty-three years together and his face still lights up when she enters a room.

It is much more than she deserves.

He takes her out that night to celebrate their anniversary. Three days before Christmas, they all exclaim. What on earth made you two pick such a ridiculous day to be married?

And Michael and Irene just laugh, they always laugh, and let the questions fall away.

He takes her to their favorite steak place on the water, overlooking the bright dazzle of Manhattan across the river, and he orders champagne and shrimp cocktail and their finest filets of beef, and then, when she thinks all the good things have been accounted for, he gestures to the waiter, who carries over an enormous box tied with shiny white paper and silvery blue ribbons.

He watches, his blue eyes wide with pleasure and pride and more than a touch of anxiety, as she carefully unwraps the gift. (When she was little, in that long-ago land, she tore into packages with greedy glee. There were always more presents, there was always more of everything right around the corner.)

He holds the box while she plunges her hands into the soft nest of snowy tissue paper, then she gasps at what she finds.

"Michael!" Her eyes meet his and she cannot disguise the wonder in her voice. "Where did you get this?"

A samovar! A magnificent Russian samovar that sends her spinning back through time to those golden years that are more golden in memory because they will never come again.

He tells her the story of the restaurant in Brooklyn, and she feels her walls and fences, so long in place and so very high, begin to crumble. Is this love? Is that what she

*feels for him? When did it happen ... why didn't she
know ...*

*She wants to tell him, but she hasn't the vocabulary for
love, and he is gone before she ever finds the words to
tell him all he means—and all he would ever mean—to
her.*

AIDAN MADE HIS way quickly down the corridor to the
elevator bank, pushed the Down button, waited five seconds, then opted instead for the staircase. He startled a
pair of X-ray techs who were taking a break on the landing. Their bodies were pressed close. Yin and yang. Part
of the same eternal puzzle. They turned their heads toward
the wall. He pretended he didn't see them.

Sometimes you had to grab happiness wherever you
found it.

He was learning—oh, yeah, he was learning all right.
He hoped it wasn't too late for him. Last night he'd had
a glimpse of something wonderful, someone wonderful,
but his track record didn't inspire hope. There was still a
chance for Kelly, a chance for her to break free of old
sorrows and guilt and build something wonderful for herself. He had screwed up too many times, let himself stand
clear of love for way too long to make him believe he
could ever do the same.

He pushed open the door marked *First Floor* and
quickly got his bearings. Down the hall, two lefts, a sharp
right, the huge swinging doors that led to the ER. He had
long ago learned that the secret to access was all in the
attitude. Act like you belonged there and you did. It was
as simple as that. Nobody questioned his presence as he
scanned the huge open room for Maddy. Central hub that
served as the nurses' station. Doctors in lab coats milling
about. A tech wheeling a portable cardio machine. A por-
ter mopping a spill near the door to the lavatory. An old
man with terrified eyes in Cube 1. A little boy holding
his arm and crying in Cube 8. Curtains strung across other
openings for privacy.

He walked past each cubicle, listening. Finally he heard

a familiar voice, and the sound hit him like a jolt of pure adrenaline. Maddy's voice. He absorbed the sound, the feel of it, into his bloodstream.

He stopped in front of the closed curtain. "Maddy," he said. "It's Aidan."

The curtain drew back and he saw it all in an instant. Rose standing near the head of the bed. Hannah, pale and disoriented, her tiny body in constant motion. Fingers pulling at the covers. Talking, talking. Strange words he had never heard before. Nonsense words with an oddly familiar rhythm. The fear in Maddy's beautiful eyes. The brief surge of joy on her face when their hands touched. The sound of a heart—his own—coming back to painful, hopeful life.

A chance . . . even if it's one in a million . . . there has to be a chance for us.

"How is she?" he asked as they stepped into the corridor.

"They don't know," she said. "Her symptoms suggest any number of things."

"Any one in particular?"

She was trembling. He hadn't noticed that before. "Meningitis."

He reacted on instinct and so did she. He opened his arms to her and she moved into his embrace. Through clothes and muscle and bone he felt her heart beating in time with his.

He asked the name of the doctor, the residents, what tests they were running. He kept her talking, kept her focused on detail, not emotion, and after a bit the trembling slowed.

"No fever is a good sign," he said, aware of Rose's curious, but not unfriendly, gaze.

"I know," she said, resting her forehead against his shoulder for a second longer. "That's the one thing that's keeping them from ordering a spinal tap."

"Kids are resilient," he said. "They bounce back from things that would knock us flat."

"I know," she said again.

"They'll figure it out any minute, and once they get those meds flowing, she'll be her old self."

Maddy tried to smile, failed, then tried again. "I want to believe that."

"I believe it," he said. "She's going to be fine."

She met his eyes. "I'm so sorry about your grandmother."

"So am I," he said.

A doctor, flanked by a pair of eager med students, descended upon Hannah's cubicle. He could feel Maddy's focus shift to her daughter. As it should be.

She asked what room Irene was in and was about to say something when Rose joined them.

"They have some questions, honey," Rose said to her daughter, "and I don't seem to know the answers."

Maddy was away in a flash.

"I'm sorry to hear Irene is declining," Rose said. "She has always been a role model for me, one of the few successful working women around when I was growing up."

"There wasn't much Irene couldn't do when she set her mind to it."

"Did you know that she's one of the people I spoke to when I was thinking of cashing in my 401(k) and opening the Candlelight?"

"You went to Irene?"

"Before I went to my banker." She smiled at the memory. "She probably gave me better advice. You were still fighting fires, so you wouldn't know how instrumental she was in the formation of the Small Business Owners Association."

"You're right. I didn't know any of this." No surprise that Claire hadn't told him.

"We should talk sometime," Rose said. "Your family and mine go way back. I owe Irene a great deal. The last few years have been so busy—I wish I'd found time to thank her."

"She's in 312."

Rose seemed to hesitate. If he didn't know better, he

would think she was afraid. "You wouldn't mind?"

He shook his head. "I'd appreciate it."

She cast a longing glance toward the curtain pulled across Hannah's cubicle, then straightened her shoulders. "Let's go," she said.

ROSE WAS GONE.

Maddy stood in the middle of the chaos of the emergency room with her arms wrapped across her chest and tried not to cry.

The doctors were still in there with Hannah. Poking. Prodding. Shining lights in her eyes, her nose, her mouth, her ears, tossing questions at Maddy faster than she could answer them.

Where have you been recently.... Have you traveled abroad.... Is she in school.... Do you have a phone contact.... Can you provide a list ...

When she asked why they wanted to know, what were they thinking, where did they think this was headed, their answers provided little comfort.

We don't know.... It could be ... We're worried about ... Symptoms consistent with ... Move swiftly but with great caution ...

They were moving Hannah up to the third floor to free up space in the ER. The plan was to run a spinal tap— they called it a lumbar puncture, as if that made it sound more friendly—if no other explanation for her symptoms revealed itself within the next few hours. At the moment there wasn't an OR available, but the second one opened up, Hannah would be top priority.

Maddy stepped out of the crowded cubicle, looking for Rose. She had been out there minutes ago. Maddy had heard her talking to Aidan. The sound of their voices had given her comfort. Her mother hadn't been there for Hannah's birth. She hadn't been there for her granddaughter's baptism. Maddy had believed she would never forgive her mother for cheating them all of something meant to be shared. But the relief she felt knowing Rose was on the other side of the curtain had almost been enough to wipe away the past. She needed Rose's strength, her determination, her belief in bending fate to meet her own needs.

She needed her mother, and, once again, her mother was nowhere to be found.

A fine anger began to burn deep in her gut.

"Good news," said one of the nurses. "They found a room on three. We'll move her up as soon as they send somebody for her."

Maddy nodded her thanks. The hot coal of anger had grown so big it was choking her. She had cried herself sick the afternoon she gave birth to Hannah, praying that she would look up and see Rose standing in the doorway to the labor room, but of course that had never happened. Through the entire nine months of her pregnancy she had yearned for her mother. Longed for her presence. Sometimes she dreamed about her. But Rose had kept her censorious distance, ashamed perhaps of Maddy's single state or, more likely, disappointed that her unambitious daughter had chosen the most traditional path of all.

A huge orderly with a clipboard tucked under his arm smiled at Maddy.

"Hannah Bainbridge-Lawlor?" he asked.

Maddy nodded and gestured toward the cubicle. "She's ready."

You should be here, Rose, Maddy raged as she walked behind the rolling bed that bore her baby girl. Not for her. It was too late for that. She should be there for Hannah.

Disappointment, strong as bile, burned through her as the elevator climbed to the third floor. Hannah deserved better. Wasn't that why Maddy had moved clear across the country, so her little girl could be surrounded by family and old friends?

Well, where were they? Where was her family? Where were her aunts who usually couldn't wait to stick their noses in her business? Where were her happy-go-lucky cousins? Where were the nieces and nephews? Where were her old friends, the ones who claimed they would always be there for each other, through good times and bad?

But most of all, where was her mother?

Anger followed her down the corridor, past the nurses' station, and it finally exploded into fury when she saw her mother leaning over Irene O'Malley's bed as if it were the only place on earth she needed to be.

Chapter Twenty-seven

ROSE SPOKE GENTLY to Irene as she sat next to the bed. It was clear the old woman was as much a part of the next world as she was part of this one, and Rose could only wonder what supreme act of will or stubbornness kept her clinging to life.

She opened her heart to Irene. She thanked her for the help she had given her along the way. She told her about Maddy's homecoming and the pure delight that was Hannah. Her voice broke when she tried to talk about her granddaughter and she was grateful to Aidan when he stepped in and tactfully changed the subject.

She had just managed to pull herself together again when she looked up and saw Maddy looming in the doorway. She felt a fist grab her heart.

"Hannah." She could barely say her granddaughter's name. "Is she—"

"They put her next door," Maddy said in clipped tones. "She asked for you. I told her you'd left."

Rose felt her cheeks burn with heat. "You were busy with the doctors. I asked Aidan if he would mind if I said hello to Irene."

The look of betrayal in Maddy's eyes sliced straight through to the bone. "Gotta keep those business contacts fresh, don't you, Rosie?"

She turned on her heel and disappeared.

Something inside Rose snapped, but she managed to control it long enough to kiss Irene on the forehead and murmur an apology to Aidan, who was standing in the corner of the room, looking supremely uncomfortable.

"Obviously my daughter and I have some unfinished business," she said in an attempt at humor that fell as flat as her expectations.

Maddy was striding down the corridor toward the elevators, her long legs eating up the distance much faster than Rose could match. She broke into a run designed to make her look foolish and vulnerable, two things she would normally never allow.

"Maddy, please!" she called out, her dignity rapidly falling by the wayside. "Wait, Maddy, please!"

Maddy didn't break stride. She reached the elevators, hesitated, then pushed open the door marked *Stairs*.

Rose was no athlete, but her adrenaline was pumping hard and fast. She felt herself gathering speed as she sprinted past the elevators just as Maddy was about to disappear through the doorway.

"Rose! Is that you?"

Oh, God.

Maddy stopped where she was. Rose kept moving toward her.

"Rose DiFalco! I heard you were here."

Rose knew how a deer felt during hunting season. Isolated. Trapped. No place left to run.

"Good to see you, Carol. How are the grandkids?"

Carol placed her hands on her heart and beamed a megawatt smile. "They make the whole thing worthwhile," she said as her smile dimmed. "I hear your grandbaby is in ER."

Rose was painfully aware of Maddy standing in the stairwell, watching and listening to every word.

"She is," Rose said, praying the elevator would show up and whisk the woman away.

Failing that, a tornado would be nice.

"I'll stop by the chapel on my way home," Carol said. "A little prayer never hurt, right?"

"Right," said Rose. "We appreciate it." Prayer was probably all she had left at this point.

She turned toward the staircase. Where was the elevator? Why wasn't there a crowd of people milling about? Why was Maddy just standing there, recording it all like a reporter at the scene of a crime?

"Rose, while I have you here—"

Rose moved toward the door. "Carol, I'm sorry but I must run. I have to—"

"Just one second," Carol said. "We still need the signed consent form so we can send your records to the Breast Cancer Institute for study."

Five years of secrets, of elaborate excuses and complicated lies, up in smoke, and all it took was a simple request from an overworked office assistant with one more item to check off on her To-Do list.

It was so pathetically ridiculous that Rose wanted to laugh. She did laugh, bending over at the waist, holding her stomach, big painful full-body laughs that almost split her in two.

"Rose?" Carol took a step closer. "Are you okay?"

Rose only laughed harder. Tears streamed from her eyes and down her cheeks.

"Mom?" Maddy was standing beside her, a cautious hand on her shoulder. "Is everything all right?"

Was it possible Maddy hadn't heard Carol? Was there still a chance?

Her laughter tightened up into choking sobs. Please, God, maybe she hadn't heard. . . . *Please, God, I want her to know. . . .*

The elevator chimed.

"I hate to leave her this way," Carol said, "but I need to get back to my desk."

"Go," said Maddy, forcing a smile. "I'll stay with her."

"I'll say a prayer for your daughter."

Maddy thanked her. So polite. Maybe she hadn't done such a terrible job with her after all.

Carol stepped onto the elevator and just before the doors closed, she called out, "Give me a yell when you find out something."

"What's your extension?" Maddy asked.

"Just ask for Carol in Oncology," the woman said. "They'll find me."

And the jaws of the trap snapped shut.

MADDY'S FOCUS NARROWED until there was nothing in the world but her mother.

"Tell me," Maddy said, her tone steely-hard and un-compromising.

Rose lifted her head and looked up at her. "I think you already know."

"You have cancer."

"No," said Rose. "I *had* cancer." She forced a shaky smile. "A very significant distinction in certain circles."

"I don't understand. How could I not know this?"

"Very simple," Rose said. "I didn't tell you."

"How long?"

She heard her mother's sharp inhalation of breath, the pause, the shaky exhalation. The ex-smoker's canto. "A long time."

"*How* long?"

"Five and a half years."

"Jesus!" She backed away from Rose. "When were you going to tell me?"

"I wasn't," her mother said. "But Lucy has been—"

"Aunt Lucy knows?" Rose nodded. "Who else? Gina? Denise? The Loewensteins? The Armaghs?" She tried to lower her voice but failed miserably. "Am I the only one who doesn't know?"

"Lucy knows," Rose said, tears still streaming down her face. She hesitated. "And your father."

That little piece of information hit Maddy like a kick

in the gut. "You're telling me that Bill knows?" *My father? Daddy?*

"When Irma was dying." Rose's voice had been reduced to a whisper. Maddy had to lean closer to hear her words. "I didn't mean to tell him. I didn't want to, but she was so frightened and I—"

"If you're looking to score points as a humanitarian, don't bother."

Rose turned and punched the Down button.

"You can't leave now," Maddy said, starting after her mother. "You can't drop a bombshell like this on me and walk out."

"Of course I can't," Rose shot back. "That's your job, isn't it? You're the one who walks out when the going gets tough."

"Unfair," Maddy said, her voice shaking with outrage.

"Is it?"

"Look at me, Rose. I'm not running. I'm not walking out."

"This isn't the time," Rose said over her shoulder, "nor is it the place."

"Maybe not, but here we are and I'll be damned if I'm going to let you walk away from this. You *owe* me, Rose. You owe me an explanation."

"You may not like it."

"Try me."

"*There* you are!" Aunt Lucy seemed to appear from nowhere. "I've been looking all over for—" She stopped, looking from Rose to Maddy. "What's wrong? I know it's not Hannah. I was just in there."

"She knows," said Rose.

It took Lucy a second, but then her lovely face broke into a huge smile. "Oh, thank God! Honey, I told you it was time, didn't I? I'm so glad you don't have to walk around with that terrible load on your mind any longer."

"Maybe we should open a bottle of champagne," Maddy said, glaring at the two women. "A toast to keeping secrets . . . where would a family be without 'em?"

The elevator clanked into position. The doors creaked

open and a score of DiFalcos spilled out. Aunt Toni and
Aunt Connie. Gina and Denise and their kids. More cousins and nephews and nieces than Maddy could take in.
She was passed from hug to hug, moving on an unexpected wave of love and support. They brought food with
them and newspapers, knitting projects and coloring
books. *We're here for the long haul,* their actions proclaimed. *You're not in this alone.*

Rose was crying softly, her forehead resting against
Lucy's soft shoulder. Maddy felt a quick stab of guilt but
pushed it away as the others gathered around the two sisters. *Your choice, Rose.* Over and over, in every given
situation, Rose had always made the choice to be alone.

Her sisters and nieces and nephews and cousins and
friends would have been there for Rose, gathering around
her like a human shield, protecting her from outside in-
vaders. They would have ferried her to doctors' appoint-
ments, held her hand during chemo, driven her to
radiation. They had done it for their own before. Rose
was their blood. They would have done it for her, too.

Maddy would have been there for her mother as well.
She would have put aside old differences and come home
to help her through. That was what families did when they
were given the chance.

But Rose never gave any of them the chance.

Look at them over there with Rose. Look at the kindness on their familiar faces, the love and concern. In that
throbbing mass of family love only Lucy knew Rose's
story. Only Lucy had been given the opportunity to hold
Rose's hand, a gift whose value Maddy was only now
beginning to fully understand.

Maddy slipped away from the knot of family and
moved quickly down the hallway. She felt numb and
bruised. Too much was happening. Her little girl's illness,
Rose's revelation, the sense that she was beginning to see
her family clearly for the first time in her life. She had
been gone for almost half her life. She was a virtual
stranger to most of them. But they loved her just the same.
It was a revelation to her. They had opened the circle wide

enough to let her slip inside and bring Hannah with her. They were her tribe. Her people. Even if she packed her bags and disappeared for another fifteen years, they would be here waiting for her when she came back. The circle would open wide again.

The third-floor lounge swarmed with people. She saw Kelly's boyfriend, Seth, at least a dozen familiar faces from around town, Claire and Billy Jr. She ducked into Hannah's room seconds before the dam burst, and the flood she had been struggling to hold back finally broke free.

AIDAN SAW MADDY disappear into Hannah's room, three doors down from Irene. She looked exhausted, terrified, on the ragged edge of losing it.

The hell of it was, she had every reason to be scared shitless. He'd overheard the doctors talking in the hallway and it was clear they were flying blind. The kid was sinking fast, and unless somebody threw her the right lifeline they were going to lose her.

If he needed proof that God had left the building, he was looking at it.

At least Irene was leaving with all flags flying. They had begun to arrive an hour ago, people who had crossed paths with Irene over the years and been the better for it. Each new revelation reminded him of how little he knew about the woman who had raised him and Billy.

"I'm pulling for her," Tommy said. "This town won't be the same without her."

"She put me in touch with Charles at the bank," Julie said. "I doubt I could've gotten the coffee shop renovated and relaunched without her help."

"I owe her big time," said Mel Perry. "She wrote a school recommendation for my kid the lawyer. Made all the difference."

Jack Bernstein tried to say something, but the hitch in his throat rendered him mute.

The crowd in the third-floor visitors' lounge overflowed into the corridor. It seemed to Aidan that Grandma Irene had touched the lives of almost everyone in town and they were determined to thank her before it was too late.

He and Kelly watched, astonished, as one familiar face after another stepped into Irene's room and whispered a few words of friendship. It was a thankless exercise. Irene gave no indication that she was aware of any of them, but still they came. He sat there taking it all in, wondering about the secret lives people led and how they intersected with each other in the strangest and most profound ways.

But it was when Claire showed up with Billy Jr. that he nearly lost it.

She hugged Kelly, then grabbed him by the biceps, her tone fierce and loving. "Not for her," she said. "For us."

Their family. It was worth fighting for.

The DiFalcos were there in force, too, gathered together to support Maddy and Hannah in every way they could. All of the sisters. The cousins. Spouses, current and ex and almost. Nieces and nephews. A huge outpouring of love that spilled over onto Kelly and him until you couldn't tell who belonged to whom.

Gina spent a few moments at Irene's bedside. He didn't know what their connection was, but at this point nothing would surprise him. Denise. Toni DiFalco and her husband sipped coffee and watched the kids. Rose sat by herself near the window, her body language an expression of sorrow in its purest form.

Minutes passed. An hour. He got up to stretch his legs, grab a can of juice from the kitchen fridge at the end of the corridor. His head ached from the continuous low buzz of conversation, from playing host at a party nobody wanted to attend.

Maddy was in there, leaning against the sink, holding a can of orange drink to her forehead. Her eyes were closed. Dark shadows were clearly visible.

"Pretty crowded out there," he said. The things he wanted to say had no place in this room today.

Her eyes flickered open and she offered him a weary smile. "I'm surprised the staff doesn't kick some of them downstairs. Looks like O'Malley's on a Friday night."

"Ten years ago maybe." He had the feeling his own smile was almost as weary. "Our Fridays aren't what they used to be."

"How is your grandmother?"

He shook his head. "It won't be long." A beat pause. "Hannah?"

"They don't know." She placed the can of orange drink on the counter and wrapped her arms across her chest. "All of the advances in medicine, all of the expensive equipment they keep telling you will save your life—" Her voice broke and he looked away while she regained her composure. "If they can't pinpoint the cause after the lumbar puncture, then . . ." Her words trailed off.

Neither one of them needed a road map.

He grabbed the can of orange drink, popped the top, then handed it to her. She murmured her thanks, took a long swig, then handed it back to him. He could taste her warmth on the metal rim. They stood there for a long time, leaning back against the counter, leaning into each other.

"I owe you breakfast," she said, taking another sip of orange drink.

"Name the day."

"The second Hannah's out of here, we'll—"

He held her as she cried, shielding her with his body from curious eyes. He wanted to tell her that Hannah was going to be okay. He wanted to tell her that nothing bad ever happened to the people you loved, but she would know he was lying. Bad things happened every day of the week. The only sure way to keep your heart from breaking was to lock it away. But that wasn't living. It had taken Aidan a long time to figure that out, but now that he had he wasn't about to let her go.

BILL BAINBRIDGE SHOWED up around suppertime. Rose flew into his arms and didn't let go for a good five minutes. Maddy watched from the entrance to Hannah's room, eyes wide with shock, as her parents kissed, looked deeply into each other's eyes, then kissed again.

They're in love, she thought in amazement. More than that, it was clear they always had been. She was too tired in body and soul to question any of it. If love showed up, you would be a fool to show it to the door.

Bill enveloped her in a bear hug, and the enormity of what was happening took on an even darker edge of foreboding.

"I thought you were some place woodsy and midwestern," she said, trying to lighten the mood.

"I still am," he said. "Just thought I'd use up a few of those frequent-flyer miles I've been accumulating and come admire your snow."

He had always been a terrible liar.

He tried hard not to show how much or how deeply Hannah's condition affected him, but he seemed to age as he stood there by her bed, her tiny hand in his, and talked to her.

"Go for a walk with your old man," he said to Maddy after he wiped his eyes with his handkerchief and stuffed it deep into his pants pocket. "I need to stretch my legs."

"Hannah's doctor should be here any minute," Maddy said. "He promised to let me know when they're taking Hannah up for the tap."

"They'll find you," he said.

They walked past Irene's open door. The room lights had been dimmed and Maddy could just make out the slight figure of the old woman as she moved restlessly in the bed.

She turned away.

"It's a hard life," Bill said as they neared the nurses' station, "and sometimes we don't leave it with quite the grace we'd hoped for."

"She's a fighter," Maddy said. "I guess you don't live over one hundred years if you don't know how to fight."

"True enough," he said, "but sooner or later the time comes when you need to stop fighting and let go of the past."

They paused by the window at the far end of the corridor and looked down on the parking lot below.

"I'm glad Rosie finally told you the truth."

She could feel her spine stiffen with anger. "She didn't exactly tell me." She explained how the truth had actually come out.

"But now you know," Bill said. "Now it'll finally make some sense to you."

"Make sense? What are you talking about?"

"When you were pregnant with Hannah," he went on, oblivious to her confusion. "Why she didn't come out and help you."

"I don't get it," she persisted. "I don't see what one thing has to do with the other."

"For a smart woman you can be mighty dumb when you put your mind to it." He fiddled with a mended latch on the window. "You're good with numbers, Maddy. Think about the timing and tell me what you come up with."

She saw it all in an instant. The evasions. The flimsy excuses. The times when Rose sounded like answering her phone took took more energy than she had to offer. The missed Christmas.

"Oh, God," she said, "that's why."

Bill nodded. If she didn't know better she would think his blue eyes were damp with tears. "She didn't want to put a damper on a happy time," he said. "And, let's be real honest here, she figured if nobody knew, she wouldn't have to deal with all of their worrying on top of everything else."

"Dad, I—"

"Go," he said. "And thank God for second chances."

ROSE WATCHED THEM until they disappeared around the bend in the corridor. She could count the times on one hand when she had been able to indulge herself in the pleasure of watching the man she loved and the daughter they had created walk down a corridor together.

A small pleasure in the grand scheme of things, but all the diamonds in the world would fall short by comparison. Both tall. Both rangy. Both with that long, loose stride

Rose always thought of as quintessentially west of the Rockies. She had carried Maddy for nine months inside her body, but you would never know it to see them together. Her genetic material was nowhere in sight.

If only Hannah had been walking with them, her shiny blond hair bouncing on her shoulders and—

No. Don't think about it. Think positive thoughts. They were going to get this whole thing figured out any minute now, and before you knew it Hannah would be her old bouncy self.

She refused to believe anything else was possible.

It felt good to sit there surrounded by family and dear friends. If positive energy meant anything, Hannah would get well in record time and Irene O'Malley's passing would be gentle and swift. She could never remember a time when she had felt more connected with her family or with Paradise Point. She hoped Maddy felt even a tiny portion of what she was feeling right now. If she did she would understand that she was loved.

That she had finally come home.

Her eyes closed and she began to drift. She could work eighteen-hour days at the Candlelight and leap from bed the next morning eager for more, but worry exacted a different toll from a woman. Exhaustion tugged at her like the undertow near the Point. Sly and seductive. Relentless. Pulling you away from shore until there was nothing you could do but give in to its demands.

A hand on her shoulder jolted her back to earth. "I'm not asleep," she said. "I was just resting my eyes."

You would think a woman would recognize her own daughter's touch, wouldn't you? But they had never been touchers, Rose and Maddy. No spontaneous hugs or arms slung around a waist for them. There were days when breathing the same air was about as close as they cared to get.

Maddy sat down next to her on the bench seat. An inch was all that separated them. Rose wasn't sure they'd been this close at any point since Maddy left diapers behind. She felt almost drunk on her daughter's nearness.

"You didn't have to go through it alone." Maddy spoke softly. For Rose's ears alone. "I would have come home to help you."

"I wasn't sure you would," Rose said, looking down at her nails, "and that would have hurt more than anything the doctors could have done to me."

"The day Hannah was born I was so sure you would show up. Every time I heard footsteps I looked up, expecting to see you standing in the doorway."

"I wanted to be there," Rose said. "More than you'll ever know." She had been desperately ill from chemotherapy at that time. Struggling to pull herself through from one day to the next while maintaining the illusion that none of it was happening.

"We could have helped each other," Maddy said. "Neither one of us should have been alone."

"I dreamed of you every night," Rose said. "I hung the Polaroids of your beautiful belly from my lamp shade. They were the last thing I saw every night when I went to sleep."

"You shouldn't have had to go through any of it alone."

"I had Lucy to lean on," she said. "I hadn't planned to, but thank God it happened that way."

Maddy's lovely face, both familiar and strange to her, began to crumple, and Rose's heart ached in response.

"I didn't say that to hurt you."

"I know," Maddy whispered. "All this time I thought you stayed away because"—her face contorted with remembered pain—"because you didn't love me."

"Oh, honey!" She pulled Maddy into her arms and held her tight. "That's the one thing that will never happen."

Chapter Twenty-eight

GRANDMA IRENE CONTINUED to hang on through the evening. The doctors couldn't explain it, even though they tried to cobble together an AMA-approved explanation. The nurses just shook their heads and chalked it up to two things: the will to live and the will of God. Two things you didn't learn much about in medical school.

Kelly's father suggested she and Seth go out and grab themselves some pizza or a burger some place, but she wasn't hungry. The DiFalcos had brought a ton of food. So had Aunt Claire and some of the old guys who hung out at O'Malley's.

Seth was sitting with Tommy and Mel Perry watching some television special about the NFL. Kelly tried watching with them, but she felt unsettled and restless. Maddy and her mother, Rose, were looking sadder by the minute, and it was all Kelly could do to keep from crying every time she thought of Hannah. How strange was it that someone right there in Paradise Point ended up winning the samovar she had wanted for Grandma Irene.

She was glad now that she hadn't won it after all, especially after seeing Grandma Irene's reaction. Her great-grandmother's cries still echoed inside her head. The last thing Kelly had wanted to do was cause her any pain and she hated herself for making such a big fat issue of the stupid teapot.

At least Hannah loved it. She smiled as she remembered the little girl pulling the samovar from its hiding spot in Rose's closet, so eager to make pretend tea. Kelly had been the same way at Hannah's age, living deep inside an imaginary world of fairy princesses and flying carpets. Her imaginary friends had seemed more real to her than the kids who sat beside her every day in school and she had the feeling it was the same way for Hannah.

How could everything change overnight? This time yesterday Hannah had been a healthy little girl rummaging through her grandmother's closet for hidden Christmas presents. Now she was—

No.

She forced the scary thoughts from her mind. Thoughts had power and she refused to allow anything but positive, healing thoughts about Hannah.

Her father was sitting next to Irene, thumbing through a magazine. It was so dark in the room that she didn't know how he could even see the pages, but she supposed it didn't matter. He was just flipping the pages the way Toni DiFalco fingered her rosary beads.

Grandma Irene was muttering something under her breath, strange sounds that her father ignored, but that unnerved Kelly. It was like the old woman was trying to tell them something but they no longer spoke the same language.

"Could you move your chair, please?" she asked her father. "I better give the samovar back to Maddy before I forget."

He nodded and shoved aside so she could get by.

Grandma Irene started at the sound of his chair scraping against the tiled floor. Her eyes fluttered open, deep blue even in the half light.

"Dad." She kept her voice soft and even. "Dad, Grandma's awake."

He looked over at Irene, then shook his head. "Her eyes are open, Kel, but she's not awake. The doctors explained it to me."

Kelly met Grandma Irene's eyes and smiled.

"She sees me," she said. "I smiled at her and she blinked in response."

He put down his magazine. "Kel, I don't want to see you reading anything into reflex actions. She doesn't know what's going on."

"I think she does."

Irene extended her right hand toward Aidan. Her gaze was focused full on him.

"Just a reflex?" Kelly asked, heart pounding with excitement.

She saw her father swallow hard and her heart went out to him. He loved Grandma Irene. If only things could have been different for all of them. If only they could have been born into one of those big happy families like the DiFalcos. The DiFalcos were noisy and not great when it came to staying married, but they loved each other and they weren't shy about letting you know it. You could do a whole lot worse.

Her father reached out and placed his hand over Irene's. Kelly's eyes swam with tears. He looked over at her and nodded. She put the samovar on the floor and rested her hand on top of his. Tears streamed down her cheeks.

Irene's cloudy gaze moved from Aidan's face to Kelly's, and she had the sensation of being hugged. Oh, she knew what the doctors would say—"She doesn't really see you!"—and what Aunt Claire would say—"That romantic imagination is going to get you in trouble one day."—but the sensation was so strong, so real, that she could actually feel the arms around her and the warmth of the embrace she had never known.

"I—"

Kelly and her father exchanged glances. This was more

than the odd sounds Grandma Irene had been making now
for hours.

Aidan leaned closer. "Did you say something, Grandma
Irene? It's Aidan. I'm here with Kelly."

There was no doubt about it. Irene's gaze left Kelly and
settled definitely on her father. She was afraid to breathe,
afraid to do anything that might break the spell.

"Ah . . . I . . . I . . ." Grandma Irene's eyes closed.

"No!" Kelly's voice rang out despite her best efforts at
controlling her emotions. "Please, Grandma! What were
you going to say?"

Irene's lids were so thin that they were almost trans-
parent. They fluttered open one more time, and there was
no mistaking the clarity of her gaze.

Or the emotion behind it.

She looked straight at Aidan. Kelly heard a low sound
deep in the back of his throat and she prayed he wouldn't
cry. She didn't know what she would do if he cried.

"My blue-eyed boy . . ." Grandma Irene said, her voice
the sound of a soft breeze. ". . . always loved you . . . always . . ."

MICHAEL WAS WAITING for her.

*How funny life was. All these years she had expected
it would be Kolya at the end, young and handsome and
strong, smiling in that endearing way that had always
touched her heart.*

*Not once had she expected it would be her husband
instead, Michael O'Malley with his sad eyes and kind
heart.*

*A surge of joy filled her and suddenly she was no longer
afraid. He knew that she loved him! She saw it in his eyes,
his smile. Perhaps he had known long before she had
come to realize it herself. She prayed that was so.*

*How lucky she was . . . how little she deserved that luck.
She had lived selfishly, allowing herself to dwell on a past
that was long gone while the miracle of the here and now,
all the wonderful things that were real and wonderful and
hers for the taking, slipped through her fingers. She had*

*sacrificed a family's future for dreams of a past that ex-
isted only in her fading memories. What a fool she had
been to waste the most precious gift of all, the gift of
today.*

*She looked down at Aidan and his daughter and all the
love she felt for them, all the love she had hidden away
for all the long years of her life seemed to spill from her
fingertips, showering them with blessings that glittered
like diamonds, that shimmered like stars.*

*It would be different for Aidan and his children. She
had felt it the moment her words blossomed in the air
between them, known the precise moment when those
words took root inside his heart. It was too late to give
him the gift of the past, but the future was still his for the
taking.*

*A wife he loved and who loved him in return . . . three
beautiful daughters and a strapping son . . . such a wonderful life . . . she wished she could be there to watch it
all unfold, but the look in Michael's eyes told her that it
was time to say goodbye.*

MADDY HEARD THE soft sound of crying coming from
Irene's room.

Claire lowered her head. Billy Jr. and his sister pulled
closer together. Big, strong Tommy, the bartender at
O'Malley's, was blubbering into an enormous white handkerchief while her hard-nosed cousin Gina leaned against
the wall, crying openly.

She wondered how Aidan and Kelly were doing. Irene
O'Malley had lived an exceptionally long and full life,
but that didn't mean the people who loved her found it
easy to let her go. There was always unfinished business,
things you wished you had said, and a few you wished
you hadn't heard. She whispered a prayer for Irene and
one for Aidan and Kelly as well.

How long had it been since she'd prayed? It seemed
that she had murmured more urgent prayers today than
she had since she was a little girl making her first com-

munion. So far, however, it seemed her prayers were falling on deaf ears.

Tom was in with Hannah now. He said he couldn't
explain it, but a warning bell had gone off inside him
when Maddy's e-mail arrived that morning and he hopped
a ride on a friend's corporate jet to be there with his youngest child. "Hannah will be so happy to see you," she had
said as they hugged briefly. The expression in his eyes
said it all. Hannah was his daughter and he loved her.
Maybe he didn't love her the way Maddy wanted him to,
but the deep, unbreakable connection was there and she
thanked God for it. Hannah's life would be the richer for
it.

His wife, Lisa, had come upstairs with him and quietly
charmed both Maddy and Rose with a Hannah story they
had never heard. She met everyone, visited Hannah, then
excused herself ostensibly to get a bite to eat in the cafeteria downstairs.

Maddy liked her. After all the months she had spent
hating the woman's very existence, she found herself glad
that Tom had chosen so well for himself and for Hannah.

So many wonderful things had happened today. Miracles, if you believed in everyday wonders. The amazing
changes in her relationship with Rose. The promise of
discovery with Aidan. Her father's quiet strength. Tom's
love for his daughter. The loving circle of family and
friends who had gathered together because that was what
you did when one of your own was in trouble.

So many things to be thankful for—if only Hannah
weren't lying in that cold and sterile hospital bed, growing
sicker with every moment that passed.

The lumbar puncture was scheduled for ten-thirty. "We
don't expect to find anything," the specialist had told her
with the flat tone of a man with better things to do. "Just
ruling out all the possibilities." Another forty-five excru-
ciating minutes to endure, followed by the endless wait
for results. She couldn't project herself that far into the
future. It frightened her too much. These doctors knew so
much about the mysteries of the human body. They could

peer into the tiniest recess, into the secrets of DNA, and yet they couldn't figure out why her little girl was dying. Things like that happened all the time. In a world that demanded explanations that could be charted on a graph or fed through a computer, sometimes life threw a curve-ball that couldn't be charted or graphed or understood and she was afraid this was one of those times.

She had to face the truth because if somebody didn't come up with an answer soon, Hannah was going to slip right through their hands.

Irene's door opened and Aidan stepped out. Claire walked over to him, gave him a quick hug. They spoke quietly and she returned to her children. His eyes moved swiftly over the assembled crowd until they found Maddy's.

She knew instantly that he had found what he had been looking for. He looked younger somehow; his sorrow over Irene's death carried within it a sense of peace that Maddy could feel across the room.

She stood up and walked toward Aidan and Kelly, searching for the right thing to say and the right words with which to say it but nothing seemed adequate. His eyes never left hers and she suddenly realized exactly what was different. Somehow his grandmother's death had freed him from the burden of sorrow that he had carried like a shield, a barrier between his heart and life's many slings and arrows and joys. She didn't know what had transpired in his grandmother's last minutes on this earth, but they had obviously had a profound effect on Aidan.

She whispered a prayer for Irene O'Malley's soul then, without a word, she and Aidan hugged. Her forehead rested against his chest for a second, just long enough for them both to register the rightness of the connection be-tween them, the healing power of touch.

Kelly watched them, her expression a blend of curiosity and affection, and on impulse Maddy made to hug her as well, but a very familiar shopping bag came between them.

"The samovar?" She felt every bit as puzzled as she sounded.

Kelly's face blazed with color. "I was just about to give it back to you."

"So I see," Maddy said, "but how on earth did you get it in the first place?"

"Rose let me borrow it earlier today. I thought maybe Grandma Irene would recognize it or react, but . . ." She shrugged. "Didn't happen the way I hoped it would." She handed the bag to Maddy. "I know this sounds crazy, but maybe you should show it to Hannah. You never know. She loves it so much that she might respond."

Maddy clutched the bag to her chest. "Kelly, she doesn't even know the samovar exists. It's a Christmas present."

"Uh-oh." Kelly's cheeks blazed an even brighter shade of red. "I forgot it was supposed to be a secret."

"She knew about the samovar?" A buzz of awareness tingled along Maddy's spine as she thought about Hannah's sudden yearning for hot tea in a glass, the smattering of Russian, the grown-up sorrow in the little girl's eyes.

"She showed it to me last night," Kelly said. "I felt weird being in Rose's bedroom like that, but Hannah was so cute about it being our secret that I—" She shrugged. "You know."

"I know," Maddy whispered, tears filling her eyes.

"Hannah wanted me to drink pretend tea with her but I—" Kelly made a face. "It looked pretty grungy when she poured it into her glass."

"How's Hannah doing?" Aidan asked.

Maddy shook her head. "They've checked everything. They even made us bring samples of the foods Hannah ate yesterday to make sure she hadn't been accidentally poisoned." The lab was also running tests on Hannah's toothbrush, her bathroom cup, her pillowcase, and a clipping of Priscilla's fur in their search for answers.

Her peripheral vision caught sight of Claire and Father Donato approaching. Jim Donato had been serving at Our

Lady of Lourdes for as long as Maddy could remember. Her stomach knotted as she noticed the vestments draped over his arm.

He greeted Maddy warmly, expressing his concern for Hannah and promising to add her to the prayer list. Maddy thanked him, while her knees went weak with relief that he hadn't suggested last rites for her little girl.

She excused herself and moved away as Father Jim explained to Aidan that while nobody knew with certainty how long the spirit lingered with the body after death, he believed Irene's soul would be well served by the ministering of last rites. Irene had been a parishioner at Our Lady of Lourdes for as long as anyone in town could remember and Father Jim was determined to ease her way along the road to heaven as best he could.

Aidan, who had eight years of Catholic school under his belt same as Maddy, agreed and the family disappeared into Irene's room.

Funny how all those hours spent studying the catechism came back to you when you least expected them. The drawings of the happy children marching out of confession without the weight of sin on their shoulders. The picture of a beatific soul hovering above a still body while the priest gave extreme unction. Page after page of mysteries that no one walking the earth could possibly understand.

The older she got, the less she understood the hows and whys of life. One little decision fed into another and another and suddenly you found yourself back home with your family, back in the town you'd left behind and the people you thought you loved best from a distance, struggling to figure out if you really belonged there or if it was just another stop along the way to somewhere else. Or maybe you sat down at the computer one night and clicked on an auction Web site and there it was, a magic lamp masquerading as a battered rusty teapot with the power to change your life forever. One decision leading into another and then another and before you know it you find yourself with more love than you had ever dreamed existed. Random luck or the hand of fate—how could you possibly know the difference when you were smack in the middle of it all?

She glanced down at the samovar cradled in her arms as the familiar voices of family and friends rose and fell around her—Rose's voice, Aidan's, her father's rumble, so many of them—all blending together as they waited and prayed for Hannah. If prayers meant anything, if love could work miracles . . .

One voice climbed above the others and she turned to see Tom standing in the doorway to Hannah's room. The old saying about blood running cold suddenly made terrible sense.

"Come here," he said, his voice both familiar and strange. "Hurry!"

She felt like she was moving in slow motion, pulling herself through a heavy dreamscape as she made her way toward Hannah. She was distantly aware of the sudden absence of sound, the spongy feel of industrial carpet beneath her feet, the sharp taste of fear.

Maddy's heart threatened to snap in two at the sight of her mother leaning over Hannah's bed, stroking the little girl's cheek. Her father stood behind Rose, his hand resting lightly on her shoulder.

"She opened her eyes," Tom said as Maddy joined them. "I think she tried to say something, but—" His voice broke and he looked away.

"Honey." Maddy, still clutching the shopping bag, leaned over the bed. "I'm here, Hannah. Mommy's here."

Hannah struggled against the sheets and blankets. Rose placed her hands against the child's shoulders and tried to calm her, but Hannah wriggled away from her.

"She's stronger than she looks," Rose said.

"Hold this." Maddy thrust the shopping bag toward Tom.

"What is it?"

"A very long story," Maddy said as she reached for her daughter. If Hannah recognized her she gave no indication. She recoiled from Maddy's touch, murmuring some-

thing under her breath, words and phrases that made no
sense at all to anyone in the room. Maddy's fear escalated.

"I should have told you I gave Kelly the teapot," Rose
said. "I wasn't thinking clearly this morning."

Maddy shook her head. "It doesn't matter, Mom. None
of us was thinking clearly." She pulled Hannah's struggling body against hers and held tight.

Tom reached into the bag and pulled out the samovar.

"Put it back!" Rose snapped. "It's a present for . . ."
Her gaze angled toward Hannah who was squirming in
Maddy's arms.

"She knows," Maddy said over her daughter's shoulder.
"She took Kelly up to your room to show it to her last
night."

"It looks like Aladdin's lamp," Tom said. "Bet she
loves it."

Show it to her, Kelly had said. *She loves it so much.*

"Come over here," she said to Tom. "Hold the samovar
up so Hannah can see it."

He did as she told him. No questions asked.

"You have to hurry up and get better, Hannah," Maddy
crooned to her daughter. She felt light as parchment in
her arms. She could almost feel her spirit oozing out
through her pores and floating away. "We'll have a tea
party with your beautiful magic lamp . . . you can invite
Aladdin and Jasmine . . . I'll even let you wear your Jasmine pajamas to bed every night next week . . . just open
your eyes, Hannah . . . come back to us . . . please come
back . . ."

Please, God, don't take her from me . . . please!

"Maddy." Tom's voice was low, urgent. "She's opening her eyes again . . . I think she's coming out of it!"

Rose's sob filled the room. Bill coughed loudly and
looked down at his boots.

Maddy's heart beat so quickly she had trouble catching
her breath.

She laid Hannah down against the pillows and took her
daughter's hands in hers.

"Come on, honey, you're almost . . . just open your

eyes . . . that's a girl . . . open your eyes and everything's
going to be all right . . ."

". . . take care . . ." Hannah said softly. ". . . take care of
my blue-eyed boy."

"Blue-eyed boy?" Bill mumbled. "What blue-eyed
boy?"

"Must be one of her dolls," Rose said.

A doll, the postman, Brad Pitt. Maddy didn't care. All
she cared about was that her daughter was coming back
to her. Hannah's eyes fluttered open. Her gaze drifted
from the ceiling to the IV pole to the samovar gleaming
at the foot of the bed. She lifted her eyes to Maddy and
for a second Maddy saw the woman inside her little girl,
and a shiver of recognition rippled through her body and
was gone before she could acknowledge it.

Maddy's father stepped out into the hallway to get a
nurse, and when he told the crowd of friends and relatives
the good news you could hear the cheers from Paradise
Point to Philadelphia.

Aidan cried when he heard. And he wasn't alone.
Kelly, Seth, Rose DiFalco, her sisters, their children, their
children's children, Maddy's father, Tommy from the bar,
Jack Bernstein, the good folks who frequented
O'Malley's, Tom and Lisa—they all cried. Sprawled on
leatherette sofas, taking turns in the one comfortable chair,
alternating runs to the local Wawa for coffee and bottled
water and bagels with cream cheese, the crowd of friends
and family had stayed there through the night. They had
come together to send Irene on her way with all flags
flying and they stayed to make sure Hannah didn't leave
them before her time.

He had the feeling Grandma Irene would have liked the
way things turned out.

Her last words had freed him. Did she know? He hoped
so. He wished he'd had one minute longer with her so he
could thank her. Love had changed everything.

The Loewensteins and the Armaghs dropped by with
the keys to the Candlelight. Rose, detail-conscious,
devoted-to-her-work Rose DiFalco, had completely for-

gotten about her home and her guests. The crowd roared with laughter at Rose's reaction to finding out her paid guests had scrubbed the kitchen, the bathrooms, done three loads of wash and walked Priscilla before locking up.

She told them they were welcome back any time, on the house—and next time they wouldn't have to do the cleaning up afterward.

No doubt about it: A new world was forming right before his eyes.

Maddy saw it, too. She saw that this was where she belonged. In this town. With these people. As part of a loving, brawling, imperfect family who loved her and loved her daughter, too. As part of a circle of strangers who had become friends overnight because they freely gave the one gift that mattered: their hearts.

Hannah was chattering up a storm, once again the happy outgoing little girl she had been before grown-up problems had turned her life upside down. Love could work miracles. All Maddy had to do was look around her for proof.

"Nothing wrong with her imagination," Rose said dryly as Hannah launched into the third retelling of her story about an old lady who told her to go home where she belonged. "That child's going to be a writer one day, you mark my words."

Hannah looked at the samovar that now rested on the nightstand and almost yawned. "I don't like Aladdin anymore," she announced. "I want Barbie's Dream House."

Which was when Maddy knew everything was going to be all right.

She slipped from the room with the laughter and high spirits still ringing in her ears. Relief had drained her. Joy had just about knocked her flat.

She sank onto the lumpy sofa in the visitors' lounge and closed her eyes.

Aidan was seated next to her when she opened them. She liked the feel of his arm around her shoulders, the touch of his fingers against her upper arm. His warmth. His strength. His loving heart. She rested her head against his chest. The beat of his heart, the smell of his skin, everything.

"I owe you breakfast," she said, stifling a yawn.

"There's a bagel over there on the table," he said, his voice a pleasant rumble beneath her ear. "How does that sound?"

"I mean a real breakfast." Another stifled yawn. "Eggs, coffee, the whole nine yards."

Neither one of them moved. There was so much ahead of them, so many things that needed doing. A memorial service to plan. A little girl to take home where she belonged.

A future to explore.

"I'm not in any rush," Aidan said. "How about you?"

Maddy smiled into his sweater. "No rush at all," she answered.

Chapter Twenty-nine

O'Malley's—three days later

IRENE O'MALLEY WAS laid to rest on Tuesday morning in the small cemetery behind Our Lady of Lourdes and it seemed to Aidan that all of Paradise Point showed up to say goodbye.

That night the doors to O'Malley's were thrown open and the drinks were on the house.

"Don't let anyone say we don't give our own a big send-off," Aidan said as he pulled another couple of drafts and slid them down the length of the bar toward Mel Perry and his wife.

"She was one in a million," Rose DiFalco said, sipping her margarita. "We'll never see another like her."

"The best," her sister Lucy said. "She blazed the trail for the rest of us."

"Salt of the earth," Jack Bernstein's father said over the rim of his Guinness. "Her word was her bond. You don't find that anymore."

Aidan winked at Kelly, who was sitting at a table with Seth, Gina, and Tommy Kennedy's oldest granddaughter.

The stories about Grandma Irene had been flowing more freely than the Guinness. He had heard from people in five states, old friends and colleagues who had read about Irene's passing and felt moved to offer their prayers and, almost to a person, an anecdote about Irene's generosity. He wished he had a tape recorder to capture the stories. The side of his grandmother he had first glimpsed the other night at the Candlelight through the eyes of Rose and Lucy and their guests was becoming more real with every memory shared.

Kelly stood up and walked over to the bar. "Gotta go," she said. "I'm baby-sitting."

"Hannah?"

"Just for an hour. Maddy said she has something for you that she wants to deliver in person."

The possibilities were enough to drive a man to his knees but he wasn't about to speculate on them with his daughter.

"Take the truck," he said, tossing her the keys. "There's still a lot of snow out there."

"You worry too much."

"So I've heard."

She leaned across the bar and hugged him and his heart melted. This time next year she would be up in New York City, a student at Columbia, taking her first giant steps into a future that didn't include him.

He watched as Seth got her coat and held it for her while she slipped her arms into the sleeves. Kelly looked up at him like the guy had hung the moon. Part of him hated the kid's guts and would gladly ship him off to a South Pacific atoll for the rest of his life. The other part grudgingly admitted his little girl had chosen well.

"No, it doesn't get any easier," Rose DiFalco said as he turned back to the bar.

"That's not what I wanted to hear."

"Maddy's thirty-two and she can still give me sleepless nights."

She gave him one of those mother looks he had come to recognize and he was smart enough to keep his big mouth shut. It was still early in the game. You didn't declare yourself to the mother before you'd taken the daughter out on the first date. Not even if the sound of the daughter's voice made you feel like you were seventeen again and discovering it all for the first time.

He poured the DiFalco girls another margarita each then pulled himself a Guinness.

"To Hannah," he said, raising his glass.

"To Hannah," Rose said.

Lucy touched her glass to theirs. "To life!" she said. "Accept no substitute."

The Candlelight

"I won't be more than an hour," Maddy said as she threw on her coat and grabbed for the shopping bag and her purse. "If Hannah needs anything—"

"Don't worry," Kelly said, laughing. "Believe me, I know the number for the bar."

"Not that I think you'll have any problems," Maddy said, lingering at the door, "but just in case—"

"Ms. Bainbridge, the snow's blowing into the house."

Maddy glanced over her shoulder. At least a quarter-inch of the white stuff covered the tops of her boots. "Okay, well then I'd better get going." She looked from Kelly to Seth. "There's plenty of food in the fridge. Rose went a little crazy for Hannah's welcome home dinner. Help yourselves. You'd be doing us a favor."

Kelly pointed down at the snow trailing across Rose's expensive runner. "Ms. DiFalco will have a cow."

"You're right. She will have a cow." She checked for her wallet, her keys, her composure. "I'm out of here. Remember if you—"

"Call you at O'Malley's. I know!"

Maddy slid her way down the steps and across the yard to her car. Kelly and Seth must think she was totally nuts. Maybe she was. The thought of seeing Aidan, even for a few minutes, made her feel downright giddy with happiness.

"Get a grip," she told herself as she started the car. "You're a grown woman. Start acting like one!"

This wasn't even their first date. That wouldn't happen until the weekend. All she was doing was driving over to O'Malley's to raise a glass to Irene and return the samovar to its rightful place of honor over the bar, where it belonged. Hannah's interest in it had been short-lived and who could blame her? The final results weren't in yet, but the hospital lab was reasonably sure there had been some kind of chemical reaction between the chlorinated tap water and the sea-damaged metal finish inside the samovar. Hannah's pretend tea had triggered a dramatic allergic reaction in the little girl that unfortunately had presented atypical symptoms that led them down the wrong path. If Kelly hadn't mentioned that Hannah drank water from the samovar they might never have made a connection at all.

Maddy thought the doctors had seemed a little too eager to jump on this explanation, especially in light of the fact that Hannah had already regained consciousness long before the first test results on the samovar came back, but she wasn't quibbling. Let them call Hannah's recovery the result of medical sleuthing but she knew better and so did everyone who had been in the little girl's room when it happened. Even Rose agreed that something else had been at work that night, something more powerful than medicine, more enduring than magic. Love had brought them all together in that room and it was love that had brought Hannah back to them. Nothing would ever convince Maddy otherwise.

She glanced over at the samovar on the seat next to her. There was little doubt in her mind that this was the same teapot that had graced the original O'Malley's more than fifty years ago. She had closely examined the scan Aidan had sent her, comparing every leaf and vine with the samovar she had won at the on-line auction and, as far as she could tell, it was a perfect match.

The thought that the samovar was about to come full circle sent a ripple of wonder up her spine. She wished Aidan could have presented the samovar to Irene but seeing it displayed in a place of honor at O'Malley's, where it belonged, would be almost good enough.

It wasn't a magic lamp. It wasn't even a workable teapot any longer. But somehow that samovar had managed to link a part of Irene's past to Aidan's present and now it was pointing toward a future that suddenly seemed brighter than Maddy had ever dreamed.

O'Malley's

Aidan sensed Maddy's presence before he saw her. An awareness that began at the base of his spine and radiated outward like joy.

"Where ya going?" Barney Kurkowski from the fire station hollered. "The party's just getting started."

Aidan didn't break stride, just elbowed his way through the throng, and out the back door.

He didn't feel the cold. He didn't feel the ever-present ache in his leg and hip. The snow felt like summer rain. The icy steps meant nothing to him because he was walking on air.

Her coat was buttoned all wrong. Her scarf was askew. Her knit cap was pulled down over her eyebrows. Her eyelashes were heavy with snow. Maddy was lugging her mammoth purse and a shopping bag that bulged like the samovar that had started it all. Her nose was Rudolph red and her eyes watered like his leaky kitchen faucet. Her breath billowed before her in the cold night air like the sails on a schooner. She was the most beautiful woman he had ever seen in his life and, just like that, in the space of a heartbeat, he fell the rest of the way into love.

"IT'S TEN DEGREES out there," Rose muttered as she and Lucy watched from the bar window. "They'll catch their death."

"They won't notice a thing," Lucy said. "They're in love."

"In love?" She looked at her sister and frowned. "They barely know each other."

"That's how it was for you and Bill," Lucy reminded her. "Why shouldn't it be the same for your daughter?"

Rose sighed. "You see how that turned out."

"Yes," said Lucy with a knowing laugh, "I certainly do."

Rose had the good grace to blush.

They heard the sound of voices drifting toward them from the street. Aidan's low rumble followed by Maddy's delighted ripple of laughter.

"We shouldn't spy on them," Rose said.

"We're not spying," Lucy said. "We're family."

Maddy and Aidan stood together in a pool of street light. Their embrace was so seamless they cast a single shadow across the snow. He brushed a lock of hair off her forehead. She touched his cheek with her hand. Simple gestures from the vocabulary of lovers that still had the power to break your heart if you let them.

The last few days had been filled with moments of such pure happiness Rose thought her heart would break open and spill diamonds and rubies at her feet. Hannah's recovery. The miraculous change in her relationship with Maddy.

Bill Bainbridge.

Bill would be back for the Christmas holidays. No promises had been made. They were far beyond that. Neither one could say what the future held for them but she knew beyond question that the only man she had ever loved would always be a part of it.

"You're crying," Lucy said as Maddy and Aidan dissolved into a kiss. "And here I thought this was what they call a happy ending."

"No," said Rose as she took her sister's hand, "I think it's what they call a great beginning."

Author's Note

MY MOTHER'S LAST words to me the day before she died were, "I love you."

My last words to her were, "I love you, too."

I think about that sometimes, about how lucky I am to have that memory to hold on to now that she's gone. Two thousand one was a difficult year for my family. My father's six-year battle with cancer was nearing the end when life threw a nasty surprise our way. My mother, my healthy happy mother, was diagnosed out of nowhere with rapidly progressing terminal cancer and our lives changed in an instant. We had forty-six days to say everything that needed to be said, forty-six days to store up enough memories to see us through.

I was with her when she died. I held her hand and felt the birdlike flutter of distant wings that was her fading pulse beat. Five months later I sat beside my father when it was his turn to say goodbye. A moment before he drew his last breath, his eyes opened and a smile—such a wonderful smile!—lit up his face. His gaze was fixed on a point somewhere over my left shoulder. He opened his arms wide and he cried out, "Visy! Visy!" (his pet name for my mother) and he died before the sound faded from the room.

I like to believe she came for him, that his last moment was one filled with the joy of seeing her again. I can't prove it. I can't offer facts or figures or photographic evidence. All I know is what I saw and heard and felt in that room—a sense of deep joy, of something so much greater than anything I had ever known before that I'll carry that knowledge with me for the rest of my life.

When I think about my mother, I see her in the kitchen. I grew up in a two-family house in Queens. I was an only child with a vivid imagination and a mother who didn't fit the June Cleaver mold. She wore Capri pants and ballet flats. She had modeled professionally when I was a baby. She believed the kitchen was truly the heart of the home and her oil painting supplies shared counter space with her spice rack and blender. I thought every little girl in town had to push aside a tube of thalo green when she sat down to her lunch of PBJ and a glass of milk. She taught me that the paintbrush was mightier than the broom and that if given the choice between reading a good book or polishing the furniture, the book won out every time.

Maybe that's why she's always in the kitchen in my dreams.

She is healthy—always healthy—and smiling and overflowing with life. We don't hug or touch but I can feel her presence like an embrace.

I see her at the old range from my childhood, the big one with the grill in the middle, in the apartment where I grew up and it feels so right, it seems so normal, that I am shocked to realize this can't possibly be. She's dead. She is gone. I was with her when she left us. She can't be here. But my eyes can't deny the proof standing there, glowing with life and love, in front of me. I don't know what to say to her. She has been someplace I can't even imagine. I fumble for words. "So," I say at last, "have you bumped into anyone you know?" And she looks at me and laughs that wonderful laugh and says, "Only our old pets! Isn't that wonderful?" And if there was any doubt at all that this was my fey and spirited mother, they vanish in that moment.

She was an instinctive cook who loved cookbooks and recipes but never paid much attention to them. She added pinches and dollops and smidgens and she never tasted while she cooked. Can you imagine! Never once. And yet she turned out delicious meals night after night, year after year.

Your macaroni and cheese, Ma. Where did you get the idea to toss in chili sauce?

And the Spanish rice—what's the secret? Is it the sprinkling of cayenne? Write it down, please, right now before it's too late.

I could have asked her for her recipes anytime. Over a cup of tea, maybe, or while chatting on the phone. But I waited too long. Wouldn't you know it? I waited too long to ask for her secrets. Once the doctors had peered deep into her core, once the pronouncement had been made, I couldn't do it. Asking her for the secret to the recipes she cooked especially for me, to make my life easier, to fill my freezer, to give me more time to write, was like admitting the doctors might be right, that she was terribly sick and that before too long there would be no more "CARE packages" from her house to ours.

The day after she died, my father handed me her jewelry box. "It's yours," he said, pushing it toward me. "You know she wanted you to have everything." *Your inheritance*, she used to call it with a wicked smile on her face. The lovely pieces she came to later on in her life and cherished because now she had something to leave to me when she died.

But you know what? She was wrong. Those rings and bracelets, pretty as they are, can't hold a candle to her pots and pans, her slotted spoon and potato masher. I found a box filled with recipes and clippings and scraps of paper and my heart soared! No diamond could make me half as happy.

Everything I know about making a home a haven I learned from her. Everything I know about loving well I learned from her. Everything I know about the wonder of daily life, the miracle of the every day, I learned from her.

She also taught me to believe in the world that exists just beyond the reach of our five senses. I believed in

Santa Claus and the Tooth Fairy and the Easter Bunny
(although I'll admit I had a bit of trouble with the rabbit)
for longer than I'm willing to admit, and I knew, like my
mother and her grandmother before her, that there is much
more to life than we'll ever know while we're here living
it.

Maybe that explains our fascination with the samovar
that had belonged to her stepmother, Margie. Margie was
the second of my grandfather's five wives and the love of
his life. She was a successful decorator in the 1930s—a
time when high-flying careers for women were a rarity—a
woman who lived in a Fifth Avenue penthouse and rode
around in her own limousine, and somehow met and fell
in love with one of NYPD's finest: my grandfather. Of
course, that's another story for another time.

The samovar held the place of honor on Margie's credenza and my mother spent many happy hours playing
with it while she daydreamed about fairy princesses and
a genie who couldn't wait to grant a few wishes for a
deserving little girl.

Like mother, like daughter, I guess. That same samovar
held the place of honor on our credenza when I was growing up in Queens years later and I can't begin to count
the hours I spent waiting for that reluctant genie to finally
make his appearance and whisk me off to Disneyland so
I could set up housekeeping with Spin and Marty.

I'm looking at that samovar right now as I write this.
It sits on a glass tabletop not ten feet away from where
I'm sitting. The samovar must be well over one hundred
years old by now and it's beginning to show its age. I
don't have a daughter of my own to inherit Margie's
magic lamp, but one of the best parts of being a writer is
that words make all things possible. After years of waiting
for the samovar to pop out a genie, it popped out a story
instead. One about mothers and daughters, about love and
sorrow and the unexpected blessings that sometimes come
our way when we need them most.

Some books practically write themselves. Others come
kicking and screaming into the world. I began *Shore*

Lights in sorrow and ended it in joy. We've all heard that famous bit of advice given to writers from the beginning of time: Write what you know. Well, this time I listened and wrote about the most puzzling and beautiful and mysterious topic of them all. *Shore Lights* is a love story, but it's one that begins the moment a woman hears those magic words, "You're going to have a baby."

Somewhere I think my mother is smiling.

And now, a special preview of Barbara Bretton's

GIRLS OF SUMMER

Available from Berkley Books in November 2003!

ELLEN O'BRIEN MARKOWITZ believed God had better things to do than tap into the prayers of thirty-something single doctors, but she was hoping the Almighty would be willing to make an exception and help her out just this once.

Please, she prayed silently. *Please let it all be a bad dream.*

She opened one eye and peered across the rumpled expanse of bed. He was still there. She hadn't imagined him, hadn't conjured him up from a combination of too much champagne and two years' worth of dreaming. Hall Talbot, Shelter Rock Cove's most-beloved OB-GYN, her good friend and colleague, was snoring softly not two feet away from her, sprawled across her extra-firm mattress like he belonged there. Even in postcoital repose he managed to look like your average middle-aged Adonis.

His silvery-blond hair shimmered against her pale blue sheets. His muscular torso loomed gorgeous in the gathering light. She remembered how he had looked last night when she slid his white shirt off his fine tanned shoulders and—

She stifled a groan and buried her face in her pillow.

In the grand scheme of things, it really wasn't such a terrible mistake. People slept with the wrong people every day of the week and somehow Earth managed to keep on turning. She and Hall had been good friends before last night and there was no reason to think their friendship couldn't survive a night of passion.

Even if he had called her by another woman's name at a very inopportune moment.

And this came as a surprise, Markowitz? The first two things she had learned when she moved to Maine were her phone number and the fact that Annie Galloway Butler was the love of his life.

He blamed it on the champagne and went out of his way to make it up to her in some amazing ways but the damage had been done. There were three of them in that bed and Ellen already had too much experience being second best. Everyone in Shelter Rock Cove knew that Hall Talbot had carried a torch for the former widow Galloway for more years, and through more failed marriages, than anyone cared to acknowledge. Not even Annie's marriage to Sam Butler had dimmed Hall's devotion. It had taken the birth of a perfect baby girl to force him to acknowledge the fact that he had lost Annie before she had a chance to find him.

Hall and Ellen had attended Sarah Joy Butler's christening yesterday as honorary members of the family and the sight of that beautiful baby, that miracle of love and fate, had turned Ellen's heart inside out. She could only imagine what it had done to Hall. The Galloway and Butler clans descended on Shelter Rock Cove en masse, filling Sam and Annie's little house with food and music and laughter and enough love to make you believe in happy endings.

The only time Ellen had ever felt more like an outsider was at one of her father's infrequent family gatherings where she needed a name tag in order to be recognized as part of the clan. Family always did that to her. All of those shared genes and stories were like a private club, the kind that didn't want her as a member. When Hall suggested they split early, she was almost pathetically grateful.

"Hungry?" he asked.

"Starving."

He avoided Cappy's where they were bound to run into someone who would ask them about the christening and drove over to the Spruce Goose, a small inn on one of the back roads between Shelter Rock Cove and Bar Harbor. Good food, better lighting, the kind of place where you could pretend to be someone you're not and maybe get away with it for a little while.

Loneliness had a way of playing tricks on even the smartest women and apparently she was no exception. Hall had needed someone last night and she had needed to be needed by him.

It should have been enough but it wasn't. Not even close.